The women of
MYSTERIA

Charlene Houtenan is the voluptuous local Realtor, who knows a hot property when she sees one. And when a new werewolf appears in town, she's going to make a move he can't resist.

See her seal the deal in New York Times *bestselling author MaryJanice Davidson's "Alone Wolf."*

Harmony Faithfull is the new minister in town. She's having a crisis of faith—in herself—until she finds a buck-naked man in her garden, a former demon who unleashes the devil inside her.

Watch her find heaven in national bestselling author Susan Grant's "Mortal in Mysteria."

Candice Cox may be Mysteria High's sexiest teacher, but after five husbands, she's burned out on romance. Until a former student—a drool-worthy werewolf—makes her howl at the moon . . .

Get hot for teacher in "Candy Cox and the Big Bad (Were)Wolf" by P. C. Cast.

Genevieve Tawdry is a witch with a bad case of unrequited love for the owner of the local bar. But is his sudden change of heart the result of a love potion—or a literally breathtaking passion?

Belly up to the bar in "The Witches of Mysteria and the Dead Who Love Them" by Gena Showalter.

MYSTERIA

MaryJanice Davidson

Susan Grant

P. C. Cast

Gena Showalter

BERKLEY SENSATION, NEW YORK

THE BERKLEY PUBLISHING GROUP
Published by the Penguin Group
Penguin Group (USA) Inc.
375 Hudson Street, New York, New York 10014, USA
Penguin Group (Canada), 90 Eglinton Avenue East, Suite 700, Toronto, Ontario M4P 2Y3, Canada
(a division of Pearson Penguin Canada Inc.)
Penguin Books Ltd., 80 Strand, London WC2R 0RL, England
Penguin Group Ireland, 25 St. Stephen's Green, Dublin 2, Ireland (a division of Penguin Books Ltd.)
Penguin Group (Australia), 250 Camberwell Road, Camberwell, Victoria 3124, Australia
(a division of Pearson Australia Group Pty. Ltd.)
Penguin Books India Pvt. Ltd., 11 Community Centre, Panchsheel Park, New Delhi—110 017, India
Penguin Group (NZ), Cnr. Airborne and Rosedale Roads, Albany, Auckland 1310, New Zealand
(a division of Pearson New Zealand Ltd.)
Penguin Books (South Africa) (Pty.) Ltd., 24 Sturdee Avenue, Rosebank, Johannesburg 2196, South Africa

Penguin Books Ltd., Registered Offices: 80 Strand, London WC2R 0RL, England

This is a work of fiction. Names, characters, places, and incidents either are the product of the authors'
imagination or are used fictitiously, and any resemblance to actual persons, living or dead, business
establishments, events, or locales is entirely coincidental. The publisher does not have any control over
and does not assume any responsibility for author or third-party websites or their content.

MYSTERIA

A Berkley Sensation Book / published by arrangement with the authors

PRINTING HISTORY
Berkley Sensation edition / July 2006

ISBN: 0-425-21106-1

BERKLEY SENSATION®
Berkley Sensation Books are published by The Berkley Publishing Group,
a division of Penguin Group (USA) Inc.,
375 Hudson Street, New York, New York 10014.
BERKLEY SENSATION is a registered trademark of Penguin Group (USA) Inc.
The "B" design is a trademark belonging to Penguin Group (USA) Inc.

PRINTED IN THE UNITED STATES OF AMERICA

10 9 8 7 6 5 4 3 2 1

CONTENTS

Introduction

✳

Once upon a time in a land closer than anyone might be comfortable with, a demon high lord was sent to destroy a small, starving (and, let's face it, weird) band of settlers who were fleeing the last town they'd tried to settle in (a place eventually known as Kansas City, Missouri, the Show Me State, which did indeed show them tar and feathers and the road west). The group was composed of magical misfits and outcasts: a bloodaphobic vampire, a black-magic witch and her white-magic husband, a pack of arduous (translation: humphappy) werewolves, and a man named John who had gotten confused and joined the wrong wagon train. When the demon spied this ragged, rejected bunch, he (for a reason known only to himself but which had to do with uncontrollable random acts of kindness) decided not just to spare them, but to create a magical haven for them.

And so, nestled in a beautiful valley in the Rocky Mountains, the town of Mysteria was founded. Over the years, it became a refuge for creatures of the night and those unwanted by traditional society. No one—or thing—was turned away. Magic thrived, aphrodisiacs laced the pollen, and fairy tales came true.

The first settlers eventually died (those that weren't already dead or undead, that is), but they left pieces of themselves behind. The vampire invented a powerful blood-appetite suppressant for any other vampires with a fear of blood. The witch and the warlock created a wishing well—a wishing well that swirled and churned with both white and black magic, a dangerous combination. The hump-happy werewolves left the essence of perpetual springtime and love (translation: they peed all around the boundary of the city, so that everyone—or thing—that entered or left Mysteria was, well, marked). John, the only nonmagical being in the group, left his confused but mundane genes, founding a family that would ultimately spawn more humans of nonmagical abilities who remained in Mysteria because finding their way out was just too much like geometry.

Each of the settlers thought, as their spirits floated to the heavens—all right, some of them went straight to hell, the naughty sinners—that their best contribution to the fantastical town of Mysteria was a happily-ever-after for their descendants. If only they could have known the events that would one day unfold . . .

MORTAL IN MYSTERIA

Susan Grant

For my three children:
Connor and Courtney (the human ones)
and Tala (the furry one).
All my love.

One

The dirty, sweat-soaked demon dropped to his knees. His hands, bound at the wrists with chains, rested awkwardly at the small of his back. Nevertheless, he formed his mouth into a smile he hoped appeared as contrite as his posture. *'Tis better if you do not infuriate the boss any more than you have already*, he thought. "I am prepared to pay for my transgressions, Master."

"And pay for them, you shall!" The Devil's forked tongue darted out to moisten thin, malice-curved lips. "I have thought long and hard about your crimes," he hissed with the very faintest of lisps. "Now, prepare to receive your sentence, Demon."

"Aye, Master." All the demons were named "Demon" down here in Hell. To their master they were all but indistinguishable. Only Lucifer stood apart, with his trademark black goatee, the horns, the pitchfork, and the crimson suit. Proof that the whimsies of fashion in Hell had been at a standstill since the birth of time.

Fashion? Hell's bells, didn't he have more important things to worry about? Like losing his head, or some other body part of which he'd grown fond? The demon winced. His concentration simply wasn't what it used to be after the century of torture he'd endured for his crimes. Or had it been two or three centuries that he'd been paying for his terrible deeds? It had become difficult to keep track. Ah, but what was an extra century or two in the grand scheme of things? He'd existed for more than ten thousand years, tasked to bring the worst sort of doubt into the miserable, pitifully abbreviated lives of human beings. Far from being just any demon, he was a demon lord, and one of the most ancient of them all: the Demon High Lord of Self-Doubt and Second Thoughts, the bane of many a human failure, simpering creatures all too eager to listen to the fears that he could so easily plant in their weak minds. *You can't*, he'd whisper until they believed it. *You won't. Try, and you will surely fail.*

Countless men who could have ruled the world had never stepped beyond their front doors because he'd made them doubt their abilities, made them afraid to take chances, to risk failure. Nor were women any safer from his dark murmurings through the eons. He'd frightened countless wenches, silencing their voices by playing up their fears of sounding too shrill, too stupid, too . . . different.

Humanity's failures—he'd been the force behind so many of them. Until that fateful day when he'd glimpsed true courage and couldn't bring himself to destroy it, giving the Will-to-Go-On to a small, starving band of settlers wandering in the snowy woods of the Rocky Mountains. He wasn't sure exactly why he'd spared them, why he'd given them the inner strength to push themselves until they reached warmth and shelter, but he had—and it had felt damned good, too. In fact, it had felt so damned good being good to the damned that he repeated the deed all around the globe, losing himself for years in a virtual frenzy of beneficence. That is, until he was finally caught red-handed in the midst of one of those random acts of kindness, a crime considered so heinous that Lucifer himself had marched upstairs and dragged him back down to Hell.

On the positive side, he'd come out the other side with all his body parts intact, the important body parts, at any rate. It could have gone much worse for him. And perhaps it still would. The devil, as always, was in the details.

The demon bowed his head. "Tell me what I must do to appease you, Master."

"There will be no appeasement! None! There is but one fitting punishment for such atrocities. Banishment!"

The demon's head jerked up. "Banishment?"

"Yes." The fiery red orbs that passed for Lucifer's eyes narrowed to pulsing slits. "I hereby banish you from Hell."

It cannot be! The demon had expected a reduction in rank, the loss of freedom to come and go as he pleased, perhaps, but permanent eviction? His salary, his benefits— *phoosh*, gone! Just like that. Hell's bells, he'd slaved ten thousand years—for nothing! Done the Devil's deeds only to end up like this: out of date, out of use, and without a transferable retirement plan!

"Is this truly to be forevermore?" the demon almost croaked, knowing how the Devil so enjoyed toying with his minions.

Lucifer chuckled. "Not really. I have made you mortal, as well."

"Mortal . . ." The mere word tangled around the demon's tongue like a serving of snake entrails.

"Never fear. Because of your newly finite life, you won't have many years to fret your fate. Consider it a favor for your years of service to the Dark Empire." Lucifer waved a clawed hand. "No need to thank me."

A growl rumbled in the demon's throat. Of all the many things he'd like to give Lucifer at that moment, thanks was not one of them. Yet, something told him it wasn't mortality itself he needed to fear as much as the locale in which he would suffer it. "Where am I to be sent?"

"Why, to the very epicenter of your initial act of kindness."

Lucifer spat out that last word. Literally. A glob of moisture sizzled in one of the many fires burning deep within the bowels of the earth. "Mysteria. I trust you remember the place."

He remembered it, all right. Remembered it all too well. The settlers he'd helped had founded the village.

The demon shifted his weight on aching knees as he mulled over his options, which were near zero, as far as he could tell. Time was running out to reverse course, so he did what he did best and sowed the seeds of self-doubt. "Are you certain this is the best plan for me, Master? The best punishment? Are you absolutely sure?"

The Devil's voice turned deadly. "What do you mean?"

"What if it doesn't work out? What if they don't want me amongst them?" *You can't . . . you won't. Try, and you will surely fail. . . .* "Imagine it, the Demon High Lord of Self-Doubt and Second Thoughts living across the street, mowing the lawn. Coaching Little League?" The demon curved his lips into a between-us smile. "Absurd, is it not?"

Lucifer shrieked in incredulity. The sound of a thousand screams filled the chamber. Goblins and gargoyles somersaulted through the shadows, fleeing the chamber as a rumbling began under the cold stone slab of a floor. "Your dark magic does not work with me!"

"I'm merely suggesting that you look at all sides of the equation—"

But Lucifer continued to roar. Somewhere far above them, on the surface, the ground also shook. The demon half-wondered how many casualties there would be this time. But that was no longer his job. He'd been fired. He would no longer be tasked with planting defeat in the survivors' minds, riddling their psyches with despair. At that, something close to relief filtered through him. *Doing good has taken the fun out of doing evil.*

Aye, it had. The demon sensed he'd never be 100 percent good. Yet, neither could he ever return to being 100 percent bad.

Lucifer grew in size until he towered above the demon,

his clothing splitting and hissing as muscled flesh bulged and tore it apart. Horns sprouted from a ridged skull, curling upward, until they, too, were lost in the swirling mist of the chamber. Finally, he spoke. "I do not doubt, fallen one. I do not err. I do not have *second thoughts!*"

That much was obvious. Couldn't Lucifer have made the point without all the needless death and destruction? Without the unneeded suffering? A growl vibrated deep in the demon's throat. He'd witnessed such showy outbursts many times during his long existence, but this time, for the first time, a reaction to the master's wrath formed inside the demon, as if he had a temper of his very own.

He made fists. It caused the manacles to bite into his wrists, pain he welcomed as a ball of heat swelled and exploded in his chest, a conflagration he couldn't recognize or explain, for he didn't have feelings. Never had. He couldn't have performed his duties if he'd been created any other way. And yet, he felt something now, aye, something too wonderful and terrible to absorb, a sensation too new and yet inexplicably ancient at the same time. The pressure built and built until something finally gave.

The demon gasped in shock. It was as if his very core had wrenched open, releasing all he carried within him. The vileness, the blackness, he realized. The evil.

For half a breath he was so frighteningly hollow, he wondered if he were about to implode; then into the vacuum rushed something so sweet, so indescribably wonderful, that he nearly sobbed. What was happening to him?

"I'm sorry," the demon whispered on a ragged breath. It was the only way to express what had boiled up inside him. "I am so very sorry. . . ."

"You don't look sorry," Lucifer hissed from high above.

The demon glared up at him. "Ah, but I am. Sorry for all the centuries of sowing doubt, of turning back those beings better than I. I am sorry for the evil I accomplished in your name. In fact, I hereby repent!" *Aye, take* that, *you gutless stinking mountain of dragon offal.*

"You . . . re-*what?*"

"I repent. R-e-p-e-n-t." Was that not an Aretha Franklin song? Or was he confusing his tunes? The demon gave his head a shake. There they went again, his thoughts wandering. One thing was certain, something had happened—*was* happening—inside him, and he was helpless to stop it.

To stop the emotion, sharp and pure, filling him with anger, resentment, shame at his past. And hope—hope despite the completely overwhelming odds against him. *Now you are just like the humans*, he thought.

"I ask forgiveness for all the deeds I ever did in the Dark One's name," he said quietly. "Aye, I truly do."

Lucifer's voice was deadly. "I never forgive. You should know this, my minion. You of all the demon high lords should know."

"It wasn't of you that I made my plea."

Lucifer's molten eyes pulsed and glowed, his fangs glinting in the cast-off light. "What?"

"You heard me." Angry now, the demon flicked his gaze upward—*heaven*ward—to make his point clear.

Only the fretful twittering of goblins interrupted the shocked, appalled silence. Then, a strange noise stuttered past Lucifer's parted lips. The demon marveled at that. It was the first time in all of history that he could remember hearing the Great Satan sputter.

Then, all hell broke loose.

Two jets of searing red lava shot out from the Devil's eyes and hit the slab where the demon crouched. Rocks exploded, pummeling him as he fell backward. The air was on fire, something that the demon should have been used to— Lucifer lost his temper often; they'd all been charred now and again—but this was different.

This was worse.

The demon spun in the center of a tornado, wrenched and torn in every direction, inside and out. He could no longer see or hear. And, after a blessed while, he could no longer feel the pain that wracked him.

Bathed in white light, he floated. *Is this what it feels like to die?* If so, perhaps he would not mind. But he knew, even as he tumbled into oblivion—or, rather, into the forested slopes of Colorado—that Lucifer would never let him get away as easily as that.

TWO

In a clear, sweet voice, Harmony Faithfull concluded her Sunday service: "Now, go in peace and enjoy this beautiful day the Lord has given us."

The sound of her six-month-old puppy's tail thumping on the hardwood floor was all that broke the perfect silence.

"Thanks, Bubba." Harmony looked up from her hand-written sermon, which had taken all of ten minutes to read to the six rows of pews. Six rows of *empty* pews, lined up like abandoned soldiers on the pristine, knotty pine floor.

There should be scuffs marring those planks, she thought longingly, lost buttons in the corners, and crushed Cheerios. And under the pews, wadded-up Kleenex, handbags, and colorful hats . . .

Harmony sighed and neatened the lectern. "It's nice to know someone appreciated the homily today."

You're talking to the dog again.

"Yep. And when you're not talking to the dog, you're talking to yourself." Crossing her eyes, Harmony shut off the halogen reading lamp and the microphone. Sometimes, she wondered what she possibly could have been thinking—

her, a city girl, relocating to Mysteria, a tiny hamlet in the Rockies, assuming she'd make churchgoers out of the locals here, who, um, weren't like any people she'd ever met anyplace else. There were supernatural happenings in the town, you couldn't miss them, really, and she had her suspicions that more than a few of the townsfolk had supernatural abilities. But God loved all creatures: great or small, good or bad, moral or immoral. Mortal or . . . ?

Harmony stopped that train of thought before it jumped the track. She was here because after two tours as an air force chaplain, she'd been looking for a new challenge. *It looks like you found it, girl. In spades.*

Six months ago, the church had been a tumbledown farmhouse with a barn on five overgrown acres. With the help of her father and brothers, she'd renovated the house, which now did double duty as a public place of worship and her personal living quarters, a cozy little home located in the back. She'd even stitched the white eyelet curtains herself in a spurt of delirious domesticity. Then her family had returned to Oakland, leaving her to grow her flock. Except that, aside from a few curious townspeople, no one had showed up.

Have some faith. Give it time.

Time . . . she had plenty of that lately.

Well, she'd simply have to drum up a little of the faith in herself that she'd always seemed to be able to drum up in everyone else. After all, she was Harmony Faithfull, the daughter of Jacob Jethro Faithfull IV, Oakland's most famous, and often infamous, but always ebullient, pastor of South Avenue Church. Daddy was a man who could fill football stadiums and concert halls with worshippers, who often traveled hundreds of miles to hear him speak. Charisma and the good word, it was a potent combination.

Harmony thumped her fist on the podium, and the puppy jumped. "It's in my genes," she said out loud. "I can't forget that. God sent me here because I have a job to do."

Bubba seemed to agree, a long pink puppy tongue draped over one side of his open mouth.

Harmony crumpled one of the sheets of lined paper she'd

used for her sermon, crushed it in her fist, and aimed the ball of paper at the wastebasket across from the pulpit. It clipped the rim and spun inside. "Two points!"

She tapped a finger against her chin. "Maybe we can start an after-school basketball team. What do you think of that, Bubba-licious?" The puppy wagged his long black tail.

The idea of an after-school basketball team had worked for her father and some inner-city kids when he was fresh out of divinity school. The hoops had brought the children, and then the mothers, who'd dragged the fathers and the boyfriends, and within the year there was an entire community with Sunday potlucks and a fifty-two-member choir. Not that she could picture any of the O'Cleary great-grandkids shooting hoops, but it'd be a start. It was all about getting people through the door.

MYSTERIA COMMUNITY CHURCH. ALL FAITHS WELCOME. That last part she'd painted onto the sign as an afterthought when weeks had gone by and nary a lost soul tromped through the door. Well, save Jeanie Tortellini, the town sheriff, and sometimes Candice, the high school English teacher. They'd drop by to see how she was settling in, staying for chitchat and coffee but not the good word. But then, Harmony firmly believed everyone was welcome here, for whatever reasons they chose to come. If they preferred their so-called magic, fine, but Harmony's calling was to let them know God watched over them as well. As a child, her parents had taught her that a true heart excluded no one, and that the church was the heart of the village.

Except in Mysteria, where that honor was held by Knight Caps, the local bar.

Harmony sighed. How could she convince the townspeople to congregate here instead? At least on Sundays. What did she have that they couldn't find anywhere else? Well, besides the obvious, she thought with a vertical glance.

"God, I need your help. Show me how to fill up this church, and I'll do the rest. Please." Harmony squeezed her eyes shut and prayed. Prayed until her head throbbed and her eyes hurt. Prayed until she was all prayed out. And then she started wishing, plain old wishing, like you would on a four-leaf clover, or a star, because sometimes, even in matters of the spirit, and maybe *especially* in matters of the spirit, you just had to stack the deck. "Show me how to bring the towns-people here," she whispered. "Give me a sign." *I'm waiting, watching, eyes wide open, Lord.*

The floor rumbled. Was that the old furnace kicking on? No, it was warm today, too warm for the heater.

The earth moved again. Harmony frowned at her drinking glass still sitting on the podium. The water was rippling like San Francisco Bay on a windy day. No, the rumbling definitely wasn't from the furnace. It was coming from somewhere outside. Strange. Everyone knew a major fault line ran through Missouri. But Colorado?

One good jolt almost threw her to her knees. Then it was quiet.

Bubba started barking. In an instant, he'd transformed from drowsy puppy to barking, fur-covered projectile. Zero to sixty in 2.8 seconds, nails scrabbling for purchase on the hardwood, he flew out the front door.

"Bubba!" Grabbing the gauzy cotton of her skirt, Harmony hurried after the dog to the flower garden she'd planted near an ancient, gnarled apple tree. THE GARDEN OF EDEN, according to the ornamental iron garden sign that her sister Hope had mailed her as a housewarming gift. "Bubba! Bubba, come here!"

Three women jogged past on the road fronting the church. They were feminine confections coated in spandex, bling jingling, ponytails bouncing. One woman carried a broomstick gripped in her hand. Hmm, that was a little different, but maybe it was good for the arms. They waved, and Harmony, smiled, waving back. Now she remembered them—the Tawdry sisters. They had the most brilliant hazel eyes that almost seemed to glow. There was something else unusual about them, too, but Harmony couldn't place her finger on exactly what. But they, like the rest of the women in town, were always nice, if a little racy.

Black lace bra types, Harmony had dubbed them in

private. Not meaning any disrespect. Her own sisters were black lace bra types. Not that Harmony had anything against a woman knowing her own charms or being confident about sex. God had never dissed procreation. In fact, He encouraged it—within the context of a committed, monogamous relationship, of course. *Nothing you need to worry about, given your current state of isolation.*

"Ain't that the truth?" Harmony followed the puppy across the lawn. Birds chirped; bees buzzed. The sky was a pure, clear blue. And the sunshine, the scent of pine, she could almost taste it. Face lifted to the sun, she inhaled deeply and became so carried away by her appreciation of the outdoors that she swept right past the naked man who was the target of Bubba's frantic barking.

The naked . . .

. . . man?

Harmony froze, the skirt falling out of her hands. There was no naked man.

Oh, yeah? Then how do you explain the afterimage that just seared itself onto your retinas?

Heart thumping, Harmony whirled around. Yep, there was a man there, and he was most definitely naked, sprawled on his side among the flowers, one thick, muscled thigh thrown forward, the sunshine bouncing off his butt.

Three

Wow. Eyes wide, Harmony stood there, staring, rooted to the ground, as if her foot were locked in cement. She'd asked God to send her a sign. But she'd never expected anything like this! The best naked man she'd ever seen, she decided with no small amount of half-crazed, hormone-driven, lust-fueled objectivity. And she'd seen her share of naked men.

Hmm. That didn't sound right. But it was true, naked men in her life had been a buck a dozen. Only she just hadn't slept with them. Her one affair, in college, was a pleasant but distant memory, and since then she'd spied naked men, fairly frequently, glimpses here and there, in and out of locker rooms, military field hospitals, and in the desert, where there hadn't been much privacy when she'd served as a pastor in Iraq. . . .

Focus, Harmony. There is an unclothed hunk-a-love lying in your flower bed.

Right. And what in the name of heaven was he doing there? Men didn't just fall out of the sky. *Ask and ye shall receive.*

"Harmony," she warned herself.

She dropped to her knees, her fingers going to the unconscious man's corded neck to feel for a pulse. His skin was tanned, perfectly smooth. Midnight black hair curled long and loose around his neck. Taking a closer look, she saw he appeared flushed, as if he were sunburned or had stood too close to a fire. More likely, he'd collapsed after a night of carousing. He was going to be pretty embarrassed once he realized he'd left wherever he'd been hanging out without his clothes.

Bubba growled, low and deep. "Shush, boy," Harmony soothed. "It's okay. I know martial arts, and you have sharp teeth. If he turns out to be the town serial killer/rapist, we'll team up and put him away. Until then, Bubba, you behave."

Harmony pressed her fingers to the man's neck. There . . . she felt a heartbeat . . . slow, distant, almost forlorn. It was if he'd grown tired of living.

She sat up straight. Gosh, that was a weird thought. Tired of living? Where did that come from? If anyone was a mind reader, it was her great-grandmother Eudora, who was said to be a "seer." But as a child growing up in the Faithfull clan, the mere mention of Eudora's psychic talents would have earned Harmony the threat of having her mouth washed out with soap, if not the real thing. Yet, as Harmony studied the stranger's face, the resignation there, the weariness, she could almost believe it true that he was ready to surrender.

Well, she'd fix that. No one was giving up the ghost on her watch, especially not dressed in his birthday suit and crushing her best zinnias!

"Hello? Sir? Are you okay?" Bubba's brown eyes were wary and huge as Harmony tapped the man on the shoulder. "Come on, up and at 'em. You can't sleep here all day. People will talk."

Not even an eyelash twitched. She took hold of his solid shoulder and shoved. "Okay, Sleeping Beauty, time to rise and shine. I'll even brew you a pot of coffee to help things along. I make a mean pot of java, too."

No response, not even a snore. He was dead to the world.

As a last resort, she switched to her air-force-officer voice. "Wake up, soldier! *Now*. Move, move, move!"

The man cracked open one eye, and then the other. At first she thought she saw a red glow, but it seemed to be a trick of the sun, because his eyes were beautiful, reminding her of the mellow gold of good scotch, the kind her father would reverently pour out in a glass once each week, late on Sunday night. "Now that God's work is done, Harmony," he used to tell her.

"Hell's bells." Sleeping Beauty frowned, squinting as if the bright sunshine hurt his eyes.

"It lives," she teased.

He peered at the Garden of Eden sign, his parched lips forming whispered words. "I'm dead."

"You're not dead. Not even close."

He turned toward her voice and his confused eyes filled with curiosity, maybe even wonder. "But . . . ye are an angel."

"Thanks for the compliment, but no. I'm a flesh-and-blood woman."

His head fell back to the dirt with a soft thud. "Dragon offal . . . goblin scum, he is." His accent was strong, a cross between a Scots burr and a bad Captain Hook parody. "The bastard did it, he really did, and now I'm here. Aye, and mortal, too. Mortal in Mysteria."

"Is that kind of like sleepless in Seattle?"

Groaning at her joke, he flung his arms wide and rolled onto his back.

Glory be. Her mouth went dry as she looked him over. For injuries, yes, that was it. Before she administered emergency caffeine, she'd better make darn sure he wasn't wounded.

Anywhere.

She gave him a thorough inspection. After all, it was her citizen's responsibility. Her pastor's duty.

He was built . . . incredibly, amazingly, *enormously*, and that's all she'd let herself think on *that* subject, dragging her eyes away from where she shouldn't have been looking in the first place. There wasn't an ounce of fat on him. Or a single scar. He was as sculpted as a statue of a Roman warrior, except with body hair, the perfect amount, too, short and coarse and dark.

Something drew her eyes back to his face, where she discovered he was watching her with something close to amusement. "You seem, uh, to be all in one piece," she quickly explained.

He flashed a blinding grin. "You like what you see, then."

She stopped her blush before the heat of it could reach her cheeks. She'd grown up with four brothers, two older, two younger. Like heck, she'd let the fact that a man was sprawled naked in her garden in all his admittedly very magnificent glory distract her.

"As a matter of fact, I don't like what I see." Was that the hurt of a wounded ego that flashed in his eyes? Certainly it was surprise. "I don't care for the sight of a man facedown drunk in my flowers on a Sunday morning—butt naked. But considering that I just got done praying for a sign, I suppose I shouldn't complain, because I didn't spell out the specifications!"

She tugged off the butter yellow sweater she'd been wearing over a matching shell and thrust it at him. "Here, put this on."

Sinew and muscle corded his arm from wrist to shoulder as he peered curiously at the sweater dangling from his fingers. It looked tiny grasped in his hand. Clearly, he didn't know what do to with the thing.

She waved her hand. "Cover up." *Your huge wing-dinger*, she almost shouted. "For modesty's sake." Although modesty was way more her issue than his, it seemed.

He pushed upright, clods of dry dirt sprinkling down as he sat up. Tight, defined stomach muscles brought new meaning to six-pack abs. She almost sobbed with relief when he spread the sweater over his private parts.

"I am not drunk," he argued.

True, his eyes were clear, not bloodshot, as he swept his

gaze around the garden, lawn, and church. And he was in top physical form, too, gifted with the well-hewn body of an NFL running back—powerfully muscled, without a linebacker's bulk. Carving a body like that took time. Alcoholism didn't lend itself to keeping regular workouts.

"What happened to you?" She folded her arms over her chest. "It usually doesn't rain naked men. At least not in the six months since I've lived here. Unless it's a seasonal thing."

His lips twitched, his gold-brown eyes sparkling, as he sized her up in an approving way. "If it is seasonal, lass, then we had better take shelter."

"Clothes first. Where'd you leave them?" she asked as calmly as she could as he didn't seem to care that he wore none.

He glanced around. "They took everything. Left me with nothing."

"You were robbed?"

"Aye, you could say that." His expression grew bleak all over again. "Robbed and abandoned."

"Oh, no. I don't like hearing that. Everyone's so nice around here, law-abiding folks. I can't see anyone doing something like this. It makes me sick to find out it may be otherwise."

"Nay, lass. They were not from here. They were from . . . the south. Aye, that's it."

"Oh, you mean Colorado Springs?"

He shook his head.

"Pueblo?"

"Nay. Far, far to the south. Farther south than you have ever been, lass."

Mexico, she thought, nodding. "That's okay. We'll get them. Just because they skipped out over the border doesn't mean they're home free. You can use my phone to call Jeanie—Jeanie Tortellini," she added at his blank look. "She's our town sheriff. And a good one, too. She'll file a report."

He frowned. "Nay. No reports. Will do no good."

"If you don't let her know, the thugs who did this to you will do it to someone else next time they cross the border."

Tiredly but firmly, he said no. " 'Tis over. 'Tis done."

"Wow," she said in a quiet voice. "Just wow."

He glanced at her strangely. "Wow?"

"You were robbed, beaten, stripped, and unceremoniously dumped in a pastor's flower bed. You have every right to be angry."

"I *am* angry."

"Yet, you haven't uttered one grumble of vengeance or head bashing."

" 'Tis no use, truly, to wish for such things." He seemed to be ready to say more but stopped himself. "None of it would do any good. 'Tis done."

"That's exactly what I mean by wow. It's not easy to forgive and forget. A true man of mercy; that's what you are."

A look of pain crossed his face. "Aye, and 'twas my downfall, too," he muttered.

"Mercy is never wrong! Never. In fact, showing mercy is good for you. And not only for your body—" She threw her hand over her heart. "Forgiving is good for your soul."

He choked as alarm lit up his face. "Can you tell if a man has one—a soul?" All at once cynical and wistful, his expression revealed nothing of the reason behind the odd question.

She explained gently, as if to a child. Perhaps, spiritually, he was still very young. "Some people have rotten souls, and some have beautiful, generous souls, but no matter what, they have one. You, me. No exceptions to that rule. Everyone has a soul."

He made a skeptical sound, but the longing in his face was clear as he rubbed his cleft chin. "How do you know so much about souls?"

"It's my job. See that church? I'm the pastor." As much as she loved her chosen calling in life, she deflated a little. Once men found out she was a pastor, they stopped thinking of her as a woman. From then on, they only wanted one of three things: absolution, friendship, or free counseling.

"A woman of God," he said with dawning surprise. "You are a nun."

A laugh burst out of her. "It seems like that sometimes, but no, I'm not a nun. I can marry, have a family, just like anyone else." *I can have hot, feverish sexual fantasies about well-built naked men. I can feel so horny I can't see straight. I sometimes think of "celibacy" as a four-letter word.*

She thrust out her hand. "I guess I should introduce myself since you obviously don't know who I am. I'm Harmony—Harmony Faithfull." He grasped the tips of her fingers with a cool, dry hand. There was gentleness cloaked in that strength, softness that he seemed to want to hide, but that she recognized anyway, putting her at ease when common sense told her she should be feeling the opposite. *Just like when you sensed he'd grown tired of living.* "And you are . . . ?" Ironic how she could know what every pore on his body looked like but not his name. "You have a name, right?" she teased when he didn't immediately answer.

His dark brows drew together in concentration. She was about to suggest he see a doctor for shock or a possible concussion when he blurted out sheepishly, "I am called Demon."

"Oh. That's a favorite of mine. My nephew's name is Damon, too."

"Demon—*Damon.*" He looked up, brightening. "Yes, I am Damon."

She smiled encouragingly. "Damon what?"

Again he concentrated.

Boy, he sure did seem rattled. But after all he'd been through, it was understandable. "Damon, you really need to see a doctor."

"Nay."

"But—"

"I am Damon," he announced. "Damon of Mysteria."

"Damon of Mysteria. It doesn't sound familiar. Or maybe I just don't recognize you without your clothes."

A devilish glint sparked in his eyes, sending shivers from

her neck downward, flipping the "on" switch attached to all the neglected places in between as the sensation plunged to her toes. "Well, lass," he said, winking, "I dinna think you can say that any longer."

Four

Do not blush, Harmony. Do not. She stood up so fast that she got light-headed, her rational side praying that she didn't faint, while at the same time the wanton tart she was fast becoming argued that there were far worse fates than landing in that incredible lap. "No, I guess I can't say that any longer. Next time I see you around town, naked, I'll know it's you," she retorted. Turning on her heel, she took a couple of steps and stopped. "Coming? I have some clothes inside I think will fit. I'll brew a pot of coffee, too. You look like you could use it."

"Nay," he winced, "nothing hot. Water."

I'm with you all the way on the water, bud. Only, I'll take mine ice cold and in the form of a shower!

Damon pushed to his feet, her sweater pressed between his massive thighs. Harmony was five-nine, but he towered over her, taller than all her brothers, even Jake Jr. He had to be six-foot-five at least.

That long shadow fell over Bubba, who until now had been hanging close to Harmony. The puppy growled and backed up, teeth bared, fur rising in a ridge along his spine.

"Hey, boy. It's okay," Harmony soothed, but the puppy started snarling and wouldn't quit.

Damon turned one hand palm up as he focused on the dog. His gold-brown eyes were arresting as it was, but now they grew so intense that they appeared to glow. It was a much different heat from what she'd seen when he'd caught her staring at his, uh, equipment. Not quite human, Damon's gaze was animal-like in its intensity and focus, almost as if he were communicating with her dog, wolf to wolf, so much so that she half-expected them to start howling any minute as something went back and forth between dog and man. Then, spell broken, Bubba wriggled over to Damon to lick his hand, that cute little tail wagging furiously.

"Wow. He likes you."

"He trusts me," Damon corrected. "The like will come in time."

Mmm. The guy had a way with women *and* dogs, she thought. An interspecies charmer.

They started walking toward the house. The road on the other side of the picket fence was empty of cars and joggers. Thank goodness. If anyone saw the new pastor going inside her house with a naked man . . . well, she'd never be able to get anyone to believe the *real* story.

Even *she* didn't believe the real story.

Bubba pranced alongside them as they walked up the porch steps leading to the door at the back of the chapel where Harmony's living quarters were located. Stepping into her small, cozy living room, Damon looked painfully out of place: a towering, hard-featured, rugged man in the midst of everything small and soft. Or, it could be just that he was naked.

In five seconds flat, she'd found him some work clothes that belonged to her largest brother. When Damon returned to the kitchen after changing into a pair of Jake Jr.'s faded Levi's and a gray, oil-stained, long-sleeved Henley T-shirt, her hunch was confirmed: everything was too tight and too short. At least the buttons and zippers weren't popping. Yet.

"Have a seat, Damon. I'll fix you something to eat and drink."

Looking a little lost, Damon sat at her small table, smoothing large hands over the lace cloth. It was as if everything were new to him, everything a wonder. Even her, she realized with a tiny twist of her heart when his gold-brown eyes found hers for a moment before focusing on the glass of water she nearly spilled in his lap. It was more than her current state of isolation—or intuition; this man did things to her, plain and simple, with his ancient eyes and surprisingly young soul.

She reached into the fridge for a leftover apple pie, a baked ham, rolls, mayo, and mustard. Big men ate big; that, she already knew from the five super-sized men in her family. Grabbing utensils and napkins, she dropped a slice of ham in Bubba's bowl on her way back to the table, where she cut Damon a huge slab of pie and slid the plate next to the overloaded one that held a lumberjack-sized ham sandwich. After she made herself a much smaller sandwich, she carried her plate to the table to sit across from Damon as he downed his water with thirsty gulps. She poured him some more. "Feeling better?" she asked after he finished the second glass.

"Aye." He winked, pressing the back of his hand to his mouth, in a truly medieval way, to dab at the droplets of water left behind. "How can a man not feel better, taken in with kindness, tended by such a beautiful wench?"

She lifted a brow. "Wench. Is that Scottish for strong, capable, intelligent woman, I hope?

"Nay. 'Tis old English. Old, *old* English."

"But you're Scottish, aren't you? The brogue."

"I do have a brogue, don't I? You can thank my ex-employer for that, lass. His sense of humor knew no bounds." He winked at her and lifted the ham sandwich, sniffing it, his eyes closing. His pleasure in the scent was so palpable, his anticipation so sharp, that by the time the breathless second had passed and he'd dived in with a hearty bite, her throat was dry and she was left wondering what she'd just witnessed.

Did he approach all activities with the same explosive, all-consuming passion?

Harmony . . . behave.

Damon was thorough, but neat. Hardly a crumb escaped him. In short order, the massive sandwich was gone. Next, he turned to the slice of pie, hesitating for a moment as if he'd remembered at the last minute that he'd better use a utensil in her presence. In no more than four shovels of the fork, the pie was gone, too.

"More?" Strangely drained, she shoveled another slice onto his plate, and he started on that, too, without taking a breath. She might as well fix him another sandwich, because he was still going strong. "Something must appeal about my cooking, or you haven't eaten in about a thousand years."

"Ten thousand," he said, wiping his mouth and hunting around for more food. She slid the pie plate toward him and let him serve himself, which he did with as much grace as speedy efficiency. When the first bite of pie reached his mouth, he closed his eyes, savoring the taste, and was that a shudder that ran through him?

Fascinated, she balanced her chin on her hand, smiling as she watched him. "I don't know what to make of you, Mr. Damon of Mysteria."

"Make of me whatever you wish, fair maiden."

"Fair maiden. I like that better than wench."

His gaze went soft again. "It fits ye better, too."

She swallowed against the feelings his gentle, sexy tone fired up inside her. Sitting straighter, she tried to gather the scattered shreds of her professionalism. "Maybe you'd better call your family to let them know you're okay."

He shook his head. "There is no one."

"No one at all? You're not married?" She immediately bit her lip.

But he'd turned thoughtful. "Nay . . . never thought of it. My livelihood would have made such a pairing difficult. Impossible, rather. But, perhaps now that has changed. . . ." When he returned his attention to her face, it was with such bold intensity, such raw consideration, that this time she did blush.

Harmony got up too quickly, sloshing water out of the

pitcher. She grabbed a dish towel and started mopping at the puddle. Damon grabbed her wrist.

All at once, his thoughts burst inside her skull. His experiences, his emotions, too. They spun in a blur too fast for her to interpret, like subtitles set on fast-forward, but in those few heartbeats, she was able to gain a sense of the man: his confusion, his lack of guile, and his genuine fear—something she sensed he was not used to feeling.

Harmony, you're not Great-grandmother Eudora. You're insane. Your overactive hormones are finally taking their toll. You should have stuck to talking to the dog.

She studied his big hand and then his face. She didn't know how to explain what had just happened—nor did she want to. Her brain felt like a snow globe that had been shaken too hard. If he let go, maybe everything would settle down. "I'm a third-degree black belt," she said softly. "And my dog will rip your throat out if you try anything stupid."

Bubba protested with a little whimper, looking from her to Damon and back again. Harmony had the sudden feeling that she might not want to test the puppy's loyalties.

Damon let go. "I did not mean to frighten you."

Harmony sat back down, her heart thumping. What had just happened? Somehow, she regained her composure. "I'd like to help you. But to do that, you're going to have to tell me how you came to be under my apple tree." She left out the naked part. Those were details he could fill in. "I'll keep in confidence what you tell me."

Damon leaned forward. The maple café chair creaked under the shift in weight. "The true story?"

She leaned forward, too. "No," she whispered. "I want you to lie to me."

He took a deep breath, and then spilled. "I am the ten-thousand-year-old Demon High Lord of Self-Doubt and Second Thoughts, or I was until I was kicked out of Hell by Lucifer for committing random acts of kindness. After centuries of torture, I forget how many now, I was made mortal and banished to live out my days here, in Mysteria, the site of my original crime of beneficence."

Harmony stared at him. Damon stared back, as serious as they came. "I was just kidding about the lying," she said.

He opened his mouth to say something then seemed to change his mind. He drummed blunt-tipped fingers, glanced out the window as if seeking inspiration before returning his gaze to her. "I worked for a corrupt employer for many years. I carried out my orders until I learned what it was to be good. I learned that I liked being good over being bad. My employer punished me for it—for changing—and then he . . . he did *this* to me. He let me go. And so now I'm here, in Mysteria. With no home, no job, and"—he cleared his throat—"no clothes."

"You've been through hell, haven't you?" With a bit of an alarmed expression, he agreed. She shook her head sympathetically. He was a strapping, healthy guy down on his luck; admitting he was jobless and homeless couldn't have been easy.

Jobless. Homeless. *Here.*

Inspiration hit like a thunderbolt straight from heaven. "I have an idea." She opened her hands so Damon could see the calluses, cuts, and paint stains. "I've been looking for someone to hire—a handyman and groundskeeper. It'd be a huge help to have someone here for the heavier work, so I can concentrate on the church. The fields haven't been planted, the fence needs repair, and the barn needs fixing. I'd like to make it into a social hall, eventually, maybe a school, or even a gym, and I thought if I had some help, it'd leave me more time for recruiting more parishioners. In fact, any parishioners." She sighed.

"No one comes?"

She shook her head. "Just this morning I asked God to help me. To show me how to bring people here. I asked for a sign. And what do I find in my yard? A naked Demon. Oh! I meant Damon. Sorry!" She threw her face into her hands to muffle the giggles bubbling up.

Through her fingers, she heard Damon assuring her, "'Tis an understandable mistake," in a surprisingly earnest tone.

She peeked between her hands and saw that his expression matched his dead-serious tone of voice. Her giggles turned to laughter. Something must have struck Damon as funny because he, too, fell into genuine laughter, rich and deep.

Finally, she got hold of herself, wiping her tears. "Oh, that felt good. I needed it, too. I think this is what's known as divine intervention."

Damon's sparkling eyes seemed at once impossibly ancient and like those of a newborn baby. "Aye, more than you know, my fair maiden."

"If I'm the fair maiden, then you can be my knight in shining armor. My hired knight. How does that sound?"

He dipped his head once. " 'Tis a fair offer."

They exchanged a smile that left her feeling cheerful and optimistic and warm all over. Really, really warm. Then she thought: what was she saying? Her smile fell as reality set in. "I can't afford to pay much."

He lifted his hands as if to say he didn't care.

"Actually, I can't afford to pay you at all." She pushed back from the table. "I'm sorry. I made a promise I can't keep. I'll give you a ride back to town."

"I don't require money. I'll work for . . . sustenance."

She shivered at the look in his sexy eyes, the way he drew out that last word.

"Food," he clarified. "And a place to lay my bones at night."

Bones . . . bones . . . she tried to keep her mind out of the gutter. "Okay." Why was she whispering? She thrust her hand at him. "Deal."

He took her hand, and she got the most curious feeling that he'd rather lift it to his soft lips than shake it. "You've been kind to me, Harmony Faithfull. Yet, you ask nothing in return."

"Why wouldn't I be kind to you?"

The hard line of his lips softened into an expression of surprise and pleasure. "That question alone answers mine, lass." He searched her face in a deeply intense, almost intimate way that made her go all squishy inside. Then he murmured, "Your goodness, it sits around ye like a halo. Are ye sure you're not an angel?"

Her smile came partly out of pleasure from his compliments, and partly out of the irony of being viewed as an angel. While her attraction to Damon was definitely heavenly, it was anything but angelic. "Very sure. Kindness exists outside heaven, too, you know."

"I've not much experience with kindness. With goodness."

"We'll have to change that," she said, her heart squeezing again.

"Aye, we will. . . ."

He released her, then, and she slid her hand under the table. Closing her fist, she secretly held on to the feel of him.

Five

Harmony stood on the porch as Damon strode off to the barn to arrange his new home in the hayloft with bedding, supplies, and a box of Oreos (the taste of which had rendered him nearly orgasmic).

Damon held no menace—raw, smoldering male sexuality, yes, but not menace. But she was an urban girl, born and bred, and it was always wise to make sure a person didn't have a record a mile long. She considered herself street smart, observant, and never blindly trusting, but she wanted to make darn sure Damon's looks, charisma, and charm—not to mention her hot-running blood and his miraculously timed arrival—weren't interfering with her better judgment. Having his fingerprints checked out was the way to go. Any employer would do the same thing.

Harmony returned to the kitchen and wrapped the glass Damon had used with a paper towel. Carefully, she slipped it into her backpack and slung it over her shoulder. "Come on, Bubba. Let's go shopping." She needed to buy Damon some work clothes that fit, but first she'd pay a little visit to Jeanie Tortellini, the sheriff.

She cut across the field to where a stand of aspens and tall pines marked the beginning of the Rocky Mountain National Forest. After turning right, a quick walk on a dirt trail would bring her right up behind the Mysteria police station and jail.

Bubba jerked on the leash and started growling. "What, boy, another naked hunk?" At this rate, she'd have a whole staff of them working for her. Not bad for a single girl. But part of her didn't want an army of muscles at her disposal. She'd rather have Damon, who engaged her on all levels, swinging from weary and jaded to boyish and full of wonder in the space of a heartbeat.

The puppy tugged hard on the leash and tried to run into the woods. Harmony held on with both hands. "Bubba, stay!"

Jeanie Tortellini burst out of the forest with a tall blond man trailing behind her. His wrists were bound with her police belt. The loose end Jeanie gripped in her fist.

Bubba broke into a full-fledged bark. "Hush, boy!" Harmony tried to quiet the pup.

Jeanie's smile when she saw Harmony was genuine, if not a little startled. "Good morning!" She used her free hand to brush loose strands of hair away from her face. With pink cheeks, messy hair, and strangely bright eyes, Jeanie looked as if she'd been in a scuffle. But it was the woman's appearance of having dressed too quickly that puzzled Harmony the most.

Jeanie's hand went to her uniform shirt as if she, too, just realized the buttons were in the wrong holes. It must have been quite a struggle, her apprehension of the lawbreaker.

Harmony stopped about twenty feet from the pair. "I was on my way to see you. I need a favor." She stole a glance at Jeanie's prisoner. His white-blond hair swung around his waist, some strands tied in braids. And were those pointed ears peeking through the spun-silk hair? A bit of an unfortunate birth defect, because with his archer's quiver, dark green tunic, and thigh-high leather boots, he was a dead ringer for Legolas from *Lord of the Rings*. "But, I see you're busy."

"I was," Jeanie said. "But I'm not now."

Making a quiet sound, the prisoner cast Jeanie a smoldering glance, and Jeanie's mouth quirked in the barest of smug little smiles. Harmony got the feeling that there was more going on than she probably wanted to know. Par for the course in Mysteria.

"Behave." Jeanie tugged on the belt and I'm-too-sexy-for-my-suede-tunic Legolas lowered his eyes dutifully. He had the perfect male pout, sullen and sensual. "How can I help you, Reverend Faithfull?"

Harmony unwrapped her paper-covered package. "I hired someone at the church this morning—a groundskeeper." Deciding it was better to keep the lurid details of Damon's arrival to herself, she moved the paper so Jeanie could see the drinking glass. "He's not from around here, and as much as I think I believe what he's told me about his background, it pays to be sure he's not wanted for a felony. Can you check out his fingerprints?"

Jeanie took the paper-wrapped glass. "No problem." The sheriff slid her gaze over the prisoner. Harmony could almost feel the electric surge of their eye contact. "If that's all you needed, I've got to get this bad boy under lock and key."

Legolas's mouth curved. The idea of a lockdown seemed to invigorate the sexy pseudo-elf. Or did he just like being called a "bad boy"?

"Thanks, Jeanie," Harmony said, unable to keep from staring at the man's pointy ears. "Stop in for coffee this week."

"I'll be there. And be careful with your new help. If you need me, just call."

"Will do."

Jeanie grinned and gave Harmony a little salute. Then she frowned at Legolas, using the belt to jerk him forward. To Harmony, his stumble seemed a little staged.

Harmony gave Bubba's leash a much gentler tug and continued toward town, and the One-Stop Mart, which conveniently did mean one stop in the true rural tradition of general mercantile stores. Since Wal-Mart hadn't yet invaded Mysteria, and probably never would, it was the only place she'd be able to find work clothes for Damon.

Puffs of pink pollen whooshed with each of her footfalls on the path, drifting in cotton-candy mounds, a phenomenon that no one seemed to be able—or was willing—to explain to her, and that included the town physician, who Harmony swore, even if she wasn't supposed to swear, that she'd spied waving a wand as she drove past his office the other day. A wand, as in magic wand, a fairy-godmother model, too, she assumed, because it had sported a shiny star at its tip. Harmony couldn't imagine what the handsome but terminally distracted Dr. Fogg had been doing, circling the wand over old Mrs. O'Cleary's white-haired head, but the very next day, when Harmony had seen Mrs. O'Cleary at the One-Stop, not only was the old woman's arthritic limp gone, but her snow-white, overpermed pin curls had relaxed into soft, shiny blond waves! It was just the sort of weird, supernatural happening Mysteria produced in abundance.

And you expect people to come to church when the local doctor can perform miracles? How could she compete with that? *How?*

After tying Bubba's leash to the bike rack in front of the store, Harmony pushed open the door to the market. Tin chimes clattered against the glass, and air thick with the scent of vanilla, peppermint, and old cardboard hit her nostrils with her first full breath. A cloud of pollen that had collected by the threshold spun in a powdery pink tornado. Unintentionally, Harmony inhaled a stream of the stuff and sneezed. Eyes tearing, she grew warm all over. Not as warm as when she was around Damon, but the same parts were involved. It was really distracting.

Mrs. O'Cleary beamed at her from behind the counter. She looked ten years younger than the last time Harmony had seen her—before her visit to Dr. Fogg. "It looks like love is in the air today, Reverend Faithfull!"

"It's the pollen." Harmony dabbed at her eyes. "I think I might be allergic."

The woman winked. "Who's the special man?"

Harmony's heart fell to the plank floor with a thud. Or at least it felt that way. "I don't understand what you mean."

Mrs. O'Cleary winked and wagged her finger. "Don't deny it. I know just by looking at you, young lady. You're in love."

"What you see is my love for my work, Mrs. O'Cleary. I love this town and the people in it."

"Pah." She waved her hand.

"I haven't been dating anyone. I haven't met anyone." Except for Damon. Harmony's face flooded with heat. "I haven't known anyone long enough to be in love."

"Silly girl. Time makes no difference. Sometimes you just know."

Sometimes you just know. Harmony thought of Damon and her heart contracted. Then she shook her head. She couldn't let the eccentric residents of Mysteria—or the pink pollen—get to her. It was her job as pastor to be the voice of reason—of God—in this town. "I need to pick up a few things for the church," she said, changing the subject as she stepped sideways down the aisle that contained everything from baseball caps to panty hose—and a display of Hanes underwear.

"Nails? Plaster? A nice . . . long . . . screw?"

Harmony shot the old woman a startled glance. The knowing amusement she saw in those crinkly blue eyes almost made her blush. "I hired someone at the church. He needs clothes."

The old woman grinned wickedly.

Harmony tried not to react. "*Work* clothes," she explained, choosing jeans, shirts, thick cotton socks, and boots, hesitating only when she turned her attention to the Hanes display. Boxers or briefs?

Harmony could feel Mrs. O'Cleary's eyes boring into the back of her head. "Do you need a particular size?" the woman inquired helpfully.

"Extra large. I mean, he's not fat. He's just . . . large." *Incredibly so.* She squeezed her eyes shut. *Just shut up, Harmony.* She chose several pairs of boxers in generic colors like beige gingham check and powder blue, studiously avoiding the designer black silks that practically begged to jump into her arms. *Would Damon look awesome in those, or what?*

Or did he look best in nothing?

In nothing, she decided.

Harmony, please. He's your employee.

Not trusting her facial expression, Harmony kept her chin buried in the pile of clothing in her arms and dumped the entire pile of clothes on the counter by the cash register.

Mrs. O'Cleary smiled at the Hanes packages as she rang them up. Harmony paid for the purchases with as much self-consciousness as if she were buying a package of condoms.

It was a relief to return to Bubba's innocent, unquestioning eyes. With several heavy shopping bags hanging from her hands, she headed home with the puppy. The closer she got to the farm, the faster she walked. And the only reason she could come up with was that she anticipated returning home to Damon a little more than she felt comfortable admitting.

Six

Sated with a belly full of the divine delicacy called Oreo—
and he'd eaten every last one in the box—Damon sprawled
on his back in bed in the hayloft to the rear of the vast empty
interior of the barn. Sunlight leaked between the timbers and
provided the only illumination. He breathed deep, sampling
the air. The scent of Mysteria had not changed much in three
hundred years, aside from the oily background odor of fossil-
fueled machinery and the more acrid smell of electrical
equipment. The barn smelled like dust and hay, and faintly of
livestock that had not lived here for a year or more. Although
his animal-sharp sense of smell was fading rapidly, he could
still pick out the faint pungent odor of mouse droppings and
that of the young black dog. Despite so many different
scents, Harmony's scent stood out above all else, perhaps
because he'd so focused on it. Her essence was on the
wooden handles of the tools, on his very skin.

  She had not the scent of another male about her; he'd
noticed that straightaway, glad he'd held on to his demon's
sense of smell long enough not to have to guess. She was
free, unattached.

Smiling, he wedged his hands behind his head, laced his fingers together as he inhaled the lingering scent of the beautiful lass. Harmony had ordered him to get some rest, and he was trying—without much success. He had not done the labor required, he supposed. Tonight, it would be different, for this afternoon, he'd start work. Aye, but there were some other labors he had in mind when it came to Harmony Faithfull. Exhausting labors he would more than care to try.

"Ah, lass," he murmured, "ye are beautiful; no denying that. Inside and out." He liked the way she listened to him, so very carefully, how she'd taken him in and given him shelter with few questions asked.

Harmony's open and generous heart was something that not all humans possessed; but rarer still was her uncanny ability to look him in the eye and sense his needs, his fears, even—a gift that brought great risk for him. If the lass ever discovered that he had no soul, she'd be repelled by him, would even fear him.

"Everyone has a soul," she'd insisted.

Bah! 'Twas an observation based on her innocence of creatures like him, a demon that was never meant for a mortal life, a good life. He was a monster created out of darkness and intended to remain in the shadows, carrying out the Devil's deeds. The fact he was here at all was due to the Devil's whim, and the Devil's whim was never good, not in all the ten thousand years Damon had watched Lucifer in action.

There was only one solution: stay far enough away so that Harmony didn't discover his dark secret, and yet close enough to savor the way she made him feel: warm, happy, hopeful—just the sort of emotions to which he was unaccustomed and woefully ill-equipped to sort out. He couldn't have her, not in the way he wanted, but he could do good deeds for her, become indispensable in other, less intimate ways. Perhaps this was Lucifer's plan all along, this punishment of placing him within arm's reach of a woman like Harmony Faithfull, without being allowed to truly touch her.

Damon could think of no crueler sentence.

A scrabbling noise in the barn dragged him to full alert.

He peered into the dim light, scanning for an obvious explanation for the brief sound. His demon eyesight was still strong enough to discern what crept down there in the shadows. Although he saw nothing, he knew he was no longer alone.

A dark creature had joined him.

With stealthy quiet, Damon vaulted off the sleeping berth and landed in a crouch, hands up and ready for battle. "Show yourself!"

"She likes you," rasped a voice from the shadows. "Yes, she does."

Hell's bells, 'twas a goblin! Useless monsters, always underfoot. "Too many eyes," Damon growled. "And too few brains."

The creature came into view. It had the dark green skin of a frog, gleaming and lumpy with boils. That the little goblin hadn't called him "Lord" reminded Damon just how far he'd fallen.

No, not fallen. *Risen.* Damon had to think differently now.

The little monster waved something at him. "I have me a souvenir."

Between the goblin's spindly fingers was a long strand of wavy dark hair. Harmony's hair. Damon's heart dropped. If the goblin brought part of Harmony back to Hell—any part: a fingernail, this strand of hair—it would forge a link between the underworld and this farm, and would make other night creatures more brazen. They'd come looking for souvenirs of their own, mementos far more precious.

Damon advanced on the goblin, snarling, but the goblin danced out of his reach. "No, no, you can't have it, mortal. It's a prize too sweet. A prize all mine. Mine, mine, mine. Soon she will like me, too. She will like me, she will, better than you." A slimy, warty tongue darted out between the goblin's lips and slid down the entire length of the hair, a sensation Harmony would feel in her sleep night after night unless Damon ended it here.

Rage boiled up inside Damon and made his blood burn.

Snarling, he grabbed for the little beastie, but it slipped out of his grip. Fury was making him sloppy. In the past, he'd always acted efficiently and without emotion. Now anger drove him. Aye, anger and fear.

Slow down. Concentrate. Damon forcibly unclenched his teeth and extended an open hand. "Give."

"No, no, no. Oh, no. Mine, mine, mine. All mine, not yours."

"But all Hell-born are brothers, yes?" The mere thought of pledging a blood bond with a goblin almost made him puke. " 'Tis simple. You help me, I help you." He advanced another step. "Give me the hair and no harm will come to you for your trespassing."

"Harm, harm will never come," the goblin sang. "Your powers are gone, yes, they are." Spinning in a careless little pirouette, it waved the strand of hair like a victory flag.

Damon watched. Waited. His gentler tone had made the thing careless. Lost in celebrating, the goblin spun closer.

Damon bolted forward and grabbed the creature by its skinny wrist before it could dart away. The goblin shrieked in surprise; its lips pulled back in fear, revealing rows of yellowed, needle-sharp teeth. "Ouch, mortal. Hurts—hurts, it does!"

Damon brought his face very close. "Unfortunately for you, I'm not yet mortal enough to care."

With the wriggling, screaming goblin in one hand, he strode across the barn. "No, no, no!"

"I think yes." Damon reached for a bucket and threw it under a spigot, turning on the water. A few drops splashed onto the creature's belly and sizzled like hot oil.

The beastie screamed in agony and fright. "No! Not that! My lord and master, not that."

"Ah, so I'm your lord now, eh?" Methodically, Damon filled the bucket. "Interesting how desperation breeds respect."

"Master, Master, please. Let me go!"

Grim, Damon shut off the water and turned to the goblin dangling from his grip. Its eyes were wide, each blinking at different rates. Thin, blistered fingers curled around his forearm. Damon could feel a rapid pulse in the press of its fingertips. Harmony's hair still curled from one knotty fist.

One dunk was all it'd take to silence the despicable creature forever.

Frantic yellow eyes searched his face. Damon knew he looked fearsome to the goblin, what with the rage he felt glowing in his gut. Sensing its demise, the goblin went very still. "I'll do anything, Master, anything."

Damon lowered the goblin until its bare feet hung inches from the water. Fear trembled through its thin frame. "Mercy," the goblin wailed. "Oh, please. Mercy!"

Damon went very still. *Mercy . . .*

Harmony's words echoed in his memory. *"You're a true man of mercy."*

But was he? Damon swallowed, frozen to the spot, almost forgetting about the struggling goblin that was so far too panicked to sense Damon's hesitation, his weakness.

Nay, not weakness! Mercy was not a weakness. Mercy was never wrong!

'Twas it not time to prove he believed it?

Damon turned his attention to his prisoner. "Give me your prize, goblin. Give it to me and I will let you live."

The goblin's little hand unfurled. "Here, Master. Here, here. You take—please take."

Damon snatched the curly black strand and slipped it into his trousers pocket. Then he brought his nose very close to the little creature's maw. The goblin's breath was fetid and warm. Wisely, the creature chose silence, or Damon might not have trusted himself to maintain his compassion. "Never come here again—you or your cohorts. For if you do return here, 'twill not go well for you the next time." He lowered the creature, slowly, until its heels just barely brushed the water. A sizzle and a scream brought a smile of satisfaction to Damon's face. "Not well at all . . ."

He threw the goblin to the ground. "Go! Return here and ye will perish."

"Don't want to perish. No, no, I will go, go." Gasping,

the goblin scrabbled, limping, across the hay-strewn floor and disappeared into a small Hell hole that opened only wide enough to allow the creature to disappear.

Sniffing the air one more time to check for subdemons, goblins, and other dark creatures, Damon had almost convinced himself there were none close by when another dark form came barreling into the barn, snorting and snuffling. A breath away from flinging the creature into the wall, Damon saw that the intruder was Harmony's dog.

Bubba leaped up on him, black eyes shining: a wriggling, roiling mass of pure eagerness—eagerness to see him, to smell him, and above all to please. Damon scratched him behind the ears. "Aye, I'm glad to see ye, too."

Next, Harmony swept through the door, her arms filled with bundles. She'd changed clothes from earlier. Her blouse was pink and form-fitting, worn over faded blue pants that hugged every inch of her long, firm legs. The flesh of her ankles peeked out between the pants and pink-and-white rubber-soled shoes.

"Down, Bubba!" Harmony's hair bounced in a mass of dark ringlets around her shoulders. "Damon does not want to be mauled."

Mauled by the dog, no, Damon thought. *But mauled by you, lass, well, that would be an experience to be savored, indeed.*

"I'm sorry, Damon. He's all over you."

"'Tis not a bother." Damon took the pup's head in his broad palms and held eye contact with the squirming animal. *Be still, boy. Be still.*

The dog immediately sat on its rump. Only its tongue fluttered.

Harmony laughed. "How do you do that? It's amazing. I'm going to start calling you the dog whisperer."

"'Tis a lot like whispering," he conceded, sorry that the talent to communicate with animals would soon leave him. With one last affectionate rub behind Bubba's floppy ears, he turned his full attention to Harmony. His heart gave a little leap at the answering spark of interest he saw in her eyes.

She was full of life. She filled him with life.

Harmony smiled and reached for him, and his breath caught as he waited for her touch, but all she did was pluck a piece of straw from his shirt. "I thought you were going to rest."

He glanced at the portion of the floor where the Hell hole had opened. It was gone. Only displaced straw indicated where the struggle had taken place. His shoulders sagged as he dashed an unsteady hand across his forehead. He hadn't been weary before, but he was now. Battle, he'd overheard many a mortal warrior state, exhausted a man.

But his weariness was more a mental matter than a physical one. After tonight he might no longer be able to detect such monsters before it was too late. *How then, will you protect Harmony?* Hopelessness threatened to swamp him. Like the tumultuous sensations coursing through him in Harmony's presence, he did not know quite how to quench such emotions. *You must fight to control them, then.* Aye, fight as he'd earlier fought to control his desire to take Harmony to the kitchen floor and make wild love to her. A shudder ran through Damon at the thought. In the silence of his mind, he tried to pray, though he knew not how. Who would listen to a prayer from a soulless demon? Certainly not God. As for the angels, he'd made enemies of most of them. Instead he simply made a plea: *Help me to keep the lass safe. Give me the strength.*

"You're exhausted," he heard Harmony say.

"I've rested long enough, lass. It's time to put me to work. You name the task, anything at all, and I will devote myself to its thorough completion."

Another contemplative spark flashed in her brown eyes, quickly quenched, but not before he felt the answering heat in his loins.

Hell's bells, living in her presence was going to be torture. *Lucifer, you have truly crafted the ultimate punishment.*

Rather hoarsely, Damon said, "Show me where I might find the tools of my labors."

Harmony's gaze dropped. Then the red patches on her

cheeks flared and she cleared her throat. "Oh, tools. Right. Everything's over here." She walked away very fast, but somehow he knew she wanted him to follow. "Everything you need. Thanks to my brothers and Home Depot."

"The men in your family have chosen well for you." Damon selected a shovel, hefting it into his hand, and heard the tear of fabric. He glanced down with dread at the same time Harmony made a small sound. His shirt had split, exposing much of his chest and torso.

Harmony ran off. For an instant he wondered if he'd scared her off for good, but she hurried back to him with the bundles she'd carried into the barn. "These are for you, and none too soon." She shoved the packages into his hands, her attention shifting somewhere else, as if she were both tempted and afraid to look at the strips of fabric hanging from the ruined shirt. "New work clothes—and in your size, too. Now you don't have to worry about them coming off until they're taken off!" Her eyes squeezed shut, as if the comment about taking off clothing had embarrassed her.

"Lass, you've given me too much as it is—"

Her hands came up to stop his protest. "Don't worry about the cost. We'll work it out."

"Aye. That we will."

She met his eyes and blushed deeply, and he wasn't sure why. Again, Damon tasted the air, trying to gather more information to help understand her baffling reactions—and his. She desired him, as he desired her. She could not hide the fact. It hung in the air, it permeated his senses.

Harmony's attraction to him, combined with his for her, was sharp and powerful, fueling passionate thoughts of sliding his hands under the garments she wore to feel the heat of her bare skin, which only exacerbated the sexual hunger building with each breath he took. As if that wasn't bad enough, he reacted physically with the thought, growing rock hard with a new-to-him ache that left him barely able to breathe. It reminded him of the sensation when Lucifer set fires so intense that they sucked all the air from the chambers of Hell. Only this was nothing close to suffocation!

Damon clutched the bundle of clothes to his lower abdomen, sharply relieved at having a way to cover up as sexual desire, a cataclysm of need, boiled up inside him. Never before had he been forced to face his reactions to a mortal. To a woman. To anyone.

But ye will have to behave. You're a man now. A good man.

Good, good, good, good. If he chanted it, it might sink in. Good men did not drag women like Harmony to their mouths to kiss deeply as they fell, clothes scattering, to the ground, where he'd kiss her everywhere else—

Damon made a sound in the back of his throat. *Good, good, good . . .*

A chiming little tune rang out from Harmony's pants, startling Damon as much as it did the lass.

She tore her eyes from his, mumbling something about taking a "call" on her "cell phone" as she pulled a little silver rectangle from her pocket. "I should have guessed," she said, reading the glowing numbers. "What is it about fathers and timing?" She pushed a button and spoke into the phone. "Hi, Daddy!"

While Harmony was otherwise distracted, Damon, trying with all his might to block the distraction of her scent, grabbed a pickax off a hook on the wall.

She had a family, he thought, and then wondered at his surprise. Of course she had a family. All humans did. Unlike him, they weren't born of shadows and darkness, the Devil's spawn.

"I'm doing great. How are you and Mama? And Great-grandma?" Harmony nodded, smiling as she listened. Then her grin faltered. "What did Great-grandma say?" Harmony's gaze shifted to Damon and darted away. The red patches were back, one on each cheek. "No, I haven't had much time for a social life. No, really! I've been too busy—yes, busy with the church. Oh, yes, the people here are wonderful. Just great. I'm so happy—you're *what*?" She almost dropped the cell phone. "You're coming here? In August?" she squeaked. "No, it'll be no trouble. I can't wait to see you,

Daddy. Look, I gotta run. Church business. Give my love to Mama and everyone else. Miss you."

Harmony sighed as she wedged the cell phone into her pocket. "Why did I do that?"

Damon shook his head. "Do what, lass?"

"My father's coming for a visit, in less than two months. With the entire family!" She pressed her fingertips into her temples, muttering, "And they're dying to see the thriving church community I just told him about."

"You dinna tell him that," Damon pointed out tactfully. "I was listening."

"My father made a guess based on what I told him, and I didn't deny it. That's just as bad! I lied to a pastor—and I *am* a pastor!" She glanced heavenward, appearing truly repentant as she murmured a prayer. Then she wiped her hands on her pants. "Well, there's only one thing to do, Damon, and that's to make what I told my father true. Somehow, I'm going to come up with a way to reel in the townspeople to this church on Sundays—and fast." She started walking to the door. "When all else fails, cook on it."

"Cook on it?" he asked and she laughed from where she stood near the open door encircled by sunshine streaming around her like a halo.

"When I have problems to solve, I head to the kitchen. I think the best when I'm cooking things. Always have, always will. Since this is a big problem, you'll have a big dinner to look forward to."

Damon remembered the food from the midday meal and salivated. His stomach grumbled so loudly that he was surprised she didn't hear it.

"Home-made fried chicken," she muttered as she walked away, already deep in thought. "Mashed potatoes and gravy . . . buttered corn . . . peach cobbler for dessert . . ."

He watched her go. *Well, lass, ye are not in this alone, no matter what ye think.* This was his chance to help her, to prove himself worthy of her generosity. If his fair maiden needed a knight in shining armor, then that was what she'd get. While he worked at his assigned labors, he'd come up

with a way to help her, though he knew not how a former demon could help fill a church with the faithful.

Aye, but he'd figure it out. Yes, he would, and quickly.

There was no time to change into his new clothing. In his
new and very mortal life, there wasn't a moment to waste.
Not having eternity before him cast everything in a different
light, in fact. Although he'd developed a certain respect for
humans when he'd committed his crimes—no, his deeds—
of mercy, only now that he was one of them did he fully appreciate the humans' courage in facing a finite life. With the
puppy trotting after him, he strode out into the sunshine with
the promise that he, too, would brave his mortality like the
man he was—or at least like the man he hoped one day to be.

And so it was that Damon of Mysteria officially began
his new life as a mortal: by digging postholes to shore up a
weakened section of the front fence.

Seven

After an hour of working outside, the weather grew so hot that sweat soaked through his ruined shirt. Tossing aside the tattered garment, he continued bare-chested.

After a dozen more strikes of the pickax, he scented something new and different in the air—something far more pleasant than his sweat. Damon looked up, the ax held in midair. Three women stood across the fence, staring at him.

Their sexual interest washed over him in pheromone-laden waves. There was the aura of the dark arts about them but not evil, nay, none of that, but sorcery and magic. And their brilliant hazel eyes were afire with a light all of their own. For one panicked moment, he thought they'd figured out what he was; then he realized they were more interested in what he was now. Or at least what of him existed below his neck.

Bubba didn't growl, which told Damon that Harmony knew these women even if he did not.

Slowly, Damon lowered the pickax. "And who might you pretties be?"

The wench with long dark hair stepped closer to the fence. Her face was serious, but her sensuality smoldered.

"Genevieve Tawdry. And these are my sisters—Glory and Godiva."

"Hello, stranger." Glory twirled a finger in her red hair as she licked her lips. Her bosom was ample, would make many a man happy, and she eyed him with the kind of come-hither smile that had remained unchanged down through the ages. Mortal men would take it as an invitation to share in the bounty of her body. *You are now mortal, too, Damon, are you not?*

Aye, he was. But as much as he found all three wenches attractive, it was only Harmony he desired.

The wench named Godiva observed him with perceptive eyes. She had a powerful magic about her, this silver-haired witch. Could she tell his origins? He hoped not. If Harmony were to find out through her friends that he'd come from the depths of Hell, she'd banish him from her church for good. He wouldn't lie to her, when that time came, but the longer he could put off the truth, the better. "If I'd bumped into you before," Godiva said, "I'd have remembered. You're new here."

"Aye, I am." 'Twas not really a lie. It had been three hundred years since he was last here; it was almost like being new in town all over again. He stood proudly, the ax resting on his shoulder. "I'm the new church groundskeeper."

"Really." Glory exchanged a speculative glance with her sisters. "We didn't know there'd been an *old* groundskeeper."

"There wasn't. I'm the first." Damon folded his hands on the tip of the shovel handle. His shirt gapped open and three pairs of hungry eyes shifted to his chest. Their sexual interest thickened the air.

The trio paused to whisper among themselves, glancing at him often, sometimes even his face, but mostly from his neck down. Damon noticed the shopping bags they carried. They'd been on their way home from shopping when they'd spotted him and stopped dead in their tracks. If townsfolk regularly passed this close to the church, why then couldn't they spare a few moments more and visit on Sundays?

An idea began to form. A magnificent idea. Harmony needed a way to lure the townsfolk inside the church. Perhaps he was the answer to that problem.

His body had been put to far worse uses, certainly. And he'd spent ten thousand years planting doubts and fears. Could he not do the same with the women in the town, but planting interest to attend Harmony's church instead? He wouldn't be able to convince them in his typical fashion, for he'd lost the ability to circumvent free will when he was banished from Hell, but he could influence others, especially female others, in a much more primitive way. Aye, an *age-old* way.

Damon's mouth curved in a slow smile he was sure all three women felt to the very tips of their toes. Then, stretching his arms over his head, he worked a kink out of his back. The women looked faint as he hefted his pickax. "Alas, I cannot dally any longer. I am behind in my labors. Reverend Faithfull will beat me if I dinna get back to work."

Glory's lush mouth fell open. "Harmony beats you?"

"Only if I misbehave," he confided in a deep and sexy burr.

One of the witches made a small, soft sound.

"But I'll be doing maintenance on the church on Sunday— Sunday morning."

"What time?" Glory whispered.

"A quarter to nine." Damon winked at her, picked up the pickax, and went back to work. When he next glanced up, the sisters had walked away, but as they disappeared around the bend in the road, he saw them murmuring and giggling among themselves.

Aye, he'd planted his seeds of interest. If things went as he hoped they would, by next Sunday, Harmony would be reaping what he'd sown.

Eight

On Sunday, Harmony stood on the front lawn of the church, watching in happy amazement as woman after woman filed in for the nine A.M. service. Smiling and shaking hands, she welcomed the women she'd previously seen only at the One-Stop, the gas station, or on the streets of the town.

In uniform, Jeanie Tortellini walked up to her. Harmony couldn't help thinking of Legolas. In fact, the other day when she'd visited the sheriff, the jail cell had been empty. Although she often wondered what had happened to the sexy elf, she hadn't come up with a tactful way to ask the question.

"You've got yourself a nice crowd this morning, Harmony," Jeanie said.

"I do." Harmony tried to keep the bewilderment from her voice. It was only 8:45 and the pews were already one-third filled. With eager women. "And you're here, too, Jeanie. I thought you had to work Sunday mornings."

"I do. I'm here on official business."

Harmony lifted a brow. "What kind of business?"

"Crowd control."

Before Harmony could ask how the sheriff knew there'd be a crowd at church, Marie, the UPS driver, poked her head in their little huddle. "Where did you hide him, Reverend?"

"Hide who?"

"Your new groundskeeper."

"You mean Damon?"

Jeanie shook her head as if Harmony was beyond all help. "Yes. Damon. He's hot. If you haven't noticed."

"And if you haven't noticed," Maria put in, "you might want to stop by Dr. Fogg's office and take a gander at the eye chart, because I would say you need those peepers examined."

"Or get her heart checked to see if she has a pulse," Jeanie teased.

Harmony supposed it shouldn't surprise her that it hadn't taken long for word to get around about Damon. Almost as much as they appreciated the attributes of a good-looking man, the women of Mysteria loved juicy gossip, particularly when the latter concerned the former. Everyone, it seemed, even the pets, had a libido running in constant overdrive. Maybe it was that strange pink pollen. Nevertheless, she mumbled something about it not being professional to view her new employee in *that* way, which was such an obvious lie that the sheriff's eyes twinkled in merry amusement.

"Ooh, there he is now." Maria hurried off to where a small crowd of women had gathered around Damon, watching as he fiddled with a repair to the door frame at the front entrance of the church. Why was he doing that now, of all things, right when services were about to start? He'd been busy with the fence all week, and she'd assumed he'd take Sunday off, which was his free time by rights.

Laughter rang out from the group of women surrounding Damon. He appeared to be charming the panties off them as he ushered them inside. As if he'd sensed she was watching, he turned and caught her gaze. Immediately, his expression changed into something warmer, more personal, telling her that he viewed her differently from the other women.

Differently, because he thinks you're a nun, Harmony.

Harmony shifted her attention to Bubba, who sat adoringly at Damon's feet, the cute little traitor. But who could blame the dog? Damon occupied Harmony's thoughts day and night, too. Especially at night. She'd added an extra two miles to her daily jog, but it didn't seem to be helping.

Jeanie lowered her voice and spoke in her ear. "If I can tear your attention away from the groundskeeper hunk for a second, I have the information you requested."

Harmony's heart skipped a beat as she whirled around. "Damon's fingerprints."

"Uh-huh. And I don't have anything on him."

"Great!" But Jeanie appeared more troubled than relieved. Harmony frowned. "Isn't that good?"

"I mean I have *nothing* on him, Reverend. Nada. Zilch. We ran his prints and not a thing came up."

"What are you saying—that he doesn't exist?"

Jeanie spread her hands. "My research went beyond prints. I have friends in high places, and they helped. As far as the government goes, no. He's never applied for a passport, or registered to vote. He's never paid taxes, either, but then he's never held a job that required even the simplest background check. It goes without saying that he's never seen the inside of a prison—which was what you were worried about, right?"

Harmony thought back to the day it seemed that Damon had literally appeared out of nowhere in the garden. "What if he switched identities? What if he's a fugitive trying to escape his past?"

"We'd have picked it up. Prints are prints. I had an expert check them out, too, a CIA buddy who owed me a favor. Your hunk's fingerprints showed no evidence of being altered surgically or by any other method." The sheriff shrugged. "I don't know what else to say, but that he's clean. Real clean. Count your blessings."

"I will." Harmony took a steadying breath. "Speaking of blessings, I'd better get this service started."

She left the sheriff's side in a happy daze. "He's clean," she whispered to herself. "Real clean." Her intuition had been right—she wasn't falling for the devil's spawn, after all. Next time she had her doubts about anything, she'd listen to her instincts. *Thank you, Great-grandmother Eudora!*

Harmony breezed past Damon, hitched herself just high enough on her tiptoes as she passed by to whisper in his ear, "Dinner at six-thirty. Inside. Dress nice."

It would be the first time since the day he'd arrived that she'd invited him to dine in the kitchen. Not knowing if he had a record or not had hardened her resolved to wait before taking the chance. Now, she knew.

The glimpse of his shock slipping quickly into pleasure lingered in her mind as she took the pulpit with true excitement coursing through her. She was finally beginning what she'd come to Mysteria to do. Her smile was contagious: a chain reaction reflected by the happy faces of the townswomen. But when her gaze settled on Damon, who stood in the doorway a few careful steps outside the church, she felt a bolt of pure energy. How could he not be heaven sent?

Harmony raised her hands and belted out a hallelujah. Her heart, filled to bursting in more ways than one, was in every single syllable.

At dusk Damon showed up at her front door with a thick bouquet of wildflowers. He'd showered and combed his hair. Although he had only work clothes to wear, he'd ironed them and she decided that no matter what he wore, everything or nothing at all, he was the most gorgeous man she'd ever seen. And tonight he was all hers.

"Thank you," she sang out, taking the flowers. "They're beautiful." The heat in his eyes was especially intense as he took in the sight of her in the red-hot form-fitting sheathe dress she'd bought on impulse in town after the service was over. Sometimes even a pastor had to break the rule of resting on Sundays. "You look very nice tonight, too, by the way." She came up on her toes and planted a kiss on his cheek. A nun's kiss. She wanted more, she thought as she stepped back.

Behave, Harmony. Be professional.

Damon's whiskey-gold gaze glinted, as if he sensed her inner battle. "You have the devil in your eyes tonight, Damon of Mysteria," she said, imitating his accent.

He looked suddenly troubled. "Sorry, lass. I dinna mean to."

"It's just an expression! You can be so literal, at times."

He flashed his famous smile, one tinged with relief. "Aye, and tonight you've got a bit of the devil in ye, too, I see."

Because I'm hoping to find a little piece of heaven in your arms.

"Sit, make yourself at home," she told him while she wedged the flowers into a water-filled glass vase and placed them on the kitchen counter because already the little eating table was half-filled with plates. On the stone in a cast-iron pan, four bone-in country ham slices, each a quarter-inch thick, sizzled in butter. While she finished cooking, she chattered from nervous excitement. The artificial barrier she'd erected between herself and Damon, one held in place by her lingering worries that he was a criminal, had crashed into so much dust. "So, how about that attendance at church today, huh? It's a miracle! A real miracle."

"Nay. Take credit where credit is due, Harmony. Word about your church has spread far and wide. 'Twas only a matter of time."

"Hmm. I'd like to believe it. But where were all the men?"

Damon's smile faltered. "Were there no males present?" he asked innocently.

"Except for you and Bubba, that crowd was a hundred percent female, and don't pretend you didn't notice. It doesn't make sense. But I guess it's not gracious to look the Lord's gift horse in the mouth."

Especially not with Daddy coming. A robust church community was a source of Faithfull pride. She couldn't let her family down.

Oh, but they'd be impressed with Damon, though, she thought happily. He was such a gentleman, so much like her brothers. And when all-seeing Great-grandmother Eudora stepped through the front door, one look at Damon and she'd see him for what he truly was!

Oh, yes, things were looking up. Yes, indeed.

She tried to forget about the strange gender imbalance at church and instead focused on the pleasure of cooking and Damon's company.

With a spatula, she flipped the ham steaks. "I'm fixing us ham and red-eye gravy. A Faithfull family favorite. Ever tried it?"

"Nay, lass. But I canna wait." Damon closed his eyes and inhaled the aroma. Even from the stove, she could see the shudder that rumbled through him.

She couldn't help laughing. "In all my life, I can't say I've ever had more pleasure cooking for anyone."

His smile was brilliant, as if he savored her compliments as much as he did his food.

She bustled about the stove, crashing pots and pans onto the burner as she hummed to the music playing on the stereo. Damon watched her with an affectionate, amused gaze that made her heart beat even faster. "My mama made me and my sisters help her with Sunday supper since we were little girls. We'd turn up the radio and listen to our favorite songs. Sometimes we'd dance more than we'd cook, and Mama would scold us." Harmony gave her butt a defiant little shake. Her tight, red-sheathed butt.

The look on Damon's face sent heat shooting up and down her spine. *Harmony, behave yourself.*

Do I have to?

It was almost like being a teenager again, except that the voice of reason she battled was her own.

She turned back to the stove and heard a loud scratching noise behind her. Damon growled, "Trolls—be gone!" Then there was a splash, a prolonged sizzle, and an abbreviated squeak.

Nine

Whirling around, she caught Damon just as he sat back in his chair. He looked shaken and was trying to hide the fact.

Harmony's brows went up. "What was that? What just happened? What did you mean by a troll?"

Damon flushed. She'd never seen his face color like that before. "'Twas a . . . mouse," he explained. "We call them trolls in Scotland."

"Oh." She pondered that. Then she glanced around her clean kitchen, the spatula gripped in her hand like a weapon. "Where's the mouse? I haven't had a problem with mice before." That's when she saw the puddle. And on the table, Damon's empty glass.

"I chased it off," he explained. "They dinna like water." As if he were reloading a six-shooter, he refilled his glass from the pitcher on the table.

Harmony stared at the puddle. "That's weird."

"What is?"

"The water's smoking. No, that's steam."

"Condensation."

"Hmm. Well, it is a little humid tonight after that thunderstorm." Before she could get to the puddle with a dish towel, it had evaporated. Humidity wasn't the problem. But she wasn't sure what was. Except that there had been a mouse that Damon called a troll that had disappeared as quickly as the puddle he'd made on the floor.

Keeping her eyes open for rodents, she mixed brown sugar, a half cup of brewed coffee, and a cup of water for the gravy, stirring until the sugar dissolved.

From behind, she heard Damon's chair scrape backward. *Not another one.* A splash and a startled squeak signaled a hit. Almost too fast to register on her retinas, something larger than a mouse but smaller than a bunny darted out through Bubba's doggie door, something that had appeared to run on two legs, not four, though she was sure it was a trick of the eyes.

Delighted barking from outside told her that the puppy had given chase to whatever it was. "Damon, I don't think they're mice."

Panic flashed in his eyes, as if he didn't want her going down that road. "What else would they be, lass?"

"I mean, I think they're rats. Why are you acting so worried? Is my hulking, six-foot-five knight afraid of little rodents?"

"Nay." *I am afraid for you,* his eyes said.

What a sweetie. He took his role of protector so seriously that it had extended to pest control. She wanted to hug him, but her hands were sticky with sugar. "I don't like mice, but I'm not afraid of them, Damon. The desert rats we had in Iraq were way worse, and I saw cockroaches in Biloxi that were as big as small horses, so don't worry about me." Despite her big talk, she did react with a little shudder as she envisioned mice scampering through the house at night, popping out of the medicine cabinets in the dark, nesting between her bedsheets. "Do you know where they're coming from?"

"I've seen one or two in the barn," he mumbled.

Where he slept. Again, she shuddered. "I'll buy some traps tomorrow. Or a cat—a hungry cat! I just want them gone before my family gets here."

"Trust me, lass. I dinna want the little beasties around, either." He said it like he meant it, too. She was confident that tomorrow, the rats would be history.

Harmony drizzled gravy over the ham steaks. Red-eye gravy was thin in consistency but potent in flavor. Her mouth watered in anticipation. Careful not to step on any stray creatures, she carried the platter to the table, setting it down amid bowls of mashed potatoes, vegetables, and biscuits.

"Oh, I baked us a special dessert, too." She carried the cake to the table and announced proudly, "Devil's food!"

Damon choked on the water he'd just sipped.

"What's wrong? It's just chocolate on chocolate, and I know you love chocolate."

"Aye, I do," he rasped. "The name—it merely startled me, lass."

"You're so darn cute sometimes, Damon of Mysteria." Tossing aside her apron, she grabbed a book of matches and stood next to his chair to light some candles. He smelled clean, like coconut soap. His skin radiated heat and his personal scent that she found so distracting. She wouldn't mind a chaste kiss. *Get real.* She craved a real kiss, a hot, deep, toe-curling kind of kiss, the kind she daydreamed about when she was supposed to be working on her sermons.

His hand slid around her waist. "Cute? I dinna know if I'm that, lass, but ye do make me happy. Very happy."

He's never felt like this before. He's never been this happy. She shook off the strange, unbidden thought. Why were those things jumping into her head? It always seemed to happen when he touched her.

Harmony tried not to think about latent seer genes coming active, and instead turned around in the circle of Damon's arms and slid her arms over his shoulders. "You make me happy, too."

They'd never touched like this, so casually, so intimately. It had never been for the lack of wanting to, of course, but suddenly she wondered what in the world she was waiting for when it came to that real kiss she'd been wanting. And so she bent down and brushed her lips over his.

Just a taste, that was all she intended, but his lips were soft . . . warm. Perfect.

Damon made a soft sound of pleasure in his throat, opening his mouth to hers as his fingers slid into her hair at the back of her head to bring her closer. Her tongue brushed his, and soon they were kissing more boldly, her hands framing his jaw.

The next thing she knew, she was in his lap with her butt nestled between his hard thighs. Damon didn't just kiss; he savored her, relished her, drawing out the tender kiss the same way he'd delighted in every morsel of food from the day he arrived. Maybe even more so, made her feel as if she were the best thing he'd ever tasted, that his appetite was endless, insatiable, and that it wouldn't stop here, that he'd want more and more and . . .

Damon released her like a hot potato. "Good, good, good," he mumbled into her hair.

Laughing and gasping, Harmony rested her cheek against his jawbone. "Good. It was definitely that. Good, good, good."

"I dinna disagree. 'Tis why I'm trying to remind myself to behave."

She rubbed her thumb across his lower lip. "A good man, you are, Damon. A gentleman."

He glanced away, as if suddenly afraid of what she'd see in his eyes. "I haven't always been good, Harmony."

"The corrupt job with the corrupt boss . . ."

"Aye."

"But you're starting over. You have a new life." *You're clean,* she almost blurted out, but she couldn't tell him that, couldn't admit she'd checked up on him. It seemed a betrayal of everything he'd been so far, which was nothing less than, well, than good. "Only God's perfect, Damon. The rest of us do the best we can."

It always amazed her how his smile transformed his face.

His bone structure was strong, and he could look almost cruel when his expression was serious, but whenever he grinned, he became so roguishly handsome it took her breath away. "I will always do my best for you," he said, pulling her close again. "Better than best."

Folding her in strong arms, he hugged her to his chest for the longest time, as if she somehow anchored him here on earth. The thought made her heart ache when she remembered how lost he seemed when he'd first arrived. Then, he pressed his mouth to her forehead in a kiss so achingly tender that it left her awash in goose bumps all the same.

Bubba crashed through the dog door, and they jumped apart.

"He's got something in his mouth." But Harmony only caught a glimpse of the rat-sized thing in Bubba's mouth before Damon blocked her view with his big hand. "Hey!" She tried peeling his fingers from her eyes. "I want to see."

"Nay. 'Tis not a pretty sight." Damon held her head to his chest with his left hand as he threw something with his right. She heard more water splash and a shriek. Did rats shriek? Several pairs of paws scrabbled on the floor. Then two loud swishes of the dog door and a lot of barking told her that whatever Bubba had caught managed to escape.

Harmony wriggled off Damon's lap. "I'm going after Bubba."

"Nay, lass. He'll be fine."

"What if the rat bites him?"

"The troll—er, rather, the rat—'twill have disappeared underground before the pup catches up."

"Underground? What are they—part gopher?"

From outside, Bubba yipped in frustration. Apparently, the rodent had indeed disappeared down its hole.

Harmony tugged on the hem of her blouse to recover some of the modesty she'd thrown to the wind. To forestall any further interruptions of dinner, of kisses, or of anything else, she shoved an empty chair in front of the dog door. Then she plopped down in her chair, clasped her hands under her chin, and whispered a quick and silent prayer to compose herself before saying grace. "Thank you, Lord, for the bounty we are about to eat. Thank you for bringing Damon here to help me." *And thank you for making him the most amazing kisser in the whole wide world!* "Amen."

For the first time in her presence, Damon murmured "amen," too. It sounded rusty on his lips, as if he'd not had much practice with prayer. It didn't trouble her; she'd seen inside his soul. He was cleaner and purer inside, where it counted, than some pastors she'd run across.

"Sometimes, lass, I dinna know if I have brought you help or harm."

She shook her head in confusion.

"Your thanks to God," he explained. "You gave thanks for my help, such as it is." He waved at the chair blocking the dog door. "It seems I have brought you more harm than good."

"You mean the rats? You can't blame yourself for that. We probably stirred them up when we cleaned out the hayloft."

He made a scoffing, grumbling sound in his throat.

"We'll get rid of them tomorrow. Besides, like I told you, they don't bother me that much. They bother my mama, though, so as long as you eradicate them before she gets here, I'm happy."

"I will try," he said with such pained seriousness that she put down her fork and knife to stare at him. "I'll do everything I can, lass. Everything. Until then, you must promise me never to be alone with them. Never fight them without me at your side."

"They're not monsters, Damon," she said with a laugh. "They're rats!"

He laughed weakly.

"And I know you'll slay them for me, brave knight, right?"

"Aye, fair maiden," he said with more vehemence than what seemed to fit the task. "'Tis my job to slay the beasties."

Nevertheless, through the rest of the supper, Damon acted edgy. Peering around the kitchen as he ate, he squinted at the corners, studied crevices, kept watch on the dog door she'd blocked.

When they'd finished, they didn't linger over conversation. Damon appeared too distracted. Harmony walked him to the back door. The air was warm for nighttime in these parts. Distant thunder echoed from somewhere over the Rockies. "It's going to be a hot one tomorrow," she observed, trying to act casual though she was acutely aware of his body so close to hers.

He turned to her. "Thank you for tonight."

"My pleasure."

"Aye, your pleasure will always be mine, lass."

Harmony gulped. Sigh. He had no idea. . . .

He stood there for a moment, studying her with a look that ping-ponged between desire and regret, then, chanting "Good, good, good" under his breath, he bid her good night as any respectable gentleman would a nun and walked away.

It was all she could do not to follow him back to the hayloft.

Behave, Harmony. Although she wasn't sure how much longer she'd be able to do so.

Pressing a cool glass of water against her cheek, she watched him go, wondering just what it was going to take to bring out the devil in Damon.

Ten

The next Sunday the men began trickling into church to see where the women were going. With every passing week more townsfolk came, until Harmony had to ask Damon to build her some more pews.

He did so gladly, though it took him away from his pet project, the installation of an expansive automatic sprinkler system surrounding the church. "The beasties don't like the water," he'd explained.

He must be right: ever since the water had been coming on every night, there hadn't been any more problems with rodents in the house. And as a side benefit, the lawn looked great, too. Unfortunately, they now had a glut of water-loving garden slugs to deal with. But at least those hadn't tried crashing dinner. Yet.

It was Sunday, T-minus one week and a day until her family invaded Mysteria, and Harmony was in the midst of delivering her sermon to a full house. Standing a few careful steps outside the half-open door, her loyal knight Damon stood guard, his arms folded over the end of a pitchfork as he leaned against the outside wall. Although he never stepped foot inside the church—"'tis not right," he'd insist so mournfully—he always listened carefully to her weekly message. Often she'd work in little things she hoped might help him escape his dark, mysterious past, something he remained reluctant to share. "I wasna good," he'd say in his brogue. Yet, without a criminal record anyone could unearth—and Jeanie had never stopped trying—how bad could he have been?

No sooner than Harmony conjured the thought than an unseasonably cold breeze whooshed inside the church. "Bad, bad," the wind seemed to whisper, a crackly, desiccated noise like the scratch of crinkled brown leaves on the sidewalk in autumn. With one hand fisted in the fabric of her cotton skirt to keep it from flying up, she tried to snatch back her papers from the whirlwind, but it only blew harder, whipping her hair around her face. "Evil," it hissed, drawing out the word. "Evil demon, baaaaad."

Then the wind surged in velocity, gushing between the pews, tossing off hats and whipping hair, until it hit Harmony full on and whirled around her like her own personal tornado, scattering the pages of her sermon. "Bad . . . bad . . . bad . . ."

Something pressed in on her mind, bitter, distasteful, like a taste of bile. She mentally flung it away. "The basement's unlocked," she shouted to her dispersing flock. "It may be a tornado. Get inside, take shelter!" But the wind erased her words.

"Baaaaaaaaaaaaaaaaaaad," it rasped.

Stay away. Harmony shut her eyes and shoved. She didn't know what it was that she heard in the wind, only that whenever it touched her mind, she shuddered, repulsed.

"Reverend!" Jeanie Tortellini tried to assist her but the wind blew the woman backward.

"I'm okay!" But was she? She had to squint against the whistling gale in order to see. Damon was no longer at the door. Knowing him, he was outside helping others. "Find Damon. You two make sure everyone's okay. Get them in the basement if you have to." Barking the orders, the blind trust, it reminded her of when a missile had struck outside the field hospital in Iraq and she and the doctors were trapped inside. "Go, Jeanie! You know what to do. I'll be right there."

Jeanie ran off. As Harmony struggled as if swimming upstream to follow, she glimpsed Dr. Fogg, as calm as could be, observing the scene like the scientist-physician he was, jotting down notes on his Blackberry as he evacuated the building along with the rest of the townspeople.

Finally, Harmony fought her way outside to the porch. Outside, shadows arced and swooped. Birds. First a rodent invasion, now a bird invasion?

The wind subsided the moment Harmony exited the church, as if it had tried at first to keep her from doing so before giving up.

That's a weirder thought than the talking wind. No more of that, okay?

"I'm sane," she muttered. "Really I am. I just live in Mysteria, that's all—" She froze on the top step, her mouth falling open. The scene before her was so inexplicably impossible that her mind almost couldn't process it.

What at first glance she thought were birds weren't. "Flying monkeys?" she whispered. Good heaven, they were! From their little gold-trimmed suits to their Dixie-cup hats, they were replicas of the winged assistants from the movie *The Wizard of Oz.*

As if that weren't bad enough, Damon stood in the eye of the furry hurricane, fighting back as if the whole thing were personal.

Eleven

Damon swung his pitchfork at the flock of subdemons. "Be gone! Back to your Hell hole!" But with his powers reduced to what he could conjure as a mortal man, he could do little more than issue threats.

The subdemons had started emerging from a Hell hole in Harmony's vegetable garden while she was preaching. More and more of them. Damon had tried to get them all stuffed neatly back down the pit before church was over. He could turn on the sprinklers, aye, and wash them all away, but what a muddle it would make, melting, sizzling subdemons everywhere. And how would he explain the little articles of clothing left behind? Nay, 'twas better to scoop them up by the pitchforkful and shove them back to Hell before Harmony emerged from the church.

He'd actually gotten ahead of the game when the winds began. Filled with dread, Damon turned around, a wriggling subdemon, caught by the collar, still dangling from his pitchfork as townspeople poured out of the church.

Hell's bells. He should have known Lucifer would not let him win, would keep trying to sabotage the trust Damon had built in Harmony. For if Damon were to win over Harmony Faithfull, Lucifer would lose. Over the past few weeks, the Devil had shown no signs of giving up on his quest to assure the defeat of his ex–demon high lord.

How many incidents such as this had there been over the past months? Too many to count. First there'd been the goblin in the barn, then the minitrolls in Harmony's kitchen. Now this, a flock of subdemons in the middle of the lawn in broad daylight on a Sunday morning, the most brazen violation yet! Well, except for the naked incubus he'd found sneaking through Harmony's bedroom window one night, but that may have been only a coincidence, the wrong window on the wrong night for the unfortunate dark creature.

Damon redoubled his efforts to get rid of the subdemons, but they swarmed. He'd seen a lot of scenes during his long years working for the Devil, but few as chaotic as this one unfolding on the front lawn of Mysteria Community Church. Townsfolk ran every which way, complicating his efforts to chase the beasties from the churchyard. Damon attended to the subdemons while simultaneously trying to joke about the infestation to impart calm to the crowd. Even for Mysteria, this was a strange happening, although many of the locals took it in stride. It would not be so in any other town.

Competing with the subdemons' raucous noise were the howls of the O'Cleary great-grandchildren, who ran wild like little demons themselves. Damon fancied that he'd like a family of his own someday, but two minutes spent with the O'Cleary offspring was almost enough to convince a man to drop all thoughts of procreation.

And then there was Dr. Fogg. His hair windblown, his tie whipping in the breeze, he pushed spectacles up the bridge of his elegant nose with one hand as he crouched down low, attempting to entice a subdemon with a broken Saltine cracker. Consorts with elves, that one does, Damon thought. The same with the sheriff. Damon could smell an elf a mile away, and even with his demon's senses almost gone, he knew well what the doctor and especially Harmony's friend

Jeanie did in their spare time. Elves, too sexy for their pointy ears, they were. The town jail stank of them.

Damon knocked several more subdemons unconscious and dragged them to the Hell hole, shoving them back into the earth. "Tell your master his efforts are in vain. He'll never destroy me. He'll never turn me back the way I was before!" A derisive sound came up through the Hell hole, like a deep belch. The warm, moist breeze ruffled Damon's hair. 'Twas Lucifer himself answering him.

Damon's lips pulled back over his teeth. "Are you such a coward that you send your minions to do your dirty work? Why don't you come out and fight me yourself?" Damon raised the pitchfork. "Come on. Come up here and fight like a man. I may be mortal, but I'm ready for ye."

"Damon, who are you talking to?"

At the sound of the familiar voice, Damon's heart plunged into his stomach.

Harmony sounded poised at the razor's edge of hysteria.

"Dinna be afraid, lass!" With a sweep of the pitchfork, he took out several of the more brazen of the subdemons before her eyes, her wide, brown, disbelieving eyes. Some of the creatures lay dazed on the ground. A few crawled, pulling their broken bodies toward the Hell hole in the garden. Damon puffed up his chest and assured her, "They'll soon be gone."

"Gone . . ."

"Aye." That's when he noticed how brightly her eyes glowed, how her lips were so pale and tight, contrasting with her flushed cheeks. But what he noticed most of all was the shovel gripped in her white-knuckled hands, as if she meant to clang it against the side of his head. Nay, she was not frightened, not at all; she was as furious as the wind that had whipped her long hair and skirt only moments before.

Harmony's glare intensified. "Gone, like those so-called rats you found in my kitchen?"

Instinct told him no answer he gave would be the right one.

"Gone where, Damon? To the south, maybe? Isn't that where you told me you were from, Damon? Farther south than

I've ever been? You weren't talking about Mexico, were you?" Harmony ducked as a subdemon swooped low overhead. Then she advanced on him, her nostrils flaring. "Were you!"

Damon hesitated, the pitchfork raised in midair as his heart sank. A thousand alternate explanations came to mind, but with those excuses, would he not be slipping back into the lies that so characterized his previous life?

"Nay," he said gently. "I was not talking about Mexico. But I can explain. I . . ." *Say it*. He jerked his pitchfork at the sky. "I was one of them."

Harmony's eyes went wide. "A flying monkey?"

"Nay, lass! I was a demon."

Twelve

There was a terrible pause. Then Harmony asked, "A *demon* demon?"

"Aye, a demon demon."

"This is the truth, Damon. You swear?"

"I do."

Harmony made a strangled sound and raised her shovel high. For a moment, Damon was sure she'd whack him in the head, but she struck at a low-flying subdemon instead, and then another as they wheeled overhead, taunting him.

"Why didn't you tell me?" *Clang*. A subdemon fell to earth, another victim of Harmony's vicious swing. "Why didn't you?"

"I did! That very first day. In the kitchen. Ye thought I was lying." As she stared at him, he saw her gaze turn inward and knew she remembered. "But ye took me in all the same. Deny it you might, lass, but ye are as close to an angel as I've ever encountered."

She snorted. "What do you know about angels? You're a demon."

"*Was* a demon, lass. I was fired. Terminated without benefits."

Crash. Thwap. A little red hat sailed down to the grass. "Benefits. Oh, please. Hell has a retirement plan?"

"They did, once," he muttered. "No longer, it seems."

"Is nothing sacred anymore?" Her sarcasm was as sharp as a blade. "Well, there's always social security." *Thump.* Another subdemon dropped from the sky.

Water erupted from the grass, engulfing them in a drenching cold spray. Shrieking accompanied the deluge, but human shrieking this time. Semihuman, Damon qualified. Mrs. O'Cleary's great-grandchildren had somehow turned on the sprinklers. Any subdemon unlucky enough to be hit hissed and sizzled, screaming as they dissolved into little piles of doll-sized clothing.

"Who turned the sprinklers on?" Jeanie Tortellini ran across the churchyard, yelling, trying to regain control. The preteen Desdaine triplets, Withering, Scornful, and Derisive, whooped in delight. "How come no one's watching these kids?" she demanded of the parents who were wisely hiding behind some lawn chairs.

"Wait!" Harmony yelled to the woman. "Leave the water on! It's . . . it's killing them." She swung her glare around to Damon. "Just like what happened to the wicked witch in *The Wizard of Oz.* She melted. You knew this all along; you prepared for it by installing these sprinklers. And here I thought you were just a fan of irrigation!"

At that moment, Damon again understood that the best answer was no answer.

The lawn turned into a sea of mud. Children squealed with laughter as they grabbed the sprinkler heads and aimed water at the subdemons. Harmony's pumps made sucking noises. She snarled and threw her shoes one at a time at the creatures, striking one and knocking off its little red-and-gold hat. A jet of water clanged off the handle of Damon's pitchfork. He lost his balance. Harmony tried to steady him, but she slipped. They went down hard in the mud.

He turned to find her lips an inch away from his. His body was wrapped around hers as they lay sprawled on the ground, the same body that now reacted rather briskly to that pleasant discovery. He'd come to enjoy the sensations of his new body—advantages to being mortal that he'd never realized. But also disadvantages, one of which was poor timing, he decided quite quickly upon noting the fury contorting Harmony's face. "I should have been happy talking to the dog!"

Damon shook his head. "I dinna follow, lass . . ."

"I should have been satisfied with the simple things, the solitude, but no, I had to want more. A full house on Sundays." She gulped several breaths. "But what did I get? Demons and flying monkeys!" She threw down the shovel.

Her face was streaked with mud. He reached up to wipe her cheek with his thumb, but she recoiled as if she feared him. Feared what he was. He couldn't blame her.

"I kissed you, Damon!" she accused. "I kissed you!"

Aye, and he'd not stopped thinking about it, either.

"I cooked for you. I bought you underwear. I . . . I wanted to *make love* with you!"

You could have heard a pin drop in the sudden silence. Damon wasn't sure which one of them looked more shocked by her confession.

Then there was a loud whoosh. Water gushed out of a hijacked sprinkler and, aimed by mischievous little hands, ricocheted off a metal fence post, zinged overhead, and clipped off one of the chains holding the Mysteria Community Church banner over the church door. As if in surrender, the banner slid off the wall.

A fitting end to a terrible day.

Harmony watched the sign fall. Looking as if she were about to cry, she stopped herself and dashed the heel of her palm across her eyes. Muddy water streamed from her hair and dribbled down her ruined dress.

"Lass . . . ," he tried, lifting a hand to her. Then he hesitated, fearing her vulnerable stance was deceptive, that if he touched her, tried to hold her, she'd snap like a too taut spring and fly away from him. As it was, she pushed to her feet without another word and went to join Jeanie in restoring order.

Damon watched her go. So much had changed since he'd come to Mysteria, and yet so little. He was as much a reason for doubt and second thoughts as he ever was.

An oddly pitched scream tore into his self-pitying thoughts. He saw an O'Cleary child go down under the weight of several angry subdemons, a situation missed by others in the chaos. Subdemons were dark creatures with little power, but enough of them could kill a small human. Could kill a child.

Damon surged to his feet, the pitchfork in hand. A half-dozen strides brought him to where the child's thin legs kicked. Damon grabbed one beastie by its collar and threw it to the ground. Then he dragged the remaining creatures off the frightened child.

The little girl's face was without color, her blue eyes wide and tear-filled. "Are you hurt, little one?"

She shook her head, but her lower lip trembled. "Scared?" he asked gently, coming down on one knee.

She nodded, her mouth wobbling. Damon lifted her fist, which was still clamping a plastic water gun. He smiled. "Would ye like to get them back?"

She grinned. "Yeah!"

"Then let's do it." He hoisted her under his arm. "Fire away!" With the child pumping water out of the little toy gun, he chased fleeing subdemons to the Hell hole, followed enthusiastically by a wildly barking Bubba and a herd of miniature O'Clearys. When every last one had either melted or vanished into the depths of Hell, Damon lowered the little girl to the ground. Her skinny shoulders felt so delicate under his hands. A sudden rush of emotion threatened to swamp him, a sensation still so new. This child encapsulated all that was fragile and good on this earth; all that he'd hoped to protect, to cherish. "What is your name?"

"Annabelle," she answered in a tremulous voice.

"Bullies, that's all they are, Annabelle. Ye canna be afraid.

Your goodness, 'twill always win out. Ye are stronger than them. Far stronger. Do ye understand?"

Annabelle nodded, and he touched a fingertip to her little freckled nose before rising to his feet. His breath caught in his throat when he realized Harmony had been watching him the entire time, her face so full of pain that he had to turn away from her horrified gaze.

Damon trudged to the sprinkler timer box to shut off the water, but before he reached the shutoff valve, and as everyone began to come up from the basement and from behind chairs and under tables—just as everyone thought it was safe—little Annabelle O'Cleary fired off one last salvo with the hose, aiming the water at her parents as her brothers and sisters, not appearing a wee bit sorry, fled the scene.

Damon wrested the hose from Annabelle's little hands. "Off with ye now, little hell-raiser." With grudging admiration, he sent her on her way. Then he tended to the shaken townspeople, working his charm as best he could to coax assurances that they'd return to church the next week. All the while he felt Harmony's gaze on him, and his face burned in shame.

Jeanie sauntered up to him. "I've seen a lot of unusual goings-on in this town, but not this. What were those animals?"

"Are they not from Mysteria?" Damon tried charming the sheriff with one of his smiles, but her gaze sharpened.

"It won't work, Damon. Not with me. And just for your information"—she bobbed her chin in Harmony's direction— "it won't work with her, either. I want the facts, not the glossed-over version."

"Aye, I know," he said with a sigh. "I'd tried to keep it from her so I wouldn't lose her, but now that I have, secrets do me no good. In Satan's army, there is a hierarchy. At the apex are the demon high lords, Lucifer's commanders. Then there are the foot soldiers, the scores of classes of underlords, demon worker-bees, and subdemons. They can take the form of almost any monster, from ant-size on up, and with more ways to intimidate, frighten, and kill than can be counted. New versions are created every day."

"Like . . . Demon 8.0," Jeanie joked, jotting down the information.

"That is a way to look at it," Damon said sadly, gazing over at Harmony, who refused to meet his eyes.

Jeanie noted the exchange and put down her notepad. "You're in deep shit, aren't you?"

"Deep, really deep, aye."

"We Mysteria women call it doghouse deep. And there's only one thing you can do. Go fix it."

"I dinna know if it's possible."

"Her job is to forgive, Damon. That'll be the easy part. All you have to do is to convince her to put her heart into it." She chucked him on the arm. "Good luck. I know you can do it."

Could he?

Damon found Harmony in the barn, washing mud off her hands and face at the work sink. Harmony turned around, wiping her hands on her soiled skirt. Water and tears had smudged the makeup under her wide, expressive brown eyes. She studied him for a moment, as if he were a stranger. Then she blew her nose in a paper towel. "No wonder you didn't like devil's food cake."

His chest hurt. "Yes, I have a past, of which ye know little."

He told her everything, as best a man could summarize ten thousand years of walking the earth.

"Ten thousand years." Harmony's voice came out as a squeak. "A *hundred* centuries."

"Aye, but I've lived more in these past few months than in all the time before." He told her the story of the starving settlers of Mysteria, how he'd given them the Will-to-Go-On, how he'd repeated such acts all around the globe until Lucifer found out and captured him. He told her about the torture, his being made mortal, and finally how he'd woken, dazed and naked, in her garden, terminated and pensionless. "I thought he was done with me, then, Lucifer was. But 'tis clear he's not yet finished. And for that, lass, I am truly sorry . . . for what you've suffered as a consequence. And 'tis about you, for the Devil does not want me to have something good, you see. Then I'll have won. If there's one thing I know about Lucifer—he does not like to lose."

"Is everything okay in here?" Jeanie Tortellini poked her head in the barn.

"Fine!" they both shouted a little too quickly.

The sheriff shot Damon a you-poor-bastard wink. "The water's off, Reverend; I locked up the church. Everyone's gone home—it's a ghost town out there." Jeanie clamped her mouth closed, as if realizing that was a poor choice of words, given Harmony's profession—and mood. She held up a little gold-trimmed red coat. "But on the plus side, there are enough doll clothes left behind to supply every little girl's collection in Mysteria." She sniffed at the garment and grimaced. "Once they've been through the wash, that is. Hey, I'll be down at the jail, so call me if you need me." Jeanie waved good-bye and slid the door closed.

Damon sighed. It was time to pack up his things, tidy the hayloft, and leave. But there was one last thing he had to say. "I am sorry, lass. I know those words do not come close to making up for all the disasters I've wreaked here, but know this: What I did, what I said, I did in hopes it would keep ye close—close to me. Know that. But I see now what I feared most has come to pass. I've lost you," he finished valiantly and turned away.

"Damon, please."

He stopped.

"You haven't lost me."

His head snapped around. "Say it again, lass. I dinna think I heard you."

The ends of her luscious mouth curved slightly. "You haven't lost me."

A harsh breath escaped him. He hadn't lost her; somehow, he hadn't chased her away.

What if Lucifer learns of this?

Damon squeezed his eyes shut. *Dinna think of it.* Like he'd told the child Annabelle, good always triumphs over evil, and he must summon the faith to believe in it.

"I lost sight of something today, something very important." Harmony brought her hands together, clasping them tightly as if she were nervous, nervous as he. "The best sermons are lived, not preached. I'll never forget the day my great-grandmother Eudora said that to my father, when she disagreed with something he'd done. She'd have scolded me today, told me the same thing, when she saw how quickly I wanted to condemn you. Seeing that God's forgiven you, it might be a little arrogant if I didn't. Ya think?"

"Only God's perfect, Harmony," he said, reminding her of her words to him shortly after he arrived in Mysteria. "The rest of us do the best we can."

"Yes, we do." Her eyes were luminous with tears as she walked to him and lifted a trembling hand to his cheek. He pressed his hand over hers as his emotions soared to heaven. "It doesn't matter what you were before, Damon. It doesn't. I had a calling to come here, and when I did, nothing was what I'd expected. But I knew God watched over everyone who lived here, whether they chose to see it or not. And then you came, and through you I fulfilled my calling here, through love. You're so full of love, Damon. What went down before doesn't matter. You're a beautiful man with a beautiful soul, and that's all that counts."

His mood crashed immediately. A beautiful soul? "Lass, I was a demon, born of shadows. I know you've insisted that all humans have a soul, but I was not created as you were. The Devil crafted me, not God."

She propped her hands on her hips. "Is this why you've never wanted to step inside the church?"

"I feared holy retribution—plagues, lightning strikes, and the like."

Harmony snorted. "Oh, puleeze. You'll have to find another excuse." She poked him on the chest with her index finger. "You can't fool me when it comes to souls, sir. I'm a Faithfull. Knowing souls is in our blood. I saw what you did to help little Annabelle O'Cleary. A man with no soul never would have done that, alleviated a little girl's fear, or have run around afterward, convincing everyone they needed to come back to church next week, and not to be scared—and they believed you, Damon. A man with no soul never would exude the zest for life that you do, or the energy, your ability to make people laugh and feel comfortable. A man with no soul never would have . . . never would have . . ." Her finger trailed down his stomach, and she blushed deeply.

"Never would have what, lass?" he coaxed.

"Never would have made me fall in love with him." She smiled softly. "With *you*."

Damon's heart crashed against his ribs. She loved him! 'Twas everything he'd ever wanted, for so many hundreds of years, to know love, to experience the pure and simple joy of it, the giving and receiving. To be human enough to share himself with someone else, to sacrifice. And now that it was placed before him, this miracle, he was all but paralyzed for fear of breaking the spell.

"Oh, lass," he managed stupidly. "Are ye sure?"

"Never been more sure of anything in my life."

Slinging an arm low around her waist, he drew her close. "Never been more sure," she whispered against his lips. In the next instant, he was kissing her, falling head over heels into the well of joy that was this woman, who said she loved him. *Loved him!* Who said he had a soul.

From the conviction in her voice, he believed her. He remembered the feeling that had surged into him the moment he'd defied Lucifer. But even that explosion of joy and rightness dimmed with the knowledge that Harmony Faithfull loved him. Wanted him.

Then something Harmony had said earlier came crashing back into his mind. "Lass, forgive me if I misunderstood you out there on the lawn, but didn't you mention you'd wanted to make love with me?"

"Yeah, I did." She grabbed his butt and hauled him close. "And if I don't do it soon, I might explode!"

"Hell's bells, so will I." Grinning eagerly, he swept her off her feet and carried her swiftly to the bedchamber in her house.

Thirteen

Together they fell onto the bed. Harmony laughed, exhilarated; being with Damon was like riding a roller coaster, and now it was perched precariously on the highest hill.

Damon's weight pressed her deep into the mattress. It felt delicious. *He* was delicious! Her hands slid everywhere, his muscled back, his abs, the thickly muscled arms. That amazing body, she had it all to herself—and everything else that came with it. Yes, everything else, and God forgive her for going after it so greedily.

"Kiss me," she told Damon, her fingers curling in the damp fabric of his shirt. She dragged him down to her mouth and kissed him, hard and deep. Dark, sweet heat. Slick and wet. The rasp of his whiskers as she explored with her tongue. He was the best thing she'd ever tasted, and she was hungry for more.

A deep sound rumbled in his chest in reaction to her eagerness. Shyness hadn't entered her mind, only that she'd wanted him like this for so many weeks.

A beautiful man. A beautiful soul.

But he was a demon! Satan's helper.

Mortal in Mysteria • 85

He's starting over. A new life. He's clean, real clean, remember?

As for his kiss? Hoo boy, it burned so hot it made Hell look cold. She'd gladly pay penance for that decidedly unholy thought—but tomorrow. Not now.

"Mmm," she murmured as they kissed. "Mmm." Smiling, she tore through the buttons on his shirt.

The scrape of Damon's teeth on the side of her throat made her shiver as he fumbled with the waistband of her skirt. His hand slid up her inner thigh, and she could feel him tremble. When he touched her between her legs, the spasm of pleasure was so intense that her body gave an involuntary little jerk. If that was what his fingers could do, then she could only imagine—

"Too many clothes on ye, lass." Her panties came off next, and the rest of their clothes went every which way.

Damon flipped her over, kissed her behind her knees and made her giggle. " 'Tis my first time, ye know," he told her as he trailed kisses up her spine, pausing to lick a sensitive little place between her shoulder blades that she never knew existed.

"First time what?" she gasped, delighted with his creativity with all the places he found to touch with his tongue and his lips.

"My first time making love."

Harmony rolled over to stare at him. Sometimes lip reading helped with communication, especially when the messages were garbled. "You're not a virgin."

"Aye, I am."

"Listen, if this is something you've come up with to make up for the whole demon thing—"

"Hush." He pressed a finger to her lips. " 'Tis the truth. Ye are my first." He didn't seem bothered by the fact in the least, nor hindered by any lack of confidence, she thought, as he pulled one bra strap down, then the other, lowering the lace until he found her nipples, lavishing each with attention as if they were made of the finest, most delectable chocolate. "No need to worry, lass. I know exactly what to do."

She tipped her head back to the pillow and moaned. "I can't argue that, baby." Her sexy Scottish hunk was a virgin! She nearly whooped with delight. "You don't act like it's your first time."

"I've experienced little, aye, but have seen much," he murmured as he concentrated on pleasuring her. "Pagan lovers mating inside stone circles on Midsummer Eves . . . Viking wedding nights, the harems of Arabia . . . Roman orgies."

Pagan mating rituals? Harems? Roman orgies? "Damon, honey, I don't know if we're on the same page."

"I know the difference, love, between what I saw and this. Trust me. My instincts are good." His arms bulged with muscles as he did a push-up over her, dipping his head to kiss her neck. Then he flipped her over and bit her on the butt. She squealed, and he laughed, soothing where he'd nipped her with kisses, then tossing her over again only to enter her, thickly, deeply. Her breath caught as her back arched, and she made a little gasp of surprise. Damon's expression shifted from astonishment to tenderness to hunger; his eyelids fell half-closed, and the softest groan of pleasure slipped out after he breathed her name. Although she could feel the intensity of Damon's emotions pressing on her mind, all she needed to know was right here, written on his face, everything he felt being with her, out in the open.

Her belly squeezed as he pushed slowly deeper, filling her, stretching her. She was glad he was going slow. It had been a long time for her, and she hadn't expected he'd take her this quickly. But maybe foreplay wasn't as popular in ancient times as it was now. Then again, she hadn't been waiting ten thousand years to "do it." Only since college, which had sometimes felt as long.

Yet, her body was ready for him—whoa, more than ready. The mere weight of his body pressing her into the mattress had her panting in anticipation.

"Ye are my first," he squeezed out in a harsh breath. "My first, aye, my only, and my last." Clutching her hips possessively, he pushed all the way home, sending shock-waves clear down to her toes.

He moved slowly, at first, not hesitant but most definitely reined in. She drew her knees higher on his hips, squeezing him with her thighs, to hold him there, to hold him close. Gradually, he gained confidence with her moans of delight. And when he finally found his rhythm, it was all she could do to hold on and ride the storm.

Just when she thought it couldn't get any better, he rolled onto his back, pulling her with him, somehow remaining deep inside her.

She straddled him, astonished, her hair tumbling over his chest. But he moved her backward so his hand could slip between their bodies. And watched her, as she'd watched his reactions earlier, his fingers dipping between her legs where she was so wet, teasing, circling, as he thrust faster and deeper. Her head fell back. "Damon . . ."

Tremors fluttered in her stomach, sharpening, hot, so hot. The quivering built to an ache that swelled until it was almost unbearable. She couldn't breathe, couldn't speak. Heaven help her, she never knew it could be like this. Never knew it could be this good.

Damon touched her again, and her climax took her; she cried out, grabbing the bedsheets, as if to keep herself from flying away.

In the midst of it all, Damon went rigid and gasped her name. It seemed to go on for a long time for him, his release, powerful and intense. Then, as he collapsed in a panting heap on the mattress, he reached blindly for her and pulled her close.

Sweat dampened his skin, and hers. Exhausted, she kissed him, tasting salt, inhaling his scent.

"Ah, Harmony, love." His deep voice vibrated in his chest, his breath hot against her ear. "Ah, my sweet angel."

She came up on her elbow and smiled at his stunned expression. "Happy?"

"Aye . . ."

"So, it was everything you hoped it'd be?"

He let out an amazed chuckle. "If this is what it feels like to be human, lass, then I've but one thing to say."

She grinned, trailing her fingertips over his lips. "What's that?"

"Immortality is highly overrated."

Much later, they lay abed, dozing, limbs tangled after making love yet again. Damon couldn't get enough of Harmony, but was trying to control his appetite so as not to hurt her. She didn't seem to have suffered overly much, though, he thought with a smug smile.

He gathered her in his arms as she slept. Deny it she might, but Harmony Faithfull was as close to an angel in human form as he'd ever encountered. And he would know. It'd been many thousands of years since he'd crossed paths with the angels, and even then it was to do battle with the archangels, like Michael and Gabriel, fearsome warriors, equals to him in all ways of war. But it was the stories of the lesser angels that had always captivated him through the long centuries. Sweet, they were said to be, and mysterious, beautiful enough to bring a mortal man to tears, he'd overheard some humans say. Some of the angels were so pure of heart and intentions that they could lure a demon from the inexorable pull of the depths of Hell to the plains of the mortal world. Aye, Lucifer raged for many days after losing one of his best demon high lords in such a fashion. Pompeii was the result of that particular tantrum. Damon knew, because he'd been dispatched on assignment to do Lucifer's dirty work immediately after. Memories boiled up: *Fire . . . the stench of cinders and death. A sky roiling with black, sulfurous smoke.* Damon had walked the destroyed streets of the city, feeling nothing, simply doing what he'd been brought into existence to do: planting fear, doubt, and second thoughts, and accomplishing it with no emotion at all. He may have lost his demon's heightened senses, but not the memory of how it felt to have the darkness inside him, the coldness. How it felt to be empty.

"Unlike now," he murmured, burying his face in Harmony's curls. "Unlike now . . ."

Time seemed to stand still as the sun slowly rose. It reached the level of the windowsill and spilled into the bedroom, waking Harmony. "I suppose we should get up." Her voice was thick from sleep and spent passion.

Damon pulled her close. Slid his hand down her warm belly to find her moist and hot. "Why not stay abed a while longer?"

"Mmm." Harmony turned in his arms and they kissed, and then he loved her, slowly, carefully, savoring her. Afterward they drowsed in each other's arms. Damon had never imagined this sort of contentment existed. This happiness. He did not want the day to arrive and interrupt it all. And apparently, neither did his lover.

They dozed a while longer until Bubba came to the bedside, whining to be let out. Since more than dogs could squeeze through the dog door in the kitchen, Harmony kept it locked at night.

Damon offered, "I'll take him." Naked, he flung open the door to the solitude of the backyard, scratching his chest as he yawned and waited as the dog trotted onto the lawn.

Bubba lifted his leg and did his business, but instead of returning, he darted across the lawn, barking his announcing-visitors bark.

"Who's here?" Harmony called from the bed.

Damon squinted toward the road. "Someone's driving through the front gate. 'Tis a large, silver boxy vehicle."

"Is it a Humvee?" Harmony's voice sounded a wee bit strange.

"I dinna know," he said. "But the license plate says . . . *#1 Pastor*."

"Oh, no! No, no, no." Harmony leaped out of bed, tripping in the tangled sheets as she shoved one arm into her robe and then the other. Damon's heart sped up at her panic. "They're here. I can't believe they're here. Why do these things always happen to me? I try to live a godly life, and I *do* . . . well, except for last night, and I don't regret that for a moment, but this—this is just so typical of my life." She whipped the robe around her lush body. "I am so busted."

Damon grabbed her shoulders and steadied her. "Tell me. Who is in that car?"

"My father. My family. They showed up one week early!"

Fourteen

After the initial burst of panic from the shock of her family's unexpected arrival blew past, Harmony forced herself into combat mode. It was like the time in Iraq when the shell hit right outside the hospital.

She shoved the rumpled quilt over the sheets, collected scattered pillows, and arranged them hurriedly, wondering where she could arrange Damon where no one would notice him but quickly coming to the conclusion that not a single nook or cranny in the farmhouse would hide a six-foot-five-inch-tall ex-demon.

The doors to the Humvee slammed. Her heart tumbled as she peeked around an eyelet curtain. "They're unpacking the car, they always do it before coming in, and they're slow. It'll buy us some time, but precious little. Just enough time for a shower, I think." She slapped her hands on his gorgeous bare butt and pushed him toward the bathroom. "We have about two minutes. Maybe less. So I'm coming with you."

Damon appeared delighted by that fact, until remembering the car in the driveway. Harmony pulled him under the gushing water with her. "This is going to be the fastest shower you've ever had."

They soaped each other hastily.

Harmony grabbed blindly for two towels as water from her soaked hair streamed over her face. "Here's the plan. I'll get dressed and go meet them. You go out the side door—grab anything, tools, whatever, make it look like you were working—and I'll bring them inside and distract them with breakfast."

He brought his hand to her cheek, a calming touch. "I willna do anything to embarrass you."

"I know, honey. I know. You'd never embarrass me, Damon. I'm proud to be with you. It's just that . . ." She waved at the bed. "This isn't exactly proper behavior for a pastor, and especially for Reverend Faithfull's daughter."

He pressed a hurried but heartfelt kiss to her lips. "You dinna need to explain. I know what to do."

Harmony uttered a prayer of thanks for Damon's understanding as he grabbed his clothes and hurried out the side door.

Somehow she got herself together, pulling on yoga pants and a T-shirt. She secured her thick mass of soaking wet curls atop her head, jamming in a couple of pins to hold it in place, and burst outside, where Bubba pranced and jumped around her family and their suitcases. Car doors slammed, and her family bustled around the luggage, chattering and laughing, clearly excited to be there. Harmony smiled, her heart filling at the sight of them: Daddy tall and graying, but still so handsome, looking strangely underdressed in his sweatshirt and ironed Levi's; Mama, regal as always in her role as Reverend Jacob Jethro's wife but as light on her feet as the star athlete she once was when she met her husband at their high school track meet; Harmony's oldest brother, Jake Jr., was busy unloading the trunk—one thing about the Faithfulls, they didn't travel light. And Robbie had come, too, at sixteen the youngest Faithfull, attentive and respectful as he helped Great-grandmother Eudora step down from the rear passenger seat.

Harmony gulped, her stomach dropping. What would the woman see? What would she know? Too much already, Harmony thought, remembering the phone call with her father, when Eudora seemed to know about Damon.

Walking carefully, methodically, Eudora leaned on her cane. As always, she was dressed to the nines: a sapphire blue skirt set, with clusters of pearls clipped on her ears and around her neck, and a chocolate brown wig slightly askew. Step by careful step, she walked around the front of the truck, sucking on her false teeth. Her cane sank into the squishy, damp grass, and she stopped. Frowning, she shook her head in disapproval. Wheeling a bright red suitcase, Mama joined her to stare at the clods of displaced sod, the gouges and skid marks, the broken sprinkler heads, pieces of tattered cloth, and someone's forgotten sneaker.

The ruined yard.

"Hell's bells," Harmony whispered. She hadn't realized so much damage had been left behind. Her shaking hand crept up to the little cross she wore around her neck. *Lord, give me strength—oh, and the creativity—to come up with some really good answers to their questions*. Then, with her mouth formed into the biggest, most welcoming smile she could muster, she glided out to them, her arms wide open. "Wow, isn't this just the best surprise!"

In the next instant, she was swallowed up in a huddle of love, hugs, and kisses.

"We were going to spend this week in Rocky Mountain National Park," her father explained, "but when we saw the exit leading to Mysteria—"

"We simply couldn't pass it by," Mama finished for him. "I had to see my baby."

Eudora grasped Harmony's hands in hers. Her skin was once the color of rich caramel; now it was almost transparent over a network of bluish veins. Despite mild palsy, her grip remained as powerful as her intense gray-brown eyes. "Ah, you're happy, girl, aren't you?"

"I am, Great-grandma," Harmony replied shyly. "Very happy." *She knows what you did last night*. The thought popped into Harmony's mind, clear and simple. Her first instinct was to look away, to break the eye contact, but she stayed strong. Fact: Eudora knew what was going on between her and Damon. No way could she hide it. The best Harmony could hope for was for Great-grandmother not to say anything.

"What happened here?" Mama waved a manicured hand at the lawn.

"Um, a circus," Harmony blurted. *Good one.* "Yes, we had a bit of a circus here yesterday after services." That wasn't really lying, was it?

Mama brought her hands together in delight. "Isn't it wonderful, Jake? Our girl's as creative in spreading the good word as you."

Harmony shrank back in shame as her father puffed himself up. "I'm proud of you, Harmony. So proud of what you've done here in so short of a time."

Oh, boy. If you only knew.

"You got someone to put in sprinklers," Jake commented. "Looks like a first-class job. You didn't do it yourself, did you?"

"I did," said a familiar deep voice.

Harmony's heart bounced as Damon strode toward the group, a length of PVC pipe and a new sprinkler head in one hand, his other hand extended in welcome. "I'm Damon, the church groundskeeper." Dressed in clean clothes, his hair brushed neatly away from his freshly shaven face, Damon looked so bright and alert that no one would ever guess he'd been doing anything other than . . . well, than what he'd been doing all night.

Harmony blushed; she couldn't help it. "I'd been looking for someone to hire, a handyman and groundskeeper, when Damon came along looking for work. He's been wonderful, such a help, a blessing, truly."

At her gushing, Damon seemed almost bashful. The part that touched her the most was that it wasn't an act. "Reverend Faithfull needed someone for the heavier work so she could concentrate on the church. I've been busy making repairs and working in the fields"—he pulled a plump ear of corn from his overalls pocket, to the obvious delight of her family—"and once Harmony approves the plans I've drawn up for the barn, Mysteria Community Church will have a new social hall and gym."

"We will?" Shocked, Harmony watched Damon withdraw a folded piece of paper from his pocket. On it was a detailed drawing that he'd clearly spent a lot of time on and that she'd known nothing about. "Well," she said, "as you can see, Damon is indispensable."

Eudora cackled and patted his hand. "I see a lot of things about Damon."

Harmony's smile was wooden at best. Why, oh, why did she have to have a seer as a great-grandma? Why couldn't she have a normal family, who wouldn't be able to tell that she'd acquired a decidedly out-of-the-ordinary boyfriend?

"You're a good boy," the old woman said. Then she winked. "Good, good, good."

Damon coughed. It was the first time Harmony had seen him blush.

Eudora ran an admiring gaze over Damon's muscular frame, nodding, her eyes crinkling, then she gave Harmony an admiring, conspiratorial he's-hot wink before hobbling away to lead the clan to the house.

Harmony sidled up to Damon as her family walked on ahead. Pointing to her eyes, she whispered, "She's a seer. She can read thoughts sometimes. Just don't say it out loud."

"But she knows, lass. She knows what I am."

"She knows what you *were*." Harmony took a deep, calming breath. "And all we have to do is keep the rest of the family from finding out."

It was like old times with the family hanging around the kitchen counters and table just like they did in the big house in Oakland. After everyone had had a tour of the property, the church, and the house, Harmony prepared a late brunch, laughing and catching up.

Bacon sizzled in a cast-iron pan; grits bubbled thickly in

a pot, while Mama stirred gravy for the fluffy, towering biscuits in the oven. Eudora sat at the table, sucking on her false teeth, while the men argued about basketball. "We didn't have basketball in Scotland," Damon was telling them.

"Hoops after breakfast," Robbie decided.

Her father wouldn't hear of letting Damon sneak away to work, and held him captive in the kitchen as if he were already a member of the family. Damon soaked up the noise and laughter. Harmony's heart squeezed tight when she realized that this was something he'd never had—a family.

This was all going much better than she'd expected. When was the other shoe going to drop?

It's not going to drop. After yesterday's disaster, what could happen today that would be worse than that? Smiling, Harmony set the table, expanded with two extra leaves, and placed a strawberry dipped in powdered sugar as a garnish next to each person's antique china coffee cup.

She straightened, admiring the festive look the fruit and china brought to the table, and was about to tend to the bacon when in the corner of her eye she saw something move.

She blinked. Surely it was lack of sleep playing tricks with her vision. *Please, Lord, let it be that.*

She waited for more movement. Nothing. She was seeing things.

As soon as the food was ready, everyone sat around the table. Damon, bless his sweet heart, pulled out her chair, taking cues from her father and brother Jake, who did the same for Mama and Eudora.

Even though only one-third of the Faithfulls were in attendance, they were a noisy group, and the conversation filled the small kitchen. Dishes were passed around. When everyone's plates were filled, they joined hands to say grace.

In the hush that came over the room, Harmony's coffee cup scraped sideways. Her hand shot out, stopping it. "Fly," she explained urgently, her heart in her mouth. "They're really in abundance this time of year."

The moving cups had been no trick of her eyes. She prayed for inspiration, for an excuse, an explanation, anything at all to hop into her head and out her mouth, but the prospect of monsters from Hell appearing while her family was here had all but paralyzed her.

"Hold Great-grandma's hand, baby," her mother urged. "Your father wants to say grace."

Ever so reluctantly, Harmony withdrew her hand from the cup and slid her fingers back into Eudora's cool, dry palm. As Reverend Faithfull's resonant voice boomed, everyone's eyes were closed, except for Harmony's. Eyes wide open, she stared at the cup. But from across the table, she heard a soft scrape. Heart pounding, she watched three of the cups slide across the table, pushed by the strawberries. Switching positions, the cups moved around in some sort of paranormal shell game. Harmony made a squeak, and both Eudora and Damon squeezed her hands.

"He plays with you because you don't know how to fight him," the old woman whispered. Instinctively, Harmony knew her great-grandmother meant the Devil himself. "If you fight his evil with goodness, he'll lose interest and cease his games. Not forever, mind you, but for now."

Damon murmured back, "My powers, they are gone."

Eudora clucked in disapproval. "They're different now, your powers, not gone, and stronger than ever for the enemy you will face for a lifetime."

Mama opened an eye. "We will discuss the flies once your father is done speaking."

They were silent for a moment, then their furtive whispering continued.

"Harmony has never accepted she has powers," Eudora continued, "but she's come into them now. It's what drew you to her, Damon, and her to you. And what still attracts Satan to you both. He feels the power, the power of good, and it threatens him."

With that scary thought lingering in the air, Harmony's father finished grace. "Amen," they all said, and with a clattering of plates, silverware, and voices, the brunch began.

Harmony's appetite had vanished. Damon sat tense and ready for battle.

"Who moved the strawberries and mugs during grace?" Jake Jr. asked, laughing. "You, Robbie?"

His little brother looked indignant. "It wasn't me."

"When we were kids, we used to play pranks when everyone's eyes were closed during grace," Harmony explained to Damon. To the others, she said, "I . . . um, thought it'd be fun to take a trip down memory lane."

Everyone moaned at her. "Harmony . . ."

Her laugh was brittle. "Sorry, it was too much fun to resist," she said, thankful for the chance at an excuse for the displaced cups.

Then her strawberry bounced into the air. She snatched it. Before she could take a bite out of it and pretend nothing was wrong, she saw a tiny green creature hanging from the stem.

A little green man.

"Ah!" She dropped the berry into her grits with a noisy plop. Her mother glanced at her sharply. "A caterpillar," she explained breathlessly. "The countryside is full of them." Where did the green man go? Was it drowning?

Then Damon's cup jerked forward. His hand slammed over it. "Aye, nothing we do seems to stop them." Then he leaned over and whispered in her ear. He sounded sick at heart. "Snotlings."

"What are those?" Her voice sounded strained and shaky, and a little bit crazed. "Wait, it doesn't matter. How do we get rid of them?" She reached for the pitcher of water, and he caught her hand.

"Water has no effect," he whispered. Harmony could see her family trying to catch a snatch of their hushed conversation. "They are the smallest of the green-skinned races. The orcs and goblins use them as slaves for simple tasks because they're not intelligent creatures."

A snotling peeked out from under her father's plate. Harmony watched in dread as her father cut into his strawberry with his knife and fork. "They seem smart enough to me."

"I mean, they are not a threat on their own to other creatures. They form gangs to attack."

Jake Jr.'s strawberry rolled to the edge of the table. He

caught it in his palm before it leaped off the edge. "Your table needs leveling, kiddo," he informed Harmony. "The food is rolling off."

She made a weak laugh. "There's still so much to do around here." Something green darted across her plate. She squished it under a biscuit. Her mother frowned at her, as if she were a child playing with her food. But that impression was better than the alternative.

The fork on Great-grandma's plate rattled. Utterly calm, Eudora covered it with her napkin. What if Daddy's plate was attacked next? Or Mama's? What if they saw they weren't caterpillars or flies? Perspiration trickled between Harmony's breasts. Her heartbeat was erratic. She was never going to make it through this meal without passing out. Short of screaming fire, how was she going to evacuate her family from the kitchen?

"Bullies," Damon muttered softly. "That's all they are. Ye canna be afraid. Goodness will always win out. We are stronger than them. Far stronger."

"Then why do they keep returning?" Harmony whispered.

"Because they can," Eudora said. "Damon is correct. You have the power to eliminate them."

"We've tried. Nothing works."

"Call a pest control company," Jake Jr. suggested, biting into a piece of bacon.

"Monday," Harmony mumbled. "I'll give them a call. If I'm not dead by then."

The old woman frowned. "Satan torments you because your panic makes it fun. Take away the reason for his amusement, and he'll forget about this place and move on. Not forever, mind you, but for now."

Harmony tried to read the woman's mysterious expression. "How do you know so much about Satan?"

Her eyes seemed suddenly ancient. "Oh, we've crossed paths before."

"Grandma . . . please." Daddy shook his head. "Let's keep our mealtime conversations on happier things. Heaven, for instance, as opposed to Hell."

Eudora placed her hands in her lap, primly, but Harmony didn't buy it for a moment. "It's always good to be grateful for what we have so much in abundance in this family," she reminded him. "Our goodness."

Murmurs of agreement went around the table.

Eudora continued with her little homily, addressing her father, even though Harmony knew the lesson was intended for her and Damon. "Because of your position and power, Jake, Satan toyed with our family more than once. He places temptation in our path, tries to ruin us, but I'm always ready for him. Always ready."

She took Harmony's hand and Damon's and brought them together under the table. Damon's fingers were hot and dry. Her body gave a little leap, remembering the feel of that hand sliding over her bare skin, doing the most amazing things. . . .

A cup clattered against a plate. Harmony squeaked and tried to pull away, but Eudora hissed at her. "No."

"But—"

"No!" Eudora placed her arms over Harmony's shoulders, Damon's, too, and drew them close. "Believe in your power to defeat him, and you will. Fill your minds with goodness, and together push it outward. He'll not be able to stand against you."

"That sounds too simple."

"It is. That's what too few people remember. Good and evil. Right versus wrong. Yes versus no. There's nothing complicated about it. Good repels wickedness. If it were otherwise, the world would have gone to hell in more ways than one eons ago."

"Aye," Harmony heard Damon murmur, as if he understood.

"Hold it right there, you three." Robbie pushed back from the table. "Great picture!" He snapped a shot on his digital, and in the distraction of showing everyone the image, Eudora spoke under her breath to Harmony and Damon.

"Whenever it seems the Devil is near, join hands and think of goodness—of God."

"Like a séance?" Robbie asked.

Eudora frowned at him. "Eat your eggs. Go on," she urged Harmony and Damon. "The two of you. Try it. You are weak alone and most powerful together against the force of evil. Gather the light of goodness around you, the power, and then use it to fight Satan—to thrust him away. Let the light expand out from you, then push. Together, you will not lose."

"Grandmother," Daddy warned.

"Hush, boy! Can't you see I'm teaching a lesson here? What is it with this family sometimes?" Eudora made a cluck of annoyance. "Together you can fight him off. And in fighting him off, you can fight *them* off."

"The snotlings," Harmony whispered.

"Now, let's practice. Close your eyes and hold hands."

Damon's hand closed over Harmony's as he shut his eyes. Their arms rested on Eudora's lap, on the bright blue wool of her skirt.

"You, too, girl. Close your eyes."

"Yes, Great-grandma." Oh, how she didn't want to listen! Not with little green men on the loose. If her mother were to see them, or Daddy, then the explanations would have to follow, and they'd learn about Damon—

"Now," Eudora growled.

Harmony squeezed her eyes shut.

She could hear something scratching on her plate. Maybe the snotling was trying to dig out from under the biscuit. If she could just squish it back down . . .

But Damon held fast to her hand. Eudora pressed her hands over their clasped ones. "Think of good . . . as hard as you ever have."

Harmony pursed her lips and concentrated, thinking of heaven and light, of faith and eternity . . . and the quiet hush of a snowy morning, of the softness of a baby's head, the ripple of grass in the fields . . . the tenderness of Damon's kiss, and that way he looked at her that morning in the twilight of dawn, when he'd held her so close. . . .

To her amazement a sense of assurance came over her, a strange and quiet confidence. And then, she sensed the press of Damon's mind against hers, the first time she'd felt him reaching out to her with his thoughts. Taking a deep breath, she opened up and let him in.

A burst of light exploded behind her eyes. Damon's hand convulsed in hers, and Eudora made a quiet sound of approval. "Yes, children. That's what you do. Now fight. Push."

Gather the light, Harmony thought. *Gather the light and throw it outward*. In her imagination, she visualized pooling her strength with Damon's, and together they chased away the shadows, letting the light seep into every crevice, letting it pool and overflow, until there was no darkness left.

The table started vibrating. Harmony's eyes shot open. The orange juice in everyone's glasses shook, and the silverware rattled.

"He's angry," Damon murmured.

The shaking continued and Mama made a gasp. "What is it, Jake? An earthquake?"

"A small aftershock to one we had some time back," Damon explained with utter calm.

The little kitchen chandelier swung crazily, and juice splashed on the tablecloth. But Harmony wasn't afraid anymore. She had control now. "Bring it on," she told Lucifer and gripped Damon's hand with all her might. "I'm ready to kick some devil's ass."

"Harmony!"

Harmony smiled a bit sheepishly at her mother's incredulous glare. "Sorry, Mama. It just slipped out. Great-grandma's got me all fired up about good versus evil."

Her brothers laughed.

A tearing noise dragged all their gazes upward. The tremors had knocked the chandelier loose. Plaster sprinkled down. It dropped a couple of inches, swinging on its wire. Then it plunged to the table with a mighty crash.

The tremors stopped. Bracing herself, Harmony glanced around the table with the fallen chandelier looking like a gaudy centerpiece. The strawberries were behaving like strawberries were supposed to behave. Same with the cups. And no little green men cavorted over the tablecloth.

"Yes," Harmony whispered. "Yes. Thank you, Great-grandma."

Cackling softly, Eudora patted Harmony on the thigh and resumed eating her breakfast. Jake Jr. moved the chandelier to the floor, and Mama plucked a piece of plaster out of her coffee. After a few nervous comments about the rarity of earthquakes in the Rocky Mountains, the conversation returned to its normal volume and enthusiasm.

"A toast," her father called out and raised his glass of orange juice. "To getting to know our daughter's new friend. Damon."

"Do you think you can join us for Christmas, honey?" Mama asked him. Then her apologetic gaze swerved to Harmony. "Or will that be too soon?"

Harmony smiled. "No, not too soon at all. I'm kind of hoping he'll be staying around for a while."

The look in Damon's gold-brown eyes was one she'd never forget. "Aye, lass. I'll be around for a while. As close to forever as heaven allows."

Harmony was terrified no one would ever return to church after the flying monkeys, but as the week went on the casseroles started arriving, brought by sympathetic towns-people, and even cookies, baked, incredibly, by the terror triplets Withering, Scornful, and Derisive. Jeanie stopped by, of course, and the Tawdrys, Mrs. O'Cleary, and her great-granddaughter Annabelle, all impressing the Faithfulls with their good words about Harmony and Mysteria Community Church, while Damon devoted his energy to acting the part of the perfect suitor, an ex-demon trying to win the hand of the preacher's daughter. It drove home the uniqueness of Mysteria. Everyone was welcome here, no one was ostracized, no matter who—or what—you were.

When the crowds returned that next Sunday, Harmony smiled from the pulpit at her father, looking so proud as the guest of honor in the front pew. Next to him were her brothers, Mama, and Great-grandmother Eudora, whose hand rested affectionately, and rather appreciatively, on Damon's rock-hard thigh.

Later that night, after the Sunday dinner dishes were cleaned and put away, and her family was gathered around the television in the living room, Harmony and Damon sneaked outside.

Taking her hand, Damon led her to the garden and under the apple tree where he'd landed naked only a few months before. Fireflies floated all around them. Frogs and crickets provided a ceaseless chorus. Damon slung his arms low around her waist and pulled her close. They stood there simply holding each other. With soft, warm lips, he nuzzled her neck. "Good, good, good," he murmured.

She giggled. "They'll be gone tomorrow and we'll finally have some private time to . . . well, you know."

"Aye, I do know. How could I forget? I've thought of it day and night, lass. Day and night." He slid his hands over her butt and pulled her closer. Yes, he was thinking about their lovemaking, no doubt about it. His body made that fact obvious.

She tipped her head to gaze up at him. "At one time, you weren't too happy about being mortal in Mysteria. Does this mean now you are?"

Damon chuckled. "Aye. 'Tis all I ever want to be."

"When I used to look at this church, all I could see was its emptiness, but it was my emptiness that was the problem," she confessed. "And then you came and everything changed."

His handsome face was luminescent with love. "This is only the beginning. 'Twill get better and better with us." Swallowing nervously, he crouched down on one knee. "Forgive me if I dinna do this properly." Then he clasped her hands in his. "Harmony, will you do me the pleasure of one day taking me as your husband?"

She whooped then slapped a hand over her mouth. "Yes," she mumbled joyfully through her fingers. "Yes."

He lifted her up and swung her around, kissing her hard. Then, with devilish intent and one hell of a bad-boy grin, he carried her swiftly away from the house to where the lights didn't reach.

And so, the fair maiden married her dark knight the following spring, and all was right between them . . . or as right as life could be in the strange little hamlet of Mysteria.

That was, until they began to wonder if demon genes could be passed on to their children, the first of which arrived within the year. But that is a story for another day. . . .

ALONE WOLF

MaryJanice Davidson

Acknowledgments

Thanks to "the girls": Susan, Gena, and P. C. for their support; they made this such a fun project, I was bummed when it was time to turn it in.

Thanks also to our editors at Berkley for their enthusiasm for Mysteria and its, ah, interesting inhabitants. Without their thumbs-up, this book wouldn't be here.

Thanks also to all those who wrote me asking about the goings on in Mysteria; the girls and I got kind of curious about that, too. So here you go.

Author's Note

The events of this novella take place three months after the events in *Bewitched, Bothered, and Bevampyred,* available at www.triskelion.com, and a year after the events in *Derik's Bane* (Berkley Sensation).

Also, triplets aren't necessarily evil. And most horses don't behave like the night mare. But there are, of course, exceptions.

Prologue

✳

The house sat in the center of two gently rising hills, looking like a jewel on a beautiful woman's bosom. It was, in fact, the color of crushed rubies; the shutters were black. It was a two-bedroom in the Cape Cod style, two stories, one and a half bath, with an assumable mortgage at a fixed rate; the heater and central air were both up to code.

Inside, the walls were the bland color of good cream; the floors were oak. There was a dishwasher, but no garbage disposal. The house was built in 1870, and so was sorely lacking in closet space. Still, at sixteen hundred square feet, it was of a respectable size; the perfect starter home.

Of course, it was haunted. In 1914, one of the roofers (hired to fix the holes brought by the Big-Ass Hailstorm of the Spring of '14) fell off and, after dying, had the bad manners to linger. But she was helpful, really; a squeaky door would magically fix itself, the heater, though thirty years old, ran without a hiccup. If her views on the doings of the Mysteria City Council were noisily and frequently expressed, it was a small price to pay for never having to call a handyman.

The backyard went straight back, like an arrow, and the garden sat at the top of the yard like an arrowhead. It had grown over, of course, but could be brought back again; it was the right size for a salsa garden, or perhaps some cutting flowers.

The front yard ran straight up to the road and was small, almost an afterthought. There was no sidewalk; just a paved driveway that led to the small detached garage.

In the front yard was a sign: white, with stark black lettering. It looked like a For Sale sign, but the largest letters read FOR CRYING

and the rest of the sign read:

. . . out loud, think about what you're doing! This is a weird weird weird town. There's a reason this house has been on the market going on ten years. Think carefully before you so much as set foot on the lawn.

(It was a large sign.)

Then, in smaller letters, accompanied by a red smiley face: DON'T FORGET TO TAKE A BROCHURE!

The house sat like a jewel, and waited.

One

His first memory was of the moon, a shining, broad black face with the whitest teeth and the darkest eyes beaming down at him. When he checked his medical records years later and did the math, he figured out it would have been his third trip to the hospital; his second broken arm.

Mama Zee, the most sought-after foster mother in the county, had taken him home after signing all the paperwork (her righteous name, according to the most-helpful chart, was Ms. Zahara J. Jones) and put him in the battered wooden crib in her tiny third bedroom. (Willie and Konnie were in the other bedroom, and Jenna slept on the foldout couch in the living room.)

He did not remember the foster father breaking his arm, or the other foster father breaking his *other* arm, and he did not remember doctors or the hours of pain, but to the end of his days he would remember her smiling face. That, and waiting. It seemed he was always waiting: for a ride, for a class to start, for a job, for a hug, for a friend.

He was just a dumb baby then, and didn't know what the

moon really was, but for a long time that was how he thought of her: Mama Zee, the moon.

In the end, he always came back to her. He loved the moon, but could not stay: for one thing, the noise drove him fucking nuts. Mama Zee *always* had kids around. There were always toys underfoot; the cupboard was always stuffed with little applesauce containers. Even as a small boy, at four, at six, at nine, he would have to get out, wander about on his own for a while.

After a while, the cops never ever caught him; he was too quick, and too quiet. But he always came back, and after the first two times, when Mama Zee saw that no matter how many times she smacked him with the dish towel or yelled, no matter what she did or how she worried, he would leave, he was compelled to go. But he always came back. And so she didn't worry. Or, if she did, she never spoke to him about it.

She even gave him a book once (well, she gave him lots of books, many times, but this one he remembered especially) about a kid named Jack who could travel between dimensions; his family called him Traveling Jack. "That's like you," she told him, "you just can't stay in one spot, boyo. And that's fine."

Well, no, he thought. *I can't stay here, is what it is.* But he didn't say it out loud. He'd bite off his own fingers before he'd say something so mean to her.

In fact, the entire neighborhood treated Mama Zee as a bomb that might blow up in their faces, because they knew *he* was quick, and quiet. And strong.

Mama Zee had all the help she needed getting groceries delivered (and because she usually had between three and seven foster kids at any one time, the milk bill alone was staggering), all the extensions needed to pay local vendors, and nobody ever broke in.

Occasionally, on his travels, Someone Bad would take it in their head that he might have something they wanted. It always went badly for Someone Bad and the older he got, the easier it got.

At first he put up with it, because he knew the bloody nose, the black eye, the whatever, would be all better in a day or two, sometimes less, depending on the moon. It was the price you paid for choosing not to sleep under a roof; that, and cold feet.

And then, one day it was like he had a lightning flash, only inside his brain. And the flash was made up of words: *Not today, pal*. He was nine when he realized he could make a grown man cry. It was shockingly easy.

He wasn't a bully (Mama Zee would have smacked him half to death with that dish towel), but he'd crunched up quite a few of them.

He wasn't very good in school—something about sitting still in a classroom reminded him of Mama Zee's noisy, toy-strewn living room. But he was good at other things.

When he got big—and thanks to Mama Zee's cooking, he got *really* big—he found out people would pay to get and keep a bully out of their lives. Pay a lot, sometimes. And sometimes it wasn't a bully; it was an ex-husband or a mean boss or a bad cop (but really, under their outside skin, they were all bullies). And the older he got, the more they paid him. Almost like if he didn't do the job, they were afraid he'd do them, so they practically threw money at him.

Of course he wouldn't; he was still a little nervous about Mama Zee's dish towel, though he had twelve inches of height and sixty pounds of muscle on her, and she was old; she was fifty-four. But the people didn't know that, and so they gave him money.

He didn't know what to do with it; he tried giving it to Mama Zee, but she only took enough to pay off her little house in Revere. He knew better than to talk her into retiring; the moon did not get tired of changing the tides, and Mama Zee loved kids. And she wouldn't move to a nicer neighborhood. She wouldn't take a car, either; not that a person needed one in that area.

He paid for Jenna's college; she was grown now, and still sleeping on the couch. She took it with thanks, and moved out, and Mama Zee didn't say anything, but he heard her crying later. Only it was the good kind of crying, so he wasn't sure what to do about that. In the end he did nothing.

Finally, Mama Zee said to him, "You're grown, boyo. Don't you want a place of your own?"

He just shrugged; his skin was itchy and he kept looking at the door. The new kid, Bryan, had colic. It was noisier than usual in the small house on Winthrop Avenue.

"Stop that twitching and pay attention to me; you can go soon enough. Don't you ever think about getting a girl and settling down?"

"No," he told her, and it was the truth, naturally. He couldn't imagine lying to her. Like he couldn't imagine taking a woman for his own, and cursing her as he was cursed. He would never.

That made her look sad, for some reason, and she slammed a cup of applesauce in front of him. She felt better when he ate.

He hated applesauce.

He got a spoon and started eating.

"You should take some of that money and buy a house of your own," she finally said. She watched him eat every bite of the pulped fruit. "Your own house, where it can be as quiet as you want it. And then, maybe . . . the rest will come."

"Okay," he said.

"Because—I've been thinking about this a lot, boyo, and you can't be the only one. The only one in the whole entire world. Right? You can't."

He shrugged.

"Just because you never ran across another werewolf," she added sharply, as if he had contradicted her, "doesn't mean there aren't any others out there. If only your birth parents—"

She stopped talking, and he was glad. He had never known them, but he didn't like them. They had been killed in a car accident, and left him.

"You need to go," she added, nicer. "Go and find someone like you, maybe a whole bunch of people like you. Not that there's anyone exactly like you, boy." She looked at him closely. "No, you're one of a kind."

He grunted.

Mama Zee got up, opened the fridge, unwrapped a raw hamburger, put it on a clean plate, and handed it to him. "Thank you for eating the sauce. I don't think you—"

"Get enough fruit and vegetables in my diet," he finished for her. He used the same spoon to wolf down the raw meat.

"Don't be smart, boyo. You gonna do what I said?"

"Sure," he replied.

Two

Cole Jones stared at the small red house, then looked back down at the map of Colorado folded in his hand, then back up at the house.

Mysteria.

Specifically, 232 Roselawn Lane, Mysteria, mail code 678. No city, county, or state.

He had literally followed his nose here; for that matter, he wasn't entirely sure where *here* was. Certainly, the small town hadn't been on any map. Small, charming, and quiet, he had found it mesmerizing and interesting. And the smells! The fields smelled like newly mown hay (a good trick in autumn), the main street smelled like fresh pie, shit, even the town dump hadn't been bad. Just interesting.

And it was so quiet. The little red house sat alone on the lane, and there wasn't a crying baby for miles—downtown Mysteria was almost five miles away. A true country house. He had assumed, being city born (well, city raised) that he wouldn't like the country, but the quiet seemed to him like the most marvelous thing.

There was, in fact, only one house for sale, and he was

looking at it. He had read the puzzling yard sign three times, and almost smiled. It didn't frighten him; it made him want to sprint to the bank and throw all his money at the first teller he could sniff out.

And speaking of sniffing, he could smell the small car seconds before he heard it. And in another minute, there was the groan of poorly maintained brakes, a door slamming, and he turned to see a short, chubby brunette with a nipped-in waist, wonderful deep breasts, and sweetly plump thighs

(ummmm)

hurrying toward him.

"I'm sorry," she called to him in the flat accent of a Mid-westerner, probably upper North Dakota or Minnesota, "have you been waiting long?"

"Yes."

"Oh." She appeared to mull that one over for a moment, then said, blinking, "I'll be glad to take you inside for a tour."

Her eyes were the exact color of oak leaves, greenish brown, and large. Her brows were a shade darker than her hair, almost black. She was very pale, like a marshmallow. A juicy, gorgeous, mouth-watering marshmallow. He was almost knocked over by the—by the *intensity* of her. It was like she was more there than other people. He had never smelled anything like it.

"That's fine," he said, trying not to be overtly sniffing. Maybe she'd think he had a cold. Or was hooked on coke. That would be great!

"What's fine?"

Juicy and intense, but not the sharpest claw in the pad. "A tour. But you don't have to. I'll take it."

"You *what*?"

She was staring at him, but that was fine; he was used to it. It used to make him mad when he was younger, to have someone gape right into his eyes, challenging, gawking—it always made him feel like hitting, or biting. But he didn't mind anymore; he figured he'd outgrown his youthful temper. He was old, twenty-seven.

"I have a cashier's check," he added helpfully.

"Er, what? I mean, great. The down payment—"

"For the asking price." He pulled out the piece of paper and tried to hand it to her, but her arms were frozen at her sides and she was opening and closing her

(red-lipped, rosy, like berries, like ripe berries)

mouth like a bass.

She looked down at herself, and he looked, too. A green suit, a white blouse. No stockings. Black pumps. Then she looked around, as if wondering if what was happening was actually happening. Finally, she said, "Er, yes. Ah, look, Mr. Jones, I have to tell you, this—Mysteria, I mean—this isn't—I mean, it's a great town, the greatest town in the world, but—but it's—I mean, it's—" She took another look at him, audibly gulped, then smiled. A real smile, one that made her eyes crinkle at the corners and a dimple pop up in her left cheek. He couldn't help it; he smiled back.

"On second thought," she said, "I think you'll fit right in here."

"No," he said, "but I like the house anyway."

"I'm Charlene Houtenan."

"I know," he said, and shook her hand, and ignored the impulse to nibble on her knuckles and tell her she smelled like wet clover.

Three

". . . And if you'll sign here . . . and here . . . and here . . ."

He signed patiently: *Cole Jones. Cole Jones. CJ. CJ.*

". . . and we've got the cashier's check, and these are your copies—I must say, this is the fastest closing I've ever done, and I've been a Realtor since—for a long time."

He ate more pie, and tucked the wad of paperwork into the folder she offered him, then dropped it on the seat beside him. They were doing the closing at Pot's on the main drag in Mysteria. He was glad. The pie was amazing.

"And I guess that's it." Charlene was resting her small chin on her hands and staring at him as he wolfed down his third piece. "Congratulations, Mr. Jones."

"Cole," he told her again.

"Right. And I'm Char."

"Right."

"Do you know what her secret is?" she almost whispered.

"No."

"She puts seaweed in the crust."

"Umm."

"And she also sells them to go," Charlene added, "in case

you wanted, you know, not to worry about fixing supper tonight."

Pot "My full name is too hard to pronounce" herself came up to their table. She was awesomely tall, the tallest woman he had ever seen, and too thin. He could see her skull beneath her face; see the bones stretching through on her limbs. Her hair was the greenish color blondes got when they spent the summer in the pool. Her eyes were the oddest green he had ever seen on a person, the color of the Boston harbor on a good day. Her eyebrows were so light and fine, they nearly disappeared into her face.

"Fourths?" she asked, drumming abnormally long fingers on their table. Her voice was low and slurring. Her nose was a blade.

"No. But I'd like two more chicken pies to go."

She placed two blue pie boxes, tied neatly with white string, on their table, then put the check on top of the box.

"Thanks, Pot. I've got it," Charlene said quickly, snatching the check before Cole could put down his fork. Pot nodded and made a graceful exit.

"You don't have to," he said, chewing. If Mama Zee could see him talking with his mouth full, there'd be hell to pay. "I have money."

"Ha! You're a homeowner; you're poor now."

"Okay."

The café door opened and three girls trooped in and, though he knew it was rude, he stared a little. He had never seen identical triplets before; they were like preteen Barbies: all blonde hair, perfect teeth, and tans. They were identically dressed in khaki clam diggers, red shirts, and white flip-flops, as if it was August instead of September. As one, they looked at him with their blue, blue eyes, then marched up to the counter where there was a pickup order waiting.

Over the muted hum of voices, he heard one of them ask, "Who is *that*?"

"Someone too old for you," Pot replied.

"Oh, yuck," the second one said. "Pot, that's gross."

"New guy?" the third one asked.

"Obviously," Pot said, popping open the cash register and dropping the triplets' money into the drawer.

"Touch-ee! What's wrong, Pot, red tide getting you down?"

"As a matter of fact, yes. Good-bye, girls."

"Nice," the first one said.

"So rude!" the second one said.

"One day we'll learn to cook as good as you," the third one threatened, "and then you'll be out of business."

Pot laughed at them, the sound like a spring trickling through the woods.

"You'll rue the day," the first one said mildly, trotting out behind her sisters.

"Those were the Desdaine triplets," Charlene said as the door whooshed closed behind them. She was grinning a little. "You should be nice to them; when they take over the world, they might spare your life."

"Umm," he said, scraping the plate. Seaweed in the crust? Whatever was in the crust, it was buttery, flaky, tangy and salty and mouth-watering. The chicken was tender and juicy, the vegetables perfectly cooked.

He could hardly wait to get to his new house and reheat another one. Assuming he had a microwave. Or a kitchen. Maybe he should have had the home inspected after all. . . .

"Excuse me," Charlene said as she got up to pay the bill. Another woman was manning the cash register, and Pot glided up to his table. She smiled at him and he saw her teeth were small, like pearls, and pointed, like thorns.

"Hello," he said politely.

"Mr. Cole."

"Will you come over to my house tonight?" he asked.

"Indeed. Eleven o'clock?"

"Yes. It's—"

"I know which one it is," she said, then glided past Charlene, who was looking at him with not a little hurt in her gaze. It puzzled him, and as usual, when he didn't know what to do, he did nothing.

Four

He did have a kitchen. Spotless, with the longest counters he'd ever seen, and the smallest microwave. A chicken pie just fit.

He prowled around the house, extremely satisfied, and made a mental note to get the computer and land lines hooked up in the morning. He had already called Mama Zee to tell her he had moved, er, somewhere, and was now a homeowner full of pie. She had been surprised, but delighted, puzzled over his address, but determined to send him a case of applesauce as a housewarming present. He would rather have a case of manure, but of course didn't tell her that.

When the ghost spoke, he was so startled he nearly fell down the stairs. He'd had no warning; it wasn't like she had a scent.

"Just so you know, your name on the deed doesn't mean this is your house."

"That's exactly what it means," he replied, recovering.

"Okay, well, what I meant was, it doesn't mean you belong."

"I've never belonged anywhere."

The ghost yawned. "How sad, boo-hoo."

He was looking out windows, in closets, smelling corners, and peeking into bathrooms. "Where are you?"

"Mind your own business, homeowner."

"Char told me a roofer was killed working on the house."

"So?"

"So, what do you want?"

There was a long, puzzled silence; Cole had the sense no one had asked her that before. "I guess I want what anybody wants: to putter around in my own house, to be left alone."

"Okay."

"Chatty, aren't we?"

"Um. What's your name?"

"Also none of your business."

"But we're roommates. You probably know my name."

"It's Rae, all right? And don't go thinking we can get all chummy and such. You're still green, homeowner, talk to me when you've been in this town for a decade or so."

"Okay."

"And no women coming and going at all hours of the night, either!"

"Pot is coming at eleven."

"Goddammit!" the ghost cursed, then sulked and wouldn't talk to him anymore, which was a relief.

Pot was early and, interestingly, did not knock. Just walked right in. She smiled like a shark when she saw the two empty pie plates on his counter.

"Hello," he said.

"Hello."

He cast about; what was polite? What did normal people *say*? "Thanks for coming."

"I couldn't resist. I'm sorry to be so early, but I was very anxious to see what was on your agenda."

Right. Time to get to it. He appreciated her directness; it was a trait he rarely ran across. "I'm different," he said, "like you."

"Not like me."

"Okay."

"I'm a river nymph," she explained patiently, "you're a werewolf."

"I don't know what that is," he admitted, as startled as when the ghost had first spoken.

"Which one?" She opened his fridge, sighed happily when she saw it was full of food and drink, and helped herself to a bottle of water.

"A river nymph."

She drained the bottle in two gulps, something he had not thought physically possible. "Couldn't you tell by looking at me? By my scent?"

"You smell like the deep end of the pool," he told her.

She grabbed another bottle, popped the top, chugged it down. "Yes, indeed. There are two rivers that run parallel to Mysteria—"

"There are?" He was startled; he'd only seen one on his way in.

She grinned again, showing her pointy teeth—good, he imagined, for eating raw fish. "You have to really be looking to find the other one. Or, I have to be inclined to let you see it. Never mind, it's not the point. Potameides Naiad, that's me, and have you noticed how dry it is in here?"

"Potameides is much nicer than Pot," he told her.

"I don't care," she told him, working on bottle number three, "and I doubt you do, either."

"Why do you make pies and run around in a hot kitchen all day?"

"Mysteria is my home; in that small way, I contribute to the community."

"But why are you here?"

"I had planned to ask you the same thing. This is my home now, that's why." She looked at her floor, and her long, greenish blonde hair fell forward, obscuring her face. "I saw you and thought—maybe—we were kindred spirits."

"Are you looking for others like you, too?" Perhaps they would team up. They'd have to stick to the coast, of course, and he would be sorry to see his red house go, not to mention Charlene, but the entire reason he was even here was to—

"No. I know where my people are; they can come to me whenever they wish. I was banished."

"Banished from the river, Pot?"

"From a particular river, so I came here." She lifted her head and stared at him defiantly; he felt like he might slip and drown in her glare. "And it's Queen Potameides, were-wolf."

"Sorry." A displaced queen! Who was a river nymph, no less. Evil triplets. Gorgeous Realtors with heart-shaped butts. And it was only his first day. "Maybe your people will relent, soon."

She laughed without humor. "I doubt it, Mr. Jones. I've been here for over a hundred years. Not long for my people, but long to be away from friends."

"I'm sorry."

"It isn't your problem. Why were you sent away? That's really what I must know. Particularly if your people are having the same, ah—difficulties—as mine."

"Oh. I wasn't sent away." He didn't think. "I was raised by ordinary humans." If Mama Zee had heard him refer to her as ordinary . . . he shuddered, then went on. "I never knew my birth family."

"And you're a werewolf? But that's terrible!" Queen Potameides seemed genuinely distressed, which was pleasant, as she'd just met him. "Did the humans ever lock you up, or—"

"No. My foster mother understood. She's the one who made me go away. In a nice way," he added, since the river queen looked alarmed again. "To find others like me."

"Oh. Well, there's a werewolf in town—"

"There is? Where?" He looked around as if the creature was hiding in his kitchen.

"His name's Justin, but calm down, he's actually out of town right now. But he could answer your questions when he returns, I'm sure."

"Thank you, Queen Potameides."

She smiled shyly. "I am pleased you don't share my particular woe. When you find your people, will you leave?"

Er. Uh. Good question. Back in Revere, he had assumed Mysteria would be a stepping stone. Now he wasn't so sure. He liked the house. He liked Charlene. He loved the pies. He liked the river goddess. In one day, he'd felt more at home, more real, than in his entire childhood in Massachusetts.

Maybe he could commute to the werewolves. Maybe they wouldn't insist on his living with them. Maybe—

"Hey, Pot, looks like you're done. Don't let the door hit you in your damp ass on the way out."

"Shush, Rae," the queen said sternly, and the ghost hushed. "You don't have to put up with that one if you don't want," she added to Cole. "There's an exorcist in town who could get rid of her like *that*." She snapped her fingers, which squished; the ends were wrinkled and damp, as if she'd been swimming all day instead of baking.

"Ha!" the ghost crowed. "He wishes. He's been trying to exorcise me for years."

"It's true," the queen added in a low voice. "His heart really isn't in it. He knew Rae in life, you see."

"Also," Rae summed up, "he couldn't exorcise a ghost if you threw them in a blender together."

"You're mistaking compassion for weakness," the queen said. "Again."

"Has anyone ever told you, you smell like wet dog?"

"You *dare* speak to me that way again, dead thing, and I'll . . ."

"Drip through me? Make water stains on the floor? Hock a big ole salty loogey into one of your pies, which I can't eat anyway, so why would I give a crap?"

"Ladies, ladies. Don't fight. It's all right," Cole said, wondering what he would do if they did fight. Try to stop them? Leave? Distract the queen by filling the bathtub? "It's all right," he said again.

"How?" the queen demanded. "How is it all right?"

"She—the, you know—" He gestured vaguely to the air.

"The *ghost*, you idiot," the air snapped back.

"She doesn't make any trouble," he finished unconvincingly.

The queen sighed. "That's what they all say."

"Squirt it out your ear, Potty."

"Thank you," she replied with the dignity of a centuries-old royal line, "for your hospitality, *Mr. Jones*. No need to see me out."

Fortified with Aquafina, the queen left, every step a squish. Cole took a minute to mop up the tracks, feeling oddly cheerful. There was a werewolf in town (well, would be soon), he had a roommate who never gave him any trouble (so far . . . and not too much) and didn't eat baby food (probably) or get colic (again, probably), the queen could cook, and the realtor had a terrific body. It was like a smorgasbord of thought: where to go, what to do, what to think about first?

Exhausted, he went to bed.

Five

The next morning, after breakfast at the café, he asked where Charlene was.

"The range," one of the triplets told him. They were sitting across from him in his booth, watching with amazement while he ate. He was a little amazed himself at their interest.

And his own, in Charlene. He'd stopped by her small Realtor's office (on the outside, it looked like a small, weather-beaten Cape Cod, though they weren't on Cape Cod . . . right?) on the way to breakfast, but it was locked, with a Closed sign hanging in the window. Well, after her commission from yesterday, she could probably afford to take a day off. And he was used to eating alone.

Not that he was eating alone this morning. "The range?" he repeated, mopping up the juice from his blueberry pie with the crust from his apple pie.

"The shooting range. East end of town. Where do you put it all?"

"I run it off."

"Oh," the second triplet said. They were again disconcertingly dressed alike, this time in felony schoolgirl outfits of red plaid skirts, white blouses, white knee socks, and black loafers. If they didn't smell so strongly of immature female, he might have been in trouble. As it was, he pitied their parents: it would be hard to keep the boys away. "You know, there are other places to eat in town."

"Yes. Where is the range?"

"We'll show you."

"That's all right, Withering. Just give me directions."

"I'm Withering," the third one pouted, kicking one of her long legs. "That's Derisive."

"No, it's not."

"How do you know? We got up and switched around when you were ordering your lunch delivery."

He shrugged. He had no intention of explaining to the preteens that they had distinct smells, and slightly alarming ones: cinnamon, cloves, and nutmeg. Sharp smells, and not comforting in females. He preferred his women to smell like flowers, grass, or—

"Charlene."

"What?" Scornful asked.

"Where is she?"

"We really will show you—no tricks," Withering promised.

"But you have to tell us something," Derisive added.

"Your deep dark—"

"I'm a werewolf," he said, already bored with their preteen weirdness. He hadn't liked seventh-graders when he *was* one.

"That's it? Just like that? 'I'm a werewolf.' "

"It's not a secret," he explained.

"It's not?" the triplets chimed. "We have all kinds of secrets," Derisive added. "You'd lose your hair just thinking about them."

"It's not a secret," he reminded them. "It's why I'm here. To find more of my own kind."

"Well, that's admirable and all, but you probably shouldn't just blurt it out to anybody you see."

"Not even here?"

"Welllllll . . ." The sisters looked at each other. "Maybe here is okay. Goddess knows it's a weird place. But still, if we didn't have to drag it out of you, or trick you . . ."

"We couldn't trick him," Scornful said.

"Yes, you could," he corrected. "I'm not very smart."

"About that," Withering said, looking at him thoughtfully, "I wouldn't be so sure. You're staying for a while, Mr. Cole? You bought Rae's house?"

"It's my house."

"Right," Scornful said.

"Better run that one by Rae," Withering added.

"Or just run," Scornful suggested.

"Welcome to Mysteria," her sisters finished in eerie unison.

Six

He found Charlene at a small outdoor shooting range on the east end of town. The triplets had, at the last second, disdained to accompany him, instead giving him a map that disappeared as soon as he saw the range with his own eyes. Disappeared like a trick: *poof*. He spent five minutes trying to find it in his car before giving up. He wasn't in Kansas anymore, Toto.

Not that he had needed it; the smell of gunpowder and spent casings was very strong on this end of town; he would eventually have stumbled across it himself. Still, it was good to know the triplets could be helpful when they wished.

He had seen silver slices of the mysterious second river on the road out of town, but every time he got close, it turned out to be a mirage. He could smell water, but it could have been from the river on the other side of town.

Meanwhile, Charlene was gamely plugging away at a series of turkey-shaped silhouettes about fifteen feet away from where she was standing. The silhouettes were made of iron, and he could hear the bullets plinking and whining off of them, and smell the stench of gunpowder. It was so bad he almost didn't go up to her, but the fact that she overwhelmed even those bad smells decided him. Also, the sight of her butt in denim.

He found a spare set of earphones at the shooter's table, slipped them on, then said, between her shots, "Shouldn't you be a little farther away?"

She didn't turn around, just kept banging away in the general direction of the targets. The gun in her hand was so big she could barely hold it upright. It made him feel slightly ill to look at it. Hunting with lead and pieces of metal seemed kind of . . . he wasn't sure. Cheating? If you couldn't bring someone down with your hands and feet and teeth, it—

"Don't you have a hot date with Pot?"

"No."

She slipped the earphones off her ears, popped the cylinder on the revolver, set it on the small, waist-high stand, and turned to face him. "And you better watch out for the triplets. They could get a guy like you in big trouble."

"Thank you for the advice."

"Is it true?"

He blinked. "Is what true?"

"That you're a werewolf?"

"Sure."

"Is Pot helping you—you know—find others of your kind?"

"No."

"Oh." Interestingly, her scent went from sharp suspicion to sweet surprise—honey over oatmeal. It made for a pleasant change from the gunpowder. "Well, maybe I can help you. I've, uh, had some experience in this stuff."

"Selling houses to werewolves?"

"No, no. I'm a . . ." She paused dramatically, then rushed out with, "I'm a vampire slayer!"

"But I'm not a vampire," he said mildly.

"That's okay, I'm not really a slayer. I'm more like a vampire beater-upper. I don't like killing them. Hey, the undead are people, too."

She was lying. But he was so used to it—people lying

like they breathed—that it wasn't especially alarming. He assumed that she was stressed and tense about her job(s), and couldn't tell him the full truth about her night business. But a vampire beater-upper might be handy, if she could—

"I've run into lots of werewolves," she assured him. "I bet I could help you find some of your kind."

"One of my kind lives in this town," he reminded her.

"Right, right. But I meant, your herd. Find your herd."

"Oh." He almost smiled at her, and didn't at the last minute. His smile made people afraid. "That would be good."

"Yes, indeed, I've seen more creatures of the night than you can shake a stick at," she continued, slipping her tinted shooting glasses off her face. And now she was telling the whole truth . . . probably a truth anyone living in Mysteria could tell. "We'll get you hooked up."

"I'd like to get hooked up," he said, and this time he did smile. Oddly, she wasn't afraid; instead, she blushed prettily, and he wondered just how important finding the others really was.

Seven

"The first thing we ought to do," Charlene was telling him after they had parked in front of a small house north of Main Street, "is leave Justin a note."

"A note?"

"I told you, I'm pretty sure he'd be helpful to you, but he's out of town right now."

"For a vampire slayer—"

"Vampire beater-upper."

"—you're not very aggressive."

"I'm a little bit of a pacifist," she admitted, scribbling something on a piece of stationery and getting out to slip it into the mailbox.

"Now what?" he asked.

"Uh . . . we wait until Justin reads his note?"

"Isn't there anything else we could do? Isn't there an underground contact you can call, or e-mail?"

"Oh, sure, *loads* of them. Tons. But right now, they're all sleeping. See?" She pointed to the sun, fat on the horizon and tinting the clouds orange. He couldn't believe it was almost evening. They'd been driving around and chatting all day as she gave him a tour of his new town. "Everybody's resting up for their nightly battle against the scourges of the underworld."

"Oh."

"So, why don't you come over to my house for supper? I stuck a roast in the Crock-Pot this morning; there'll be plenty."

"Oh." He thought that one over. If he went to her house, there would be food, and her company, and that would be pleasurable. But he would want to—

"I guess you don't want to," she said, and blood had rushed to her face again, that charming blush.

"I do want to," he assured her. "I'm just not sure I'd want to leave."

"Well," she said, blushing harder and starting the car, "who said you'd have to leave?"

Pot roast was awkward, but delicious. He couldn't get what she'd said out of his mind. She was so *there* it was driving him crazy; he wanted to be done with potatoes and carrots and meat and just get her on the floor and fuck her until they were both slick with sweat and out of breath.

But you didn't just do that. He was pretty sure. There were women in his old neighborhood, of course, but nobody like Charlene. What was the protocol? Goddammit!

He was never more aware of being a werewolf than when he wanted to get laid. Sex made the difference between species yawn like a chasm, a bottomless one. Because he knew when the woman wanted to do it, but she rarely came out and said it.

So he had to sit there (at the movies, at dinner, at a car show, whatever) and pretend he couldn't smell her lust. And she pretended she wasn't giving off enough hormones to make him feel like he was losing his mind. The whole thing made his balls hurt.

Charlene wanted him. He wanted her. She'd joked about him spending the night. She'd made him supper. She was helping him find his—what was the term? Herd. His herd. And she'd been helpful in a hundred other ways, too, professionally and personally.

So—what? Jump on her? Ask for seconds? Get a refill on his milk glass? Ask her out for the next night and go home and try to sleep with a raging hard-on? (He didn't know about other werewolves, but masturbation had always seemed to him silly and wasteful.) What?

"Do you want a refill?"

"No," he snapped.

"Cripes, sorry. Well, why don't we just get to it, then? But let me clear the dishes first."

He sat like a lump while she cleaned off the small kitchen table, rinsed dishes, put the milk back in the fridge.

Had he heard her right? Get to it? Get to what? Maybe she had a slide show all prepared, or puppets in the closet, or something. It sure as shit couldn't be what he was thinking. Nothing in his life had come easy; he didn't expect things to change now.

He caught another whiff as she went by

(ummmmm)

and then realization hit and he backed up so fast his chair fell over. "You're ovulating!" he cried, and it was as much an accusation as "You're the killer!"

She blinked owlish eyes at him; her pupils were enormous, and ringed in dark green. *Nocturnal*, a voice in the bottom of his brain told him, a voice that didn't speak up very often.

"What?" she was asking. "I mean, I am, but how can you tell?"

"Because you smell like peaches in syrup. I was so distracted by all the other smells, I didn't—no, no!" He backed away from her. "I have to go home now."

She pouted. Her full lower lip actually poked out and he thought about sucking it into his— "But I wanted you to spend the night."

"No way. Not if there's a chance you'll get pregnant."

She blinked again, slowly. "But I'm on the Pill."

"You're lying." It would only occur to him later to wonder why she had lied about such a thing.

"Well." That seemed to give her pause. "You could wear a condom."

"No."

"Oh, so you're one of *those* guys."

"I don't know what you're talking about, but they don't work," he explained, as patiently as he could while climbing over the coffee table to stay away from her. "I guess latex doesn't stop werewolf sperm."

"Oh." Weirdly (what the hell was going on?) she seemed pleased at the idea. "I guess you won't believe me if I tell you I've got a diaphragm in the bathroom."

"I'm leaving now."

"But we haven't had dessert!" she wailed, gesturing to the dishes of fresh pie.

And I plan on keeping it that way.

Eight

Annoyingly, she could drive as fast as he could run, or almost, because he had barely slammed and locked his front door when she was hammering on it.

"Cole! Come on, don't be a baby. Let me in and we'll talk about this!"

"No!" he yelled back, resting against his front door. If he let her in, they were going to mate. If you put your hand in the fire you got burned, if you jumped into mud you got dirty, and if an ovulating female got too close to a werewolf, he got laid. They both did.

"Why are you acting like this?"

"I don't want a baby!"

"Then stop acting like one!"

Argh. Faulty human hearing. "I didn't say I wasn't acting like one, I said I didn't *want* one."

"But why don't you?"

"Because I don't even know you!" he lied. Of all the reasons not to mate with a healthy, gorgeous, sweetly rounded, helpful, intelligent female, not "knowing" her was the least of it. "Now get back into your car and go away!"

"You know, the full moon's over seven days away," she said. "I looked it up. It's not like you're going to burst into hair right this second."

"It's four days away," he corrected her. "Get lost."

"Are we really going to have a conversation like this through your door?"

"Not if you get lost."

She was silent. Thank God! He slumped to the floor, still throbbing, still wanting her. But he could never do that to *any* woman—curse her with a half man/half beast, a child who didn't know, and a father who couldn't help—never mind someone like Charlene. He wouldn't go near her while she was ovulating. In fact, he was starting to think it was a good idea to stay away from her altogether.

The thought made his heart hurt, actually cramp like when you swam too long and your legs burned. He ignored it; his personal feelings about someone he barely knew—

(yes, that's right, you don't even know her)

(is that the human in you, or the werewolf? maybe werewolves make up their minds a little quicker)

He slapped his hands over his eyes and shook his head. How would he know? Anyway, it was a perfect example of why he shouldn't knock Charlene up. What if his son or daughter wanted to know these things in twenty years?

What the hell could he tell him or her? "Sorry, I was supposed to find out but I got your mom pregnant and settled in Mysteria instead, and never got around to finding my people. Well, good luck and all."

Never.

He could hear Charlene rustling around the side of his house, doubtless looking for a way to get in. Silly bunny; she had no chance. He wished she would give up and break a window. Argh! He meant give up and go home, yeah, go home, that's what he wanted.

He heard a double click, and instantly realized what had happened. As Char stepped through the back door, he howled, *"Rae!"*

"What?" the ghost asked petulantly. "Nobody's gotten

any in this place for decades. I think you should go for it."

"I had no interest in it before—"

"So—what? That's an electric drill in your pants?"

"—and I'm sure not doing it if you're going to watch!"

"Oh, calm down, princess. After all these years, I've decided sex is fundamentally boring, at least from a voyeur's point of view. I'll be in the basement. Did you know the tap's been leaking since last night?"

"Go fuck yourself, Rae!"

No answer. Just as well. Somewhere, Mama Zee could probably sense he had been swearing, not to mention rude to a lady. A dead lady, but still.

Charlene was stamping down the hall toward him, her breasts jiggling with every stamp. He tried to look at her face for about a second, immediately gave up the battle, and turned to scrabble at the locked door. His fingers were suddenly too big, the lock the size of a pin head.

If the neighborhood could see him now, the neighborhood enforcer scrambling to escape from a woman who barely came up to his chin . . .

Her arms were around him and she was raining kisses on the back of his neck. He groaned and fought the door as if it was a living thing, but it stubbornly resisted him.

"Come on," she said, and there was a note of sad urgency in her voice. "I need you. In more ways than you can ever imagine."

"We can't," he groaned. He stopped clawing at the door, and stood still in her arms, leaning his sweaty forehead on the (annoyingly closed) door.

"We have to. I have to."

"I can't do it to you."

"I think," she whispered, reaching around and cupping his jeans where the zipper came together, "you can."

"You have no idea what you're getting into."

"That's okay," she said, turning him around. He kissed her, sucked on her full lower lip, even nipped her lightly. She just wriggled closer. "Neither do you."

Nine

"God, God . . ."

"That's funny, that's just what I was saying," she teased. They were resting on the living room floor, clothes strewn everywhere, and she had slid a chubby thigh over his legs and was stroking his ribs. "Repeatedly. Loudly."

It had been, to put it mildly, a hectic half hour. Kissing and sucking and stroking and sliding . . . and then they had really gotten down to business. She had been everything he imagined: athletic and indefatigable, with the lips of a devil and the hands of an angel. He wanted to go again. He *would* go again. Except . . .

"What if you're pregnant?" he asked anxiously.

"Boy, you are *really* harshing my buzz. No afterglow at all, huh? No?" She saw he was leaning over her propped up on an elbow in a pose of tense waiting, and answered him, obviously quite puzzled. "Cole, what is the big deal? I told you I was on the Pill."

"Yes, but that was a lie."

She pressed her lips together. "And the pitiful remnants of the afterglow . . . gone. Yes, okay, it was a lie. I admit, I wanted to get you into bed. Forgot about that damn nose of yours for two seconds. But I still don't understand what the big deal is. I wouldn't tie you down—what year do you think this is? What town, for that matter?"

"But the baby—"

"Ah, the baby." She said it with such admiration and longing, he was a little afraid of her.

"What if it's—like me?"

She smiled. "What if it is?"

He got up, starting putting his clothes on. "You're not getting this at all."

"Obviously. So explain it to me."

"I could never make you understand. Now get out." He paused. "Please."

"Okay, okay." She slipped into her blouse, found her underpants wadded up in a corner, stepped into them. "Your postcoital grumpiness has been duly noted."

"So has your total indifference toward the consequences of intimate relations."

"What are you, a woman now? And nobody held a gun to your head, I might add. *And* I might not be pregnant, you know. Maybe you're not the big ole stud you think you are. How about *that*?"

"I am, though," he said gloomily, holding the door open for her. She hopped out, half-dressed and trying to slip into her sneakers.

"Don't call me!" she yelled as he shut the door.

"Don't worry," he muttered.

It was only after she left that he remembered she was supposed to take him around to other supernatural creatures, try to track down his herd.

His lifelong dream, his goal, and it had all flown out of his head right about the time he ripped off her bra. Fucking great. Reason #238 to stay the hell away.

Ten

The child—not a child anymore, a woman in her thirties—had dark hair, long strong legs, and Charlene's owlish eyes. "Anything?" she was asking him, keeping well away from him, as was her habit. "You can't tell me anything?"

"I'm sorry." His voice surprised him; it was old, cracked. "I came here and met your mother and that was the end of it."

"But what about our people?"

He shrugged, then coughed an old man's cough. Though they were sitting on the porch of his beloved red house, the paint had long faded; now it was his beloved pink house. Many of the windows were broken, but he was too indifferent to fix them—he didn't feel much in the way of cold, anyway.

Charlene, of course, was years dead. It was just him and the whelp, a woman who avoided him—lived in Reno, of all places—unless she needed something.

"What about my grandparents?"

"Dead." The black mare was standing patiently on the porch next to his rocking chair and he reached out a wrinkled hand and stroked her velvety nose. "They're all dead."

"But these—these *things* happen to me all the time, things I can't control."

"I know."

"And I'm stronger than everybody. And faster. Everyone else seems like a clumsy—I don't know—it's like they're monkeys or something. I don't really feel like I belong with them."

"I know."

"I can't marry one of *them.*"

He yawned. "Then don't."

The mare nickered into his palm and he saw the For Sale sign was up again in his yard, facing the house instead of the road, and this time it read DEATH LIVES HERE.

"Dad, you have to help me."

"I can't."

"Dad."

"Sorry." The sign changed while he watched: HA. HA. HA.

"But who am I?" the woman asked as she faded from sight, like a ghost.

"I don't know," he told her fading figure. "I never knew myself, either."

The mare nickered again, almost like laughing. The sign now read: TOO BAD, SO SAD, LIE DOWN AND BE BAD.

"Gosh," Rae's voice said from behind him. "Don't you think you should wake up now? This is a doozy of a nightmare. I mean, blech."

He blinked and coughed his dry old man cough again. His hands were wrinkled claws. He looked at the horse, standing so patiently by his chair.

"Shoo!" Rae said. "Get lost! Go scare somebody else, you creepy nag!"

Startled, the horse clopped down the steps and galloped off.

And he woke up in the middle of a sweaty bed. His hands were normal. He was still young. It had all been a—

"Fucking night mares, they're always causing trouble," Rae said from nowhere, and was that a note of sympathy in her voice? "It was just a bad dream, Cole."

Or a vision of things to come. He leaped out of bed, intent on finding Charlene. He'd been avoiding her for three days, but he had to warn her. Make her understand. And if she didn't understand, he—he didn't know.

But . . . like she said, maybe she wasn't pregnant. Maybe the situation would be salvaged. He would have to leave Mysteria, but the alternative was worse. He had no animosity toward the night mare; she had shown him a future he wanted no part of, a future he needed reminding of, and given him time to fix things.

"I've got to see her," he told Rae, striding toward the door.

"Good plan, Cole. May I suggest clothes? Or at least boxers?"

"Oh. Right. Thanks again."

"I must say, you're the most interesting roomie I've ever had. Everyone else usually moves out by now."

"Can we talk about this later, please?"

"Oh, fine, ignore the ghost, see if I care. It's not like I have feelings or anything!" That last was almost shouted as he slammed the door on his way out. He made a mental note to make it up to her—how, exactly, does one make it up to a ghost?

A problem for later. Right now: Charlene.

Eleven

He bounded up the steps to her house and, before his fist could land on the door, it opened and he fell through the doorway.

"For a werewolf," she observed, looking down at him, "you're remarkably clumsy."

"Buh," he replied, because she was wearing a Vikings jersey and nothing else. He had never had much interest in organized sports, but he had a sudden urge to watch every Vikings game ever televised.

"You do not," she observed, "look well. Everything all right?"

He climbed to his feet. "Sorry about barging in on you like that." A lie, but he had to start somewhere.

"You didn't really barge," she pointed out, walking toward the kitchen, big hips rolling sweetly beneath the purple and white. "I heard you jogging down the lane—don't you ever drive? We live five miles apart, you know. Then, zip! Like the Marathon Man. Is it safe? Anyway, I had the door open by the time you came up the walk."

"Uh-huh." It all went over his head, and who cared? He had other things to worry about. He followed her, trying not to obviously sniff. "Why are you up so late? Oh, of course. Vampire beater-upper business."

"Ah. Yes. About that. I'm not."

"Not pregnant?"

She froze in the midst of pouring a glass of milk for herself. "Now how would I know that already? It's been, what? Half an hour since we did it?"

"Seventy-six hours."

She gave him an odd look and he crept closer. He needed a really good whiff of her hair or her neck, skin on skin would be even better. In fact, best of all would be—

"Riiiiight," she replied. "Anyway, I'm not a vampire beater-upper. I made the whole thing up."

"The whole thing?"

"Yes."

"You don't have dealings with the, uh, depraved underworld of the dead?"

She shook her head. He literally didn't know what to think: his mind was as blank as a broken TV. The enormity of the lie actually distracted him from the other problem. "But—why?"

"Why do you think? I wanted an excuse to be close to you. You picked out the one house for sale and bought it so damn fast, I had to think of something else. Something you wanted. The truth is, I wouldn't know a vampire if he came up and slapped me in the face."

"You're pretty close to that now," he said, getting pissed.

"Oh, Cole, stop it. You'd suck up your own barf before you'd hit a woman. And I'm sorry to sound like such a bitch."

Her switches in temperament were dazzling. "What?" he managed.

"Well, it was a crummy thing to do. I've been just sick about it and I wanted to—you know. Get all the cards on the table, as the saying goes."

"But—"

"Justin really is a werewolf, though," she added anxiously, watching his face.

Justin—some strange male werewolf—was the last thing on his mind right now. "I don't—" he began.

"I'm sure he can help you. I can't, though. I've got other stuff to worry about. Stuff you can't even dream of, so don't bug me about it," she added, going from truthful to contrite to defiant in about ten seconds.

He stared at her. "I knew you were lying about part of it, but I didn't think you were lying about all of it."

"How does it work, exactly?" she asked. "It's not like your nose is a lie detector—I mean, it is, and obviously a pretty good one compared to most people's equipment, but how could you know exactly what was a lie and what wasn't?"

The irony of the woman who claimed to be able to help him find his herd asking about something as fundamental as scenting was not lost on him.

"I just assumed you were anxious about your work—I was distracted by, uh, other things." He looked down at his hands. He should, by rights, be strangling her right now. But he had gone along with the lie, hadn't he? To get laid. To see those fabulous breasts. To be with her. The most important quest of his life and he hadn't asked any questions. The neighborhood was right: all muscle, no brains.

Charlene put a chubby hand over his, looked up at him earnestly, and said, oblivious of her milk mustache, "I really did have my reasons. I don't blame you for being mmpphhh-phargle."

She mmpphh-phargled because he tugged her into his embrace and buried his nose in her hair. Then he held her at arm's length and almost shouted, "You're pregnant!"

"I am?" She looked thrilled. "Noooooo. Really? You can really tell so quickly?"

"Dammit! Dammit! Dammit!"

"Yes!" She broke out of his embrace, clasped her arms around herself, and spun around in a tight circle. "I don't suppose you can tell whether it's a boy or a girl?"

"Charlene, this is a very serious business. You have to

stop—stop dancing around your kitchen and listen to me."

"It's more serious than you know," she reminded him, "but I'm listening."

He stopped. What was there to say now? Stay or go; it was still the same choice it had always been. Only now infinitely more complicated. He didn't handle complicated well. He tended, in fact, to handle it by leaving.

"What do you mean, more serious than you know? What's your agenda?" he asked, stalling for time. Stay or go? Have sex with her or throttle her? No, wait. That wasn't the question.

"I have to have a baby," she explained. "Do you want a glass of milk?"

"No. Why?"

"I'm a mial."

He blinked. The name meant nothing to him. "What?"

"A mial."

"A meal?"

"Mee-*all*."

"Yes, but what is it?"

"What's a human?" she retorted, scrubbing her fingers through her loose hair and almost glaring up at him. "What's a werewolf, what's a warlock, what's a night mare? What's a witch, what's a dryad, what's a vampire? What's a fairy, a goblin, a troll? It's just another creature sharing the planet, that's all."

"Yes, but what *is* it?"

"Oh, right. Uh. That's a tough one to explain. We're just—we're just another species here. There's about . . . um . . ." Her eyes slitted as she thought. "Maybe half a million of us on the planet?"

He thought of Pot, the triplets, the night mare. "What kind of magic can you do?"

She smiled. "No kind. We're pretty boring. The only thing interesting about us is our life span—the average mial lives to be about twelve."

"Twelve?" he almost shrieked. "How old are you now?"

"I'm old," she said wistfully. "Old to be having a baby. Four next month. Don't worry," she added, "it's not creepy or anything that we did it. We reach maturity at ten months."

"Wh—but—wh—"

"But Cole, listen!" She grabbed his forearms. "Listen to this! If I have a baby with a human or a human hybrid—like a werewolf or a witch or whatever—he or she will have an *enormous* life span! Fifty or sixty years, at least! Think of *that*! That's practically forever." For a moment she was looking through him, not at him. "My line could go on for centuries. We can't get a foothold on this planet because everybody else lives eight times as long, but my baby has a chance—we have a chance—"

Definitely the weirdest day ever. And this from a man who routinely turned into a wolf and ate cows. "You want to take over the planet?"

She looked shocked, as if he had slapped her. "Heck, no. We just want to have a chance. We can't get a chance, you know, because—but my baby will have a chance. My line, my name."

"Your baby won't know anything about anything," he said, almost shouting. "He'll be stronger and faster than everybody, live longer than his mother's people, be alone, die alone. You want *that*? *That's* your big plan?" He realized he was towering over her, roaring, and didn't care. "Because that's what you've got!"

"He'll have the world! He'll be able to do whatever he wants!" she shrilled back. "He'll have more than ten years to live, and that opens up anything you can think of."

"You're cursed. I've cursed you. And the baby."

"We're blessed," she snapped back, "and you're a moron. You've given the baby great gifts and you don't even realize. The life span alone is the birthright of practically everyone else here; my child deserves it, too. And she'll be strong—able to defend herself and stay safe. And *live*."

"You are," he said carefully, "a crazy person."

"Yeah, well, it takes one to know one."

"And I'm not having anything to do with this."

"Who asked you to?"

"If I walk out this door . . . ," he threatened.

She threw the empty milk glass at him; he ducked easily. "Bye!"

He walked out that door.

Twelve

※

"And then you left?"

"Well. Yes. I said . . . you know . . . If I walked out that door I was never coming back, and then—"

"She threw the glass at you and good-bye."

"Yeah."

"And you've been in town—what? Less than a week?"

He almost groaned; the full moon was a few hours away. He had actually forgotten about the moon, that's how crazy Charlene was making him. Forgotten! Christ, what next? Forgetting to eat?

"Are you sure you won't have a piece?" Pot asked, tapping the box with a bony finger.

"No."

"It's goat," she wheedled.

"I'm not hungry."

"That," Rae announced, "is seriously screwed up."

"Hush, ghost. You're not helping."

"Come on, Potty. There isn't one part of that story that isn't weird. Charlene's a mial? Whatever that is. And pregnant? All part of her plan? And she's dying?"

At Cole's fresh look of alarm, Pot quickly said, "She's dying as we all are, Rae. Everyone has a time limit. You're just too silly to acknowledge yours."

"She can talk," Rae said as if Pot wasn't sitting right there at Cole's kitchen counter. "Her people live for a zillion years. Poor Charlene! Just think, she could be dead before Bush is out of office."

"I'm going to puke," Cole said, and went to the bathroom, and did. When he came back after brushing his teeth, Pot was still there. So, presumably, was Rae.

"What are you going to do?" the queen asked.

He opened his mouth, but no words came out.

"Boy oh boy," Rae observed. "Not the sharpest knife in the drawer."

"Enough, Rae. Well, Cole? Are you going to stay here with Charlene, raise the baby? See to its upbringing after Charlene—ah, after? Or leave them and find your people?"

"Door number two," Rae added, "makes you a gigantic loser."

"That's not true," the queen interrupted. "You have no obligation to her; she admitted she tricked you."

"Which doesn't sound like it took much effort on her part."

"Rae!"

"All I'm saying is, Einstein he's not."

"As I was saying," the queen continued, sending looks of irritation to all corners of the kitchen, "you're not mates, she has what she needs of you, she has in fact released you from any obligation."

"Yep, she's totally fine living a life alone, being a single mom, dying young, and leaving your kid an orphan. Don't give it another thought."

Cole leaned over far enough to rest his forehead on the counter. It felt smooth and cool. "Why did you come over?" he asked the Formica.

"Well . . ." The queen paused. "I don't want you to read anything into this, but—"

His front door was thrown open. "My queen, your kingdom awaits!" several people shouted in unison, which was a good trick.

"—I'm leaving town," she finished.

Thirteen

"Holy Christ on a cracker with Cheez Whiz," Rae gasped, while Cole stared at the naiads—he assumed they were naiads—milling around in his living room.

"Forgive us, Queen Potameides," one of them said, and the group—there were seventeen, severely straining his living room space—went into a deep bow. "We have been from you so long, we could not remain in the front yard a moment longer knowing you were not far away, and so we—"

The queen waved the explanation away, and the guard or whoever it was instantly shut up. "Yes, yes, that's fine."

"What's going on?" Rae demanded.

"Probably the ones loyal to her overthrew the ones not loyal to her," Cole said. At the queen's unguarded look of surprise, he added, "Violence I understand."

"Yes. Ah. Yes. My cousin is dead—"

"Long live the queen!" another one interrupted. They all, Cole noticed, looked a great deal like the queen, the same long stringy hair and watery eyes, the same damp smell and long, spidery limbs.

"Right," the queen finished. "So, I go."

"This very damned minute?" Rae asked, sounding upset.

"Rae."

"I mean, you gotta leave right now, pack a bag and your swim fins and off tonight? Without a good-bye or anything?"

"Rae."

"Because that rots!"

"Rae. The river is my home, and more, my people need me."

"Well, shit!"

"You must have known I wouldn't stay forever."

"Why not? All the other freaks in this town don't seem to be in any damned rush to leave." The ghost audibly gulped. "Uh, no offense, Cole."

"That's okay," he replied. To Pot: "So you're taking the chance to go back and be with your people?"

"As I said. Don't read anything into that. Our situations are different. I'm an exiled queen and you—"

"Are a chump if you let Charlene get away," Rae said, "but we're getting off the subject. Why do you have to leave now? Because I know that look, Pot, you cow, you can't fool me, once you're in the wind we'll none of us see you again, and stop me if you heard this already but that *rots*."

"I'm of the royal family of the Naiad," Pot said sternly, "and I do not have the freedom ordinary people have. The Mississippi is a large territory and I lost it once through carelessness and—"

"The Mississippi *River*?" Cole asked. "That's your kingdom?"

"Was," Pot replied. "And now, is again. But I wanted to come by and say good-bye. In fact, you and Rae are the last ones on my list. I can't have my kingdom and Mysteria both—don't read anything into this—so I've traded the café to the triplets and their mother for, ah, future favors, and have wrapped up my other affairs. So now—"

"Wait a minute," Rae interrupted. "We were *last* on your list?"

"Well . . ." Pot paused. "I went, ah, geographically. This house is the last one."

"Fine, go then!" Rae shouted. "I never liked you anyway!"

"I will go," the queen replied, smiling, "and that is a lie. And Rae, I adore you, and that will never change, not if I rule for a thousand years."

"Go soak your head in the deep end!"

"I go, then."

One of her hench-naiads opened the front door, but before Pot could grandly sweep out, in the manner of a river queen, a tall dark-haired man blocked the doorway.

"What now?" Rae griped, but Cole could hear the undercurrent of tears in her voice.

"Aside for the queen," one of the naiads demanded.

"Shush," the queen said. "He's not one of my subjects, Mr., ah . . . ?"

"Michael Wyndham."

"Potameides."

They shook hands. "Pack leader," the tall man explained.

"Queen of the Mississippi River naiads," Pot offered. "Good night."

"See you."

She left. She took all the river people with her. The werewolf came in.

Fourteen

"Hi," the werewolf said. He was dark-haired and broad, with gold eyes, big hands, and a feral scruffiness that Cole felt and instantly responded to. He had the weird urge to kill a cow and present it to the stranger. *Two* cows.

"Hello."

"I'm Michael Wyndham. In case you didn't hear me at the door."

"Cole Jones." He didn't offer his hand to shake; he had the very strong sense that the man wouldn't want his hand. Instead, Wyndham was sizing him up and Cole saw his nostrils flaring as he took everything in. Oddly, this was in no way alarming. It was almost—comforting?

"I can't believe she just picked up and left with those other weirdos. I didn't even like her," Rae said tearfully, "but you talk to someone for fifty years, you get used to them, you know?"

Wyndham flinched. "Who the hell is *that*?"

"That's my ghost."

"Hey, pal." The tears instantly vanished. "I'm not *your* anything."

"Sorry," Cole said. He kept trying to look Wyndham in the face and his gaze kept skittering away. He had been raised to know that it was polite to look people in the eye when you spoke to them, but Wyndham didn't seem to mind. "My roommate."

"A ghost? And a river naiad. I've met an eleionomid be-fore—"

"Marsh nymph," Rae explained, before Cole could ask.

"—right, they're all over the Cape where I live. Lots of river marshes out there. And lots of witches, but that's about it. Oh, and you." Wyndham smiled in a perfectly friendly way, keeping his teeth covered, and Cole, responding to the man's natural charisma, actually smiled back.

"What—" Cole began, and stopped. Still the weirdest day ever, and getting weirder. And too many damned questions. Pack leader? What was he doing here now, tonight? How had he found Cole? What did he want?

Rae saved him the trouble. "Are you—what?—the boss of all the werewolves, then?"

"I am."

"So—what? You're here to—what?"

Wyndham was recovering quickly, and didn't seem to mind being interrogated by a dead woman. "I'm here to as-sist a member of my Pack, if he needs it." To Cole: "You don't look like you're in any real peril to me."

"He knocked up the local Realtor," Rae offered.

"Oh. Congratulations?"

"We're, uh, still working that out," Cole said. "How did you find me?"

"Another Pack member lives here. He got in touch with me—apparently there's a vampire killer in this town? Some-one who knows quite a bit about werewolves?"

"You don't sound like you believe that all the way."

"Well"—Wyndham shrugged—"I don't take chances, period. As you were new, we thought you might need a hand. And with the moon on her way"—Wyndham gestured to the window, which showed nothing but unalleviated darkness; there were no street lights this far out of town—"I thought you might be vulnerable. Normally I wouldn't travel this close to a Change, but in this case . . ."

While Cole processed this, Rae said, "Whoa, whoa, whoa. That stud wannabe Justin *told* on Charlene?"

Wyndham blinked slowly, like an owl. "My Pack keeps me informed of any potential threat, yes. Which reminds me, Cole, why didn't *you* tell me about this vampire killer?" His lips actually curled at the word "vampire," and Cole instantly knew: the boss werewolf didn't believe in vampires. But had come anyway. Perhaps he assumed Charlene was a crazy person. God knew there were enough of them in the world. Still, it was nice of him to check up, even if Wyndham had doubted anything would come of it.

And he was waiting for an answer. "My parents were killed when I was a baby," he explained. "I was raised by regular people. I mean, my foster mother." Not exactly "regular people." He prayed word of his slip wouldn't get back to Mama Zee.

Wyndham was nodding. "Yep, yep, that's what I figured. I can smell them all over you. That's not a bad thing," he added quickly. "You can probably smell them all over me— I married one."

"Ha!" Rae cried. "There you go. He married a regular person."

Wyndham laughed. "I didn't say that."

"She's no threat to you," Cole said quickly. "The vampire killer. She was just trying to—" What? What in the world could he say? Annoyingly (or mercifully), Rae remained silent.

"Are you sure? You're part of my family, even if you never knew, and I want to help you any way I can." Wyndham clapped a large hand on Cole's shoulder. It felt like a brick. "You're not alone anymore, Cole."

Then why, he wanted to ask, did hearing that—at long last—make him feel exactly nothing?

Fifteen

✳

"That was, no joke, the most amazing thing. Pot leaves, the werewolf guy shows up, and how nice was he? I mean, wow! He had kind of an Errol Flynn thing going on, did you notice? Yummy. And where'd he go already? You guys didn't even get a chance to catch up or anything!"

"He left for his Change." Change. Pack. He could hear the capital letters in his head, sensed their deep meaning. "We don't like to be in towns or cities when the Change happens." We. Werewolves. My people. Us. Our.

"How long do you have?"

"About an hour." Fifty-three minutes.

"So you have time!"

"Time?"

"You're not fooling me, pal. I heard you sticking up for Charlene. And I heard you tell him you weren't in any big rush to get out to the Cape."

"Too many tourists," he said automatically.

"Ha! The thing you came here for, the reason you blew Charlene off, it's handed to you on a platter, and what? You're all Mr. Cool, 'Oh, well, I'd love to visit, maybe for Christmas.' Give me a goddamned break."

He said nothing.

"I mean, look at the situation," Rae continued. Christ, she loved the sound of her own voice. "You've basically got a choice: go off with your people—like Pot did—or stay with what you like and marry a local—like your boss says *he* did. And he's soooo helpful: you don't have to move in with all the werewolves on the Cape. What'd he say again?"

"There are too many in the world to live in one place," he said automatically.

"I just knew you were paying attention. Aaaaaaand?"

"Any werewolf past the age of consent can live anywhere, with Wyndham's permission."

"Which he *gave* you about five minutes ago. Aaaaaaaand?"

"I don't have to choose; I can move between worlds, as his mate does."

"Ding ding ding!"

"What?"

"Cole. For Christ's sake. What are you still doing here? You're talking like I didn't hear you puke at the thought of Charlene dying alone."

Fifty-one minutes.

"And you're talking like you have a choice. When really, you never ever did."

"That's true," he said.

"So, again. Stop me if you've heard this. What the hell are you waiting for? Does that Wyndham guy have to chisel an invite on your forehead?"

"No," he said, and practically jumped toward the doorway. But before he could get it open, it opened by itself (but not really) and like magic (but not really; she probably just drove up and he was too distracted to hear the car) Charlene was standing there. Her thereness, her concentrated punch, washed over him like a wave and he wondered why he was surprised. Of course: she had a short life span; her people jammed everything they could into a dozen years. Of course they were more there than ordinary people. And how could he ever have resisted her?

"I knew this would happen," Rae said, sounding shocked. "I think I'll see if I can install free cable."

He opened his mouth, but as usual, the smarter person beat him to the punch.

Sixteen

✳

"Before you leave," Charlene began, "I've come to tell you that I've changed my mind, and no matter where you run to, I'll hunt you down like a rat."

"I met the head of the werewolves," he replied. "And it's pack, not herd."

"*And*, it's fine if you don't want to get married, but you're going to be with me until the bitter, gory end."

"Also," he added, "the baby is welcome with my people anytime; a drop of werewolf blood is as good as a hundred percent as far as they're concerned."

That gave her pause, he saw at once. Her brow wrinkled and then smoothed out, and she said, "You've been busy in the last few hours. Days, come to think of it."

"I was coming to get you," he told her.

She smiled, and it was like clouds blowing away from the bright, beautiful moon. "That's funny. I was coming to get you, too."

A split second later, they were in each other's arms. "You're not allowed to die in six years," he said into her hair, her dark, dark hair.

"Well, I've had some thoughts about that. This *is* Mysteria, you know. The oddest place on earth. Maybe we can find a spell or something. You're just as much on the edge as I am—what if you're out chasing rabbits and get hit by a truck? It could happen anytime. It's the risk we all run."

"Repeat," he said, kissing her throat, her cheeks, her forehead, her mouth, "after me: I'm not going to die in six years."

"Well . . ." She was busy kissing him back. "I won't if you won't. Er, how much time do we have before you grow a revolting amount of back hair?"

"Forty-seven minutes."

She laughed. "Plenty of time."

THE WITCHES OF MYSTERIA AND THE DEAD WHO LOVE THEM

Gena Showalter

To those of us who probably should *live in Mysteria:*
P. C. Cast, Susan Grant, and MaryJanice Davidson,
And to Christine Zika for a wonderful experience.

One

"Men suck," Genevieve Tawdry muttered, "and not in a good way."

She was tired, so very tired, of Hunter Knight's hot and cold treatment of her. He was making her crazy, laughing with her flirtatiously one moment (translation: stringing her along without giving her any actual benefits, the bastard), then dropping her altogether the next moment, then laughing flirtatiously with her again.

By the Great Goddess, she wasn't going to tolerate it anymore.

Unfortunately, lovesick witch that she was, Genevieve didn't have the strength to shove him from her life—which meant she would have to up her game. But how? Truly, she'd tried everything. Spells and incantations. "Accidental" meetings where she happened to be braless. "Accidentally" ramming her car into the back end of his Ford Explorer. Or the latest, an incident that happened only last night, "accidentally" tripping and falling into his lap at a mutual friend's wedding.

Nothing worked.

Last night had been a "cold" night. Hunter had taken one look at her in her brand-new white silk dress (no, she hadn't been the bride and yes, the bride had been pissed that she'd dared to wear the "sacred" color) and he hadn't been able to get away from her fast enough. She sighed.

What would it take to make herself irresistible to him? To hold his attention for as long as she desired it? To at last put an end to the heart-pounding tension that always sparked between them when they were together? Whatever was needed, she'd do it. Anything. Everything.

"God, I'm a stalker." Frowning, she tapped her fingers against the desk surface.

Moonlight spilled through the window in front of her, mingling with the soft glow of lamplight, illuminating the unread book in front of her. Incense burned beside her, the scent of jasmine curling sweetly and fragrancing the air.

She sat in the office of the three-bedroom home, aka den of iniquity, she shared with her two sisters, hunched over the desk, dark strands of hair falling over her shoulders. Behind her, the TV emitted a *crunch, crunch* sound, as if someone on screen was enjoying a tasty snack. A family of squirrels raced around her feet—her oldest sister's newest save-the-world-one-animal-at-a-time "project."

I don't want to be Hunter's stalker. I want to be his lover.

Over the years, he had become the bane of her existence, the mountain she'd tried to climb (naked) but couldn't quite manage to conquer. But damn it. He liked her; she knew he did. Last night, before he'd run away from her, she would have sworn to the Great Goddess he'd had an erection and had been desperate to get *to* her, not away. Desperate to touch her. Desperate to taste her.

Heat had blazed in his emerald eyes, scorching, white-hot. Enough to blister. He'd reached for her, his fingers caressing her with phantom strokes, before he dropped his arm to his side. He'd licked his lips and taken a step toward her before catching himself and striding away.

Why, why, *why* did he continually do crap like that?

If not for moments like those, she might have given up long ago and forced herself to forget him. Yet, he'd beaten John Foster to a bloody pulp for trying to kiss her. He always walked her home if he saw her in town. And it was *her* he'd called when his father had died, seeking comfort. *Her* he came to when he had a problem at work and needed help finding a solution.

That meant something. Didn't it?

"Maybe you should offer to ride him like a carnival pony," Glory said from behind her. "That always works for me."

Genevieve twisted to face her younger sister. "What are you doing in here?" she gasped out in surprise.

Glory brushed away the cheese dust on her lips. "Uh, spying. Hello. I say sleep with some other man and forget Hunter."

Always the same advice. Genevieve eased slowly to her feet. "How would you like it if I cast a spell, bringing every one of those chips to life and letting them exact their revenge against you?"

Glory's hazel eyes flashed. "You wouldn't dare!"

"Oh, really? Keep talking, then, and by tomorrow morning the entire town will be talking about the Great Doritos Death."

"Is that before or after they talk about Stalkerella and her unwilling victim?"

For several seconds, she and Glory glared at each other. Hunter was a sore spot for Genevieve; food was a sore spot for Glory.

Finally Glory expelled a deep breath, and her features slowly softened. "Evie, when are you going to realize Hunter will never want you the way you want him? He dates everything that moves and even some things that don't. But not you. Never you. He just, well, I didn't want to be the one to tell you this, but he pities you."

"He does not."

"Yes, he does."

"No, he *desires* me."

"That's delusion talking, and something *every* stalker says."

"I'm not stalking him," she said with a stubborn tilt of her chin, even though she herself had thought the very same thing. "I'm seducing him."

Her sister rolled her eyes and popped another chip in her mouth. "That's like saying murdering your neighbor is merely giving them a big send-off."

"Girls, please." Godiva, the oldest sister, strode into the room, her silver-white hair streaming behind her. She wore ripped jeans and a faded blue T-shirt, both of which were streaked with blood, dirt, and dark fur. "I've got an injured wolf in the kitchen and your arguing is upsetting him."

"You brought an injured wolf into the house?" All traces of color abandoned Glory's cheeks. "I can live with the squirrels and the wood mice, but a wolf? No way. They're dangerous killers, Diva. They like to claw witches like us into bite-sized nibblets and feast on the pieces."

"We have nothing to fear from him." Godiva anchored her hands on her hips. "He's too weak to cause us any harm."

"Where is he?" Genevieve asked, trying to push Hunter—and Glory's remarks—to the back of her mind. Her sister didn't understand. How could she? She'd never been in love, never been consumed by the emotion. Never wanted more from a man than temporary satisfaction.

"He's in the kitchen, and I could use your help."

"Of course." Following behind her older sister, Genevieve dragged a protesting Glory down the hall and into the kitchen.

Glory immediately flattened herself against the wall, surrounding herself with faux plant leaves, maintaining a safe distance from the large—very large—animal lying on the black and white tiled floor. As if she could hide with hair as vivid red as hers. Godiva bent over him, dabbing a steaming cloth over the jagged, bleeding claw wounds on his belly. He whimpered up at her, his eyes big and brown and glazed with pain.

Genevieve crouched beside her oldest sister. "What do you need me to do?"

They spent the next several hours murmuring peace spells, applying salve, and stitching the poor wolf's wounds. He drifted in and out of sleep, but through it all he responded to Godiva's every touch, recognizing her voice, her scent, and calming whenever she approached.

"He likes you," Genevieve said.

"I think he recognizes me and feels safe. I've seen him before, in the forest. I was gathering herbs, and he was watching me."

Genevieve wished Hunter responded to her half as much as this wolf responded to her sister. Since the day Hunter had saved her from gracing the dessert menu of a rabid gnome, she'd loved him.

She'd been seventeen years old at the time and he twenty-two, but she'd known she belonged with him. They'd even kissed that day, a delicious, mind-shattering kiss she'd never forgotten. Yes, she'd relived it in her dreams over and over again.

They were meant to be together, damn it. The way he sometimes treated her like a curse of hemorrhoids, no anti-itch cream in sight, had to stop! Did he think she meant to use him as a sexual toy then kick him out of her life? If so, he should love that. Did he think she meant to ruin their friendship? Well, she didn't. She wanted to love him (hard core).

She would never, ever do anything to hurt him. Well . . . she bit her bottom lip. Fine. That wasn't exactly true. Once she'd cast a seduction spell over him, hoping he would become sexually enthralled with the first woman he saw (which would have been her). Instead, she'd made nearly every woman in Mysteria, a town known for its weirdness, fall into instant lust with *him*. Even her sisters had been trapped under the spell. For days the entire female population had followed him everywhere, ripping at his clothes, begging him to make love to them.

"Even if the wolf saw you before," Glory said, the sound of her voice breaking into Genevieve's thoughts, "that's not reason enough for him to respond so favorably to you. He acts like he adores you." She frowned. "Hey, did you give him one of my love potions?"

"Of course not," Godiva said. "I think he senses that I mean him no harm."

At Glory's words, a wonderfully frightening idea danced inside Genevieve's mind, an idea she'd always discarded before—and no, she wasn't going to injure Hunter to gain his attention (although she wouldn't rule that out, the sexy bastard). What if *she* drank a love potion? What if she made herself so irresistible he wouldn't think of turning her away? She'd never dared drink one before; there were simply too many uncertain variables.

For one night in his arms, though, she was now willing to risk it. Risk the deflation of her inhibitions, the danger of enticing the love of a legion of other men. The danger of loving him forever and him only loving her for a single night. Hell, she already loved him and she didn't see an end in sight for the emotion. For Hunter, she'd risk anything. Everything. Except . . .

Genevieve uttered a sigh. Did she really want to win him because of a potion and not because he simply wanted *her*? Yes, she decided in the next instant. The stubborn man needed a push in the right direction, and she was tired of waiting for that to happen naturally. Her patience was frayed beyond repair.

Besides, if she had to watch him flirt and laugh with another woman one more time, just one more time, she'd fly into a rampage worthy of the Desdaine triplets, the town's most notorious troublemakers.

Now that she had a plan, urgency rushed through her. She glanced at the clock above the refrigerator. Ten P.M. Knight Caps, Hunter's bar, would be open for at least four more hours.

"Will you be okay on your own?" she asked Godiva.

"Hey, she's not alone. *I'm* here," Glory said with a pout.

"Oh, sorry. Will you be okay with Glory standing in the shadows and doing nothing?"

"I'll be fine." Godiva nodded. "Candy Cox should be here any minute. She's going to sit with me." Candy—oops, *Candice*—was the high school English teacher and Godiva's best friend. "My big boy is finally resting peacefully. Why? Are you going out?"

"Yes." She offered no other explanation. Neither of her sisters approved of her obsession with Hunter.

"Where are you going?" Glory asked suspiciously. She inched to the kitchen table, keeping the long length of the hand-carved mahogany between herself and the wolf.

"I'm. Going. Out."

"That's not what I meant and you know it." She paused, then her pretty face scrunched in disgust. "You're going to see *him*, aren't you?"

Genevieve's back went ramrod straight. "So what if I am? You got something to say about it?"

"Nope. Not a word. Except, if you want to make a fool of yourself over him again, go for it. Just know that the town isn't laughing *with* you, they're laughing *at* you."

Her fists clenched at her sides. "You're just begging for a piece of me, Glor."

Awakening, the wolf raised his head, his lips pulling tight over his fangs.

"Don't listen to them," Godiva cooed at him. She smothered her fingers over his thick fur, giving her sisters a pointed glare. "They're both going to rot in the fires of hell, just like Pastor Harmony says."

"Harmony didn't say we were going to hell," Glory said. "She embraces every one of every religion, and she says only evil people go to hell."

"Exactly."

As they argued, anticipation and nervousness zinged through Genevieve's veins. Not for the proposed trip into hell, but for the coming night. Now that she'd decided to do it, to love-potion the pants right off of Hunter, she didn't want to waste another minute. "Glory, I'd like to talk with you privately," she said sweetly. She motioned to the living room with a tilt of her chin. "I don't want to fight."

"I don't believe you."

"Okay, stay here then. I'm sure the wolf won't regain full strength soon and be disoriented and afraid. He won't fly into a rampage and—"

Glory jolted backward with a gasp. "Alright. Fine." One tiny step, two, she scooted around the table, around the wolf. "I'll meet you in the living room."

Dissatisfied with such a gradual pace, Genevieve reached out, grabbed her younger sister's hand, and tugged her into the next room. In the center, she whirled. She was almost bubbling over. Tonight might be the night all her dreams came true. . . . Glory's love potions were legendary. Each sister specialized in a different area of magic. While she herself wielded the darkest power, that over vengeance, Godiva's strength was in healing, both spiritual and physical, and Glory's was in love.

"I want to drink one of your love potions. And don't say no."

Glory pursed her lips and crossed her arms over her chest. "How about: hell, no."

"Please."

"Nein. Nay. Non."

She pushed out a frustrated breath. "Why not?"

"Evie," her sister said, her expression softening, "he's not good enough for you. When are you going to realize that? I'm more inclined to turn him into an impotent troll than help you win his affections."

"It's one night, Glor. What can that hurt?"

"It wouldn't be one night for you. You'd want more."

True. So true. Deep down, she hoped Hunter would be so enthralled by her that he'd become addicted to her touch. "If he doesn't want me after the potion, I'll take a blood oath never to speak to him again." A small lie, really, since she only planned to leave out one word. Never.

"Sorry."

"Please. I'll bake those eye of newt muffins you love so much."

"Oh, you bitch. I love those." Several minutes passed in thick, brooding silence, before she shook her head. "Nope, sorry. I simply can't allow you to endure more hurt because of him."

"I'll wreak vengeance upon your greatest enemy. I'll go total witch on their ass."

Glory opened her mouth, then closed it with a snap. Opened. Closed. Her hazel eyes gleamed hopefully, glowing with otherworldly power like they did just before a spell. "Horrible, painful vengeance?"

"Yes."

"Even if it's, say, against Falon Ryis?"

"Hunter's best friend? *He's* your greatest enemy?" Genevieve blinked in surprise. "I didn't know you and Falon had even spoken to each other. Ever."

Glory's jaw clenched stubbornly. "I'm not going to explain. You make his life miserable, I'll give you the potion. Take it or leave it."

She didn't have to think about her answer. "I'll take it."

Glory slowly smiled. "Then the potion is yours."

"Thank you, thank you!" With a joyous whoop, she threw her arms around her sister. Sometimes family was a wonderful thing.

"What's going on in there?" Godiva called.

Glory said, "Genevieve accidentally conjured a male stripper, and we're placing dollar bills in his G-string. Just ignore us."

"Ha, ha. Very funny," came the muffled reply. Then, "I'll be there in a sec."

"Come on." Glory extracted herself from the bear hug and flounced down the candlelit hall, through thickly painted shadows, toward their bedrooms. "It's in my room. I really hope you know what you're doing," she murmured.

Did she? Genevieve mused. Not really. Did she care? Hell, no. Thoughts of lying naked in Hunter's arms eclipsed all else. He'd trace his fingers over her breasts, roll her nipples between his fingers. He'd kiss a path down her stomach, lingering, licking . . . "Uh, can we put a rush order on that potion?"

Glory unlocked her door with a quietly muttered "Open" and a wave of her delicate hand. Instantly the thin slab of wood creaked open. They stepped inside the room.

Genevieve's jaw nearly hit the ground. She rarely ventured in there and was momentarily shocked by the total chaos. Clothes and empty food cartons were scattered all over the floor, a sea of reds, blues, greens, and sweet and sour chicken orange.

"I need a minute," Glory said, already tossing shoes and other items aside as she scrounged through the mess.

"No, you need a maid." She pinched the 38D bra hanging from the lampshade between her fingers before dropping it on top of the matching panties at her feet.

"I've been depressed and haven't cleaned. Big deal." Pause. "Ah-ha! I found you, you little sneak." Smiling, Glory jumped up. A red bottle dangled from her fingers. "Love potion number thirteen."

Genevieve frowned. "I want love potion number nine."

"Trust me. Nine sucks. You want to ride a man like a bronco at peak rodeo season, you go with thirteen."

"I'll take it." Genevieve grabbed the crimson container and gently rolled it between her fingers. Dark liquid swirled inside, mesmerizing her. This was it, the answer to her prayers. Her heart drummed in her chest, faster, faster, then skipped a beat. This innocent-looking bottle was about to gift her with the best night of her life. Eager to begin, she reached for the cork, but her sister's next words stilled her hand.

"Drink half just before you walk into the bar, not a moment sooner. Only half. Understand?" Urgency rang from her voice like a clarion of bells.

"Yes. Why?"

"Uh, hello. You'll have every man in Mysteria following you and fighting for your attention if you drink it now. And the full bottle will cause . . . too much passion in you. Now go. Get out of here before I change my mind."

Genevieve needed no further prompting. "I love you." She kissed her sister's cheek and raced to her room. Quickly she changed into the sluttiest outfit she possessed. A black dress with a V neck so low it nearly touched her navel. The hem dangled mere inches below the curve of her ass. A little uncomfortable with the amount of skin showing, she slipped on a pair of tall hooker boots that hit just above her knees.

She left her hair down, the brunette tresses hanging along the curve of her back in sexy disarray. She spritzed jasmine perfume between her breasts and swiped fuck-me-hard red gloss over her lips. There. Done.

After grabbing a quarter, she grabbed her broom and skipped outside. Flying would be faster than driving. A cool night breeze kissed every inch of visible flesh—and boy, was there a lot of it. Amid the romantic haze of moonlight, insects sang a welcoming chorus, interspersed prettily with the buzz of fairy wings. Once she'd settled on top of the skinny broom handle, careful to cover her butt so she didn't moon the entire town, she commanded the contraption to fly.

"High, high my stead will soar. Touch the ground we shall no more." As the words left her mouth, the broom inched higher and higher into the air, then sped forward, moving faster than any car. Long tendrils of dark hair whipped her face, slapping her cheeks. Plumes of pink pollen whizzed past her, leaving behind an erotic scent.

When the lights of the town square came into view, framed by towering, majestic snowcapped mountains, she lowered and slowed. She stopped at the One-Stop Mart and bought a package of condoms from the pink-haired kid at the register. Outside, she popped back onto her broom and stuffed several foil wrappers in her dress.

Ever upward she soared again, past the tall pines. White-washed wooden buildings, dirt roads, and friendly people came into view, each weirder than the next. Psychics, vampires, trolls, fairies—Mysteria turned no one away.

As she flew over the town's wishing well, a lovely arching marble structure that glittered in the moonlight, she swooped low and dropped her quarter inside. "Let tonight be exciting," she said, wanting the wish to come true with every fiber of her being. Wisps of magic ribboned in the air, curling into the sky, making her shiver. She grinned.

Soon Knight Caps entered her line of vision, the tall stone structure bursting with people, laughter, and gyrating music. She slowed. Her heart raced when she finally stopped at the side of the building. Her palms began to sweat as she hovered, hidden by the shadows. What if Hunter was somehow able to resist the potion? She swallowed the sudden lump in her throat. What if she failed to attract him? What if—

Her teeth ground together. No. No thoughts of failure. Not tonight. Tonight wishes came true.

Stiffening her shoulders, she hopped to the ground. Her broom fell with a thump. Already she could sense Hunter's presence inside. His warm essence swirled around her, layered with a subtle fragrance of sex appeal and man. With shaky fingers, she studied the bottle one last time, only then seeing the warning label on the side.

"May cause dizziness," she read. "This drug may impair the ability to drive or operate machinery. Use care until you become familiar with its effects. Seek medical attention if liquid comes into contact with eyes."

Nothing she couldn't handle, she thought, popping the bottle's cork. "Bottom's up, Evie." She drained the contents. If half would make Hunter love her for a night, just think of what the full bottle could do. There was no such thing as too much passion. The bitter liquid tasted foul on her tongue, and she felt its quick descent into her stomach. Burning, burning. So hot. She coughed and doubled over. Her blood boiled, setting fire to everything inside her. She squeezed her eyes shut and tried to scream, but no sound emerged.

Thankfully the burning soon faded as if it had never been.

Blinking, Genevieve straightened and took stock of her physical being. She didn't *feel* any sexier. Didn't feel irresistible. Still, she inched to the front entrance. *I can do this. I'm a sexual cauldron of lust.* She pushed open the doors. *I'm a sexual cauldron of lust.* The sound of inane chatter and frantic music filled her ears. Smoke wafted around her, blending with the shadows and creating a dreamlike haze.

A small part of her expected everything male to attack her as her gaze searched the room for Hunter. No one paid her any heed. Where was—her heartbeat skidded to a stop. There he was. Behind the bar. For a moment, she forgot to breathe. He was serving drinks to a twittering, giggling fairy threesome. A rush of jealousy hit her. Each fairy possessed a startling, delicate beauty, with glittery skin and gossamer wings that entranced human men, bringing out their protective instincts. Not to mention lust. These fairies were completely pink, with fuchsia hair, rose skin, and seashell garments.

Hunter looked magnificent. His disheveled black hair tangled over his forehead and hit just below his ears. Silky. Tempting. His sharp cheekbones hinted at some foreign lineage. Probably royalty. A ruthless conqueror. His nose possessed an endearing bump and a scar nicked the right corner of his lips, most likely souvenirs from a barroom brawl.

He was probably six-foot-five, a veritable giant to her five-four. Obviously he worked out. A lot. His delicious biceps stretched the fabric of his black T-shirt. Overall (and quite surprisingly) he was not a handsome man. He was too savage looking. *Predator*, his mesmerizing green eyes proclaimed. An irresistible proclamation. She wasn't sure why he'd come to Mysteria, or what made him so different from other males that she had to have him. Only him.

He laughed at something one of the stupid flirting fairies said, and her jaw clenched. He must have sensed her presence in that moment because even as he laughed, his gaze traveled across the distance and locked on her. His smile grew even wider, and he waved in a welcome—until he saw her outfit. His eyes, suddenly blazing with fire, narrowed. His smile faded into a fierce frown; his hand fell to his side.

He turned away from her.

Oh, no no no. There would be no ignoring her tonight. No giving her the cold shoulder. *I'm a sexual cauldron of lust*, she thought, stepping into the bar.

TWO

I'm dead, Hunter Knight thought. *So fucking dead.*

His blood heated as his gaze drank in the vision that was Genevieve Tawdry. Actually, he didn't have to look at her to know her appearance. He'd memorized it long ago. Long, dark brown hair that glinted red in sunlight framed a serious little face. Pert nose, huge hazel eyes that sometimes glowed and were always fringed by the prettiest lashes he'd ever seen.

As usual, she mesmerized him.

Right now, in the dim strobelight of the bar, she appeared lovelier than ever. Her barely-there dress—holy hell, she might as well have been naked. Every muscle in his body (even his favorite) hardened to the point of pain. A pair of black boots stretched up her calves, just past her knees, leaving several inches of delicious thigh visible. Cleavage spilled from the deep V of her top. *Come over here and lick me*, that cleavage said.

What he would have given to take that cleavage up on its offer.

Every time he saw this woman, he experienced an inexorable urge to strip her and ride her. Hard. Ride her till she screamed his name. Ride her till she spasmed around his cock. Now was no different. Her slender body, with its hide-and-seek curves, would fit perfectly against him. Over him. Under him.

His teeth ground together. He wanted her desperately. He'd always wanted her.

And there was no way in hell he could have her.

Loving Genevieve would destroy him. Literally. Being psychic sucked ass. One touch of Genevieve's lips at their first meeting and he'd known, *known*, she would somehow kill him if he let himself get involved with her romantically.

That didn't stop the cravings, however, didn't stop her image from constantly haunting his dreams. Hell, in that scrap of black material she now wore, she might very well cause his heart to stop or his dick to explode.

"Hunter, will you get me a sex on the beach?" a high-pitched female voice said in front of him. Fairy laughter erupted, ringing like dainty bells.

He forced his gaze away from Genevieve, forced his lips to edge into a semblance of a smile, and met the impish gaze of one of the fairies. "Sure thing, sugar. Sex on the beach, just for you. I'll even add Knight's special ingredient."

More giggling. The girlish sound grated on his every nerve.

He thought he might have slept with one of these horny pixies (maybe all of them?) at some point last year, but at that moment he couldn't remember when. Or who. Or if they'd had a good time. He didn't care anymore. Couldn't get hard unless he thought of Genevieve.

What was it about her that so obsessed him? She was pretty, but other women were prettier. Maybe it was her amazing smell. No one smelled as sweet and intoxicating as Genevieve. Or maybe it was her eyes, so vulnerable. So determined.

He mixed the requested drink and slid it across the counter. From the corner of his eye he watched Genevieve saunter to the bar, her hips swaying seductively. She eased onto a stool, mere inches from his reach. Every nerve ending inside him leaped to instant life, clamoring for her. A touch, a press. Something. Anything.

"I'll have a flaming fairy," she said. Her voice dipped huskily, soft and alluring. Menacing.

The fairies gasped at the implied threat.

His lips twitched. Genevieve arched her brows—they were two shades darker than her hair, nearly black—silently daring the fairies to comment. They remained silent. He watched the byplay in amusement, admiring Genevieve's spirit and strength. Fairies were delicate creatures, at times human in size, at others merely flickering pinpricks of light. They adored sex and alcohol, gaiety and games, but they rarely fought. Most resided in the surrounding forest and Colorado mountains, visiting Mysteria when they grew bored.

"Are you refusing to serve me?" Genevieve asked him.

"Of course not," he said, realizing he hadn't moved an inch since she'd requested her drink. He grabbed a glass. He didn't allow himself to look at her and the tempting cleavage she displayed. Lately it was becoming harder and harder (literally!) to send her away.

Maybe he should not have cultivated a friendship with her, but he'd been unable to completely push her out of his life. He just, well, he wanted to spend time with her. She amused and exhilarated him.

At least she hadn't killed him. Yet.

Every time he saw her, he asked himself a single question: is she worth dying for? Always the answer was the same. No. No, she wasn't. Not then, not now. He might crave her, he might enjoy her, but he would *not* die for her. He lifted a bottle of rum.

"Sooo . . . how are you, Hunter?" she asked him.

Stay strong, he mentally chanted. *Fight her appeal.* But damn it all to hell, the urge to wrap her in his arms and give them both what they wanted was stronger tonight than ever before. "I'm good. Busy, though. I really need to see to my other customers. You'll have to excuse me."

He turned his back on her.

Silence.

Horrible, guilty silence where everything faded from his mind except the look of pain that passed over Genevieve's face. He wished he could take back the words and say something else. Something innocent like, You look nice. Something honest like, It's great to see you. As it was, hurt radiated from her and that hurt sliced through him sharper than any knife.

"Genevieve," he said, then pressed his lips together. If he told her he was sorry, he'd only be encouraging her.

"I still need my drink."

"Of course." Well, hell. He didn't know how to handle her anymore. Always his resolve teetered on the brink of total destruction—now even more so. He needed to send her away, but he wanted her to stay so badly. *She's not worth dying for, remember?*

He inhaled deeply, meaning to relax himself, but her scent filled him. More decadent than ever before. Pure temptation. Forbidden desire. Total seduction. Hot and wild. His eyelids closed of their own accord, and his hands ceased all movement, her drink once again forgotten.

"Hunter?"

His cock jumped, hardening further. Again, his name coming from her lush made-for-sin lips was torture. Too easily could he imagine her screaming his name while he pounded in and out of her.

Snap out of it, asshole, and fix her drink.

Hunter pried his eyes open and mixed vodka, peach schnapps, and cranberry, orange, and pineapple juices into the rum. Without ever glancing in her direction, he struck a match and lit the top on fire. Yellow-gold flames licked the rim of the glass before dying a hasty death. He slid the drink to Genevieve and turned away.

"What do I owe you?" she said in that breathy voice.

"You're my *friend*." They both needed the reminder. "It's

on the house." If her fingertips brushed his while she handed him money, he'd come right then, right there. And he'd be willing to bet it would be the best orgasm of his life, no penetration required.

"Falon," Hunter called. Falon, his employee and best friend, was busy cleaning tables, but the tall, muscled male sauntered to the bar.

"Yeah?" Falon smiled a mysterious smile.

The three fairies trembled in reverence, bowing their heads in acknowledgment.

Falon had uptilted violet eyes, perfect white teeth, tanned skin that sometimes shimmered like it had been sprinkled with glitter, and shoulder-length blond hair with a slight wave. While human women lusted for him, fairy females were awed by him. They treated him as if he were a king, a god. Hunter had no idea why. Every time he asked, Falon shrugged and changed the subject.

Falon wasn't human, Hunter knew that, but he didn't know exactly what type of creature Falon was. There was an unspoken rule in Mysteria: if you can't tell, don't ask.

"Do you mind taking over?" Hunter asked him. "I've, uh, decided to call it a night."

"I don't mind at all. I like the view from the bar." Falon's gaze strayed meaningfully to Genevieve. "I've been meaning to call Genevieve, anyway. So this works out perfectly."

Falon and Genevieve? Hunter froze in place, lances of possessiveness and jealousy blending together and spearing him. *Nothing you can do about it, man. Leave. Now.* Muscles clenched tightly, he strode toward the storeroom. His home was above the bar, and the only door to the staircase was there. He'd go upstairs and seduce a few bottles of Jack Daniels. Maybe then he could wipe Genevieve's image from his mind. Not to mention the hated image of Genevieve and Falon.

"Thanks a lot, Tawdry," he heard one of the fairies murmur. "You scared Hunter away, just like you always do."

Genevieve growled. "If your greatest wish is to be

bitch-slapped, color me Genie in a Bottle because I'm about to grant it."

Hearing the embarrassment in her tone and the shame she tried so hard to hide behind bravado, he stilled. Another wave of guilt washed through him. He'd rejected this woman at every turn. He'd embarrassed her in front of the entire town more times than he could count. And she'd never been anything but sweet to him.

He knew she was shy around men. The way her cheeks pinkened, the way she sometimes stumbled over her words and gazed at anything but him, proved that. Yet she'd worked up the courage to approach him time and time again. How could he hurt her yet again?

"I, for one, am glad Hunter left," Falon said, his tone seductive. "I've wanted to get Genevieve alone for a long time."

Get her alone? That poaching bastard. *Stop. Don't think like that.* Hunter rolled his shoulders and drew in a deliberate breath. Still, the thought of Falon and Genevieve together flashed through his mind again, the two of them naked and writhing. Rage seethed below the surface of his skin.

Maybe his psychic abilities were wrong. Maybe Genevieve wouldn't be the death of him. Maybe— He ran his tongue over his teeth. His instincts were never wrong, and he knew better than to fool himself into believing a lie. He had to keep pushing her away.

Except, pushing her away might send her straight into another man's arms. Something he'd always feared.

Yes, he'd always dreaded the day she would *stop* coming to him. That would mean she was ready to move on and accept another man. His hands fisted at his sides. He hadn't meant to, but he'd cultivated a tentative friendship with her to keep such a thing from happening. Was it wrong of him? Yes. Did he care? Hell, no. The idea of her with another man always blackened his mood and set him on killing edge.

If she went to someone else tonight, to Falon, he'd—

he'd—no way in hell he was letting that happen, he decided.

Determination rushing through him, he spun on his heel. Genevieve was still sat at the bar, her shoulders hunched, her face lowered toward her empty glass as Falon spoke to her. Her hair tumbled over her shoulders, shielding her delectable cleavage.

"Genevieve," he called before he could stop himself.

The music skidded to a halt, the band members too interested in what was happening to play. In fact, everyone present went silent and locked eyes on him. Everyone except Genevieve, that is. She continued to stare into her glass, her gaze faraway, lost.

"Genevieve, you beautiful thing, I need your attention."

Finally her chin snapped up and she faced him, shock filling her luscious hazel eyes. "Did you say beautiful? Are you talking to me?"

"Is your name Genevieve?"

"Well, yes."

Oh, how she enticed him. She was all innocence, yet she possessed a wild, sex-kitten allure. It was a lethal, contradictory combination that always intrigued him. "Why don't you have a seat at one of the tables, and I'll join you in a minute."

"Thanks a lot, Hunter," Falon said, but there was a glimmer of amusement in his tone. Scamming bastard.

Genevieve's nose crinkled and her brow furrowed, the planes of her face darkening with suspicion. "Why?"

"Because."

"That's not an answer. What do you want to talk about?"

He flicked a pointed glance to their avid audience. "It's private."

"I don't understand." Then her lips—her lush, kiss me, lick me all over, fuck me all night lips—pressed together. Comprehension dawned in her eyes. She smiled slowly, seductively, yet somehow she appeared even more sad.

Now *he* was the one confused. What had made her happy and sad all at once? What did she comprehend?

"I would love to 'talk' with you," she said.

He gulped. She made it sound like they'd be going at it like wild animals on the tabletop. Maybe they would. If only she didn't tempt him on every level. Why did the Fates have to be so cruel? He desired this woman desperately, but he couldn't have her as anything more than a friend.

She eased to her feet, and he choked back a laugh when she flipped the rose-colored pixies off. His laugh died a sudden death when he saw that her dress barely fell below the curve of her bottom. His fingers itched to touch.

None of the tables were empty. Everyone watched her curiously as she crossed her arms over her chest. "You have five seconds to give me a table or I'll conjure your spouses into the bar. They'll find out what you've been doing and—"

Before the last word emerged, everyone at the tables jolted to their feet—everyone except Barnabas Vlad, the art gallery owner. He didn't have a spouse. Chairs skidded, drinks sloshed over rims. "Here, take mine," rose in disharmony. Satisfied, Genevieve skipped to the table hidden in the corner, partially covered in a shadowy haven. "I'll take yours, John Foster. Thank you."

The town pervert was too busy staring at her cleavage to respond.

"Move out of her damn way!" Hunter shouted.

John nearly jumped out of his skin as he leaped away from Genevieve.

"And play some music. *Now*." Hunter scowled at the band leader. "That's what I pay you for, isn't it?"

A few seconds later, soft, romantic music drifted from the speakers. His scowl deepened. Resisting Genevieve was hard enough; throw in a romantic atmosphere . . . God help him.

The three fairies were frowning, he noticed, and Falon was leaning his hip against the bar. "You're putting on quite a show tonight," his friend said.

"I'm glad you find it entertaining." He paused, looked away. "I'm taking a break."

"That's nice."

"You're still in charge."

"That's nice, too."

"Yeah, well, you're an asshole and if you don't wipe that smirk off your face, you're fired."

Falon's deep laughter followed him as he stormed to Genevieve's table and plopped down across from her. Once again, her delicious scent enveloped him. He shouldn't have instigated this, but now that he had he was helpless to stop.

"What did you want to talk about?" She propped her elbows on the table and leaned forward, granting him another spectacular view. Sweet heaven above, she wasn't wearing a bra.

Had he suggested they talk? Perhaps a better suggestion would be that he shoot himself here and now and just get his death over with. "We've known each other a long time," he began, fighting past the friction of sexual need working through him.

"Yes."

"And we've never discussed—" What the hell was a safe, nonsexual topic?

"Yes?" she prompted, grinning.

Her teeth were two rows of pearly white perfection. And she had a dimple. Why had he never noticed it before? *Probably because you've rarely given her a reason to smile at you, moron.* He yearned to nibble on the delectable little morsel.

"We've never discussed—" He paused yet again. The weather? No, he'd only picture her naked in the rain. Favorite places to shop? No, he'd picture her shopping naked. Favorite books? No, he'd picture her reading naked.

Ah, hell.

Is she worth your life? Now, this moment, he couldn't say no so easily.

"There's got to be *something* you want to talk about." She licked her lips, her pink tongue as lethal as any weapon of mass destruction.

They could talk about taxes at this point and he'd be

aroused. "I—how have you been doing lately?" he asked. He leaned as far back in the stool as he could, hoping distance would clear his foggy senses.

"Good."

"How are your sisters?"

"They're good." She tapped a finger to her chin, her oval nail glinting in the light. "Hunter, is there something else you want to say to me?"

He tangled a hand through his hair. Hell, yes, there was something he wanted to say to her: get naked.

How did she twist him into knots like this? He saw her, and he wanted her. He caught a whiff of her sweet fragrance, and he wanted her. He closed his eyes, and he wanted her.

Is she worth dying for?

He stared at her, watching the way shadows and light played across her lovely, serious little face. Watching the way hope flickered in her eyes, lighting the hazel to an otherworldly green.

Before the night was over, he was going to have this woman's thighs around his waist. Or head. He wasn't picky. He was going to know what it felt like to touch her curves, to know her taste. He was going to know how her expression changed when she climaxed. The future be damned.

Not giving himself time to consider the ramifications, he shoved to his feet and held out his hand, palm up. "Genevieve, would you please dance with me?"

"Really?" Disbelief and awe rained over her face before she frowned. "You don't plan to leave me in the middle of the song, do you?"

His chest constricted. He'd done that to her on numerous occasions. In his defense, he'd become so aroused holding her in the curve of his body he'd had two choices: leave her on the dance floor or fuck her on the dance floor. "We'll dance the entire song. I promise."

Slowly she grinned. "Yes. Yes. I would love to dance with you."

The moment she placed her fingers atop his, his senses screamed with approaching danger. He ignored the warning.

Here, in this moment, nothing mattered except cherishing Genevieve the way he'd yearned to cherish her all these many years.

Was she worth dying for?

Hell, yes.

Three

Oh, Great Goddess, it had worked! The love potion had actually worked.

Her hand in his, Hunter led her onto the dance floor. Where their skin touched, she tingled. He'd asked to do this; he'd even said please. She hadn't begged—not that she would have. (Okay, she might have.)

They stopped in the center of the floor, paused for a moment, facing and watching each other. Their breath intermingled—his was shallow, hers was coming in fast, erratic pants. Multihued light pulsed from the strobe above, caressing his face, and music flowed seductively.

Something she'd never seen before flittered over his expression. Something infinitely tender. Her stomach flip-flopped. What thoughts were rolling through his mind? He reached out and sifted a strand of her hair between his fingers, then brushed it from her temple. His touch electrified her.

The need to breathe was forgotten. Only Hunter existed, only Hunter mattered. His fingers slid down her shoulders, along her arms, and circled her waist. Her lips parted on a sudden gasp of pleasure. His strong arms locked around her, gathering her close. Heat zinged and crested, then his hands were, anchored on her lower back.

"Hunter," she said, unsure why she'd whispered his name. It was there, in her mind, in her blood, branded on her cells.

"Genevieve," he returned softly. "So lovely."

Throughout the years, she'd prayed he would accept what was between them. She would have prayed even harder if she'd known the sheer magnificence reality would be. Her chest pressed to his, nipples hard and aching; his strength seeped through her scanty dress. And he didn't jerk away from her, didn't run. The scent of him, heat and man, enveloped her.

Together they swayed to the erotic rhythm of the music. Several times, his erection brushed against her. Delicious. Welcome. Their gazes never strayed. Constantly sizzled.

Emboldened, she rasped her hands up the buttery soft material of his T-shirt. He sucked in a sharp breath. "I've wanted to be your lover for so long," she admitted.

"I've wanted that, too. So badly."

Her fingers played with the hair at his neck. "Some days I would have sworn you desired me. Some days I would have sworn you hated me."

"I always desired you. You're total pleasure, sweetheart." He paused. Frowned. "You're eternity."

Eternity . . . With that one word, joy and sadness battled for supremacy inside her. Joy because he was talking about forever with her; sadness because it had taken a love potion to get him to this point. However, she shoved the sadness away. Tonight was a night for magic and love. She would allow nothing else to intrude.

Tomorrow the sadness could return and erode the precious memories she had formed. As for now, she would take what she could get, however she could get it.

She'd wanted him too long.

"I'll give you eternity," she said. "I'll give you anything you ask for."

He broke eye contact and pulled her the rest of the way into his body. Her head rested on the hollow of his shoulder. "I've watched you grow from pretty teenager to exquisite woman."

A shiver stole over her skin. Was he speaking true, or did the love potion beckon him to lie and say anything that might please her? "Why did you constantly push me away, then?"

He ignored her question. "Every time you walked into a room, you consumed my attention. If you had known just how much I desired you, you would have pursued me all the more. And if you'd pursued me any more, I wouldn't have been able to resist you."

Sparks of exotic sensation pulsed through her. Unable to help herself and craving the taste of him, she grazed her lips over his neck. Her hands clutched at his back. Mmm, his skin tasted good, like expensive wine and twilight magic.

"There was no reason to resist me," she said. "I wanted to be with you."

"You amaze me." He nuzzled her nose. "You could have any man you want, but you never gave up on me."

That sad little gleam returned to her eyes, and Hunter knew he'd do anything to get rid of it. "What if I swore to never run from you again? Would you smile for me?"

In lieu of an answer, she brushed her lips over his neck once more. This time, however, she let her tongue explore, twirling, circling. He cupped her butt, lifting her slightly, and his erection rubbed the crevice between her legs. A moan tore from her. They were fully clothed, yet they were managing to make love on the dance floor, despite the people circling them.

Genevieve bit his ear. "Help me understand why you ran. Did you think I would use you? Did you think we would no longer be able to remain friends?"

He laughed, the sound devoid of humor. "No. I knew you wanted more than sex from me. I knew our friendship could survive."

"Then . . . why?"

"Genevieve," he said. The grief in her voice sliced through him, more lethal than a blade. He couldn't tell her the truth because it would frighten her away. If she knew she was going to be the death of him, she would leave him.

Now that he had her in his embrace, he wanted to keep her there. *Would* keep her there. He couldn't believe he'd pushed her away for so long. Stupid. A mistake he'd never make again. Never had a woman felt more perfect in his arms.

After all the years he'd hurt her, she deserved romance from him. Sweetness, tenderness, more than he'd ever given another.

"You have the most amazingly expressive eyes." He allowed his fingers to crawl down the curve of her bottom and play with the hem of her dress. "Have I ever told you that?"

She sucked in a gasp of air; then, as she released the breath, she relaxed against him fully. "No. You never told me."

"More fool me. Your eyes are so intoxicating, sometimes green, sometimes velvety brown, and I always feel like I'm lost in them." He brushed the side of her face with his, tickling her softness with his slight beard stubble, relishing the contact. He kissed the tip of her nose. Not dipping lower and tasting her lips proved nearly impossible. "Did you know you have three faint little freckles on your nose? When you're angry or sad, those freckles darken. I've wondered over and over again if you have freckles on the rest of your body."

"I could . . ." She gulped. Her eyes widened and filled with eagerness. "I could show you."

"Yes. I would love that." *I'm not an honorable man.* He stilled with the thought. Here she was, offering him a paradise he didn't deserve. His mouth curled into a frown, and he stared down at her. She deserved a man who could love her forever, a man who hadn't hurt her for years.

So what? he thought in the next instant. She wanted him; he wanted her. He wasn't a martyr. For what short time they had together—he knew his death was certain now, but he was past the point of caring—he would give her everything. His heart, his attention, his affection. He'd love her so thoroughly she'd savor the memories for the rest of her life.

"I truly am sorry for how I've treated you in the past, sweetheart."

"I forgive you," she said, her features sincere.

His brows arched in surprise. "That easily?"

"We're friends, aren't we?"

"Genevieve." He groaned her name as he meshed his lips into hers. She immediately parted for him, welcoming him inside. Her decadent flavor filled his mouth, so much richer than he'd ever imagined. She moaned, a needy sound, a greedy sound.

Urgency roared to intense life. Shards of her magic flowed into his cells, awakening pieces of him he hadn't known existed, crowning him with power and vitality. Warming him. He felt the pinprick rasps of her nipples against his chest and had to clench his fists in the material of her skirt to keep from kneading her breasts. Had they been anywhere else but a crowded barroom, he would have taken her. Would have pushed them both over the sweet edge of seduction.

"I want you," she breathed. "I want to make love with you."

"Hell, yes." He'd place her gently in his bed and smooth his hands over her. Work his way up and down her body with his tongue. Her legs would part, revealing the wetness of her arousal. "Stay the night with me." *Stay forever*.

"Yes. With all my heart, yes."

His cock jerked in reaction. Passion blazed in her eyes— passion for him. Only him. She smoothed her tongue over her lips, taking his taste with it. Her eyes closed in surrender, and she was the very picture of desire. Of lust and love and his most private dreams.

"Tell me what you're going to do with me, once you have me in bed," she said in a needy, aroused whisper. As if she had to know right then or she'd combust.

"What would you like me to do?" If he did half the things floating through his mind, they wouldn't walk for a week.

"Everything."

He rubbed against her, the action causing pleasure/pain flickers through his body. "Kiss you?"

"Mmm-hmm." She bit her bottom lip.

"Touch you?" He wanted so badly to drag her up to his room, to kiss and touch her *now*, but he was going to dance the entire song with her if it killed him. And it just might.

A tremor slipped down her spine. "Where would you touch me?"

"Everywhere."

Another tremor. "Yes, do that. Touch me everywhere."

"I'll taste you everywhere, too."

"Please, yes."

He licked the shell of her ear. "I'm going to make you come so many times, you'll—"

The double doors suddenly bounded open and a horde of . . . creatures burst inside the bar, surrounded by a palpable air of menace. Instinctively sensing their danger, Hunter shoved Genevieve behind his back. The music screeched to a halt. At the bar, the three fairies instantly shrunk to their tiniest size, puffs of glitter-smoke wafting from them.

Short, winged monsters with long fangs, more fur than a bear during hibernation, and razor-sharp claws formed a line in front of the doors, blocking escape. Their eyes were red and glowing; their angled, grotesque features were misshapen. Hideous.

They were subdemons, he realized.

Though different breeds were formed every day and he'd never encountered this type, Hunter recognized their scent: sulfur. As a monster hunter—pretending to be nothing more than a bar owner—he'd stalked and killed their kind most of his life. Demons, vampires, predators of the night—the scum of the earth, in his opinion. They were creatures who survived on human carnage. They were pure evil, and he despised them all.

Killing them had always been one of his favorite pastimes.

"Did someone wish for excitement?" one of them asked.

Genevieve gasped. "Oh, my Goddess. No, no. I take it back. No excitement."

"I suggest you leave," Hunter told them, the actual words nearly undetectable, laced with rage. Genevieve slipped her hand into his, and he felt a tremor rush through her. "Don't worry, sweetheart, I'll take care of this," he assured her quietly.

"No." The demon who had spoken, the tallest of the bunch—which wasn't saying much, since he only reached Hunter's navel—stepped forward and grinned slowly, anticipatingly. "I think we'll stay."

The grainy, high-pitched voice sent shudders through him. "Your kind isn't wanted here."

The creature's stance became cocky, arms crossed over his chest, legs slightly parted, his expression taunting. His dark, broken wings fluttered like an erratic heartbeat. "Your woman doesn't agree. She wished for excitement, so excitement we'll give her."

"I've changed my mind." Fighting past her fear, Genevieve stepped beside Hunter. She maintained her hold on him. Inside, her magic churned and swirled, dark and dangerous, ready for release. Sometimes the darkness of her powers frightened her more than her opponent; now she felt only fear for Hunter's safety. "He asked you to leave nicely. If you don't, I'll wreak such horrible vengeance upon you that you'll go home crying to the devil like little girls."

"We're not going anywhere until we've granted your wish. Master's orders." Laughing, the demons broke apart, knocking over tables, throwing chairs, climbing up and down the walls, and tearing off chunks of stone. Men and women, fairies and gnomes, gasped and raced (or flew) out of the way. That the gnomes, stumpy, trunklike monsters with more brawn than brain, were scared, added to her worries.

"Go upstairs and lock yourself in my room," Hunter demanded.

"I won't leave you to deal with them alone. I can make them go away." Amid shrieks of horror, the frantic pitter-patter of frightened people, and the evil vibrations of demon laughter, Genevieve raised her hands high in the air. "Burn to ash these demons shall, never a night again to prowl."

As she spoke, the demons flinched, anticipating the bombardment of her magic.

"Pain and suffering you will endure," she finished, "of this I am very sure."

Nothing happened.

Shocked, frowning, she tried again. Again, nothing.

The demons smiled slowly. "Looks like the witchy-poo has lost her powers."

More shock pounded through her; she uttered the spell for the third time. Still, no results. Why? "I—I don't understand." Why wouldn't her magic work? A side effect of the love potion? No, surely not, but Glory had told her to only drink half. The demons should be writhing balls of fire. Instead, they were chuckling and amused.

"Playtime is over," a grating voice proclaimed. The demon snarled and flashed his dripping fangs. "Get her!"

"Genevieve!" Hunter shouted as a creature lunged for her. Hunter grabbed it by the forearms and tossed it to the ground. He kicked and hit the demon with expert precision. His arms arched through the air so quickly the movements were barely visible. He ducked and spun, leaped and struck with poetic menace.

Falon joined the fray, stabbing at the monkey wannabes with broken liquor bottles and wood shards.

With the men occupied, another demon dove for her, slamming her into a table and knocking every ounce of air from her lungs. Dizzy, she sank to the ground. The only people she'd ever fought were her sisters, yet they hadn't wanted to actually kill her. Still, she knew the basics of self-defense and how to fight dirty.

Her opponent jumped astride her, pinning her where she lay. It licked its lips and tried to wrap its claws around her neck. She put her newly filed nails to use and poked it in the eyes. It howled, its attention on its pain, and she smashed her palm into its nose. In the next instant, Hunter kicked the demon away from her and grappled the hell spawn to the ground.

"Demons of the night," she chanted, standing, arms high in the air, "you will die now, I don't care how."

The fight continued without interruption.

Damn it! She glared down at her hands. Why wasn't her magic working? She felt the power of it inside her, as potent as ever, yet it refused to be released.

From the corner of her eye, she saw a demon's razor-sharp claws lengthen and slash at Hunter's chest. He didn't move in time, and blood began to ooze from the gaping wound. She gasped. Screamed. Fury and fear bubbled inside her.

"Run, baby," he panted, struggling to keep the creature from his throat.

"No, I won't leave you." Nearing panic, she grabbed a long, splintered wood shard and raced toward the battling pair just as Hunter punched the bastard in the face and rolled away. "Catch!" She tossed him the shard.

He caught it, and when the demon advanced, Hunter stabbed it dead center in the chest.

The creature burst into flames.

As the orange-gold flickers licked the walls and dissolved into ash, the tallest of the demons stopped tormenting a screaming gnome long enough to focus narrowed eyes on Hunter, who was pushing to his feet.

"You'll pay for that, human." Two other demons approached the leader's side, each of them glaring with hostility. "Oh, you'll pay."

Genevieve grabbed a beer bottle, broke the end on the bar, and held the jagged amber glass in front of her. "You'll have to fight me, as well," she said bravely. At least, she hoped she sounded brave.

"With pleasure, little witch," was the delighted reply.

"Damn it, Genevieve," Hunter said. "When this is over I'm going to teach you to obey my orders." He closed in on

the demon, and a bleeding Falon closed into step at his side.
Both men wore expressions of certain death—demon death.

Her heart drummed in her chest. *What should I do, what
should I do, what should I do?* When she'd wished for excitement, she hadn't meant *this*.

Distracted as she was, she didn't notice as one of the
demons sprinted to her. It reached her and knocked the glass
from her hand before tossing her to the ground. Suddenly
breathless, she lay still for a long while. Or perhaps she lay
for mere seconds. Her attacker jumped on top of her and she
fought like a wildcat, kicking and scratching. As it attempted
to subdue her, its rancid breath fanned her face.

"Be still!" it hissed. Its forked tongue slithered from between thin lips.

She bit its arm, the taste of salt and ash filling her mouth.

"Bitch!"

"That's *witch* to you." She worked her arms free and
clashed her hands together, then backhanded the creature
across the face.

"Dead witch." Its sharp, lethal fangs emerged, dripping
with . . . what? Not saliva. This smelled bad. Worse than
bad. Evil. Like death. It gripped her wrists and held them
down, its head inching toward her. She knew it was moving
quickly, about to sink its fangs into her neck, but her mind
processed it in slow motion.

She pulled her knees to her chest and slammed her feet
into the demon's chest. Surprisingly, it flew backward and
propelled across the bar. Gasping for air, trembling in fear,
she jolted to a sitting position.

"You okay?" Hunter panted, at her side. He dropped to
his knees. Sweat and blood dripped from his temples. His
gaze roved over her body frantically, over her ripped dress,
searching for injury.

"I'm fine. But you—"

"Look out!" Falon shouted.

Hunter whipped around; Genevieve gazed, horrified, past
his shoulder. The demon she'd kicked was flying at her, hate
in its eyes, a long shard of glass in its outstretched hand, mere

seconds away from reaching her. Instinctively, she dove to the side. Anticipating such a move, the demon moved with her. Hunter, damn him, sprang in front of her, taking the blow himself.

"Hunter!" she screamed.

Eyes wide, he looked down at his chest.

"Got him." Laughing, the demon and the rest of his cohorts raced away. Some jumped through windows, the sound of tinkling glass echoing from the walls. Others rushed out the same way they'd entered. Hinges squeaked as the front doors burst into shattered pieces.

Genevieve's mind registered only one thing. "You're hurt. Hunter, you're hurt." Still on her knees, she scrambled in front of him. Blood dripped from his chest, the glass embedded so deeply she could only see the tip.

"I'll be fine." Weakness and pain tinged his voice. "Did they hurt you? Are you cut anywhere?"

"I'm okay, damn you. I'm okay." He looked so pale, causing her panic to intensify. Not even when she'd first spied the demons inside the bar had she felt this much fear. "You should have let him stab me." Her chin trembled. "You should have let him stab me."

"I'm glad you're well." His eyelids drifted shut for a long moment. "I'd have to become a ghost and do the revenge thing if they'd harmed you."

"I need to pull out the glass and bandage your wounds, okay? I need to—"

"It's too late. Demon saliva . . . is poison, and one of them managed to bite me. Genevieve," Hunter said, his voice so raspy she had trouble hearing him. "I want you . . . to know, you were totally . . . worth it."

Her arms anchored around him, her head burrowing against his chest. His heartbeat thumped weakly, sporadically. "Hunter, listen to me. You're going to be okay. Let's get you to my sister. She's a healer." She gazed at the bar, wild and desperate. "Someone call Godiva. Call her right now."

"I'll do it," Falon said.

"My head is spinning." Hunter's forehead bobbed forward. "Help me lie down, sweetheart."

His full weight fell into her. She absorbed it as best she could, locking one hand at the base of his neck and the other at his lower back. Leaning forward, she slowly and as gently as possible lowered him. Seconds dragged by. By the time he lay completely prone, her arms burned and shook with exertion.

"I wish I could have had more time with you," he said. He didn't open his eyes. "That's my only regret."

"Stop. Don't talk like that. You're going to be fine." Her chin trembled all the harder; her blood ran cold. She tore the shirt from his chest and studied the rest of his wounds. What she saw made her mouth dry up. Long, jagged scratches ran like bloody rivers over his ribs. Several teeth marks adorned his neck, the skin already black. Already dead.

She covered her mouth with her hand to cut off her horrified cry. "I love you, and I need you. Tell me you're going to be okay."

His lips lifted in a weak smile. "I wish . . . I wish . . ." As his voice tapered to quiet, his head drifted to the side.

Genevieve screamed. "No." She gripped his shoulders and shook him. "You're going to be okay. You're going to be okay." Violently, she continued to shake him. "Open your eyes, damn it. Open them right now or I'll curse you to live in a monastery."

He didn't respond.

Falon approached slowly and crouched down. He reached out and placed two fingers over Hunter's neck. Tears filled his eyes. "I'm sorry, Genevieve, but he was dead the second the demon bit him. They produce a poison that no human can survive."

"No. No. When my sisters get here, we'll cast a spell and he'll be fine. You'll see. He'll be fine." A huge lump formed in her throat, making it difficult to breathe. "He's going to be fine," she whispered raggedly, more for herself than Falon.

Yet even after she and her sisters cast their spells, Hunter remained motionless. Lifeless. Dead.

Yes, Hunter Knight was dead. And there wasn't a damn thing she could do about it.

Four

"Uh, Mr. Collins. I think you should know something."

Roger Collins, owner and operator of Mysteria Mortuary—as well as a closet shape-shifter (spotted owl)—looked up from his desk and faced his apprentice, a freckle-faced boy with a pasty, almost gray complexion. "What's happened, hoo hoo, now?"

"Hunter Knight's body has disappeared."

Exasperated, Roger scratched his shoulder with his nose. Things like this were always happening, and he was tired of it. "Let's keep this between us, hoo hoo. No reason to alert the town." They'd only cancel the burial, and he'd be out a hefty chunk of change. No thanks. "Knight's funeral, hoo hoo, will happen as scheduled."

"Huuunnnterrrrr. Hunter Knight, you silly boy. Wake up, *s'il vous plait.*"

The voice called to him from a long, dark tunnel. Hunter tried to blink open his eyes, but it hurt too badly so he left them shut. Did lead weights hold the lids down? His mouth was dry, and his limbs were weak. Most of all, his neck throbbed.

What had happened to him?

He remembered fighting the demons, remembered Genevieve leaning over him. Remembered a black shadow swooping him up and carrying him away. And then, nothing. He remembered nothing after that.

"*Mon dieu!* Aren't you just the prettiest little thing." A soft hand smoothed over his brow. "I could snack on you all day and come back for leftovers."

That hand . . . His ears twitched. He could hear the rush of blood underneath the surface of skin. He could even hear the faint *thump, thump* of a heart. His mouth suddenly flooded with moisture. Hungry, he realized. He was so hungry he could have gnawed off his own arm.

"Well, don't just lie there. I know you're awake. Pay some attention to *moi*, you naughty boy. I saved your life, after all." A pause. "Well . . . I kind of saved your life. Maybe a more truthful saying would be I saved your death."

The voice was deep enough that he knew it belonged to a man, but it was surprisingly feminine. And that horrible French accent . . . Despite the pain, Hunter forced his eyelids apart. Dank blackness greeted him. But slowly, very slowly his eyes adjusted, and he was able to make out a rocky cavern and a silhouette. The silhouette became a body . . . the body became a man . . . and then he saw everything as clearly as if the sun were shining.

"Hello, my little love puppet," the man said. "We're going to have *the* best eternity together, *oui.*"

"Barnabas?" Hunter asked, rubbing his eyes.

"None other," he said with a proud lift of his chin.

Barnabas Vlad, owner of Mysteria's only art gallery ("art," of course, meaning pornographic photos); Hunter had come across the man only a few times. Last time he'd seen him, the man had been inside the bar. Something about him had always set Hunter's nerves on edge—something besides the fact that Barnabas often hit on him like a sailor on leave.

Right now Barnabas was dressed in a black, Oriental-styled gown, and he twirled a black parasol in his hand. Usually he wore huge blue sunglasses, but he wasn't wearing those now.

His eyes glowed bright red.

Hunter jumped to his feet, behind the stone dais he had lain upon. He winced in pain, but held his ground. "You're a vampire." He spat the word, for it was a foul curse to him.

"Oui, oui." Barnabas's glossed lips stretched into a happy, unconcerned smile. "What do you think of my outfit? It's new. Very *china doll* meets *modern society*, don't you think?"

"I think your dress needs a hole in it," Hunter snarled. "Right in the vicinity of your undead heart." His gaze circled the cavern, searching for anything he could use as a stake. There were no rocks, no twigs. Damn it. What he would have given for his COTN—creatures of the night—arsenal at home.

"Why are you looking at me like that?" Barnabas's smile became a pout, and he splayed his arms wide. "You're a vampire, too, *mon ami.*"

"No, I'm not."

"Oui, you are."

"No, I'm not."

"Oui, you are."

"No. I'm. Not. I'm a vampire *hunter*, you disgusting, vile, rotten piece of dog shit."

Barnabas took no offense and laughed, actually laughed. "Not anymore. Feel your neck. I drained your blood and gave you mine."

There was truth in the vampire's expression, truth and utter enjoyment. Everything inside Hunter froze. No. No! He couldn't be a vampire. He'd rather die.

Hesitant, hand shaky, Hunter reached up. He could taste blood in his mouth, it was true, but the rest . . . His fingertips brushed over the small, very real puncture wounds on the side of his neck. He knew exactly what that meant. *No*, he thought again. He hunted vampires; he hated them. Before

Genevieve, it had been his only purpose in life. "Now . . . you putrid sack of undead flesh." Glaring, he pointed a finger at Barnabas, wishing it were a stake. "Why would you make me a vampire? Why didn't you let me die?"

With a guilty flush, Barnabas hopped onto the dais. "I was in the bar the night those demons attacked you. When you fell, you were covered in blood and, *mon dieu*, you looked so tasty. I didn't cop a feel or anything, if that's what has you so worried."

"That's not what I'm worried about," he shouted. *I'm a monster now. I'm the very thing I despise.* He knew a lot about vampires. They were—had been—his business, after all, and he'd seen many people make the change from human to beast. Oh, they tried to fight the urge to drink.

They never won.

Always the thirst for blood, for life, seduced and consumed them. They killed the people they once loved—and everyone else around them. *I can never allow myself to see Genevieve again.* The wretched thought nearly dropped him to his knees. Nearly felled him.

Barnabas has lived in Mysteria for a long time, and he hasn't slaughtered the population. Hunter paused, blinked. How seductive the thought was and he grasped onto it with desperation. Maybe he was wrong about vampires. Maybe vampires didn't kill—

He squeezed his eyes closed. Such rationalizations were dangerous and could get Genevieve slain. No, he couldn't see her, couldn't risk it.

"Are you worried that you will no longer have a sexual appetite? You will, I assure you." The vampire's eyes stroked over him, stripped him, glowing a brighter red with every second that passed. "Despite the myths, you will function as you always did—except for the sunlight thing and the blood thing. Small prices to pay, really."

"Considering what?" he snarled. "There are no advantages that I can see."

"There are most certainly advantages." Barnabas tapped a black-gloved finger onto his chin. "You'll get stronger every day. Faster. You'll be a force no man—uh, woman—can resist. Like *moi*. After a while, you'll even enjoy taking blood. I pinky promise."

"I'll be a killer." This wasn't happening, couldn't possibly be happening. He tangled a hand through his hair.

"You won't be a killer."

"Yes, I will."

"*Mais non*, you won't."

"Yes. I. Will. Your continued arguing is really starting to piss me off."

"Do you want to fight me?" Barnabas asked hopefully. "I'm always up for naked wrestling."

Hunter bared his teeth in a scowl. As he did so, his incisors elongated. He actually felt them do it, sliding down, sharpening. He smelled the metallic twang of blood in the air—blood from a recent feeding Barnabas had enjoyed. How thirsty Hunter suddenly was. He shook with the force of it. "I can't drink blood. I just can't."

"You smell me, don't you? You want to sink your teeth into me? Go ahead. I already gave you blood, but you were asleep and didn't get to taste the sweetness of it." Barnabas motioned him over with a wave of his hand. "Taste it. You might like it. But you had better hurry. Soon my heart will shrivel up again, the blood gone, and there'll be nothing left for you to taste."

Hunter's stomach twisted in revulsion—and eagerness. He found himself stepping toward Barnabas, closing the distance between them, unable to stop himself. He found himself leaning down, teeth bared, mouth watering.

Genevieve's beautiful image flashed inside his mind. *She's in trouble.* The knowledge flooded him, his psychic ability attuned to her. Even in death. He straightened with a jolt. Blood was forgotten. Only Genevieve mattered. "Show me the way out of this cave before I kill you, vampire." He'd save her, then leave her.

Barnabas frowned. "You're not ready to leave."

"Yes, I am."

"*Mais non*, you're not."

"Yes, I am. And you're not French, so stop with the accent."

"I haven't taught you the way of our kind yet."

Rage poured through him as if he'd drunk it. "*Your* kind, vampire. I will never be like you."

"*Oui*, you will."

"No. I. Won't. Stop arguing. My woman is in trouble, and I *will* save her."

"Fine. Go. I've already fed you, so you don't have to worry about drinking for a while yet." Barnabas's eyes flashed red with jealousy. "But when the hunger hits you, you'll come back to me. I know you will."

"She hasn't stopped crying for three days."

"She refuses to eat. She barely has the energy to sit up and drink the water I force down her."

"What should we do?"

"I don't know. Great Goddess, I don't know."

Genevieve heard her sisters' hushed voices and stared up at the hole she'd blown in the ceiling yesterday. Why couldn't she have done that the night of the brawl? The morning after Hunter's death, her magic had returned to full operating capacity, but she hadn't needed it. And now she didn't care.

"Should we call a doctor?"

She rolled to her side, placing her back to her sisters. Why wouldn't they leave her alone? She just wanted peace—from their voices, from life. From the flashing, bloody images of Hunter's death.

"Genevieve, sweetie, we know you're awake. Talk to us," Godiva begged, her tone tinged with concern. The wolf she had saved plopped at her ankles and nudged her hand, wanting to be petted. "Tell us how we can help you."

"Bring Hunter back to life." Her throat ached from her crying. Raw, so raw. Like her spirit. "That's all I want."

"We can't do that," Glory said softly. "Raise his body from the ground, yes, but the risen dead become predators. Killers. You know that. The longer the dead walk the earth, the hungrier for life they become. He would eat you up and spit out your bones."

Yes, she knew that, but hearing it tore a sharp lance of pain through her. One moment she'd had everything she'd ever dreamed, the next she had only despair. *Hunter*, her heart cried.

"The surviving demons are destroying Mysteria," Godiva said. "We need your help to stop them."

"I can't." Strength had long since deserted her. More than that, any concern she'd had for the town and its citizens had died with Hunter. "I just can't."

Glory claimed her right side, and Godiva sat at her left. Surrounding her. "His funeral is today. Do you want to go?"

"No." She didn't want to see him inside a casket. A part of her wanted to pretend he was still alive, simply hiding somewhere. "Why did he have to die? Why? The love potion had worked. He wanted me as much as I wanted him."

"Uh, um." Glory looked away, at anything and everything but her sisters. "Humm."

Godiva's eyes narrowed. "What did you do, Glor?"

Pause.

"Glory!"

"Well, Evie asked for a love potion. I didn't think Hunter deserved her, and knew if he loved her for one night, then dumped her the next day, she'd be devastated."

"What did you do?" Godiva repeated.

Another pause.

"Don't make me ask again," Godiva said, raising her arms as if to cast a spell.

"I, uh, sort of gave her a power depressant instead."

"Sort of?"

"Okay, I did. But I didn't mean any harm. I thought it would be okay. I didn't think she'd need her powers."

The sorrowful fuzz around Genevieve's brain thinned. *Power depressant,* echoed through her mind. How many spells had she attempted with no results? One spell, that's all it would have taken to save Hunter. One spell, and the night would have ended differently.

She squeezed her eyelids closed, wave after wave of fury hammering through her, each more intense than the last. "He's dead because I couldn't help him. He's dead because I couldn't use my magic."

Her younger sister's cheeks bloomed bright with shame, then drained of color with regret. "I didn't think you'd need them. I didn't even think you'd notice." She clutched Genevieve's hand. "I'm so, so sorry. You have to believe I'm sorry. But think. Hunter wanted you. Not because of a potion, but because of *you*."

Genevieve's fury fizzled, leaving only despair; her muscles released their viselike grip on her bones and she sank deep into the mattress. Hunter had wanted her. Truly wanted her, without the aid of a love potion. All the things he'd said to her had come from *him*.

That made the pain of his death all the harder to bear.

I killed him. I killed him! If she hadn't decided to make Hunter love her, no matter the methods used, if she hadn't made a wish for excitement, he would still be alive. *My fault. All my fault.* Hot tears slid down her cheeks.

"Please. Leave me alone for a little while. Just leave me alone."

Hunter's funeral had begun an hour ago.

The digital clock blurred as Genevieve's eyes filled with tears. Any moment now, they would lower his casket into the ground and the cycle of his life—and death—would be complete.

Sobbing, she turned away from the glowing red numbers and mashed her face into her pillow. She'd never been so miserable. Her sisters had gone to the funeral. Genevieve simply wasn't ready to say good-bye.

She cried until her ducts could no longer produce tears. She cried until her throat burned and her lungs ached. Then she remained utterly still, absorbing the silence, lost in her sorrow. Minutes later, or perhaps an eternity, a buzzing sound reverberated in her left ear, and a fly landed on her cheek. Weakly she swatted the insect away.

"Bitch," she heard.

"Murderess."

"I wish *you* would have died instead."

Genevieve rolled to her back and blinked open her tired, swollen eyes. Three tiny fairies swarmed around her face, flashing pink. All three were female and scowling. She recognized them from the bar.

"You killed him," one of them hissed.

"You killed him," the others reiterated. "You could have used your magic against the demons, but you didn't. You killed him."

You killed him. Yes, she had. "I loved him." She'd thought her ducts dry, but stinging tears beaded in her eyes.

"How could you love him? You don't care about him. The demons have sworn their vengeance upon him for killing their brethren and are even now desecrating his grave, yet here you lie, doing nothing. Again. Someone even took his body from its casket."

"What?" She jolted upright. A wave of dizziness assaulted her, and she rubbed her temple with her fingers. "Desecrating his grave, how? And who dared take his body?"

"Does it matter?" *Buzz. Buzz.* "Your sisters are fighting the demons off, but they cannot do it without you, the witch of vengeance."

Without another word, Genevieve leaped out of bed. Her knees wobbled, but a rush of adrenaline gave her strength. Arms shaking, she tugged on the first pants and T-shirt she could find, then raced through the hallway. The wolf—what had Godiva named him?—trotted to her, following close to her heels. He was almost completely healed, and his brown eyes gleamed bright with curiosity.

"There's trouble at the cemetery," she felt compelled to explain. Trouble she would fight against. Heart racing, she grabbed her broom and sprinted outside. No one—no one!—

was going to destroy Hunter's grave. Whoever had taken him *would* return him.

Moonlight crested high in the night sky, scooping low. The citizens of Mysteria did everything at night, even funerals. A cool breeze ruffled her hair and kissed her fiery hot, tear-stained face. Moving faster than she ever had in her life, she hopped on her broom and flew toward Mysteria's graveyard. When she passed the wishing well, she flipped it off. When she passed Knight Caps, closed for the first time in years, she pressed her lips together to silence a pained moan.

Soon the graveyard came into view.

Monuments rose from the ground, white slashes against black dirt. Only a few patches of grass dared grow and the only flowers were silk and plastic. Death reigned supreme here. Broken brick surrounded the area with a high, eerie wall. The closer she came, the more chilled the air became, heavier, laden with the scents of dirt and mystery.

Her eyes narrowed when she saw the open, empty casket. Her eyes narrowed further when she saw the group of demons taunting her sisters and spitting on Hunter's grave.

Hunter's mourners must have already escaped, for there was no trace of them. Her sisters were holding hands and pointing their fingers toward the short, monkeylike horde of demons whose wings flapped and fluttered with excitement as they tried to claw their way through an invisible shield.

Both Godiva and Glory appeared weakened and pale, their shoulders slumped. Genevieve dropped to the ground, tossing her broom aside as she ran to them. She grabbed both of their hands, completing the link. Power instantly sparked from their fingertips. In pain, the demons shrieked.

"Thank the Goddess," Glory breathed. Her hands shook, but color was slowly returning to her cheeks. "I wasn't sure how much longer we could hold them off."

"There weren't this many left at the bar." Right now Genevieve counted eight. "Hunter and Falon killed a lot of them."

"They keep multiplying," Glory said. "I have a feeling we can kill these, too, but more will come. You're the vengeance witch, Evie. Do something."

Genevieve focused all of her rage, all of her sorrow into her hands. They burned white-hot. Blistering. Her eyes slitted on her targets. "Burn," she said. "Burn."

One of the demons erupted into flames, its tortured howl echoing through the twilight. Another quickly followed. Then another and another turned to ashes, until only one remained. "Go back to hell and tell the others if they ever return I'll make their deaths a thousand times worse."

The creature vanished in a panicked puff of black smoke. So easy. So quick. Exactly what should have happened at the bar.

Finished, depleted, she allowed her hands to fall to her sides. Weakness assaulted her as it always did when she used her powers to such a degree. She should have felt a measure of satisfaction. She should have felt vindicated. She didn't. Inside, sorrow still consumed her.

"Everyone must have raced home," Godiva panted. She hunched over, anchoring her hands on her knees. "We need to do something to prevent more demons from attacking."

"Like what?" Glory settled on the ground, her hand over her heart. "Genevieve warned them. What more can we do?"

Genevieve stared up at the stars. "A part of me wants them to return." Her tone lacked emotion, but the cold rage was there, buried under the surface. "I want to kill more of them."

Arms folded around her, comforting arms, familiar arms. "That puts other citizens at risk," Godiva said softly. "If Hunter were still alive, you'd want him protected. Let's give everyone else the same consideration."

She closed her eyes at the pain those words brought—if Hunter were alive—but nodded. Always the voice of reason, Godiva was right. If Hunter were alive, she would do whatever was necessary to protect him. "Do you know who took his body?" She gulped, the words foul on her tongue.

"No." Glory.

"No." Godiva.

Genevieve fell to her knees in front of the empty casket. Tears once more burned her eyes. There was a fresh mound of soil beside her, the spot Hunter was supposed to rest in for all of eternity, a gift to Mother Earth.

He's lost to me. No, no. She could not accept that. *Would not* accept that. "I want to raise the spirits of the dead to protect Mysteria," she found herself saying. No matter where Hunter's body was, his spirit would be able to find her—*if* she raised it. In that moment, she would have sold her soul if it meant seeing him one last time. "They can guard the town against the demons."

Pause. Silence. Not even insects dared speak.

"I don't know," Glory hedged. "Spirits are so unpredictable."

"Genevieve . . . ," Godiva began.

"Please. Do this. For me."

Her sisters glanced at each other, then at her, each other, then her. Concern darkened both of their expressions. Finally Godiva nodded. "Alright. We'll raise the spirits, but only until the next full moon."

Elation bubbled inside her, not obliterating her sadness but eclipsing it. *Hunter*, her heart cried again. *We'll be together again soon. If only for a little while.*

Five

"Let's begin the spirit-raising spell." Godiva removed the band from her hair, letting the long pale strands cascade down her back. She breathed deeply of the night air. "We need to be naked for this one, so no part of our magic is trapped in the clothing fibers."

"Oh, great," was Glory's reply. She remained still, *not* stripping. "This is the twenty-first century. Do we still need to strip?"

"Yes. Now hurry and take off your clothes. I need to get home and feed Romeo." Romeo, the perfect name for her injured wolf. He'd charmed her with only a look.

Already Godiva missed him. He'd become her constant companion, a comfort in these last dark days. She wished there were something she could do for Genevieve, anything to remove the haunted glaze from her sister's eyes.

Remaining silent, Genevieve removed her clothing. Godiva unbuttoned her dress and shimmied it down her voluptuous hips. The buttercup yellow material pooled at her feet. A chill night breeze wisped around them, and with a sigh, Glory, too, stripped.

"There," she said. "Now we can begin. Form a circle and clasp hands."

The tortured howl of a wolf cut through the darkness. Godiva stilled. Had Romeo somehow gotten out of the house and now stalked the woods, searching for her? Another howl erupted through the night.

"Oh, Goddess." Losing all trace of color, Glory shoved her hair out of her face. "The wolves are out. Maybe we should go home."

"We'll be fine," Godiva said, though she was worried. For a different reason. She didn't fear the wolves; she feared for Romeo. What if he got in another fight and was injured again? He might not survive this time. Her need to hurry increased.

She was just about to grab her sisters' hands when, a few feet away, her gaze snagged a silver phone and a masculine arm. Her mouth fell open. A cold sweat broke over her skin. "Girls," she whispered frantically. "Someone is taking pictures of us."

"Did you say someone is taking pictures of us?" Glory's silver eyes narrowed. "Nobody takes secret pictures of me unless I've had time to diet."

"Don't worry. I'll handle this." Cold and emotionless, Genevieve raised her hands into the air, a dark spell slipping easily from her lips.

A startled scream echoed through the night.

"What did you do?" Glory bent down and swiped up her broom.

"See for yourself."

The girls closed ranks on the tombstone, circling the intruder and blocking him from escape. They found the flip phone hovering in the air in front of a trembling, horrified man, the phone clamping and snapping its way down his body. Only after it had bitten his favorite appendage (twice) and he screamed like a little girl (twice) did it fall to the ground.

"John Foster," Glory gasped. "You big pervert. Does Hilde know you're out here? And staring at our breasts, no less?"

"Please don't tell her—your breasts are so big." Eyes widening, he said, "I mean, I don't want her to know—I want to touch your breasts." He shook his head, but his gaze remained glued on Glory's chest. He licked his lips. "What I mean to say is—double-D fun bags are my favorite."

Glory smacked him over the head with her broom. "Letch!"

"Bastard!" Godiva grabbed her own broom and popped him dead center in the face.

"This was the wrong day to piss me off, John." Genevieve didn't have her broom in hand, so she raised her arms high in the air and uttered another incantation. "You like breasts so much, you can have a pair of your own."

His shirt ripped down the middle as a huge pair of breasts grew on his chest. He stared down at them, his mouth gaping open. "What the hell! Get them off, get them—hey, these are nice." Closing his eyes, he reached up and kneaded his new breasts, a rapturous smile spreading across his face. "Mmm," he muttered.

"Undo the spell!" Glory scowled. "Undo the spell right now. We'll punish him another way."

"No, this is punishment," he cried, covering the man-boobs protectively. "I swear. Don't take them away. I've got to learn my lesson."

Genevieve did as Glory suggested, and John's chest shrunk back to its normal size. He bawled like a baby the entire time. He even tried to dart out of their circle, but Godiva locked his feet in place with a wave of her hand.

"Not so fast," she said.

His eyes widened with horror. "What are you going to do to me? I didn't mean any harm. I only wanted a peek at your boobies."

Without saying a word, the three sisters tugged at the rest of his clothing, peeling it from his middle-aged body until he wore nothing but a few teardrops. Since he'd gotten a look at their goods, it was only fair they got a look at his.

"Ew, gross," Glory said. "Maybe we should dress him again. I'm throwing up in my mouth."

"That will just waste more time," Godiva replied. "We're going to cast our spells around you."

Glory's gaze darted between his legs. "Yes, *little* John, we're going to cast our spells around you and you're going to stand there like a good boy and pray the Goddess takes mercy on your soul."

That dried his tears. "You mean you're not going to hurt me, and I get to watch you dance? Naked?" He tried real hard not to grin. "Thank you, Great Goddess. Have mercy. Oh, have mercy. Lots and lots of mercy and breasts and mercy. Amen."

"I swear," Genevieve said, "you're the scum of the earth."

"Ignore him," Godiva said after another wolf howl echoed through the night. "We need to get to work."

"Fine."

"Yes. Let's hurry." Genevieve found her broom half buried in a mound of dirt, snatched it up, and rejoined the circle.

The three sisters closed their eyes, blocking out John's image and his voice, and in perfect sync began their protection spells. Round and round they danced, their hips undulating, their hair swaying, their brooms raised high in the air. Each one chanted under her breath.

While she danced, Godiva stumbled over the spell's words, unable to push Romeo from her mind. That last howl had sounded pained. Was he hurt again? Should she go looking for him? He was one of the biggest, strongest, fiercest wolves she'd ever seen, but he possessed a gentle and loving nature and other beasts of the forest might trample him.

Suddenly Glory stopped, her breasts jiggling with the abrupt halt.

"What are you doing? Keep moving," John whined. "I'm still praying."

She frowned. "Does it feel like the ground is shaking?"

Godiva stilled, followed quickly by Genevieve. In the next instant and seemingly without provocation, Glory stumbled backward and landed on her butt.

"What's going on?" Godiva gasped as dirt began cracking at her feet. Grass began splitting. Flowers tumbled off of tombstones . . . and then the tombstones themselves tumbled to the ground. "What's going on?" she asked again, her tone more frenzied.

Glory popped to her feet, and Genevieve paled. "I think—ohmygoddess—I think the bodies are rising!"

"That can't be." Glory sucked in a breath, whirling around to scan the surrounding area. "We only called forth their spirits."

"Well, the dirty bastards didn't listen!"

"I don't understand. Did we say the wrong words?" Godiva asked.

A bony hand shot through the cracked dirt and latched onto John's ankle. Startled, he screamed and would have dropped into a fetal ball and sucked his thumb if his feet hadn't been frozen in place. All over the cemetery, bodies rose. Most were completely decayed, but all still wore their worm-eaten burial clothes. As they emerged, they limped, lumbered, and trudged toward the sisters. Deadly moans echoed across the distance.

"What should we do?" Glory gasped out, holding out her broom like a sword. "What the hell should we do?"

Agnes McCloud—a woman everyone knew had once been John's mistress—climbed all the way out of the ground. Seeing her, John started shaking like an epileptic. "Help me," he cried. "Please, help me. Free my feet."

Godiva swatted at the skeleton with her broom. "Shoo." Big chunks of dirt fell out of the dead woman's hair. "Get back in the ground. I command you."

Agnes was only recently dead from a car accident, and her face lifted into a grin when she spied John. "John! Oh, my darling Johnnie. I missed you so much."

"We've got to send them back." Glory's mouth formed a large O as she counted the number of bodies headed toward them. "They're multiplying like rabbits!"

"Demons of the Dark," Godiva shouted, "return to your graves!"

They kept coming.

"Spirits of the Netherworld, be gone!"

Still, they kept coming.

Meanwhile, Agnes had pounced on John and was feasting on him like he was a buffet of sensual delights and she had been on a year-long fast. Except, the man looked like he would rather eat his own vomit than the dead woman's tongue. That didn't stop Agnes.

If she'd had time, Godiva would have snapped a picture of the two with the flip phone. As it was, the rest of the dead bodies finally reached them and closed her and her sisters in a circle, moaning and groaning and reaching out to caress them. Having been without human contact for so long, they were probably desperate for it. Or maybe they were simply hungry and she and her sisters looked like a triple-stacked Egg McMuffin.

Glory shrieked. Godiva swatted at the bony hands with her broom. And Genevieve stood in frozen shock. "Is that . . . Hunter?"

A male form broke through the line of trees, just beyond the cemetery. His skin was intact, his features normal. Except for his eyes. They glowed a bright, vivid red. Obviously, he wasn't a corpse. But . . . what was he?

"Hunter!" Genevieve called excitedly. "Ohmygoddess, Hunter, over here!"

He turned toward the sound of her voice, and his lips lifted in relief. "Genevieve!"

They sprinted to each other, avoiding dead bodies and Genevieve threw herself into his arms. Godiva couldn't hear what they were saying. She watched as Hunter flung Genevieve over his shoulder and carted her straight into the forest.

"Godiiiiiva," Glory gasped. "Don't just stand there. Help me!"

She shook her head and continued to fight off their molesters with her broom, all the while uttering spell after ineffectual spell. Well, not so ineffectual. Each spell conjured something—just not the help they wanted. A fairy. A gnome. A gorgeous demon high lord. Why were their spells messing up? She still didn't understand. Each creature materialized at the edge of the forest and stood, watching the proceedings, grinning. One of them even produced a bowl of pop-corn and a large soda.

"Two dollars says the one with worms in his eyes snags the witch on the left," the demon said.

"You're on," the gnome agreed.

Suddenly a fierce growl overshadowed every other noise, and a pack of wolves raced into the graveyard, snapping and snarling.

"Romeo," Godiva cried, her relief nearly a palpable force when she recognized her pet.

His teeth bared in a menacing scowl, Romeo leaped up and latched onto the bony arm reaching for her and snapped it off before sprinting away.

"Give that back," the corpse shouted, chasing after him.

The rest of the wolf pack chased the skeletons in every direction. All except Agnes, who was still sucking John's face. Godiva and Glory dropped to the ground in relief.

"I never thought I'd be grateful to the wolves," Glory said. "Should we be worried for Genevieve?"

"No. I think she'll be fine." More than fine, actually. "Here, take my hand. We have to send these corpses back to their graves."

Glory intertwined their fingers. Without the fear of being eaten, they were able to concentrate on their spell. As they chanted, magic began to swirl around them, drifting through the cemetery and luring each dead body back to its grave.

Suddenly, Falon—who had not come to Hunter's funeral, for some reason—burst from the forest and came running toward them. Rage consumed his features. Godiva blinked over at him in surprise—she'd never seen him move so quickly or so lethally—and from the corner of her eye she saw Glory jolt up, panic storming over her expression.

"I'm naked," Glory said, her voice frantic. "Where are my clothes? Falon can't see me naked!" Her movements jerky, she searched the dirt, found the yellow dress Godiva had worn, and tugged it over her head.

Falon skidded to an abrupt stop in front of Glory. "Are you alright?"

His gaze focused on Glory, and Godiva was amused to realize she herself could have been a bloody, writhing mass and he wouldn't have noticed. Still, she scrambled for the clothing littering the ground, a pair of stone-washed jeans and a pink sweater.

"We're fine," Glory said stiffly. She pushed to her feet and smoothed her hair out of her face, looking anywhere but at Falon. "How did you know we were in trouble?"

A tinge of color darkened his cheeks. "I sensed it."

Well, well, well. Godiva had never seen the two exchange a single word, yet here they were, acting as if they knew each other. How interesting. Sexual attraction sparked between them, white-hot, intense. Nearly palpable.

"Well, you're too late," Glory told Falon. "We took care of everything ourselves."

Just then Romeo appeared in front of Godiva, claiming her attention. "There's my good boy," she said, reaching out for him. He dropped an arm bone at her feet as if it were the greatest prize in the world and nuzzled her with his nose. She luxuriated in his soft black fur as his tongue flicked out and licked her collarbone. "I'm glad you're okay."

"Eww." Glory balled her fists on her hips. "I know I've said your boyfriends were dogs in the past, but hello. This one *is* a dog. Don't let him lick you like that. Have him neutered, at the very least."

"He's my special sweetie." She rubbed her cheek against his. "My hero."

Glory turned on her heel. "I'm outta here," she called over her shoulder.

"I'll walk you home," Falon said.

She didn't bother glancing in his direction. "No, you won't."

"I wasn't asking. I was telling." The determined man strode to Glory's side, keeping pace beside her.

"I don't need your help, jerk-off."

"I'm giving it anyway."

Their voices faded. Romeo growled at Glory's retreating back, then looked up into the sky and howled. As he howled, his body elongated and his fur fell away. Godiva gasped and jerked away from him. Skin and muscled ridges were forming. Ribs, fingers, and toes. Bronzed skin.

"Romeo?" she asked, frightened. Her mouth went dry, and her heart pounded against her ribs. He was . . . beautiful. "Romeo?" The name emerged on a breathless catch of air this time.

Dark gold *human* eyes were suddenly staring down at her, and she drank in the most beautiful face she'd ever seen. Perfectly chiseled cheekbones, perfectly sloped nose. Full, lush pink lips made for kissing. Her gaze traveled downward, taking in the rest of him. His chest was wide and muscled, like velvet poured over steel. And his—"Oh, Great Goddess." Hello, satisfaction.

"I've been dying to do this all week, but was afraid you'd stop coddling and petting me." He grinned wickedly. "You are not mad?"

His voice was rough and husky, and so sexy she shivered. Gulping, she blinked up at him. "Not mad. Promise."

"I would like a chance to coddle *you*. Let me take you home."

To bed, echoed in her mind, unsaid. "Yes. Take me home."

Six

"You're here," Genevieve said as Hunter slid her down his body. "You're really here." She circled him, disbelief, joy, and sexual hunger eating at her. Pink pollen twirled around them.

Hunter remained utterly still. He was as harshly gorgeous as ever, only somehow more savage looking. Her heart thrummed with excitement, even as confusion rocked her. "How are you here? You aren't a corpse and you aren't a spirit, but you've been gone for three days."

Trees swayed around them, and the scent of moon-magic and jasmine wafted headily through the air. Rays of muted light illuminated the clearing.

"I . . . didn't die," he said. He stared at her neck, his eyes red. "I should leave."

"No! Stay." She bit her bottom lip. Never had she been more overjoyed, more confused. "Why are your eyes red? Wait, the red is fading. I don't understand. What happened to you?"

He didn't answer.

She forgot the question, anyway, as she reached out, hands brushing his jacket to the ground. *She* was already naked; she wanted *him* naked, too. Nothing else mattered really. Next she unbuttoned his shirt. It, too, pooled at their feet. Her fingers met his chest, paler than before but strong.

"I missed you so much," she told him. "When I thought you were dead, I wanted to die, too."

"Genevieve," he said, the sound of her name a moan of pleasure-pain. He squeezed his eyelids together. "I should go. You're safe now."

"Don't leave. Stay with me. Please."

"Something happened—"

"However you survived, I don't care. I just want you." She flattened her palms over his chest, his nipples deliciously abrasive. "Mmm. So good."

His hands tangled in her hair, and their gazes locked. "I want to kiss you."

"Do it. Kiss me."

He leaned toward her and nuzzled his nose over her neck. "You smell so good. Better than I remembered." The more he spoke, the more slurred his words became.

"Kiss me, Hunter. Please."

He paused only a moment before straightening and crushing his lips against hers. His tongue slid into her mouth, already heating, already slick and flavored with passion. He tasted like urgency. They'd been apart so long—days that seemed to have stretched beyond eternity.

Her hands tore at the button on his pants, and in seconds, he was naked. All the while, he rained little kisses over her entire face. Desire rushed through her blood. "No more waiting," she said breathlessly.

"No more waiting," he agreed. Something dark blanketed his expression, his eyes suddenly going red again. "I'm not going to hurt you," he said, his voice rough, filled with determination.

"I know."

"Good." He tumbled her to the ground. His lips clamped

around her hard, aching nipple, and his hand trailed down her stomach, raising gooseflesh. He stopped at the apex of her thighs, dabbling at the fine tuft of dark hair.

"Yes, good," she moaned.

She kneaded her hands down his strong torso, reveling in the hard muscles hidden under male skin. Power radiated from him. *My lover,* she thought dazedly. *My man. Mine, all mine.* The passion, the desire, the pleasure he gave her surpassed her wildest imaginings. And he hadn't even entered her yet.

He began sucking her nipple, his teeth surprisingly sharp, wringing another gasp from her. He licked away the delicious sting. "I'm not going to hurt you, I'm not going to hurt you, I'm not going to hurt you," he chanted.

"You can't. As long as you're with me, you can't."

"How did I push you away all these years?" His voice was strained, laden with carnal intent, heavy with arousal.

She arched into his fingers, silently begging him to move them inside her. No, wait. She stilled. Before she forgot everything but his touch, she wanted to fulfill the fantasy that had been floating through her mind for years. "I want to take you in my mouth."

Like a sea siren of long ago, she rose over him, her hair falling like a dark curtain. She walked her fingers down the muscled ridge of his chest. Scars slashed left and right over his ribs, jagged badges of past pain. This was not the body of a bar owner. This was the body of a warrior.

He sucked in a breath when she licked each of his nipples. He moaned when she cupped his testicles.

"You aren't just a bar owner," she said, voicing her thoughts and blowing a hot puff of air on his abdomen. His muscles quivered. "You're much more."

"Yes, but I don't want to talk about it. Move a little lower, sweetheart, and help me forget." He growled, and hearing that desire-rough growl made her shiver.

"Besides running the bar, what is it you do?" she persisted. She wanted to know him. She didn't want to simply be his lover, she wanted to be his confidante. His . . . everything.

A muscle ticked in his jaw. "Hunt vampires, demons, and other creatures of the night. That's how I got my name."

She circled his navel with her tongue. His hips shot toward the sky.

"Have you destroyed very many?" she asked.

"Many." An aroused breath shuddered past his lips, and his eyes closed. "Then I met you and decided to settle here and now I think it'd be a really good idea if you moved a little lower. I don't want to talk about the past anymore."

Shock brought her to an instant halt. "You settled here because of me?"

"Yes."

Surprised, happy, she sucked the entire length of his penis into her mouth. He was so big, her mouth stretched wide.

He began to babble. "I was afraid another gnome would try and hurt you, couldn't let that happen, had to stay near you, damn you feel so good, I need to get inside you. Oh, that feels good. Your mouth. Heaven."

"I love you," she said, never ceasing her up and down strokes.

His hips shot up, and he growled low in his throat. Hoarse. Animalistic. She worked him, savoring every sensation, every taste.

"Holy hell, I can't stop," he managed to gasp.

She sucked him dry.

When he lay limp, collapsed against the dried leaves and twigs, she crawled over him. Feminine power filled her, and she grinned slowly, wickedly. "I've wanted to do that for a long time."

"Not nearly as much as I wanted you to do it." Twin circles of pink painted his cheeks. "I didn't mean to go off so quickly. That just felt so good, and it's been so long, and it made me forget—" He cut himself off and pressed his lips in a thin line.

"How long has it been?" The question sprung from her before she could stop it. She didn't want to hear about his other women. Wanted him only to think of her. Her body, her mind. Her heart.

"About a year," he admitted sheepishly.

He pushed her to her back with quite a bit of force, and she smashed into the ground with a gasp.

Instantly he frowned. "I'm sorry, baby. I didn't mean to push so hard."

"Don't be sorry. I'm not hurt." Smiling seductively, she stretched her arms toward him. "I like it when you're rough."

His expression softened, and his gaze raked over her. Desire blazed all the hotter in the blue depths of his eyes. No longer red, she realized happily. Why did they turn red? Was he a demon now? If so, she didn't care. He bent between her legs, his warm breath fanning the very heart of her. Her mind blanked. Already she trembled for the first stroke of his tongue, for the ache she'd always dreamed about, for the completion she'd always wanted. Needed.

He tasted her. His tongue circled her clitoris, an erotic dance that spun her through madness, through heaven. "Hunter," she cried, arching against him.

"That's it, baby." His voice was strained. "Go all the way over the edge."

Her legs wrapped around his neck, locking him in place. The pressure . . . the building . . . an unstoppable crescendo. When he brought his fingers into play, sinking them deep inside her, she realized the pleasure had only just begun.

"I won't hurt you, I won't hurt you, I won't hurt you." His voice vibrated through her. "You taste so good."

She continued to arch, writhing, screaming her pleasure to the twinkling stars. Her magic acted as a live wire, shooting fireworks in her blood. Then, everything crested. High, so high. Her inner walls spasmed; heat exploded inside her. So much sensation, more than she could bear, yet not enough and somehow everything.

She must have squeezed her eyelids tightly shut because Hunter was suddenly hovering over her. His eyes were red again, and sweat trickled down his temples. Lines of tension bracketed that sweet mouth of his, as if he'd endured all he could and needed satisfaction.

"I'm going to enter you now, but I won't hurt you. I'm going to fill you with me, but I won't hurt you."

"Yes. Please, yes!"

"I won't hurt you." Slowly he slid inside her, his cock stretching her, filling her as he'd promised. He moaned. She gasped. Tension tightened his features. "You're so tight. I didn't expect you to be this tight."

"More. I need more. Do it, take me the rest of the way."

He required no further encouragement. He pushed the rest of the way home. Her legs tightened around him. Squeezed his waist. Her virginity tore. Destroyed perfectly. Wonderfully.

"Virgin," he said, shocked. His eyes closed. Pleasure blanketed his expression. "Never felt this . . . good. This right. I can smell the blood. So good." He licked his lips as if he'd never experienced anything so delicious and wanted to savor the sensation. "So good."

"Only you would . . . do. Harder," she rasped.

"No, savor," he intoned. "I won't hurt you. Won't . . . hurt . . . you."

Her hands gripped his butt at the same moment she rocked her hips upward, "Savor," she allowed, barely able to get the word out. She wanted him inside her forever.

His teeth bit into his bottom lip. "No, harder."

"Yes, yes. Harder."

He slammed inside, pulled back, and pounded home.

"Yes!" she shouted, loving the feel of his in-and-out penetration.

"Not. Hurt. Not. Hurt." He moved so quickly his balls slapped her. She threaded her fingers in his hair and jerked his face to her. Her tongue thrust into his mouth. Taking. Giving. Pushing her even closer to the edge.

"You can't hurt me, I swear."

He reached between their bodies, rubbed his thumb over her clitoris, and that was it. The end. She erupted. Spasmed. Arched. Screamed. Her ecstasy vibrated into his body, propelling him to the end, as well.

"Genevieve," he howled. His features tightened further and he pounded inside her a final time.

Minutes passed, perhaps hours, before their breathing settled. His eyes were so red they lit up the entire forest, and he was staring at her neck. He licked his lips. She didn't move. Couldn't, for that matter. Satisfaction thrummed and swirled inside her, the madness gone, delicious lethargy in its place. "I love you," she said.

Hunter suddenly jerked from her as if she were poison. "I have to leave, Genevieve. I'm sorry." His expression was tortured. "I'm beginning to lose control. Barnabas was right. When the hunger hit . . ." He spun away from her.

"What—what are you talking about?"

"Good-bye. I'll never forget you." He jolted into a lightning-fast run, never once looking back.

Seven

If not for her witchy powers, Genevieve never would have caught him. He moved unbelievably fast. As it was, she uttered a transport spell under her breath. One moment she was lying on the forest floor, the next she was standing in front of Hunter.

He snarled in his throat and ground to a halt. "Get away from me!"

"Tell me what's going on," she commanded. Moonlight shimmered between them, painting the forest in a magical golden hue. "Are you part demon?"

Hunter shoved a hand through his hair and turned away from her—exactly like he'd done in the past. "I lied to you earlier, Genevieve. I *did* die. After the fight with the demons, Barnabas Vlad took my body to an underground cave. He—he turned me into a vampire." His voice was laced with pain and sounded . . . tortured.

Ah. Now she understood the red eyes. She owed Barnabas a smorgasbord of human delights dinner, no doubt about it. "This is a good thing, Hunter. We can be together now."

Gaze rounding, he whirled on her. "I'm a monster. I want to drink your blood."

"Well, I'm a witch and you accepted me for who I am."

"Stop. Just stop. It's not the same. I could kill you, but your powers can't harm me."

"Yes, they can." Determined, she raised her arms in the air and summoned forth a small beam of light. Not enough to burn him, just enough to prove her point. Golden rays began to ribbon from her fingertips.

He raised his hands to shield his eyes. "Fine. Your powers can destroy me. You, at least, can control them."

She dropped her arms to her sides and the light dimmed completely.

"Even now I'm close to jumping on you and sinking my teeth into your neck, Genevieve. I'm thirsty, and I can smell the sweetness of your blood. I'm vile and disgusting and *terrible*."

"Hunter," she said, exasperated. She threw her arms in the air. Men—correction, vampires—could be so foolish. "If you want to drink from me, I don't mind." She flicked back her hair, revealing the sensuous line of her neck. "I promise."

"Argh." He spun away quickly, his body stiff, his hands clenched. "Don't do that again."

"Or what?"

"You don't know vampires like I do. Once they get a drop of blood in their mouth, they can't stop. I could take too much. I could kill you."

"You won't hurt me," she said in utter confidence. "You said so yourself, a thousand times. Bite me. Do it. Blood, blood, blood. I'll keep saying it until you get over here and bite me. Blood, blood, bl—"

Hunter pivoted on his heel and closed the distance between them. He captured her face with his hands, his eyes fierce, but he didn't bite her. He bared his teeth, sharp and white, but still he didn't bite her. "Shut. Up. I would rather live eternity without you than to know I drained you."

She saw the depth of his concern for her, and desperation churned inside her. If she didn't show him the error of his thoughts, he was going to leave her. Forever. "If you walk away from me, you're going to hurt me."

A pause.

A heavy, sickening pause.

"Genevieve." His fingers traced her mouth, then dipped to her neck. He fingered the pulse hammering there. "I won't allow myself to become a killer."

She wrapped her arms around his waist, locking him in place. "I barely survived our first parting. How am I going to live without you?" The idea alone filled her eyes with tears. After all the years she and Hunter had been apart, they deserved a happy-ever-after.

"You'll live. That's all that matters." He spanned his hands around her waist, holding her with such fervency she had trouble drawing in a breath, but she didn't care. What was breath without Hunter's scent? What was life without her reason for living?

"Bite me," she commanded him. As she spoke, she arched her head to the side. She *had* to prove to him that he wouldn't kill her. "Blood, blood, blood, bloo—"

With a pained growl, he swooped down as if he'd reached the edge of his tolerance and sank his sharp teeth into her vein. There was a stinging prick, and she gasped. A minute passed, then another, but he didn't stop. The sensations began to feel good, so good. He drank and drank and drank, and her mind began to grow foggy. Her limbs became weak. Black wisps twined around her thoughts.

"Hunter," she gasped. "I'm . . ."

He jerked from her as if she'd screamed. She slumped to the ground. Panting, he stood over her body. Blood dripped from his mouth and guilt filled his eyes. "I'm sorry. Sweet heaven, I'm sorry."

"I'm fine, I'm fine." She was panting. "I swear. You stopped in time."

"No. Too close. In the morning, I'm going to walk into the sun," he said, his voice so ragged with determination it emerged as nothing more than a feral snarl. "There's no other way. I'll keep coming for you otherwise, I know I will."

In the next instant, he was gone.

"Hunter. Hunter!" Weak, she lumbered to her feet. She screeched a transport spell, but it didn't work. Her magic had weakened with her body.

Genevieve scanned the forest. Where was he? Where had he gone? *I'm going to walk into the sun*, he'd said. "I'm okay. I survived. You didn't hurt me, only weakened me a bit." Not allowing herself to panic—yet—she stumbled through the trees. "Hunter, please!"

Branches swayed on a gentle cascade of wind. Birds scattered, soaring into the night sky, their wings striped with every color of the rainbow. If morning came before she found him . . .

"Hunter! Hunter!" She twirled as she shouted, still searching. Minutes passed. Horrendous, agonizing minutes.

He never reappeared.

Hunter made it to the caves in seconds. He'd moved so quickly that the world around him became a blur, that the five miles seemed like less than one.

Barnabas was still there, still sitting on the dais. The cave walls were rocky and bare. Bleak. Like his emotions. Hunter didn't know why he'd come here. Here, of all places. With *this* man. He simply hadn't known where else to go. He'd bitten Genevieve and had almost drained her. If she hadn't uttered his name . . . Shame coursed through him.

"Couldn't stay away, I see," Barnabas said smugly.

Dejected, Hunter wiped the sweet, magical blood from his mouth. "I'm walking into the sun, vampire. I'm too wretched to live."

"I told you the hunger would hit you, and you wouldn't be able to control it." Barnabas used his too sharp teeth to tug off one of his black gloves. "You should have listened to me, *oui?*" He *tsked*. "Now. Would you like to play a game of strip poker? I brought cards."

"No cards." Hunter could still smell Genevieve on him, could still taste her mystical-flavored blood in his mouth.

His hands clenched at his sides, and he found himself stepping toward the entrance, ready to go to her again. "Damn it." He froze. "Morning can't get here fast enough."

Barnabas sighed, and the sound dripped with dejection. "I'm going to lose you one way or the other, aren't I? Through death or through your woman, and I think I would rather it be your woman."

Hunter's eyes narrowed. "What are you talking about?"

"Sit down, and I will tell you a secret. . . ."

At last giving way to her panic, Genevieve raced into the thankfully empty cemetery and gathered her clothes. Her neck ached; she didn't care. Her fingers shaky, she tugged on the pants, the shirt. All of the gravesites were in complete disarray, dirt crumbled, headstones overturned. Where was Hunter? She had to find him before it was too late. Her fear intensified, joining ranks with her panic. Her gaze scanned the area until she found her broom. She hopped on it and commanded it to fly.

It didn't work. Fine.

Holding on to it, she ran, just ran. By the time she reached the center of town, her lungs burned and her heart raced uncontrollably. People were in their yards and on the streets, cleaning up damage the demons had caused. No one paid her any heed.

She spotted John Foster hiding behind a tree in his front yard, watching the lusciously ripe Candy Cox rake her garden. "Have any of you seen Hunter Knight?" Genevieve called.

John squealed in horror and sprinted away.

"No, sorry," Candy replied with a frown. "Hunter's dead, sugar. I doubt I'll be seeing him for a while."

Panting, Genevieve ran to Knight Caps. She searched every room, every hidden corridor, but the place was empty. Nothing had been cleaned; everything was the same as on the night Hunter died. Overturned tables, liquor spilled on the floor. Pools of dried blood.

She sprinted back outside and down the long, winding streets. Finally she reached the white picket fence surrounding her home. She pounded up the porch steps and shoved past the screen door, tossing her broom aside. "Godiva! Glory!" She was so short of breath she had trouble getting the words out.

A few seconds later, Glory stumbled out of her room. She rubbed the sleep from her eyes. The buttercup yellow flannel pj's she wore hung over her curves like a sack. "What's going on?" She yawned. "Are you okay?"

"Have you seen Hunter?"

"No. I thought he was with you. What's with his red eyes, anyway? Is he a demon?"

She didn't bother with an answer. "Where's Godiva?"

"In her room. With Romeo."

"Who?"

"Romeo. Her wolf." Glory stretched her arms over her head and gave another yawn. "I think they're having sex. Again."

"Stop playing around and tell me where Godiva is. Please. I don't have much time."

"I told you. In bed. Nice hickey, by the way." Glory paused, her gaze skidding to the kitchen. "Oh, look. Doughnuts." She breezed past Genevieve and headed into the kitchen, where a box of Krispy Kremes waited on the table.

"Godiva!" Genevieve shouted. "Get out here right now."

The handle to Godiva's bedroom rattled, then the door pushed open. Out toppled Godiva, tightening her robe around her middle. She wore an expression of concern, yet underneath the concern was utter satisfaction. "Is everything okay?"

"Have you seen Hunter?"

"No, I thought he was with you."

A warrior of a man stepped from the room and approached Godiva from behind. He wrapped his strong arms around her waist. Dark hair tumbled to his shoulders, framing a face of such golden-eyed beauty Genevieve found it difficult to believe he was real. Her mouth fell open as realization struck her. *This* was the injured wolf?

"What's going on, Evie? Is everything okay?" Godiva repeated. "Your neck is bleeding."

"Hunter is a vampire, and he plans to die with the morning sun. I have to find him. Can you transport me to him?" She covered her face with her hand, fighting tears. "I can't let him kill himself."

"You know we can't transport other people. I can transport myself, though, and—"

"You are not transporting yourself in front of a vampire, Godiva," Romeo said, his voice deep, gravelly. "We will search together. I can track humans—even dead ones—in ways you cannot."

Grateful, Genevieve nodded. She would have ridden on the broom with Godiva, but Godiva couldn't find hers. "I must have left it in the graveyard," her sister said. Genevieve still didn't have the strength to fire hers up, and Glory couldn't hold both of them. They walked.

They kept pace beside Romeo, who took wolf form. They ended up searching all night, stopping only to drink. No one had seen Hunter, and only a few people seemed surprised that they were asking about a dead guy.

Finally, only thirty minutes till sunrise, Romeo caught a trace of him. "This way."

"Hurry. Hurry." She wanted to scream in relief, in frustration, in agony. But when Romeo led them back to her house, she did scream. "Damn it! Why did you bring us here? He's—" She gasped as her gaze snagged on the man standing on her porch.

"Genevieve," he said starkly.

"Hunter? Hunter!" With a cry, she raced to him.

Eight

Hunter opened his arms and welcomed Genevieve as she threw herself at him. He twirled her around, reveling in her luscious female scent, the soft curves of her body.

"Where have you been?" she demanded. "You stupid, stupid man. I've been so worried about you. You didn't hurt me out there, okay? You didn't hurt me. You stopped in time."

"I *could* have hurt you, and that was enough reason to die." He pulled back and cupped her face in his hands. Would he ever get enough of this woman?

Tears streamed down her face. "Why are you here, then? Why?"

"I talked to Barnabas. His creator hated and feared blood like me, so he took something called a blood-appetite suppressant. I didn't think it'd work, but I took it and my cravings went away. I won't hurt you now. I know it sounds too good to be true," he rushed on, "but it's true. Trust me not to hurt you. Please. I want to be with you."

"Why do you want to be with me?" she interjected. In that moment, her relief and joy overflowed, but she needed to hear the words.

His expression became tender. "I kept picturing your face and I began to realize that even in death, you would haunt me. I began to realize that leaving you would be more vile than drinking from you. I began to realize that I couldn't leave you again. You're my reason for being. You're my everything."

She blinked through her tears, barely daring to breathe.

"Will you have me, Genevieve Tawdry? Vampire that I am?"

"With all of my heart." Laughing, she kissed him over and over again. Loving kisses, happy kisses. Relieved kisses.

Hunter hugged her fiercely. That laugh of hers . . . glorious, uninhibited, he would never get enough of it. "I want you. I want you naked."

"Uh, Genevieve," came a female voice.

Genevieve's cheeks reddened, and she pressed her lips together. She'd forgotten about their audience, he realized with satisfaction, just as he had.

"Hunter, you know my sisters."

He nodded in their direction, but his eyes were only for Genevieve. "Godiva. Glory. Nice to see you again." His fingers played with the silky soft hair at the base of Genevieve's neck. He couldn't stop touching her. He still didn't like the fact that he was a vampire. He still didn't like that he had to drink blood, even though the cravings could be controlled. But he would put up with anything to be with his Genevieve.

"You, too," they said simultaneously.

"The man with Godiva is Romeo," she said breathlessly. Her eyes closed and a look of rapture blanketed her expression. "You can meet him later."

Romeo nodded in acknowledgment. He placed a protective arm around Godiva, as if Hunter might leap off the porch and attack at any moment. Hunter tried not to take offense. He had better get used to people fearing him.

"Hunter and I are going to my room," Genevieve said. "To, uh, talk."

"Dirty," Glory added.

He allowed Genevieve to take his hand and lead him

inside, down a hallway and into her room. It was a neat, tidy space with everything color-coded and organized. The bed was made for sin, however. Black silks, crimson pillows. Cerulean velvets. "You want to talk?" he asked with a chuckle.

Her lips lifted in a sensual grin that caused his stomach to clench. She hurriedly secured all of the drapes over the windows so that when the sun rose, it wouldn't hurt him. "We can talk while you're inside me." She raced to him and tugged at his clothes. "I need you so desperately."

He slipped her shirt over her head, then pushed her pants to her ankles. She stepped out of them, completely naked. The sight of her naked beauty almost made him come, right then, right there. Supple curves, ripe nipples, milky skin. The long length of her dark hair provided a mesmerizing contrast.

"I can't wait," he said raggedly.

"No waiting," she agreed.

He took her quickly, with all the urgency he felt inside. Filled as he was with blood and the suppressant, he didn't have the slightest urge to bite her—except in pleasure. They rolled atop the bed, panting, growling, straining. Her breasts filled his hands. Her legs anchored around him as he pounded in and out.

"Hunter," she screamed as a sharp peak tore through her. He felt every spasm and it fueled his own.

He spilled inside her with a loud roar.

Someone banged at the wall. "Enough already," he heard one of her sisters say. Glory, most likely. Godiva was probably otherwise occupied. He chuckled into Genevieve's neck. Nope. He still didn't want to bite her. Relief consumed him.

Playfully she bit his collarbone. "I love you so much."

Her words filled his mind as surely as he'd filled her body. Even his heart stopped beating—or maybe it had never started up again after his death. Women had said those words to him before, but he'd never felt them in his bones. Even Genevieve had said them before. He'd never returned them.

"I love you, too, sweetheart."

She sucked in a slight intake of breath. "Do you really?"

"I've loved you from the first moment I saw you."

"Then why did you push me away for so long?" she asked with a frown. "You never really answered that question."

He placed a sweet kiss on her temple. "Sweetheart, the answer doesn't matter anymore. Let's just—"

"Please. Tell me."

Unable to deny her anything, he explained. As he spoke, she paled. Tremors reverberated through her by the time he finished. "You should have told me the truth years ago," she said. "I would have left you alone."

"I know, and that's exactly why I didn't tell you. I didn't want you to leave me alone. I loved you too damn much."

"What a pair we make, hmm? The dead man and the witch."

He chuckled. Life—or death, rather—was ripe with promise. He was happier than he'd ever been and he owed it all to the sweet, sweet witch in his arms. "I'm looking forward to spending eternity with you."

Slowly she smiled. "Eternity with Hunter Knight. Now that's something I can look forward to."

CANDY COX AND THE BIG BAD (WERE)WOLF

~

P. C. Cast

For S.L.,
with a smile and a wink.
Thanks for the . . . inspiration.

Acknowledgments

I'd like to thank Berkley, and especially my talented editor, Christine Zika, for publishing this author-created anthology. It's wonderful when your publisher believes in you.

Thank you to my agent and friend, Meredith Bernstein, who said, "Absolutely!" when I called her with this idea.

And a big THANKS GIRLFRIENDS to Gena Showalter (my partner in crime in the inception of this anthology), Susan Grant, and MaryJanice Davidson. It was such fun to work on this with the three of you. Let's do it again soon!

One

"Godiva! Wait—wait—wait. Did you just say that you and your sisters called forth the dead two nights ago?" Candice said, rubbing her forehead where it was beginning to ache.

"Yeah, but you missed the important part. Romeo was . . . *spectacular*," Godiva said breathlessly into the phone. "Who knew that poor, wounded wolf would turn into something—I mean, some*one*—so delectable."

"So he actually did more than hump your leg this time?"

"Candy Cox—I swear you haven't been listening."

"You know I hate it when you call me that."

"Fine. *Candice*, you haven't been listening," Godiva said. "He's not just a wolf. He's a *were*wolf, which means he has an excellent tongue and he humps a lot more than my leg."

Candice kept muttering as if Godiva hadn't spoken. "It's not like I don't get enough of that name crap at school. Why I ever decided to attempt to teach high school morons I'll never know." She cringed inwardly, remembering the countless times some hormone-impaired sixteen-year-old boy had made a wiseass remark (usually replete with sophomoric clichés) about her name. God, she was truly sick and tired of Mysteria High School—Home of the Fighting Fairies.

"You could have kept one of your ex-husbands' names," Godiva said helpfully.

"Oh, please," Candice scoffed. "I'd rather sound like a porn star than keep any reminders of ex-husband numbers one through five. No. My solution is to change careers. As soon as I finish my online master's in creative writing I can dump the fucking Fighting Fairies and snag that job in Denver as assistant editor for Full Moon Press."

"Honey, have I told you lately that you have a very nasty mouth for a schoolteacher?"

"Yes. And I do believe I've told you that I *have* said nasty mouth *because* I'm a schoolteacher. Uh, please. Shall we take a moment to recall the one and only day you subbed for me?"

Godiva shuddered. "Ack! Do not remind me. I take back any form of criticism for your coarse language. Those teenagers are worse than a whole assortment of wraiths, demons, and undead. I mean, really, some of them even smell worse!" Just remembering had her making an automatic retching sound. "But Candice, seriously, I don't want you to move!"

"Denver's not that far away—we shop till we drop there several times a year. You know I need a change. The teenage monsters are wearing on me."

"I know," Godiva sighed. Then she brightened. "Hey! I could work on a spell that might help shut those boys up whenever they try to speak your name. Maybe something to do with testicles and tiny brains . . ."

"That's really sweet of you, but you know that magic doesn't work on or around me, so it probably wouldn't work on my name, either." Candice sighed. It was true. As a descendant of one of the few nonmagical founders of the town (his name was, appropriately, John Smith), Candice had No Magic at All. Yes, sadly, she lived in a town full of witches, warlocks, vampires, fairies, werewolves, et cetera, et cetera, and her magic was nonmagic. It figured. Her magic worked like her marriages. Not at all. "Men are such a pain in the ass."

Without losing a beat at her friend's sudden change in subjects, Godiva giggled. "I agree completely, which is why I know exactly what you need—a werewolf lover."

"Godiva Tawdry! I'm too damn old to roll around the woods with a dog."

"A werewolf is not a dog. And forty is not old. Plus, you look ten years younger. Why do you think high school boys still get crushes on you, *Ms. Candy Cox*?"

"Put boobs on a snake and high school boys would chase after it. And don't call me Candy."

Godiva laughed. "True, but that doesn't make you any less attractive. You've got a killer body, Ms. Cox."

"I'm fat."

"You're curvy."

"I'm old."

"You're ripe."

"Godiva! Do you not remember what happened last time I let myself commit matrimony?"

"Clearly," Godiva said. "It took ex-husband number five less than six months to almost bore you to death. And he seemed like such a nice guy."

"Yes, I admit he did seem nice. They all did at first." Candice sighed. "Who knew that he would literally almost kill me? And after my brush with death, I decided that I. Am. Done."

"Okay, look. You accidentally took an unhealthy mixture of Zoloft, Xanax, and pinot grigio. It could happen to anyone, especially when she's being bored to death by a man scratching himself while he incessantly flips from the History Channel to CNN—"

"—And pops Viagra like they're M&Ms and thinks that the telltale oh-so-attractive capillary flush constitutes foreplay," Candice interrupted. "Yeesh. I'm going to just say no from here on out. Truly. I've sworn off men."

"No, I remember exactly what you said. 'Godiva'—here you raised your fist to the sky like Scarlett O'Hara—'I will never marry again.' So you've sworn off marriage, not men. And anyway, a werewolf is not technically a man. Or at least if he is, it's only for part of the time. The rest of the time he is the most adorably cuddly sweet furry—"

"Fine." Candice cut off Godiva's gushing. "I'll think about it."

"Really?"

"Yes." *No,* she thought. She hurried on before Godiva could press the point. "I've really gotta go. I'm deep in the middle of Homework Hell. I have to turn in my poetry collection to the online creative writing professor next week, and I still haven't figured out a theme for the damn thing. I'm totally screwed if I can't get rid of this writer's block."

"Well . . ." Godiva giggled mischievously. "I don't know how it'd work on writer's block, but Romeo sure unclogged me last night."

"You're not helping."

"I'm just saying—a little werewolf action might fix you right up."

"You're still not helping."

"Sorry. I'll let you get back to your writing. Remember, you said you'd think about a werewolf lover."

"Yeah, I'll think about it right after I think about my poetry theme. Uh, shouldn't you and your sisters be frolicking about the graveyard checking on the dead or whatnot?"

"Oh, don't worry about it. Our little screwup actually ended up being a good thing, what with those horrid demons on the prowl; the town could use the extra protection. And anyway, it's only temporary and the dead have already quieted down. Uh, but since you mentioned it . . . are you planning on going jogging today?"

"Yes."

"Do you think you could take a spin through the graveyard and keep your eyes open for my broom? I must have forgotten it in all the excitement that night, between Genevieve scampering off into the woods with Hunter—whose eyes, by the way, were glowing bright red—and my Romeo morphing from wolf to man rather unexpectedly. Anyway, if you see it would you please grab it before somebody flies off with it? You know a good broom is hard to find."

"Yeah, sure. If I see it, I'll get it for you. But wait, isn't Hunter Knight supposed to be dead?" Candice said.

"Well, kinda. Actually, he's a little undead."

"Isn't that like being a little pregnant?"

"Don't be a smart-ass. It's embarrassing enough for me to admit that my sister's getting some vampire action. God, I wish the girl had better taste in men, alive or dead."

Candice sighed. "Hey—don't be such a prude. If I'd chosen one of the undead I might not be unmarried."

"Candice, honey, I love you, but you are a hopeless piece of work. Now be a doll and go find my broom. Bye."

Godiva hung up the phone and sat tapping her chin with one long, slender finger. Candy was getting old before her time. Goddess knew, she really did need a lover. A young lover. A young werewolf lover. A hot, naughty affair would be the perfect thing to keep her from moving to Denver. Her fingers itched to swirl up a little love spell, but magic wouldn't work on her friend. Godiva's eyes widened and her full, pink lips tilted up. Magic wouldn't work on Candy, but it definitely would work on a werewolf. . . .

Two

Candice would never get this damn assignment done.

"You'd think after teaching for almost twenty years I wouldn't have any problem doing homework." She grumbled at herself and ran a frustrated hand through her thick blonde hair. "Poetry themes . . . poetry themes . . . poetry themes . . ." Death, time, love, heartbreak, the soul, happiness, sex . . . "Sex," she muttered, chewing the end of her well-sharpened #2 pencil. "That's one I can't write about. Like I've had sex in—"

She clamped her lips shut, refusing to speak aloud the ridiculous amount of time it had been since the last time she'd been laid. As if the last time even counted. Ex-husband number five had been, in politically correct terms, penis impaired. Spoken plainly, he'd had a pathetically small dick, and an incredibly large wallet. Unfortunately, one did not make up for the other. Candice grimaced. Quite frankly, women who said size didn't count had clearly never been with a man with a small dick. And, as if their, well, lack of substance wasn't bad enough, SDM (small-dicked men) had the same problems short men had. They were mad at the world. Like it *helped* to make up for said unfortunate short-age by being a jerk? Sometimes men just didn't make sense.

"Theme!" she said, forcing her thoughts back to the blank notebook page. She wanted to create poetry that would dazzle her professor, replete with complex symbolism, witty phrasing, and possibly even a few clever slant rhymes. What she had come up with was exactly—she glanced at the naked page—nothing.

She was, indeed, screwed (figuratively speaking).

"Okay, so write something . . . anything . . . write what you know. . . ."

What the hell did she know? She knew she was sick of teaching the Fighting Fairies and she knew she would never get married again. Well, she certainly didn't want to write about high school, which left . . .

"What the hell. At least it'll get me writing."

She drew a deep breath and let her pencil begin moving across the blank page.

Keep your Errol Flynns, Paul Newmans, Mel Gibsons
all puppets—empty masquerades.

She blinked and reread the first two lines. Not Shake-speare, but it did have a certain ring to it. Candice grinned and continued.

Tom, Dick, and Harry, too
the boy next door
I want no more.

Wasn't that the truth! Her pencil, with a mind of its own, kept moving.

You ask, what now?
Well,

And the self-propelled pencil stubbornly stopped. What now? What now? What now? She jumped as the clock in her study chimed seven times. Seven o'clock already? How long had she been on the phone with Godiva? Now she'd have to hurry to get in her five-mile jog, complete with graveyard detour, before the sun set. Crap! She absolutely didn't want to be outside alone after dusk. Weird things had been going on around town lately—and it took some doing for anything to be classified as "weird" by a Mysteria native. Candice put down her pencil and began pulling on her running shoes.

The beat of her shoes against the blacktop road was a seductive lure. The sound beckoned to him. He'd heard it while he was still deep in the woods. It had called him away from the young thing he was still licking. She snarled after him, disgruntled and unsatisfied at his premature departure. He called a hasty apology and promised to meet her and her twin sister later. Right now he had to follow the beat of her running feet, even though it was unlike him to leave such a delicious tidbit. He prided himself on his ability to satisfy. Like a modern Don Juan, his lovers could count on him for romancing as well as consistent orgasming, but the steady slapping sound seemed to somehow have gotten into his body. It pulled him away from his lover with an incredibly powerful singularity in thought.

You (beat) need (beat) her (beat). You (beat) can't (beat) stay (beat) away (beat).

The rhythmic lure thrummed with his pulse . . . his heartbeat . . . it pounded through his loins, making them feel hot and heavy. He scented the warm evening breeze. Woman . . . hot, sweaty, and ripe. And not far ahead of him. He wanted her with a single-minded intensity that he hadn't felt for anything or anyone in years. Growling deep in his throat, he hurried to catch her.

Jeesh, gross. Candice kept glancing nervously from side to side as she sprinted through the graveyard, totally annoyed that she'd promised Godiva she'd look for her broom. Not slowing down, she gritting her teeth and peered into the creepy shadows that flitted past the edge of her vision. Nope. No broom. Also no walking corpses, trolls, goblins, or fairies (whom she disliked with an intensity she knew was unreasonable—they hadn't asked to be made the school mascot and she shouldn't hold it against them, but she did). Nothing untoward at all. Just lots of spooky graves and silence. Thank God. Sometimes it was damn disconcerting to be normal in a town filled with abnormals. She shivered and increased her pace, wanting to leave the graveyard and (hopefully) anything that wasn't 100 percent human behind her.

Lengthening her stride, Candice thought that the burn in her muscles actually felt good. Godiva had been right about one thing—she did have a killer body. Sure, she'd like to lose a few pounds. Who wouldn't? But thanks to her lifelong love of jogging, her legs were long and strong. She also still had excellent boobs. No, they weren't as perky as they had been a few years ago, but they were full and womanly, without boulder-hard, anatomically impossible enhancements. And—best of all—she had seriously big blonde hair that was light enough to hide the encroaching gray without requiring too many touch-ups.

With a burst of speed, she shot out of the graveyard and pounded down the empty blacktop road that would eventually circle around and lead back to her house, which had been built, log-cabin style, at the edge of town. Maybe she could keep up this pace the rest of the way home. Hell, she might even run an extra mile or so!

Which was a lovely thought until the cramp hit her right calf.

"Shit!" She pulled up. Hobbling like Quasimodo she looked around for anything that might resemble sanctuary. Breathing a sigh of relief, she realized that the little rise in the road was the bridge that covered Wolf Creek. She could sit on the bank and rub her calf back into working order. So much for sprinting home.

She had just pulled off her shoe and thick athletic sock when she heard the growl. Low and deep it drifted to her on the breeze, tickling up her spine. It sounded too big to be a dog. It was probably a werewolf. Sometimes the damn things were thick as rabbits in the mountains around Mysteria. Candice rubbed harder at the cramp. She wasn't actually afraid. Werewolves were rarely more than annoying. They tended to come and go in packs—unerringly drawn to the town's preternatural nature, but except for a couple of gainfully employed families (surprisingly, werewolves tended to be excellent restaurateurs—must have something to do with the whole pack mentality and their love of meat or whatever) they usually didn't stick around long, and didn't interact with Mysteria residents, especially while they were in their wolf forms. They certainly didn't pose a danger, unless one was made nervous by big dogs. Candice didn't mind big dogs (as evidenced by her choice in ex-husbands one and two).

"Did you hurt yourself?"

His voice was deep, with a rough, husky sound that was very much man, not wolf. She swiveled around in time to see him step from the edge of the pine trees. And her mouth flopped unattractively open. He was easily six-foot-four and probably 230 pounds. At least. Broad shoulders seemed to stretch on forever, and a wide, scrumptious chest tapered down to a well-defined waist. And those legs . . . even through the relaxed jeans she could see that they were lean and muscular. His face was in shadow, so all of her attention focused on his body and the way he stalked toward her with a strong, feral grace that made her breath catch and her mouth go dry.

Then, as if he'd walked into an invisible tree, he stopped. He hesitated, and seemed almost confused. She could see him run his hand through his hair. He wore it long and loose and it framed his shadowy face as if he was an ancient warrior god that had only partially materialized in the modern world.

"Ms. Cox?"

"Yes!" she said on a burst of breath, totally surprised that the warrior god knew her name.

"It's me, Justin."

He started toward her again, and she blinked up at him as his face emerged from the shadows. And what a face it was! Strong, well-defined cheekbones and a rugged, masculine chin. His sand-colored hair was thick, with a sexy, mussed curl. His eyes . . . his eyes were an unusual shade of amber and were almost as inviting as his beautiful mouth.

"Justin Woods. You know . . ." He hesitated, then flashed an endearingly warm smile that was just the right mixture of mischievous and nervous. ". . . I had you for sophomore English."

She mentally recoiled. What the hell had he just said? An ex-student! So the warrior god was really a fucking Fighting Fairy. Didn't it just figure? Candice frowned, trying to pull her thoughts from the bedroom into the classroom.

"Oh, that's right. Wow. Time sure flies," she said with forced levity, feeling suddenly old and as out of date as an eight-track tape. She looked up at him, shielding her eyes from the setting sun with her hand. Yep. She vaguely recognized the echo of the gawky teenager within the man. "What was that, five years ago?"

"More like ten." He crouched next to her and nodded at her bare leg. "Did you hurt yourself?" he repeated.

"Oh, no. It's nothing. Just a cramp." He was so close to her that she could feel the heat of his body and smell him— young and virile and masculine. Holy shit, he was one wickedly sexy young man!

"I can fix that," he said. "I like to jog and I'm prone to leg cramps, especially when it's hot out like this. I know just what to do to make it go away."

Without waiting for her to respond he took her foot and propped it in his lap. Then he began to massage her cramping calf. His hands were strong and his touch was warm and experienced.

"Lie back. Relax." His voice had dropped to the deep, throaty tone he'd used when he'd first come into the clearing. "Let me take care of you."

She stared at him. She should tell him to take her foot out of his crotch and take his hands off her leg. But his touch was doing the most amazing things to her body. His fingers were sending little ripples of shock from her calf up the inside of her thigh and directly to her crotch, filling her with an unexpected rush of heat and wetness.

"Don't fight it. There's no reason to. It's just me," he said. His breath had deepened and his eyes kept traveling from her mouth to her breasts. She glanced down at herself and saw that her aroused nipples were clearly visible through her damp T-shirt and sheer white sports bra.

What would it hurt? It had been years since a beautiful young man had rubbed anything on her body. Years . . .

The thought of realistically just how many years it had been since a man this young had touched her had Candice sitting straight up and pulling her tingling leg from his warm hands. She flexed her foot and refused to meet his eyes as she pulled on her sock.

"Thanks!" she said with considerably more perkiness than she felt. "That's fine. Good as new."

"Well, at least now I know how you stay in such great shape."

"Yeah, that's me. Miss Great Shape." She cringed. Miss Great Shape? What the hell was she saying?

"I had a huge crush on you in high school," he murmured.

Her eyes widened with surprise and finally lifted to meet his. He had leaned back on his elbow and he was watching her with an intent expression that was anything but boylike.

"I thought you were the sexiest woman I'd ever seen," he said.

Candice was trapped by his frank, masculine appraisal, and the fact that he clearly liked what he saw. Her mouth felt dry and she couldn't seem to find her voice.

"You're still the sexiest woman I've ever seen."

She felt excitement slither low and hot through her belly. Lord, he was delicious! Her gaze slid from his beautiful eyes to his lips. He smiled, confident and handsome and just a little bit teasingly.

Candice blinked. *Reality, girl! Snap the fuck out of it!*

"You shouldn't say things like that," she said in her best

teacher voice, forcing her gaze from his lips and pulling on her shoe.

"Why not?"

"Because you're my ex-student!" she blurted.

He flashed the smile again and scooted forward. Brushing her hands gently aside, he began slowly tying her shoe.

"I'm of age. Well of age. I'm twenty-six."

"Twenty-six!" her voice sounded shrill. "I thought you were twenty-seven." As if one year actually made a difference. He was an infant! Practically a teenager.

"I'll be twenty-seven if you want me to be," he added huskily.

"Uh, no. A year really doesn't make that much difference." Thank God, he was done tying her shoe. Candice started to stand, only to feel his strong hands under her elbows as he helped her to her feet.

"I agree with you. A few years don't make much difference."

He kept his hands on her arms, holding her close to him. He smelled so damned good. She could feel his thumbs rubbing slow, soft circles above her elbows. That simple caress spread electric sensation from her arms all the way down to her crotch. He was wearing a plain gray T-shirt, worn thin and soft by many washings. The outline of his chest was clearly visible beneath it. He was strong and firm and deliciously big. She wanted to lean into him and lick him through the damn shirt. And then bite him. Yeah, she'd like to nibble her way down his body.

What the fuck am I thinking? She stumbled back out of the seductive cocoon of his arms.

"Our age difference is more than a few years, Justin." She tried for her teacher voice again. Unfortunately she sounded more like a breathless Marilyn Monroe.

He shrugged broad shoulders and grinned at her. "You're really cute about that."

"About what?" Her mind didn't seem to be processing correctly, and she inanely added, "And I'm not cute."

"About our age difference. And you are cute about this

272 • P. C. Cast

one thing. Other than that you're sexy and beautiful." He brushed a strand of thick blonde hair that had escaped from her ponytail out of her face. "May I walk you home?"

Candice batted at his hand. "No, you may not."

"Why not? And don't say it's because I'm too young. My age should work for me when it comes to walking." He grinned and added, "Or jogging. I don't imagine many older men can keep up with you."

"Actually, they can't," she said. Despite herself she was thoroughly enjoying their flirty banter.

"Just as I thought! So there's no reason why I can't walk you home."

"Yes, there is. I've sworn off men," she said firmly.

He threw his head back and laughed, a sound that was as seductively masculine as it was youthfully exuberant.

"That's perfect, because I'm not a man."

"Exactly the problem," she countered, finding that she was unable to keep herself from smiling in response. "You're a boy, and I don't go out walking with boys."

His amber eyes darkened. With a quick movement that was feral in its grace he closed the space that had grown between them. He took her hand in his and, without his eyes leaving hers, he turned it over, palm up, and kissed her at the pulse point on her wrist. His lips were so close to her skin when he spoke that they brushed her arm, making her shiver with the warmth of his breath. "I'm no boy." Then, eyes shining, he nipped her gently. "But I am a werewolf. So you can go out walking with me—or anything else you might like to do—and still be sworn off men."

Three

✳

What harm could letting him walk her home cause? It wasn't like he was a stranger, and he was right. He wasn't a teenager anymore. Really. He was twenty-six. And a half.

Plus, she was having fun. Justin was making her laugh with stories about botched meat deliveries at his family's restaurant, Red Riding Hood's Steak and Ale House, which bragged it was "the best darn steak place this side of Denver." She hadn't remembered him as being this charming or witty in high school. Little wonder—the only thing more self-absorbed and boorish than teenage boys were teenage girls.

Laughing, she made squeamish noises as he finished the story about the fist-sized hunk of fur that had been found in a package of ground buffalo meat, and how his dad hadn't figured out that it was really buffalo fur and not wolf fur until after he'd sheared the pelts off of each of his brothers.

"Thankfully, I was out of town on one of my many buying trips for the restaurant." He rubbed a hand through his thick hair. "I know it grows back, but still . . ."

"So, that's what you do? You work at your family's restaurant?"

"Yeah."

"Do you like it?"

"I guess."

She studied his handsome face, wondering at the sudden change in his attitude. And then an old memory surfaced. "Wait! Aren't you an artist? Don't I remember you winning the PTA Reflections Contest at the state level your sophomore year?"

He moved his shoulder and looked uncomfortable. "That was a long time ago. I don't do much art anymore."

"Why not? I remember that you were very talented."

"Just lost interest. It started to feel like just another chore—like washing dishes at the restaurant. Whatever." Then he seemed to mentally shake himself and his expression brightened. "Enough about that. I want to hear about you. So you're still teaching?"

"Not for much longer, I hope," she said.

He laughed. "How are you going to escape from the Fighting Fairies?"

"Ironically, through education. I'm working on my MFA. As soon as I finish it, I'm off to Denver to snag a job as an editor."

"Well, it'll be the Fairies' loss."

"Right now it doesn't feel like the Fairies need to worry. I'm in the middle of a poetry class that's trying to kill me; sometimes I don't think I'll ever get through it."

"Really?" He rubbed his chin, amber eyes shining. "Let's see if I remember. . . ." He cleared his throat and gave a quick, nervous laugh.

She raised her brows questioningly. What was he up to? Then he began a recitation. At first he spoke the lines hesitantly, but as he continued his confidence grew.

"If it be sin to love, and hold one heart,
Far 'mongst the stars above, supreme, apart,
If it be sin to deeply cherish one,
And hold her rich and rare as beams the sun
Across the morning skies,

Then have I sinned, but sinning gained
A glimpse of Paradise."

His voice was rich and deep and his eyes lingered on hers, causing the poet's words to seem his own. And he effectively rendered her speechless for what seemed like the zillionth time in just the short while they'd been together.

"Did I get it right?"

"Yes!" The word burst out of her stunned mouth. *Get a grip on yourself and say something intelligent before he starts thinking he's talking to a prematurely aged teenager.* "Yes, you did," she said in a more grown-up voice. "That's 'If It Be Sin' by DeMass, isn't it? Are you a poetry fan?"

Laughing, he took her hand and planted a quick, playful kiss on it.

"What I am is a man with a pretty good memory who had one hell of a hard sophomore English teacher who terrified him and pounded poetry into his head so thoroughly that more than a decade later it's still stuck there."

"Oh, God. I did that to you?"

"Yes, Ms. Cox, you certainly did."

Unexpectedly, Candice blushed. "What grade did I give you?"

"A 'C,' and I was grateful for it. And I do believe you might have also given me an ulcer as well as several painful hard-ons that semester, too." He laughed. Then, before she could sputter a reply about the C, the ulcer or (embarrassingly) the hard-ons, he glanced around them. "Isn't this your place?"

Surprised, Candice realized that they were standing in her driveway. "Yes, it is." She smiled at him and had to press her palms against her legs to stop her hands from fidgeting. "Thanks for walking me home."

"Entirely my pleasure." He studied her for a moment, and his charming smile faltered as his expression grew more serious. "I'd—I'd like to see you again," he said quickly, then held up his hand to cut her off when she automatically opened her mouth to tell him no. "Wait. Before you shoot me down I'd like you to answer one question for me. Did you enjoy talking to me?"

"Yes." The answer came easily.

"Because I'm an ex-student or because you think I'm a man who is interesting and maybe slightly charming?"

"That's two questions," she said.

"Nope—it's the same question, just with two parts. Kinda like some of those hellish essay questions you used to torture us with."

She smiled begrudgingly at him, and decided to tell him the truth. "Because I find you interesting."

"And maybe a little charming?"

"Maybe . . ."

"Then why not agree to see me again?"

"Justin, I'm forty."

He waited, looking at her as if there had to be more to it than that.

She sighed. "Justin," she tried again, "I'm forty years old and you're—"

"Yes, I know. I got a C in English, but I did better in math. You're fourteen years older than I am. You're also smart and funny and easy to talk to and very, very sexy. Seriously, Candice. Try finding all those qualities in girls half your age. It's next to impossible." When she looked like she wanted to argue with him, he took her hand and said, "Okay, if our age difference bothers you that much, how about let's not call it a real date? Let's call it . . . an exercise appointment."

"An exercise appointment?"

"You jog every day, don't you?"

"Almost."

"Will you be jogging tomorrow?"

"Probably."

"Then how about we make an appointment to jog together tomorrow?"

"Okay," she heard herself say. "I'll jog by Wolf Creek at about sevenish."

"You're awesome! See you tomorrow." He shot her a

blazing smile, kicked into a youthful, athletic jog, and disappeared into the fading light of dusk around the curve in the road.

Awesome? She cringed. *Like, wow. I am, like, totally awesome.*

Laughing softly at her own silliness, she skipped lightly up the stairs into her house. Refusing to berate herself for being a horny middle-aged letch, Candice poured herself a cold glass of water. She had the whole day tomorrow to consider if she really was going to show up for their "appointment" or not. She wouldn't think about it now. And anyway, her eye caught sight of the notebook and pencil sitting on her desk where she'd left them. She had homework to do.

Candice grinned.

She also had lines of poetry unexpectedly popping into her mind. Godiva had been partially right. Being in the presence of a werewolf had certainly unblocked her—even if an evening of conversation hadn't been exactly what her witchy friend had been recommending. Eagerly, she sat down and put pencil to the unfinished page, taking up easily where she'd left off.

You ask, what now?
Well, love comes with the night,
in the most inexplicable places
leaving the most unexplainable traces.

Candice giggled, and kept writing.

You see . . . a wolfman is the man for me!

Hmm . . . maybe she would meet Justin tomorrow.

Four

He thought about her a lot more than he'd intended to. He was supposed to show up at a keg party in the forest—rumor had it that several of the not-so-innocent high school seniors from the cheerleading squad were curious about just how well werewolves could use their tongues . . . not an invitation he had declined in the past. But tonight it felt, well, *wrong* to be rolling around the forest with girls Candice had probably taught in English class—and not a decade or so ago.

Actually, if he was being really honest with himself, his life had begun to wear on him. Or, more accurately, to bore him. He hated the restaurant. His older brothers were already firmly ensconced in management positions—hence the fact that he had been relegated to making purchasing runs for them. Not that anyone expected more of him. He'd always been "that Justin—so incorrigible and handsome!" He'd never been taken seriously. But, then again, it hadn't really mattered to him. He'd always been into having fun . . . feeling good.

When had that started to change?

He wasn't really sure. But he knew he hadn't been giving Candice a slick line tonight when he'd told her that she was smart and funny and sexy. Very, very sexy. And that he hadn't found that combination of qualities in twenty-something girls. She challenged him. She made him think. And she turned him on. He'd had no idea what a lethal mixture those things were before he spent an evening in Ms. Cox's stimulating company. He wanted to see her again. Badly. More than that, he wanted her to want him. If a woman like that could want him . . . what couldn't a man accomplish if he won the love of a woman like that?

So tonight, instead of joining the orgy in the woods he was much more interested in searching the back of his closet for an old textbook from a freshman lit class he'd taken before dropping out of the Denver Art Institute. Funny . . . he hadn't thought about his failed attempt at an art major in years. But those eyes of hers. They'd made him remember. They were mossy green—a color that cried to be painted.

Those eyes . . .

Justin grabbed the literature book and then flipped open his laptop. A few simple clicks took him to the website of Mysteria High School—Home of the Fighting Fairies. He smiled triumphantly. Sure enough, there was a complete list of faculty phone numbers.

Candice jumped when her cell phone made the little three-tone sound it did when she had a text message. She wiped her eyes, stuck her reading glasses on top of her head, and reluctantly took her nose out of Tanith Lee's *Silver Metal Lover*.

"Why do you insist on reading and rereading this book? You know what happens, and you know it makes you cry. You," she told herself sternly before blowing her nose, "are a ridiculous romantic. And you're old enough to know better." She sighed. Ridiculous or not, she truly loved the story of a robot finding his soul through loving a woman. Not that it could really happen. Even putting aside the fact that it wasn't possible to make humanlike robots, it was an impossible dream that a man could really become . . . well . . . *more* simply through the love of an exceptional woman. After all, she was exceptional (wasn't she?) and she had the unquestionable proof of ex-husbands one through five being total turds—despite her loving attempts.

Of course, a little voice whispered through her conscience, maybe she hadn't really loved any of them . . . maybe true love *did* have the power to create souls and make miracles.

"Please," she scoffed aloud at herself, "grow the fuck up."

Then, remembering what had interrupted her, Candice reached for her phone. Flipping it open she keyed up the one new text message.

> Looking forward to our "appointment" tomorrow @ 7:00. J
> P.S. you have beautiful eyes

She felt a rush of sweet excitement—a heady, intoxicating feeling she hadn't experienced in years. No matter how *ridiculous,* she had a date with a twenty-six-and-a-half-year-old man.

It took forever for it to be evening. Candice had chosen, vetoed, and rechosen what she was going to wear. Then she'd cursed herself over and over. Why the hell hadn't she agreed to a normal date? One where she could drive up in her chic Mini and meet him at a nice restaurant somewhere out of town. (Way out of town.) She'd have chosen her sexy little black dress that displayed all of her assets and hid most of her imperfections. Her makeup would have been meticulously applied. And her hair would have been Truly Big and Ready for Flirtatious Flinging About. She could have dazzled him with her experience and good taste in choosing excellent wine, and then ordered from any menu with the confidence and flair that can only be earned through maturity and experience. She, in short, would have had the upper hand.

Instead she was trying to figure out which of her rather old sports bras was the least tattered, and which cotton panties weren't totally grandma-ish. As if there was such a thing as an un-grandma-ish cotton workout panty. Why, oh why hadn't she bought new sports bras at the last Victoria's Secret sale? Oh yeah, she remembered . . . *they don't have real, usable sports bras at Victoria's Secret!*

Oh, God. Would he see her bra and panties? Just the thought made her feel like she wanted to puke her guts up.

No! Of course he wouldn't see her panties! She was meeting him for a quick jog, not a quick fuck.

Regardless, somehow she found herself in the bathroom. Naked. Staring through her fingers into the full-length mirror at her body as if she was watching a horror flick.

Looking at myself totally naked and under fluorescent lights just can't be healthy. But she continued to stare and criticize.

Sure, she wasn't awful looking. Candice forced the shielding fingers from her eyes. Okay. She wasn't really that bad. She'd been thinner and tighter, but her skin was soft and smooth, and she was definitely curvy. Maybe even lush. She shook her head, as if to clear the bizarre notions from it. "Lush" and "curvy" were not "young" and "tight-assed." There was just no way she was going to get naked in front of and have sex with a twenty-six-and-a-half-year-old. No. Fucking. Way.

Maybe he wouldn't be there. He probably wouldn't be there. Why would he want to be there? He could have just been being polite yesterday. He probably was just being nice. She had misinterpreted. He hadn't really flirted and come on to her. It was silly, really. He was so damn young. Sure, she was attractive, but please. She was almost fifteen years older. No way was he *interested* in her. Not like *that*.

"Hey there, beautiful."

She'd told herself that she was ready to see him—or ready for him to stand her up. Either was fine. Really. Whatever. Who cared? But then he was there, calling her beautiful and smiling his sexy, boy/man smile, and she felt the same dizzying rush of excitement she'd felt when he'd sent her the message the night before. And, dear sweet Lord, he was even more handsome than she'd remembered. Had she been blocking? Was it temporary amnesia? How could she not have been obsessing all day over his height and the incredible width of those shoulders, and that amazing jawline. . . .

"Hi," she said breathlessly, glad that she'd agreed to meet him at the creek so that she had an excuse other than just the sight of him to be breathing hard.

"How do you feel about trying something new today?"

His flirty smile made her stomach tighten. Oh, God, if only he knew.

Never mind. It was probably best that he didn't know.

Be normal! Talk to him!

"What do you have in mind?"

His eyes sparkled as he jerked his head, pointing his chin away from the road and into the forest. Then, with a confidant, deep voice he recited, " 'I shall be telling this with a sigh somewhere ages and ages hence: Two roads diverged in a wood, and I—I took the one less traveled by.' "

He was actually quoting poetry to her. Again. Her cheeks felt warmed by more than the short jog through the graveyard. "A little Robert Frost?"

"A very little, I'm afraid. And don't be too impressed. I freely admit to memorizing it this afternoon."

"You know, I don't remember you being this interested in poetry in high school."

"Would it help if I made my voice crack and stared, slack-jawed, at your boobs?"

"Only if your intention is to scare me out of the forest."

His smile was intimate. "That is not my intention."

She almost asked what his intentions were . . . but she didn't want to know. What if he gave her a blank look and said, "I thought we'd be friends"? She'd fucking die. But whether it'd be from relief or disappointment, she wasn't sure. She only realized that she'd been standing there silently staring at him when his smile faded and his tone became more serious.

"Candice, if you don't want to go off into the woods with me, all you have to do is say the word. I'll understand. I just thought that you might like exploring a hiking path I know about. That way we could get our exercise and still be able to talk. I don't know about you, but I've never mastered the talent of jogging and talking at the same time."

She met his eyes. His gaze was open and honest—vulnerable, even. Could he be as nervous as she felt? And then came the startling revelation—he had to be *more* nervous. She was almost fifteen years his senior and his ex-teacher. She was more experienced and more confident. She could reject him with a neatly turned phrase and a patronizing, disdainful look. She definitely had the high ground, even if she wasn't perfectly coiffed and perched on a posh chair at an elegant restaurant. Disregarding the rather ridiculous question of whether or not this was a real date, Justin had put himself in a position where he could be thoroughly humiliated and ultimately rejected by her, yet here he was, with a sweet smile on his handsome face, looking for all the world like a man who was doing his best to woo a woman.

"Do you remember the rest of the quote?" she asked, smiling softly at him.

"The Frost quote? No—I just memorized that far." His cheeks flushed a little with the admission.

"Frost concluded it, 'I took the one less traveled by, and that has made all the difference.' How about we take your path—the one less traveled by?"

Refreshingly, he didn't attempt to hide his relief with a suave turn of phrase or a knowing look. Instead he just smiled and said, "I promise that it will make all the difference."

Justin took her hand and led her into the forest.

Five

"All this time I've been jogging by the creek, and I had no idea a hiking path like this was so close."

"That's one good thing about being a werewolf. I have definitely gotten to know these woods."

He'd spoken nonchalantly, but she could feel his look and the expectant silence that screamed, "I'm waiting for you to freak out because I'm a wolf!" So she didn't respond right away. Instead she picked her way carefully over a large log that had fallen across the trail.

"You're right. Knowing the secret paths in the woods is one good thing about being a werewolf. What's another?" she asked, matching his nonchalant tone.

He hesitated only a moment. "The physical power."

"You mean when you're in your wolf form?"

Justin slowed down and studied her face. "Do you really want to know, or are you just making polite conversation?"

"I'm intrigued," she said honestly.

"There's physical power in both forms, and in both I can tap into the magic in these hills pretty easily. In this form I'm stronger than a human man. And not just physically. My senses are more acute. My memory is better." He grinned a little sheepishly. "I guess that means I should have made better than a C in your class."

"Nah," she said. "You weren't a man then. You probably hadn't attained all of your"—she paused and made a vague, fluttery gesture at him with her hand—"uh, Spidey senses yet."

His infectious laugh rolled around them. "Spidey senses? On a werewolf? Are you thinking I might be a hairy Peter Parker?"

"Oh, God, no!" she said with mock horror. "If I was going to fantasize about walking through the woods with a superhero it wouldn't be one that was really just a dorky kid. Let's try Bruce Wayne, shall we?"

"How about a happy medium? How about walking through the woods with a grown-up superhero who is modestly employed—I don't exactly have Batman's resources." The trail took a sharp upward turn and Justin stopped, pulling her gently back to his side when she started to climb ahead of him. "Want to test my superhuman powers?"

She narrowed her eyes at him. "Does this involve either: one, me being unattractively carried away by any type of a creature who has more than two arms, or two, your having the ability to see through any article of my clothing?"

He rubbed his chin, considering. "No and no."

"Then fine. I agree to the test."

"Okay. You have to hold totally still."

He walked a tight circle around her and Candice instantly noticed the difference in the way he moved. His body language was once again that of the man who had entered the clearing the day before—the warrior god who had not known who she was. He positioned himself behind her, standing so close that she could feel him draw in a deep breath. Then he bent, and whispered huskily into her ear.

"You don't wear real perfume."

She started to turn to answer him, but his words, which were spoken hot against her neck, stopped her.

"You must hold totally still."

She froze, whispering back. "What do you mean by not real perfume?"

"You don't buy that packaged and bottled stuff other women like so much and spray too much of on their bodies. Not you. Instead, you put drops of pure lavender oil behind your ears, on your wrists"—he drew another breath, then exhaled the warmth of his words against her neck—"and between your breasts. Am I right?"

"Yes, you're right."

Slowly, his hand rose to lightly, lightly caress her hair before he gently fisted it and pressed his face into it, taking a deep, hot breath. She focused on not trembling, and thought how glad she was that she'd conveniently "forgotten" to pull it up in a ponytail.

"You never blow-dry your hair. You let the air dry it. And you prefer the night air to the warmer, daylight breeze."

This time she was truly amazed. How the hell could he know that?

"Am I right?" he asked again.

"Yes," she whispered. "How did you know?"

"Your hair smells like moonlight and shadows, and I know those scents intimately." His hands were still in her hair. "Why do you prefer the night air?"

"It's something that started when I was a little girl. In the summer I'd wash my hair at night and then sit on the porch with a flashlight and read. My dad used to laugh and say that the moonlight made my hair wavy like the tide. I guess it's a habit that stuck."

"I'm glad. I like moon wavy hair," he said.

"Do you?"

Justin gently nuzzled the ear he was whispering into. "Yes."

His breath sent chills down her body that lodged in her thighs, making her legs feel wobbly and semidrunk. She was relieved when he took his mouth from her ear and moved back around in front of her. Smiling, he was once more just a handsome young man.

"Impressed by my superpowers?"

"Very."

"Good. You'll love my next display of EWP."

"EWP?"

"Extrawerewolfory perception," he said, with only a slight glint in his eyes. "So. Are you hungry?"

"If I say yes are you going to grow fur and chase down some poor helpless rabbit?"

"Maybe another time. Right now if you said you were hungry I'd simply clap my hands twice and then help you climb up the rise in the path so I could show you that I made your wish come true."

"Okay, I'll bite. I'm hungry."

He waggled his eyebrows and leered at her. "Be careful, Ms. Cox—mine is the species that bites."

Before she could respond with the pithy reply she was formulating, he grabbed her hand and pulled her up the incline. Candice glanced around, surprised that the dense woods had suddenly given way to a lovely meadow of soft grass that was dotted with blue wildflowers. Fireflies flitted in the dim evening light, looking like miniature fairies. (Candice squinted her eyes and made certain that they weren't actually fairies. God, she hated fairies.) And then her surprise doubled. Not far from the path someone had spread a large plaid blanket, on which sat a huge wicker picnic basket and a bucket filled with ice and a bottle of white wine.

"You see what happens when you date a superhero?" he said.

"This isn't a date. It's an appointment," she said automatically.

"Well, I think that depends."

"On what?"

"On the good-night kiss."

Smiling, he led her over to the picnic dinner he had so meticulously chosen, packed, and then brought out into the forest just for her.

Six

The dinner was scrumptious. Candice was amazed by the obvious care he'd taken with everything. From the excellent dry white wine from Venice and the real crystal goblets he served it in, to the decadently tender prime rib sandwiches and fresh fruit—everything was better than perfect. And that included the conversation. She couldn't believe how easy he was to talk to. He was actually smart! A closet history buff, he told her stories about the settlers who had founded the various cities in Colorado—something she knew little about because she'd always focused on European instead of American lit.

And he noticed everything. Not just the details of the meal, but he noticed when the inflection of her voice changed, when she was distracted by the beauty of the blue wildflowers (which he promptly picked for her), and when she talked about her new passion—finishing her master's and moving to Denver. He discussed the aspects of her new future animatedly. Unlike Godiva, he didn't try to talk her into staying or dissuade her from following her dream. Justin honestly seemed to understand her need to move on.

But what surprised Candice most was how easy it was for her to forget he was so young. She wasn't sure when it happened—somewhere between their discussion of the stupidity of the underfunded state education initiatives, and their mutual (and, on her part, rather blasphemous) agreement that the *Lord of the Rings* movies were actually better than the books—but Candice Cox totally stopped thinking of him as ohmygodhe'ssofuckingyoung Justin, and started seeing him as the man she was out on a date with.

"So, how's the poetry assignment coming?" he asked.

"Better, I think. At least I got a little written last night." She sipped her wine. Maybe it was the third glass of wine, or the intimate silence that surrounded them, but it felt easy for her to speak half-formed dreams aloud. "You know what's weird? I'm doing this whole master's thing so I can get a job reading other people's writing, but I think I'm finding out that I actually like doing the writing part myself."

"You want to write a book?"

"I don't know. Maybe. Right now all I know is that I'd like to write something that—" she broke off, suddenly embarrassed.

"That what?" he prompted.

She met his amber gaze. He was so sincere. Rarely had she known a man who listened as well as he did. There was something about the way he looked at her, and spoke to her—as if he thought she was interesting and smart and he honestly cared about what she had to say.

It was more intoxicating than the Venetian wine.

"I'd like to write something that would have the ability to make people feel. It could be a book, or short stories, or maybe even poetry. What it is isn't important. What is important is that what I write evokes feelings in those who read it."

His gaze was hot and intense on hers as Justin leaned toward her, resting his hand on her knee. "I know exactly what you mean. That's how I always felt about my art. I didn't care if I was painting or sculpting or just sketching with plain charcoal. I wanted people to feel what I felt."

"Why did you stop, Justin?" she asked softly.

"I don't really know. . . ." His eyes dropped from hers. "One day I was a college freshman at the Art Institute—the next I'd washed out. I'm pretty sure it had something to do with me changing my major from art to beer and women." His lips twisted in self-mockery. "A double major actually. I made stupid choices—a string of stupid choices—and then I was back in Mysteria working at the restaurant."

She wanted to tell him that it wasn't too late for him to go to college, that he could get a portfolio together and get back into the Art Institute, but she hesitated. Did he really need her to turn into a teacher and lecture him? She didn't think so, and she also didn't want to. She liked being his date and not his mentor. Candice put her hand on top of his.

"Sometimes it's easy to get lost. You let your art get lost when you dropped out of college. I let good sense get lost when I committed serial matrimony. I suppose all either of us can do is to learn from our mistakes."

"I'm glad you're divorced." He smiled and added, "Again."

"Well, I'm with you on that one."

"Do you mind if I ask why none of your marriages worked?"

"I don't mind you asking, but I'm not sure I have an answer for you, even though I should because the ending of each of them felt the same—so you'd think I'd learn how to define the problem, if not fix it." She sighed. "I stopped loving them. Each one. Actually, it's more accurate to say that I stopped liking each of them first, *then* I couldn't love them anymore. They were five different kinds of men, and, as much as I kid around about it, none of them were bad men. I wouldn't have married a bad man. Still, it didn't work out with any of them, which, naturally, points to the one common denominator—me." She glanced up at him. He was watching her intently, and not in that patronizing "I'll just let the woman talk so I can get into her panties" kind of way. His amber eyes were interested—his expression plainly said he was involved in what she was saying. Candice drew a deep breath. "I'll tell you something I've never told anyone. I think I fail at relationships because I don't have any magic."

His brow wrinkled. "But most places aren't like Mysteria. Outside of here lots of people don't have magic and they manage to have happy marriages."

"Nope. I don't think so. I don't think you have to live in totally bizarre Mysteria to have magic. See, I think the ability to have a successful, happy marriage is a special kind of magic, and that special magic exists all over the world. The problem with me is that I'm doomed because I have nonmagic, just like I have nonmarriages and nonrelationships."

"Maybe"—he reached up and cupped the side of her cheek with his hand—"you just need to quit trying so hard."

Then, amazingly, Justin leaned forward and kissed her. It was a gentle kiss, not accompanied by any intrusive thrustings of tongue and teeth. She'd worried about that when she'd allowed herself to think about kissing him. Would a twenty-something be a bully kisser? Would he blindly stick his mouth on hers and proceed to grind any and all available body parts against her? It'd been too damn long since she'd kissed a man this young—she couldn't remember how they did it. But she needn't have worried. The boy/man/wolf kissed like a dream . . . a deliciously erotic dream. His mouth was a warm caress against hers—not a demand, but a seductive question.

"You taste like lavender and wine," he murmured, his lips lingering near hers.

"You taste like sex," she whispered back before her better sense could stop the words. "Erotic and decadent, and very, very male."

He chuckled and his lips moved to her neck. "That's because I'm still using my superpowers on you." His tongue flicked out to tease the gentle slope of smooth flesh where her neck met her shoulder. "But maybe you don't believe me. Maybe you need more proof first."

"If I say I do, does that mean you won't stop?" she said breathlessly.

"I won't stop unless you tell me to."

"Then we may be here all night," she moaned.

He pressed her down into the blanket and slid his hand under her T-shirt. "I'm good with all night."

She let her hands travel up his arms to his chest. God, his body was hard! And more than just between his legs (although it was already decidedly obvious that he didn't suffer from the same unfortunate and very flaccid problem her last ex-husband had). Utterly fascinated, she tugged at his shirt until he took his hands from her long enough to pull it over his head.

Dear sweet Lord—she'd died and, despite her numerous sins and bad language, gone straight to heaven. He looked better unclothed—and that was one hell of a compliment because he had looked scrumptious with his shirt on. He was truly a beautiful man.

Then his hands were tugging up her shirt. She started to help him . . . and remembered: 1) that she was wearing her least stretched out and frayed sports bra—"least" in no way meaning that it was attractive, and 2) she was forty. Suddenly he was, once again, ohmygodhe'ssofuckingyoung Justin.

"Uh, wait. I'm—I'm not completely okay with this," she said quickly, smoothing down her shirt while she avoided meeting his eyes.

Instantly, he stopped. But he didn't pull away from her. Nor did he throw a fit because he had a hard-on and needed to have sex now. He just shifted his weight so that she was resting comfortably in his arms. Then he lifted her chin with his finger, gently making her meet his gaze.

"Did I do something wrong?" he asked.

"No. It's not you."

He cocked an eyebrow at her and smiled crookedly. "Is there someone else here I don't know about?"

"Of course not."

"Then is it that you don't want me?"

"Of course not!"

"Candice, I'm going to be honest with you. For the past several years I haven't been connected to much—not another person or a job or even a place. I've been playing at life and just letting time pass. But with you I feel a connection, and that's something I'm not used to. I want to see where it takes us. If that means going slow physically, I will. But I have to tell you that the truth is I want you more than I've ever wanted any woman in my life."

His amber eyes had darkened to the color of aged Scotch. She could feel the sexual tension in his body. She loved the intensity with which he looked at her, and the way his hands lingered on hers. And she knew if she didn't make love to this beautiful young man that she would regret it forever.

Deliberately, she sat up and, keeping her eyes fixed on his, she pulled off her shirt. Then she reached behind her and undid her sports bra, shrugging it off her shoulders. The late evening air was cool against the heat of her skin, and her nipples puckered. Justin's gaze dropped from her eyes to her naked breasts. He reached forward and took her heavy breasts in his hands, lifting and caressing them.

"God, you're beautiful," he said huskily. "Look at you! You're not some plastic girl who hasn't lived enough to know there are sexier things than fake boobs and lace bras that match their thongs that match the color they paint their toes." He bent and kissed the swell of her breast, then let his tongue tease her already aroused nipple while she moaned and arched into him. "You're an earth goddess, rich and ripe and desirable."

He pressed her back into the blanket again, his lips and tongue teasing her breasts. His mouth moved slowly down her stomach, kissing the waist of her shorts. Before she could begin to get nervous about the fact that her stomach wasn't as flat as it had been ten years before, she heard him murmur, "Your skin is like silk, and you taste like lavender-scented honey."

She probably would have let him pull off her shorts then, but he slid down, until he knelt at her feet. Smiling at her, he took off her running shoes and socks. When he kissed the arch of her foot she had a moment to think about how desperately glad she was that she'd had a pedicure just two days ago, then he moved from her foot to her calf, kneading it much as he had done the day before. Only now he interspersed his caresses with soft kisses as he made his way slowly up her leg.

"Justin . . ." His name was a moan, and all thoughts of statutory rape and moral turpitude permanently flew from her mind.

"Sssh," he breathed against the sensitive spot behind her knee. "Let me worship you like the goddess you are, and allow me to teach you what I've learned since I left your class."

"A little role reversal?" she asked breathlessly, making no move to stop him as his lips grazed her inner thigh.

"Absolutely, Ms. Cox. It's time you quit worrying about marriages and relationships and nonmagic and just relax and enjoy a man who appreciates what an exceptional woman you are and can make you feel as good as you deserve to feel." He nuzzled the leg of her shorts up so that when he spoke his mouth moved, hot and insistent, against the very top of her inner thigh. "What I've learned is how to use my tongue and mouth to bring a woman to orgasm before I fill her body with mine and stroke her into another climax and then another."

"Do you do this often?" The thought of the possibility that she might be just another in a long line of female conquests began to dissipate her horny haze.

"No," he moaned, his mouth on her skin. "Don't think that. It's you I want to taste—you I want to pleasure. I've fantasized about you for years. You have no idea how much I want you and how special you are to me. Let me make my fantasies real. Let me taste you."

When he pulled at the waist of her shorts, she willingly lifted to make his job easier. As she settled back against the blanket, her eyes were drawn over his shoulder to the darkening sky and she felt a little jolt as she realized how close it was to sunset . . . which would be followed by moonrise . . . and a nearly full moon rise at that.

Observant as ever, Justin read the new tension in her

body. He saw her eyes fixed on the sky and the clear concern in her face.

"I promise that you have nothing to fear from me."

Reluctantly, her gaze left the sky and met his eyes. "But when the full moon rises, you're a wolf, aren't you?"

"Actually, there's always a little of the wolf in me, full moon or not," he said, nipping her stomach gently and then lowering his head to taste her with a long lick of his tongue.

Her breath caught in surprise and she had to bite her lip to stifle a breathy moan.

He kissed her thigh and then smiled up at her. "Remember, your magic is nonmagic. Which means I am unable to shift my shape around you. I am in man form right now, and as long as I'm close to you I'll stay in that form." He nuzzled her thigh and kissed her again. "Let me make love to you, my sweet Candy," his voice caressed her name. "Let me be your lover."

"I know exactly what you need . . . a werewolf lover." Godiva's voice whispered through her mind. Maybe her friend was right. And why not? Justin appreciated her. He listened to her and made her feel beautiful and desirable. What was wrong with her taking a young, virile lover who wanted to worship her like a goddess? . . .

With a triumphant smile, she made her decision.

"If you can't change form as long as I'm close to you, I guess the right answer is for me to keep you *very* close to me." She pulled the young werewolf to her and let his victorious growl vibrate against her naked skin.

Justin had been right. He had learned a hell of a lot since he'd left her classroom. And his tongue . . . not only did he use it between her legs with such enthusiasm that her vibrator would forever after seem a weak substitute, but his ability to listen (amazingly enough) hadn't stopped when his dick hardened. He listened and responded when she showed him the secret place low on her stomach that was so ultrasensitive. He paid attention to that spot at the base of her neck. And his kisses . . . his kisses were an erotic adventure.

When he'd brought her to climax three times he finally

moaned that he couldn't wait anymore, and she'd reveled in the hard length of him as she guided him within her slick, ready folds. He'd tried to hold back—tried not to be too rough. She'd bit him on the shoulder and told him fiercely that she wasn't a breakable young girl—that she wanted him—all of him. His growl had been sensual music. She gripped his hard hips with her legs and met his thrusts with equal strength, urging him on until he cried her name and spent himself within her.

Seven

Godiva had known what she was talking about. Having a werewolf lover was *spectacular*. Especially such a young werewolf lover. God, she'd almost forgotten the incredibly sexy strength of a young man's body. And recovery time! Jeesh. That *boy* had been better than a recharged vibrator. Way better. She was so glad it was the weekend and there was no school the next day. They'd made love for hours, and he was still nibbling at her neck when he'd walked her home. She jumped the steps into her house two at a time. He made her feel twenty again. No! She took that back. She didn't feel twenty again—no way did she want to feel that stupid and unconfident again. Justin made her feel fabulous and forty, which was exactly what she was.

Candice had taken a long bath, delighted with the unaccustomed soreness of her body. And then, replete, she'd slept till noon. Noon! And only woke up then because her cell phone had toned at her, telling her she had a text message. She flipped it open, feeling a rush of pleasure even before she saw the text.

Are you busy tonight? I have a surprise for you.

What was he up to now? She grinned and replied:

More spidey sense?

His reply was a single word.

Better

She laughed out loud. This was fun! And, no. She wasn't going to go on and on with herself about how long it'd been since she'd had this kind of fun . . . and that she might be having *too* much fun *too* soon. No. She was just going to enjoy herself.

I think I can fit you into my schedule.

She waited impatiently for the tone that signaled his reply, and when it came it sounded like beautiful music—even though she was completely aware of how ridiculously romantic that seemed.

Be on your deck at dusk. And be ready . . .

Be on her deck at dusk? And be ready for what? But she forced herself not to text him back and ask for details. She wanted to break her old habits. She overanalyzed things ("things" being defined as "men"). She knew she did it, and she knew she had gotten worse as she'd gotten older.

"Not this time," she muttered as she fixed herself a cup of her favorite green tea and stuck a couple pieces of toast in the toaster. "This time is going to be different. This time I'm not looking for a husband; I'm looking for fun."

Candice took her tea, toast, a pencil, and the pad of paper she'd started writing her poem on the day before out onto the wonderful wood deck that wrapped the length of the back of her house and looked out into the woods that surrounded

Mysteria. She curled up cross-legged on the comfortable wicker rocker that sat beside the little wicker table.

It was such a beautiful day! The woods, always magical (literally and figuratively) looked like a romantic dream come to life. All that it lacked was the knight and the white horse and . . .

Good lord! What was happening to her? She was making her own self sick.

"Snap out of it and get to writing so you can get to the good stuff tonight." Then, humming "Tonight, Tonight" from *West Side Story* she looked at the partially written poem.

> *Keep your Errol Flynns, Paul Newmans, Mel Gibsons*
> *all puppets—empty masquerades.*
> *Tom, Dick, and Harry, too*
> *the boy next door*
> *I want no more.*
> You ask, what now?
> *Well, love comes with the night,*
> *in the most inexplicable places*
> *leaving the most unexplainable traces.*
> *You see . . . a wolfman is the man for me!*

She smiled and began to write from there.

> *True, hair in the sink is copious,*

Two hours later she should have been frustrated and annoyed. She was, after all, staring at the same line she'd written earlier and nothing else was coming. Well, not exactly nothing. She'd written line after line after line, but nothing seemed to work. Nothing could begin to capture the new, crystal bright feeling of happiness and expectation that was building inside of her, and that was the feeling she wanted her poem to evoke.

"Ah, hell! Never mind. I'll write it tomorrow." She had a date to get ready for, a really hot date at that, which called for eyebrow plucking, leg shaving, a full pedicure and manicure, and lots of hair primping. Not to mention that she was going to dig through some of the boxes she'd moved into the basement to find what she'd done with her really sexy lingerie.

"Tonight I will not be wearing a sports bra and grandma panties," she promised the air around her. Had she not been so busy trying (unsuccessfully) not to giggle like a girl, she would have noticed the gaggle of pink-winged fairies who, overhearing her, had taken off in a burst of silver glitter and musical laughter out over the trees, heading in the direction of their favorite witch's house.

Justin wanted to do something special for her. He'd been up most of the night thinking about what he could do—and about her. Her skin and her body . . . he'd never felt anything as lush and inviting. So this was what it was like to be with a woman versus a girl! Twenty-somethings paled in comparison to Candice. And he could talk to her! He'd actually talked with her about dreams he'd thought were long dead. He couldn't remember the last time he'd even thought about painting, yet here he was, heading to her place with the huge book he'd checked out from the library, one with glossy, full-color pictures of famous pieces of art, tucked under his arm. With his other arm he carried a bag filled with several cuts of prime fillet steaks from his family's restaurant, each broiled and spiced to perfection, and one of the brightly checked tablecloths they used in the dining room. He smiled as he got closer to her house and left the road to circle around to her backyard. When he could peer through the thick trees and just barely make out her deck, he put the book and the bag down, spread the tablecloth out over the leafy ground, and opened the boxes, letting the aroma of expensive steak waft in the light evening breeze.

He didn't have long to wait. He heard their giggles and the whirring of their wings before he saw them. Then, poof! He was standing in the center of a cloud of fairies who, as soon as they spotted the steaks, squealed with pleasure and began a dive-bomb-like descent.

"Wait!" He growled menacingly and stood protectively over the delectable meal. The fairies paused, midswoop. "If you want the steaks you have to do something for me."

Four of the glittering miniature nymphs glided toward him. They were only about as big as an outstretched hand, but their beauty was not diminished by size. They smiled coquettishly at him.

"We know you, wolfman," the four trilled together, magically harmonizing. "We've often watched you pleasure females in the forest." They ran their hands suggestively down their naked bodies. "We would be happy to do *something* for you."

He quickly put his hands up, as if fending off an attack. "No, no, no. You don't understand. The favor I need is not quite so personal."

"What a shame." They pouted prettily.

"Do you want the steaks or not?" He already knew their answer. Fairies craved red meat, but they never got enough. They could really be a pain in the ass; they were almost as bad as termites or fleas. His dad had to spray the restaurant for them monthly.

"We want the meat!" the entire group answered together.

"Good. Then this is all I need you to do." He picked up the thick art book and then hesitated before he opened it to one of the three pages he'd marked earlier. "Do you know the teacher who lives in the cabin right there?" He pointed through the trees at Candice's house.

As a group the fairies nodded.

"You know what she looks like?"

They nodded again, causing their long, shining hair to sparkle and glisten and float around them like slightly tarnished, then glittered, haloes.

"Excellent. Here's what I need you to do . . ." Justin opened the book. The fairies flocked around him, making curious little cooing noises as he gave them their orders.

Candice was going to be totally surprised!

* * *

Candice was sitting in her wicker chair sipping an excellent glass of chilled chardonnay when he stepped out of the forest and onto the grass of her backyard. There was just enough light left in the dusky sky to see that his smile was reflected by the sparkle in his amber eyes.

"Hello, Ms. Cox," he said mischievously.

"Hello, Justin," she said in her best teacher voice. "Did you stop by for a little detention?"

"I don't know." His grin widened. "I think I've been a pretty good boy lately."

"Yes, you certainly have," she said, feeling suddenly very warm.

"Not that I wouldn't like being locked in a room alone with you."

"So my surprise has to do with locks?"

"No, Miss Impatient. Nothing like that." He climbed the deck stairs and leaned down to kiss her lightly. "You look beautiful tonight. Love the short skirt."

Candice didn't think she'd ever been so grateful for having good legs.

"Thank you. Wine?" she offered.

"I'd love some, thanks."

She poured him a glass of sun-colored wine. Just before he sat in the empty wicker chair across from her he looked out toward the forest, raised his hand, and yelled, "Action!"

Instantly, the sky over the trees began to glitter like Fourth of July sparklers, and the breeze carried the sound of silly feminine laughter to them.

Candice scowled. "Fairies. What are they up to?"

"Keep watching," Justin said, sipping his wine.

"I do not like fairies," she grumbled. Still frowning, she looked back at the sparkling sky and gasped. A picture was forming from the glistening fairy dust.

"Oh, my God! It's the *Mona Lisa!*"

"Keep watching," Justin repeated.

Mona Lisa's face changed. Candice mouth fell open. "It's me!"

Justin laughed and lifted her hand from where it rested on the little table. He kissed her palm. "Yep, it is."

Candice was still staring at the glowing portrait when the picture shifted and changed. Now she was looking at a hauntingly beautiful woman with long red hair who was sitting in a small boat.

"Waterhouse's *Lady of Shalott*!" Then it, too, changed and she was watching herself frozen in time as the lady who was cursed to sing her last song as she floated down to Camelot.

Entranced, she watched the picture dissipate and begin to form again as another famous woman. This time it wasn't a painting the fairies were reproducing. It was the eternally graceful statue of the winged Nike. And then, as if the Greek gods had ordered a miracle, Candice's face and neck, even her long blonde hair, appeared to complete the glorious statue. Candice laughed and clapped her hands.

Justin hardly glanced at the fairy artwork. He couldn't stop looking at Candice. Uninhibited joy had transformed her face from pretty to stunning. Everything inside him screamed, *Her! She's the one I'm meant to be with!*

Candice gasped again as the new painting took form. "This is one of my all-time favorites! *Meeting on Turret Stairs* by Burton." She made a happy little cry. "Justin! It's us!"

Then he did pull his eyes from her to look at the sky. Sure enough, the incredibly romantic scene of the knight passing his lady on the narrow stairway had been altered so that it was the two of them. The knight was kissing his lady's arm as she leaned dramatically against the stone wall of the castle; both of them were clearly overwhelmed by a desire so real it seemed to leap off the painting and become tangible. He hadn't told the fairies to re-create this scene—just as he hadn't told them to put his face in any of the paintings—but he was glad they'd added to his instructions. He'd have to remember to bring them a couple more steak dinners. Soon.

The fairy dust painting faded slowly, leaving only the darkening sky. Finally Candice turned to him.

"How did you do that?"

Her eyes were alive and her face was slightly flushed. He wanted to push the little table that was between them out of the way and take her in his arms and kiss her until his touch was what made her eyes sparkle and her face flush.

"Magic," he said.

"But magic doesn't work on me."

"It worked on you tonight." He took her hand and kissed her palm again. "Maybe you just needed the right partner to find your magic."

"Or maybe your magic is so strong that even I can't stop it."

"I like that. I like that anything about me could be strong enough to attract you."

"Everything about you attracts me," she said, her voice low and sexy.

"Show me. Show me how much," he said.

Without speaking she stood up and led him into her house, through the cozy kitchen, the comfortably decorated den, and into her bedroom.

"I want to undress you," she said. "Is that okay with you?"

He bent and kissed her softly on the lips. "Anything you want is okay with me, as long as you still want me."

"I can't imagine not wanting you," she said, guiding him over so that he stood beside her bed while she sat on the edge of it. He was wearing a black pullover, and she skimmed it up his body and over his head, letting her fingers trail lightly down from his shoulders over his naked chest and abdomen, loving the way his body shivered at her touch. Then she unbuttoned his jeans, taking her time to slowly unzip them while her lips teased his chest and her fingers caressed the hard lump that was pushing against his pants. When she finally got his pants undone she stood, and then, hooking her fingers in his waistband, slid the jeans down, pressing her body against his as she did so.

On her knees in front of him, she took him in her hands. He was hard and hot and his body jerked and quivered under her hands. When she closed her mouth around him he moaned her name, and had to lean against the bed to stay standing.

"Your mouth," he rasped, "is a dream. A very sexy dream."

"Wet dream?" she asked when she paused.

"Oh, God, yes," he moaned.

She laughed, but before she could take him in her mouth again, he pulled her to her feet and in one quick movement, lifted her onto the bed. Lying beside her he unbuttoned her shirt.

"Now that's sexy," he said, running his finger lightly over the delicate white lace bra. "Too many women think red or black or some other godawful bright color is what men want. I don't know about other men," he murmured, "but I think white is the sexiest. You can see right through it." He circled her nipple with his finger, causing it to harden. "But there's something innocent about it. Like what it's covering has been waiting just for you." He bent over her, taking her nipple into his mouth right through the sheer lace of the bra.

Candice's breath left her in a rush. "My panties match," were the only words her lust-clouded mind could form.

Justin moved from her bra to unbutton the short cotton skirt she was wearing. He pulled it down and then knelt between her legs, gazing down at her body. She watched him closely and suddenly saw herself reflected in the desire that was so clear on his face, and knew she'd never again think of herself as old or fat or frumpy.

"Feel what you do to me," he whispered.

He took her hand and pressed it to his chest so that she could feel the racing of his heart. She let her fingers rest there for a moment, and then held the hand that had so recently covered hers against her breast.

"Feel what you do to me," she echoed.

"It's good that we're in this together," he said. "I don't think I could stand feeling all of this alone."

"You're not alone," Candice said.

"Give me a chance," Justin said. "Say you'll take me seriously, even though you think I'm too damn young."

"Justin, I don't expect—" she started.

"Expect!" he blurted. "Can't you just expect magic? Even if it's never happened to you before, can't you let me prove to you that there's more than one kind of magic in this world, and that we can make it happen together?" He leaned down and cupped her face between his hands. "I want you, Candice Cox. Not just tonight. I want you in my life. Let me make you love me."

His words scared and thrilled her. She should tell him no. Or she should lie to him and say yeah, whatever, so that they could have more good sex, and then send him on his way. But she didn't want to. It might be stupid. It probably wouldn't work. But Candice wanted more than anything else to take a chance on loving Justin. Unexpected tears came to her eyes when she answered him.

"I've waited a long time to feel like this, Justin. I can't let you go now," she said.

He smiled and wiped the dampness from her cheeks. "Well, you had to wait for me to grow up."

"Hush and kiss me." She pulled him down to her.

Soon neither of them could talk anymore. All they could do was feel.

Eight

Candice slept till noon again the next day—this time curled up against Justin's body. And she awoke to his gentle caresses and they made love slowly, whispering erotic secrets as morning gave way to afternoon. They'd said good-bye like lovers had for centuries, with lots of long looks and lingering touches.

And tomorrow . . . they were meeting tomorrow. He'd wanted to see her again that night, but as he'd been kissing her good-bye for about the zillionth time, his cell phone had interrupted them. He'd taken the call, albeit reluctantly, and after he'd hung up he'd apologized, saying that it was a call from his family's restaurant. They needed him to go to Denver tonight because . . . hell. She didn't remember exactly what he'd said. She'd been too busy floating on a cloud of sexual satisfaction.

But that wasn't all it was, Candice reminded herself that evening as she poured a glass of white wine and took it to her writing desk. She was floating on more than a sex cloud. She really liked him. Her lips tilted up in a secret smile as she remembered the text message she'd received from him not long ago. It had simply said:

"Did my heart love till now? Forswear it, sight! For I ne'er saw true beauty till this night."

First DeMass, then Frost, and now Shakespeare! He was smart and interesting and so sexy she wanted to begin at his mouth and lick her way down his body . . . and then back up again. And he wanted her to be in his life—to love him. No matter how improbable or impossible, she found herself wanting the same thing. She sighed happily and sipped her wine. Creative juices flowing (along with all the rest of them), she picked up her pencil and reread the poem she'd started.

Keep your Errol Flynns, Paul Newmans, Mel Gibsons
all puppets—empty masquerades.
Tom, Dick, and Harry, too
the boy next door
I want no more.
You ask, what now?
Well, love comes with the night,
in the most inexplicable places
leaving the most unexplainable traces.
You see . . . a wolfman is the man for me!
True, hair in the sink is copious,

She grinned at where she'd stopped and, inspired, started writing.

and the house at night tends to be a mess.
But

The ringing phone jarred her. The caller ID said Tawdry, Godiva.

"Well, hi there, girlfriend. Long time no hear from." Godiva's voice was smug. "So, has anything new come . . . uh, *up* recently?"

Candice's breath came out in a rush. "Shit! You know! How the hell do you know?" Then she gasped, a horrible feeling lodging in her stomach. "Oh, no! Did you do it, Godiva?"

"Do what?"

"Don't play innocent witch with me. How did you manage it? Magic doesn't work on me."

"It might not work on you, but it definitely works on werewolves."

"You made him want me!" she shrieked, feeling even sicker.

"Certainly not." Godiva sounded offended. "All I did was to cast a lupine drawing spell right after the last time we talked. If it caught a wolf who didn't find you attractive, he would have never approached you. Think of it like baiting a hook. If the worm—which was you—wasn't juicy and tender and appealing to the fish—or in this case, werewolf—he would never taste the bait."

"Oh." Candice grinned, feeling so relieved she was weak-kneed.

"Details, please."

"Let's just say this worm has been well eaten."

They both dissolved into giggles.

"And," Candice said breathlessly, "I'm meeting him again tomorrow. Godiva, baby, he's quoting poetry to me! *Poetry!* And he made the stupid fairies make art for me. Can you believe it? He said he wants to worship me like a goddess, and, honey, let me tell you. I definitely can't get enough of that kind of attention! But it's more than just how completely sexy he is. He's smart and funny *and* totally into me. And, Godiva, I *really* like him."

"Sounds fabulous! Who is he?"

"You mean you don't know?"

"No. I told you—I just baited the hook. I had no idea which wolf would bite."

"Oh, Godiva, it's so deliciously naughty. He's *young*, and"—she dropped her voice to a whisper—"he's an ex-student of mine."

"Oh, my Goddess! How wickedly yummy. Give. Who is he?" Godiva gushed.

"Justin Woods," she gushed.

"Who?"

"Justin Woods. You know, his family are the werewolves who own Red Riding Hood's."

"Oh, Goddess."

"What? What's wrong? I know he's young, but it's not like he's still a teenager—which would be totally and completely disgusting—he's twenty-six. And a half. Practically twenty-seven."

"Oh, Goddess."

"Godiva Tawdry, stop saying that and tell me what's wrong!" Candice was beginning to feel sick again.

"I should have known," Godiva groaned. "But how could I have known? I didn't think it would be *him*."

"Godiva. Tell me."

The witch drew a deep breath and then blurted out, "He's a slut."

"What?!"

"He's the most promiscuous werewolf in town—or out of town, for that matter. The pack tramp. Truly a dog in all the worst connotations of the word."

"Oh, no . . ."

"Oh, yes. I promise you. My Romeo has told me all about him. He's the pack joke. Thinks he's some kind of furry Don Juan. He's always licking coeds and cheerleaders and whatnot."

"Cheerleaders!"

"I'm so sorry, Candice."

"And all that stuff he said to me . . ."

"You mean about making a woman orgasm with his mouth?"

Candice gasped in horror.

"Let me guess—he licked your foot and sucked your toes?" Godiva said.

"Yes," Candice squeaked.

"That's his move. He does that with all the girls—wolves—whatever."

"I may puke." She put her hand to her forehead and closed her eyes. How could she have been so damn gullible? "How about the poetry he quoted and the fairy art? Does he use that on all of his victims, too?"

"I don't remember hearing about that, but hey, come on! Just forget about it." Godiva forced perkiness into her voice. "You had a good time, right? A little fling—an unclogging of your pipes."

"He played me for a fool." Candice's voice was quiet and intense. She let her anger build. As long as she was thoroughly pissed she could keep the hurt from blossoming like a black flower inside of her.

"No, he's just—"

Candice cut her off. "No, Godiva! It wasn't all fun and games—he made it appear to be more than that. I should have known . . . I should have been smarter, but he's not going to get away with it. I said I was too old for this kind of shit, and I am. But not because I'm dried up and unattractive. I'm too old to be lied to and manipulated. So tell me the truth. He's obviously not going on a supply run for his family tonight. I want you to find out from Romeo what he's really doing."

"Uh, if I do and I tell you, what are you going to do?"

"Well, my witchy friend, I can sum that up in one word. Retribution."

He should never have agreed to meet the twins at the full moon party. It didn't matter that his intentions had been right. He hadn't told Candice the truth, which had been bothering him ever since the family restaurant supply run lie had blurted from his mouth. He shouldn't have answered the damn phone, but he'd been feeling so good there with Candice—so right—that when the phone rang he . . .

He what? He'd answered it because he'd wanted to yell

from the mountainside that he'd FOUND SOMEONE IN-
CREDIBLE! In retrospect that seemed stupid and immature.
And instead of telling the world about Candice, he'd quickly
agreed to meet Brittney and Whitney at the party that night.
There was little he wouldn't have agreed to just to get them
off the phone before Candice heard their silly female voices
on the line and dumped him right then and there.

And actually going to the party hadn't seemed stupid—
not until he'd stepped into the forest and felt the moon's call
on his blood. He'd answered that call automatically, embrac-
ing the sweet savage pleasure and heat of sinew and bone
changing and re-forming with the power of the beast. He'd
meant to show up long enough to tell the twins—and any of
the other numerous females he'd pleasured—that he was officially taking himself off the market. He meant to make a
clean split with his old life, so that he could begin his new
one. Earlier that day he'd even gone online and looked up
the Denver Art Institute. Then he'd actually begun a sketch.
Just a woman's eyes. They were green and framed with thick
blond lashes and soft laugh lines. . . .

Thinking of Candice, Justin let the moon caress his fur as
he raised his muzzle to the sky. Surrounded by young wolves
who were breaking off into intimate groups, he howled his
passion for Candice into the night.

The full moon was so white against the absolute black of the
starless sky that it almost looked silver. Sitting at the edge of
the clearing, Candice breathed deeply of the warm night air
and waited. It wasn't long before she heard them approaching through the trees. They weren't being stealthy—there
was no reason for it. They were being young and uninhibited
and very, very horny.

Godiva had been right (again). It was easy to tell which
of the wolves was Justin. That thick sand-colored pelt was as
distinctive as his eyes (and his tongue).

She stood up and stepped into the clearing. Keeping the
hand that clutched the collar hidden behind her back, she

cocked her hip and shook out her hair. With a sexy purr in her voice, she called to him.

"Justin, come here, boy!" The big wolf sitting between two blonde bitches who were drooling over him (literally) while he howled at the sky cocked his ears at her. Candice ran her hand suggestively over her body. "I have something special for you that I just couldn't wait till tomorrow to give you."

With an enthusiastic woof, he bounded toward her, his all-too-familiar tongue lolling. With one quick movement, she dropped to her knees beside him and slipped the heavy-duty choke collar around his throat.

"Arruff?" he said, staring up at her in confusion.

"Tonight you're coming with me," she whispered. When the bitches yapped at her, she grinned over her shoulder at them. "Don't worry. I'll give him back to you—but not till I've had my way with him."

He whined and squirmed as she dragged him to the Jeep she'd borrowed from Godiva. No damn way his hairy ass was going to fit in her lovely little Mini—even if she did allow dogs to ride with her, which she definitely didn't.

"Don't bother with the whining and big doggie eyes. They're not going to work," she told him. "And remember, my magic is nonmagic. You can't change as long as I'm close to you. But isn't that convenient? I hear that your favorite position is very close to a woman. Any woman. So get comfortable, fur-face."

"Thank goodness I caught you before you closed, Doctor." Candice smiled as she dragged the whining wolf into the veterinary clinic.

"Is there something wrong with your . . ." The vet hesitated, narrowing his eyes at the wolf.

"Dog," Candice supplied innocently. "Yes, there is something wrong with my dog. I need you to perform emergency surgery."

"Really? He looks healthy to me." The vet reached down and ruffled the "dog's" sandy fur.

Justin whined pitifully.

"You're a big boy, aren't you?" the vet said.

"He certainly thinks he is—which explains the emergency. I need you to cut off his . . ." Candice paused, glanced at Justin, then dropped her voice and whispered into the vet's ear.

"Well, I don't know. It's pretty late. I was just closing," he said.

"Surely you can fit him in. Pretty please, Doc?" She fluttered her lashes at him.

The vet smiled and shrugged. "I suppose I could for my favorite teacher. Go, Fairies!"

"Go, Fairies!" Candice chimed in automatically.

"If you wait here, I'll take him in the back and be done in no time."

"No! I mean, I'll come with you. If I don't stay close to him he'll change . . . into something that might surprise you."

"But you won't want to watch!"

"Of course not," she assured him. "I'll stay in the room, but I have a poem I need to finish, so I'll be concentrating on that while you take care of his little *problems*."

"Suit yourself, teacher," the vet said. "Bring him back."

Justin began to growl.

"Doc, I think we need a muzzle."

Candice settled on a metal folding chair not too far from the operating room table, careful to keep her back to the busy veterinarian and his unwillingly drugged patient. She ignored the tight, sick feeling in her stomach and, while Justin was being prepped, she picked up her pencil and smiled grimly as she finished her poem.

Keep your Errol Flynns, Paul Newmans, Mel Gibsons
all puppets—empty masquerades.
Tom, Dick, and Harry, too

the boy next door
I want no more.
You ask, what now?
Well, love comes with the night,
in the most inexplicable places
leaving the most unexplainable traces.
You see . . . a wolfman is the man for me!
True, hair in the sink is copious,
and the house at night tends to be a mess.
But if that wolfman breaks my heart,
if he thinks that we should part,
I'll wait until the moon is waxing full
that magic time when his change is soon,
(my love is quite helpless then, as a puppy . . .
baby . . . body in a mortuary)
I'd collar that fur-faced gigolo
and make a timely visit to the Vet.

Ah, well, I'm sure there'll never be a need.
I haven't seen a neutered werewolf . . .

Candice glanced up at where the vet obscured her view of the sleeping, spread-eagled Justin.

. . . Yet.

As the vet picked up an evil-looking scalpel, Candice closed her notebook.

"Doc?"

The vet paused, blade hovering above the spread-eagled "dog," and glanced over his shoulder at her.

"I'm sorry. I know this is going to seem odd, but I've changed my mind."

He frowned at her.

She gave a purposefully silly, girly-girl laugh. "Oopsie, sorry. I guess I just can't go through with it, no matter how . . . uh, naughty he's been. I'll still pay you for the neutering, though. Don't worry." She fished her checkbook out of her purse and hastily wrote the vet a check. Then she nodded at the sleeping Justin. "How long will he be out?"

"A couple hours."

"Perfect. Can you help me lift him into my car?"

Nine

Justin woke up in the ditch not far from the clearing where the party was still in full swing, as evidenced by the randy growls and breathless giggles that drifted on the night air. At first he was totally disoriented. His mouth felt like a bird had shit in it and he had a killer headache. What the hell? He'd gone to the party as a farewell to his old life, and then . . .

With a terrified yelp, his memory rushed back. Commanding his human form to come to him, he sat up, gasping and reaching between his legs. All there! He was all there.

What had happened? Why had Candice freaked out?

But even before Justin found the neatly folded note she'd left staked to the ground beside him with . . . he shuddered . . . something that looked disturbingly like a scalpel, he knew what had happened. Someone had told her about him. He was fully aware of his bad reputation. He'd never really given a shit. Until now. He opened the piece of notebook paper. The full moon had brightened the sky enough for him to easily read her bold writing.

> *Girls might think it's cute or exciting to be with a*
> *man who collects lovers like a dog collects fleas. Well,*
> *that's just one of the many differences between girls*
> *and women. Gigolo men piss grown women off. I'm a*
> *grown woman. The game you played with me pisses*
> *me off. I suggest you stick to girls. Next time you may*
> *lose more than a few orgy hours. Keep in mind,*
> *"Heaven has no rage like love to hatred turned, nor*
> *hell a fury like a woman scorned." Ah, to hell with*
> *that poetic crap. Basically, I wanted to say, GO*
> *FUCK YOURSELF, JUSTIN!*

When he returned to wolf form he didn't notice the sensual stir of his morphing flesh, and he didn't rush back to the clearing to pair up with an eager young wolf to reassure himself that everything was still in working order. Instead he padded slowly home—the garage apartment his parents pretended to rent to him as part of his salary and benefits at the restaurant, which felt as empty and meaningless as his life had become.

"You should be almost done with that awful poetry class, right?" Godiva asked her friend.

Candice was sitting on her balcony, arm resting against her little table, pad and pencil beside her. She stared out at the forest while she propped the phone against her shoulder and kept doodling on her notebook paper. "Yep. Almost."

"And that means the whole MFA is almost done, right?"

"Yep. Almost."

"And snow is almost done falling out of that giant flying rabbit's ass, right?"

"Yep. Al—" Candice frowned, realizing what Godiva had really said. "Don't be such a smart-ass."

"You know, I hear he's back in town."

"I don't want to talk about it."

"So don't talk—just listen. He's back in town, but werewolf gossip has it that he's only here temporarily. Seems he's just come to collect some of his stuff to take back to his new apartment in Denver."

"And why should I care?"

Godiva kept talking as if Candice hadn't spoken. "Word also has it that he's still not slutting around. No parties. No orgies. No cheerleaders. Not even the slightest hint of a girl-friend, wolf or not."

"Godiva! I do not give a shit. I haven't talked to him in weeks."

"Well, maybe you should!"

"I cannot believe you're saying that. You're the one who told me what a slut he was. And I saw it with my own eyes. He lied to me and was fucking every bitch in sight that night."

"Girlfriend, I told you what Romeo told me—that several werewolves told him that Justin wasn't doing anyone that night. And, as far as my excellent gossip network—which includes forest fairies, and you know those little shits live for gossip and red meat—can tell, Justin Woods has not been with anyone since the three dates he had with you."

"Two dates. And one of them wasn't even official."

"Whatever. I think you should call him."

"What! I am *not* going to call that boy."

"Oh, give it up. You know very well he's no boy."

"Again I say whatever. And he knows my phone number. If he wanted to talk to me, he'd call me."

"Candice Cox, may I please remind you that the last time you interacted with him you almost had his balls cut off, you dumped him in a ditch, and you left a scary revenge note, complete with a literary quote and a go-fuck-yourself."

"He lied to me."

"True, and circumstantial evidence pointed to his defi-nitely being an asswipe. But since then he has behaved re-spectably, by either man or wolf standards."

Candice sighed. "I can't call him. I feel like an idiot."

"Do you want me to cast a little—"

"Hell, no! Godiva Tawdry, promise me right now that you will not put any kind of love spell, or anything like a love spell, on Justin."

"Okay! I promise. But I still think you should call him."
She brightened. "Hey, I could have Romeo talk to—"

"No! God, I feel like I'm trapped in a dream where I'm
back in high school trying to figure out my locker combination and realizing I'm butt-ass naked. Just leave it alone, Godiva. If Justin wanted to see me again, he'd figure out a way to
do it." And she knew it was true. Candice had only been with
him for a short time, but she believed in his tenacity. He'd
set his sights on seducing her, and he'd certainly accomplished his goal. If he had any desire to talk to her or see her,
he'd get it done. But even though his behavior had changed
drastically since the night she'd almost had him neutered, he
had stayed completely away from her. Not that she cared.

"Candice?"

"Oh, sorry, what did you say?"

"I asked what your last poetry assignment was about."

"We have to write two poems about heartbreak. One free
verse. One sonnet. And neither can be clichéd."

"Oh, a real uplifting assignment."

"Yeah, it's just one laugh after another over here."

"Are they done?"

"Almost. I just have to finish tweaking the couplet to con-
clude the sonnet. Then I'm going to set them aside for a day
or so, and do a quick rewrite before I have to turn them in
next week."

"After you do that, why don't you and I get all dressed up
and go into Denver for some excellent Italian food? I'll even
drive."

"I'm not flying on that damn broom of yours."

"I said *drive*."

"I'll think about it," Candice said.

Godiva paused. She was almost afraid to ask the next
question, but she knew she had to. Her talent was, after all,
healing. Resolutely, she said, "Candy, what happened with
Justin really did break your heart, didn't it?" It took her
friend several seconds to answer her.

"Yeah," she finally whispered into the phone. "Isn't that
stupid?"

"No, it's not stupid. It's what can happen when we love someone, and you have rarely let yourself love anyone."

"Ironic, isn't it? And I'm the one who's been married a zillion times."

"You didn't really love any of the ex-husnumbers. But there was something about Justin that got to you."

"I wish . . . ," Candy began.

"What, honey?"

"I wish your magic worked on me."

"So do I, honey. So do I."

After she hung up, Godiva sat staring at the phone a long time. There had to be some way she could help her friend. After all, it was her fault this whole thing had happened. First, she'd cast the drawing spell that had brought them together. Then she'd spilled the beans about Justin's promiscuous ways. Who knew the wolf was going to have some big, hairy epiphany and learn to zip his pants? And now the gossip tree said that he was really getting his shit together. Seems he was spearheading the acquisition of a new restaurant for his family, and the eavesdropping fairies, who seemed to have a real soft spot for the wolf, had even heard whispers that he'd reenrolled in college. Was it just her? Wasn't it obvious to everyone that Justin was trying to make himself worthy of Candice?

And Candice was moping around like she'd been stuck in a classroom with the horrid Desdaine triplets (Godiva shuddered—Goddess! What a wretched thought! Those girls were the brat pack.). Something had to be done.

Maybe if Justin knew how miserable Candice was . . . maybe then he'd call her and they'd live happily ever after!

But she'd promised Candice she wouldn't cast any love spells on him. Godiva tapped her long fingernail against her chin. Then she smiled. Candice was writing poems about heartbreak. What if Justin were to read them? He wouldn't know that they were an assignment! He'd just think she was pining over him—which she was. That was it; the fairies would be only too happy to help. . . .

Humming to herself, Godiva began gathering four-leaf clovers . . . the little dried white things from the tops of dandelions . . . a pinch of frog snot . . . and various other delightful things she would need for the spell. . . .

Candice rubbed her neck and stretched. Well, the couplet that ended the sonnet was done. Good thing, too, it was getting dark and she should move inside from her porch. But she didn't get up. She liked sitting out there. And it wasn't because she remembered another evening on the porch, one that had been filled with hope and magic and love. . . .

No. It was just that the woods were quiet, and their somberness reflected her recent mood. It was nice to sit out on her balcony and write, even if what she wrote was damn depressing. She lifted the paper that had the final draft of both poems written on it and shook her head sadly. They were good. She knew it. But if they did evoke feelings, the feelings would be sadness, loss, longing. . . .

She put the paper down, remembering how not long ago she had dreamed of writing things that evoked brighter emotions.

What was wrong with her? So she'd had a little fling that had ended abruptly and, quite frankly, not very well. It was ridiculous that it was still making her feel this sad. She closed her eyes and rested her head against the back of the chair. What was it about Justin that stayed with her? Was it just because he'd been so damn handsome? That couldn't be it. Ex-husband numbers one and four had been very handsome men. Well, was it the sex? No. Ex-husband numbers one and three had been fantastic in the sack. She'd gotten over all of them, more easily than she usually cared to admit. So why was Justin still haunting her dreams?

Against her closed eyes the warm evening breeze had picked up. It felt good, almost like a caress against her skin. It made her think of the summer, when dandelions dried and their little white heads blew all over fields of four-leaf clovers. She sighed and relaxed, feeling suddenly sleepy. . . .

. . . Until she heard the wild flapping and opened her eyes in time to see her homework papers being lifted by the crazy wind. She leaped up, grabbing at papers, sure she saw translucent pastel wings fluttering in among the notebook pages as her poetry scattered out into the forest.

"Fucking fairies!" she screamed, running after the trail of paper.

An hour later she had still not found the final drafts of both poems. Grumbling about hanging sticky flypaper and a giant bug zapper to get rid of the fairy problem, she gave up, resigning herself to rewriting the finals again. At least she'd just finished both poems that day. It shouldn't be too hard for her to remember exactly what she'd written. . . .

He'd gone for a walk. Justin hadn't even understood why, but all of a sudden it had been very important that he take a walk in the woods, and before he knew it, he was heading south. Toward her house. He'd just realized how close he was to her little log cabin when the wind changed directions and, in a flutter of iridescent wings, two papers blew straight into his hands. He felt a jolt at the familiar writing.

Poetry . . . her poetry!

Then he started reading, and his heart clenched. Candice's words were like a mirror of what was going on inside him. Could it be? Could she really care as much as he did? He read on, and images began to form in his mind, and with them a plan. Maybe, just maybe, he could find a way to reach her.

Ten

To some people it might seem counterproductive to jog to town simply to eat a triple fudge banana split. To Candice it made perfect sense. She sat outside the One-Stop Mart and tried to tune out the sounds of the arguing Desdaine triplets as they fought over God knew what. Those monsters were always into something. And that poor sweet preacher, what was her name? Pastor Harmony? She'd somehow gotten trapped in there with those little demons. Candice could hear woman trying to end the argument before any of the three little terrors could permanently disable some hapless passerby, which was just damn brave of the preacher. No wonder everyone said she was honestly nice—that she accepted everyone no matter how magical or nonmagical (or how disdainfully horrid).

Something crashed inside the store and Candice cringed. How old were those brats now? Eleven? Twelve? She'd damn sure better be out of teaching before, like a plague of locusts, they descended upon Mysteria High. Just another reason to land that fabulous job as an editor in Denver. Candice ate her ice cream slowly, dreaming of the romantic possibilities of her future profession. She'd have three-martini lunches with authors. She'd wear amazing clothes and have a loft near downtown. She'd discover the next Nora Roberts!

"Candice! There you are. Holy bat shit! You will not believe what the vampire is displaying in his gallery!" Godiva rushed up to her friend, her large round bosoms heaving with excitement.

"More porno dressed up as art?" Candice said, interest definitely aroused. She was always up for some full-frontal male nudity. Actually, it might be just the thing to help her get over the Justin Blues. Unfortunately, Godiva shook her head.

"No. It's not porn."

"Damn. Then what's the big deal? You know I don't like those bloody pictures the vamps think are cool. I don't know why vampires are so into art, anyway. You'd think they'd choose a more, I don't know, nocturnal profession."

"Candice! Just come with me. I cannot begin to explain what you're going to see."

"Can I finish my banana split first?"

"Bring it. This can't wait."

Grumbling, Candice let Godiva shoo her down Main Street to Mysteria's only art gallery, Dark Shadows. A crowd was gathered around the front display window, and as she got closer, she realized that all of them were staring in the window, and they all were crying.

Crying? The exhibition was so bad it was making the populace cry? Sheesh.

Godiva grabbed her arm and shoved her forward so she could get a better look. At first she was so completely distracted by the beauty of the pieces and the amazing talent of the artist that she didn't understand exactly what it was she was seeing. There were two watercolor paintings on display. Her immediate impression of them was that they were dream images, and they vaguely brought to mind Michael Parks's sexy fantasy work. One was of a woman who was in a cage that looked like it had been carved from ice. All around the outside of the walls of ice were big tufts of a delicately leafed plant in full purple bloom. *Lavender*, she thought. *They're bunches of blooming lavender.* Candice looked more closely at the woman in the center of the cage. She was sitting on the floor, with one hand pressed against the nearest translucent wall, almost as if she were trying to push her way out. She was wearing only a white hooded cloak. Parts of her shapely bare legs were showing, but her face was in shadows—all except her eyes, which were large and mesmerizing with their mossy green sadness. There was something else about her eyes. . . .

Candice shifted her attention to the other painting. It, too, was amazingly rich in detail and color. It showed a woman sleeping on a bed that was in the middle of what looked to be a dark room in a castle. Mist, or maybe fog, hung around the bed, further obscuring the woman. A single tall, narrow window slit let in two pearl-winged doves, as well as a ray of moonlight, which fell across the bed, illuminating the side of the woman's face so that a single tear at the corner of her eye was visible. This woman's face was also in shadow. Her blonde hair spilled around her on the dark bed, drawing Candice's eye. What was it about her hair?

Then she realized that displayed beside each painting was a framed poem. She pushed her way farther through the sobbing crowd until she was so close to the window that she pressed her fingers against the cold glass. Candice began reading the elaborate calligraphy of the first poem.

Come, icy wall of silence
encase my weary heart
protect me with your hold, hard strength
till no pain may trespass here.
Make still my battered feelings
within your protective fortress
safe
request I this sanctuary from life's storm.
But, what of this ensorcelled heart?
Will it struggle so encased?

Or will walls forged to keep harm out
cause love's flame to flicker low
till silence meant as soothing balm
does its work too well, and
no more breath can escape
to melt the fortress of frozen tears.

Candice couldn't breathe. She felt as if someone had punched her in the stomach. Frantically, her eyes went to the second poem. It was a sonnet, and it was written in the same meticulous calligraphy.

The dreamer dreamed a thousand wasted years
Captive of wondrous images she slept
Swathed close in sighs and moans and blissful tears
Reliving promises made, but not kept.

The moon's deft watch through narrow casement fell
Its silvered light caressed her silken face
Like a dove's soft wings colored gray and shell
Shadowy thoughts frozen in time and place.

He watched her breath like silver mist depart
And he longed to join her murderous sleep
But truth rare listens to the wounded heart
Hence even hero souls must sometimes weep.

Now love's pinions can never more take flight,
Entombed forever in grief's endless night.

"They're mine," Candice whispered. Her stricken voice didn't carry above the sobs of the people around her. She tore her eyes from the window and looked frantically back at Godiva, who was standing at the edge of the crowd crying softly. She raised her voice so that her friend could hear her. "They're my poems, Godiva. I wrote them."

"Who said that?!"

Heads swiveled to the tall gaunt figure standing in the doorway of the gallery. Barnabas Vlad (a name everyone in Mysteria knew he had absolutely, beyond any doubt, *not* been born with) was swathed head to toe in black, holding a small lacy black parasol, and wearing huge blue blocker reflective sunglasses.

"Who said that she is the poetess?"

"That would be me," Candice said reluctantly.

All the heads then swiveled in her direction and Candice heard weepy murmurs of *Oh, they're so wonderful,* and *They break my heart, but I love them,* and *I have to have one of my own and the art that goes with it!*

Barnabas pointed one finger (fully covered in a black opera-length glove) at Candice. "You must come with me at once!" The vampire turned and scuttled through the gallery door.

Candice couldn't move. Everyone was staring at her.

"Let's go!" Godiva pushed her toward the gallery door, ignoring the gawking crowd. Then, still sobbing softly, she added, "And no way are you going in there without me."

Candice had been in the gallery before. It was decidedly on the dark side—walls and floor black instead of the usual clean white of most galleries. It was never well lit, and it was always too damn cold. But she liked the art exhibits, especially the gay pride exhibits Barnabas like to have. She could appreciate full-frontal male nudity, even if it couldn't appreciate her.

"Back here, ladies."

Barnabas's called breathily from the rear office. Godiva and Candice exchanged glances. Both shrugged and followed the vampire's voice.

"You're sure it's your poetry?" Godiva whispered, wiping her eyes and blowing her nose.

"Of course I'm sure," she hissed at her friend. "How could you even ask me that! They're the poems about heartbreak I wrote a week or so ago for that poetry class."

"Well, it's just that . . ." But they'd come to Barnabas's office so Godiva clamped her mouth shut.

"Ladies, I'm charmed. Come in and sit, *s'il vous plaît*." Barnabas fluttered his long fingers at the two delicate pink silk Louis XIV chairs that sat regally before his ornately carved mahogany desk. When they were seated the vampire launched into a breathy speech in his trademark poorly rendered French accent. "Do *pardon* my abruptness out there, but it's been wretchedly stressful since I put up that new display. That is no excuse for *moi* rudeness, though. It is just such a shock—such a surprise. *Mon dieu!* Who would have imagined that such a magnificent discovery would have been made at my humble gallery? Oh! How rude of me. Introductions are in order. I am Barnabas Vlad, the proprietor of this humble *galerie d'art*." He peered at Godiva for a moment, squinting his eyes so that his iridescent pink eye shadow creased unattractively. Then his expression cleared. "Ah, *oui oui oui!* I do know you. Are you not Godiva Tawdry, one of the Tawdry witches?"

Godiva looked pleased at her notoriety. *"Oui!"* she said. Now that she'd stopped crying she was able to appreciate the humor of the undead guy's foppishly fake Frenchness.

He turned to Candice with a smile that showed way too many long, sharp teeth. "And you are our poetess! You look familiar to me, *madam*, but I'm sorry to say that I have misplaced your name."

"I'm Candice Cox," she said.

The vampire's pleasant expression instantly changed to confusion. *"Mais non!* It is not possible!"

"Okay, this is really starting to piss me off. I wrote the poems a week or so ago for an online class I'm taking for my master's. I can prove it. I turned them in last Friday. Now I want to know how you got them, who this artist is who has illustrated them, and why you all"—here she paused to glare at Godiva—"think it's so impossible that I wrote them. I may be a high school teacher, but I do have a brain!"

"Madam! I meant no disrespect." The vampire definitely looked flustered. "It is just . . ." He dabbed at his upper lip with a lacy black hankie before going on. "Are you not the English teacher whose magic is nonmagic?"

"Yes," Candice ground from between gritted teeth.

"Then that is why it is impossible that you have written the poems."

"What the hell—" Candice sputtered and started to get up, but Godiva's firm hand on her arm stopped her.

"Candice," Godiva said. "The poems have magic."

"*Exactement!*" Barnabas said, clearly relieved that Godiva had stepped in.

"Magic? But how? I don't understand," Candice said.

"You saw the people. Your poems made them cry. They made *me* cry. When I looked at the paintings and then read your words, I thought my heart would break with sadness. It was awful—and wonderful." Godiva teared up again just thinking about it.

"That is how everyone has been reacting," Barnabas said. "Since I put them on display this morning. Weeping and blubbering, blubbering and weeping."

"But where did you get them?" Candice felt as if she'd just gotten off a Tilt-a-Whirl and couldn't quite get her bearings.

"They were in a plain brown package I found by the rear door to the gallery this morning. I opened it, and my heart began to break. *Naturellement* I instantly put them on display."

"So who left the package?"

He shrugged. "It did not say. There was only this note in the package."

Candice snatched the paper from his expensively gloved fingers. Typed on a plain white piece of regular computer paper it said:

*If the poet would like to work with me again I would
be willing. Tell her that I will meet her here at the
gallery tonight at sunset.*

"But there's no signature or anything," Candice said.

"Artists." Barnabas sighed and rolled his eyes.

"Okay, none of this makes any sense. The artist seems to

know who I am, but I have no idea who this person is, how he or she got my poems. I mean, I just wrote them for the online class. I typed them into the computer, attached them to my e-mail, and sent them to the creative writing professor. Then I put the originals into a file labeled with the proper class. I suppose someone at the university could have gotten to them. The only other copies were blown away one day in a freak windstorm."

Godiva shifted guiltily in her chair.

Candice shot her a narrowed look. "What do you know about this, Godiva Tawdry?"

"Nothing!" she said quickly.

"So you did not print them in such lovely calligraphy?" Barnabas asked.

"No! Not even my handwritten copies looked anything like those." Candice got up and marched to the front window. She yanked both framed poems from the easels on which they were displayed. As an afterthought she made little shooing motions at the gawking, crying people. Then she hurried back to Barnabas's office.

"Let me see them," Godiva said. Candice gave them to her and the witch studied the poems. "This is hand-lettered with a calligraphy quill—nothing computer-generated about it." She kept staring at the poetry, and suddenly her eyes widened. "It's not working!"

"What?" Candice asked.

"The magic. I'm not feeling anything." She looked apologetically at her friend as she handed the poems back. "They're perfectly lovely poems, but I'm not crying."

"So the magic's gone?" She should have known it. No way would she really have magic. She glanced at Barnabas. The vampire looked stricken.

"Wait. I have an idea," Godiva said. Flouncing herself over to the window, she grabbed one of the paintings, noting that all the criers had dried up and drifted away. She returned with the picture. "I need the poem that goes with this one."

Candice looked at the green-eyed woman in the cave of

ice, and was in the process of handing the free verse poem to her friend when she gasped and stared at the painting.

"The eyes! I knew there was something about them. She has my eyes."

Barnabas looked from the painting to the teacher. *"Mon dieu!* You are right, *madam."*

"The other one has your hair," Godiva said.

"Holy shit," Candice said.

"Give me the poem."

Candice let Godiva take it out of her numb fingers. The witch held the poem up beside the picture. Almost immediately the vampire started to sniffle. Through his tears he said rapturously, "It has returned! The magic has returned!"

"It never went away," Godiva said. "It just doesn't work without the paintings."

"That is weird as hell," Candice said.

"Madam," Barnabas gushed breathily into the silence, "I would like to commission you and the artist for twelve more poetry paintings. And I would be willing to pay you this amount of money." He scribbled a number down on a piece of pink notepaper and slid it over the desk to Candice.

She picked up the paper. She blinked. And blinked again. She could not believe the amount of zeros on the paper. "You want to pay me this for twelve poems?"

"Mais non!" He looked offended. "I would pay you this for each of the twelve poems, as long as your artist agrees to illustrate them. *"Naturellement,* I would pay the artist the same commission. I have already called my brother in Denver. As soon as you and the artist *fini,* we will have a grand opening exhibit in the city that will be *très extraordinaire!"*

Candice wasn't sure she could breathe. "But I don't even know who the artist is."

"We're idiots!" Godiva said. "Isn't there a signature on the paintings?"

"No, *madam sorcière.* I studied each painting for the artist's signature. What I found was odd, not a normal signature at all."

"Well, what did you find?" Candice asked, staring at the painting.

"In the bottom right corner of each is a miniature reproduction of a full moon. That is the only signature the artist left."

Candice sighed. "Looks like I'll be here at sunset to meet this mysterious artist."

"But I think you should go home and change first," Godiva said. "Those jogging shorts are frayed and you spilled banana split all over your shirt."

Candice was too busy wondering at the amazing events to notice Godiva's self-satisfied little smile.

Eleven

✳

Candice was more excited than nervous. She dressed carefully, purposefully picking artsy clothes instead of the boring teacher crap that hung in the front of her closet. *A poetess!* she told herself, *I'm going to dress like a poetess*.

She chose a silk skirt that she'd bought in a funky shop in Manitou Springs the last time she'd visited the Colorado Springs area. Its scalloped hem flirted a couple of inches above her knees and it made her feel pretty and feminine. She matched a sleeveless black top with it and then hung her new necklace around her neck. It was a waterfall of amber beads and she realized that she'd bought it only because it reminded her of Justin's eyes—but she couldn't seem to help herself. *This job will help me get over him. And if it keeps up it'll be my ticket out of here. Denver, here I come!* She pointedly ignored the fact that rumor said Justin was living in Denver. It didn't matter. Denver was a big city, and she'd never run into him. She didn't hang in the coed crowd. Instead of thinking about Justin, Candice slid on a pair of strappy black sandals, gave her hair one more fluff, and rushed out to her Mini.

The sun was just setting when she pulled up in front of the gallery. She was relieved that Barnabas had taken the paintings and poetry out of the display window. She really didn't want to wade through another crowd of crying people to get to the door.

Stepping into the gallery she was met by Barnabas, who was wringing his hands.

"The artist insists on meeting alone with you, *madam*," he said. "I will go, but I will be back in *exactement* one hour to hear your decision. *Au revoir* until later, then."

"But where's the artist?"

"In the rear gallery. That is where I have hung your work." With one more worried glance around his gallery, the vampire minced out the door.

Candice straightened her shoulders and walked to the rear gallery. He was standing with his back to her, studying the two paintings that hung beside the framed poems. *He's really tall,* was her first thought. He was wearing a dark, conservative suit that fit his broad shoulders well and tapered nicely down to his waist. His thick sand-colored hair was short and neatly cut. He didn't seem to notice that she was there.

"Hi. My name is Candice Cox and I'm the poet," she said, wishing she'd given more thought to how she would introduce herself.

"I know who you are," he said without turning around.

Candice blinked. Was she so excited that her ears were playing tricks on her? That voice. She knew that voice. Didn't she?

"Why did you write these poems?" he asked.

"As an assignment for a class I'm taking." She felt the air slowly being squeezed out of her.

"Was that the only reason?" He still didn't turn around.

"No," she said softly. "When I wrote them I tried to explain how I was feeling."

"And how was that?"

"My heart had been broken. I made a stupid mistake and jumped to a conclusion that wasn't the right one."

Finally, the artist turned slowly around. His amber eyes met hers. "You weren't all that mistaken."

She couldn't believe it was really him. With his hair cut and his suit he looked . . . he looked like a man who could take on the world and win.

"I've missed you, Candy."

"Justin, I—I . . ." She tried to put together a coherent sentence while her emotions swirled.

"I'm sorry!" they said together.

"I should have given you a chance to explain," she blurted out.

"No! I shouldn't have gone to that stupid party to begin with," he said. "I want you to know that I wasn't going there to be with another woman."

"I know that," she said.

He took a couple of steps toward her. "Did I really break your heart?"

"Yes," she whispered.

"Is there any way you could let me fix it?" he asked.

"Yes," she whispered again. Then she closed the space between them and stepped into his arms. He bent to kiss her, but her words stopped him. "You're the artist!"

He smiled. "I am."

"So you found your inspiration in my poetry?"

"No. I found my inspiration in the woman whose heart finally became soft enough to be broken, and when I did I understood that separately we are just a gigolo wolf and a burned-out teacher, but together . . ." His lips gently brushed against hers.

"Together we make magic," she finished for him.

Epilogue

✳

The art gallery, Dark Shadows II, was located in trendy downtown Denver, nestled between a Starbucks and a posh designer jewelry shop. It was a popular place, known for its unique exhibits and for discovering talented new artists. But even for a popular gallery, tonight's opening was busy. No, not busy—mobbed. The gallery owner, Quentin Vlad (whom everyone in Denver believed to be eccentric and odd, which was partially true . . . the other part was that he was a vampire—something that no one needed to know) was all atwitter. Dollar signs were blazing in his eyes, and he didn't even mind that he'd had to hire extra security to control the crowd. Sold! Every available piece in the exhibit had been sold within the first hour of the opening.

He could hardly believe his brother's amazing find! Who would have imagined it? A nonmagical poet and an untrained artist werewolf—put them together and they create art that evokes feelings in the people who view it *even outside the boundaries of Mysteria*!

Now that was magic.

"Fifty thousand! I'll up my offer to fifty thousand dollars!"

Quentin looked into the flushed face of the sweaty man who was staring, mesmerized, at the spectacular painting and poem that hung side by side in the central room of the gallery. "Sir, I'm sorry. I told you the first twelve times you inquired as to its price. That particular piece is part of the artist and poet's personal collection. It is not for sale."

"Everything's for sale," the man quipped. "Everything has a price."

"Not that piece."

The deep voice came from behind them. Quentin and the desperate man looked back to see a tall, handsome young man dressed in dark jeans, a T-shirt, and a black leather jacket. He had his arm around a woman who wore funky, artsy clothes. Her thick blonde hair was loose, framing the arresting green in her eyes perfectly. She leaned into his side intimately.

"No." She smiled. "Not that piece."

He bent to kiss her and, arm in arm, they strolled into one of the other crowded rooms of the gallery.

The sweaty-faced man's gaze stayed with them a moment, but soon his eyes were drawn back to the painting and the poem—as was everyone's attention. The painting was wondrous, a blending eroticism and beauty so breathtaking that it, alone, would have been an attention-getter in any gallery. But mix it with the poem that was displayed in intricate calligraphy and framed beside it, and wondrous evolved into spectacular . . . magical. As couples read the poem they gravitated together. Lone readers sighed wistfully. Some rushed out of the gallery, already on their cell phones to their lovers. Some just stood and stared, weeping silently at what was missing in their own lives. Some, like the sweaty-faced man, decided that if they just owned the piece then somehow, miraculously, love would find its way into their lives.

"It's what I want; what I have to have," the sweaty man said to no one in particular. "It has to be my story." He looked at Quentin one last time. "I really can't buy this?"

"No, you really can't."

The man's eyes moved back to the artwork. "But maybe I can get her to forgive me—ask her for a second chance." His eyes brightened and some of the desperate flush went out of his face. Quentin decided that he must be much more attractive when he wasn't so, well, sweaty and florid. "That's it! I'm going to ask her for a second chance!" He gripped Quentin's thin hand. "Thank you, Mr. Vlad! And thank the artist and the poet, too!" Then he rushed from the gallery.

Quentin grimaced and discreetly wiped his palm on his hand-tailored Italian suit. But like everyone in the room, his eyes were pulled unerringly back to the wall where the art was exhibited. The painting was almost life-sized. The medium was textured oil, so the nudes looked rich, their skin almost alive. Their bodies were twined together in an intimate embrace—erotic yet loving—sexual and sensual. Their faces were indistinct, and Quentin thought then, as he had the first time he'd seen the piece, about the brilliance of the artist. He'd created a painting that allowed each viewer to imagine his or her own face within the scene. But the woman's hair was distinctive—thick and long and blonde. The man in the painting fisted it in his desire as it cascaded around her shoulders. Quentin shivered. Even he was not immune to the passion in the piece. His eyes shifted to the poem and, again, he was captured in the poet's web as he read:

Second Chance

Remember when it went wrong,
When the fabric of our universe tore . . . frayed . . .
dissolved?

But then you turned back time
and we escaped from the prison of withered desire
I flung my arms wide and embraced
passion newborn.

Because you turned back time
I dance naked, joyously teasing the fiery sun,
safe in the knowledge that even Apollo's
warmth cannot compare to
the heat of your caresses.

When you turned back time
I found the way to nurture
soft, sweet words
in my emerald meadow
I wound around you, a clear, cooling stream
soothing and nourishing,
helping you, in turn, to feel renewed.

And in that renewing
        found my own magic
        with you.

Beside the poem hung a placard that told about the artist and the poet. It read:

The medium of our work is not important. It varies from piece to piece. We do not focus on techniques or styles. We simply focus on the same thing we'd like you to focus on—the true magic of love, which will always transcend time and disbelief. May all of you live happily ever after. . . .

—Justin and Candice Woods